Wind-Up Toy: All Wound Up

David Owain Hughes

WIND-UP TOY: ALL WOUND UP

DAVID OWAIN HUGHES

Darkerwood Publishing Group
Colorado, U.S.A.

Darkerwood Publishing Group
Colorado, U.S.A.
First Paperback Printing, August 2016 - U.S.A.

ISBN: 978-1-938839-07-8

Cover art by Kevin Enhart

See the back of this book for more information about the author and his work.

TABLE OF CONTENTS

FOREWORD

by Chris Hall (DLS Reviews)

"It is always by way of pain one arrives at pleasure." - *Marquis de Sade*

I must admit, I'd planned on giving one of David Owain Hughes' novels a read for quite some time. We'd been in contact a couple of times in the past - with him being a horror author hailing from nearby Taff's Well, and me being a horror book reviewer based in sunny Porthcawl, our paths crossing was quite frankly pretty much inevitable. Nevertheless, for some reason or other, I'd not got around to giving one of Dave's tales a full dissection over at www.dlsreviews.com.

Of course, that all changed back in February of 2016, when I happened upon a Facebook post from Dave promoting his next new release (keep your sordid puns to yourself, Dave). Set in Porthcawl of all places, *Wind-Up Toy* was billed as being an extreme horror novel with one fucker of a sleazy undertone to it. To be honest, I was sold with it having Porthcawl as the backdrop alone. Extreme horror and a hefty slice of seediness just sealed the deal.

I immediately got in touch and so we agreed to meet along the Porthcawl seafront for a couple of pints and a chat about horror. Dave picked the venue for our meet-up. Now for those who don't know the area, in Porthcawl there's a veritable abundance of fine establishments for enjoying a quiet ale or two. Of course, out of all those on offer, Dave picked the grubbiest, seediest, gloomiest drinking hole along the waterfront.

Not really knowing the fella, I simply put this down to him not being all that familiar with the locale. Now I know differently. His choice in where to meet was invariably my first glimpse at the man that is David Owain Hughes. The rough around the edges, grinning horror fanatic, with an unhealthy fixation for firm-legged women in tights. Or is that Simone? I forget who's who sometimes.

Half a year's passed since then. Over that time, for better or worse, I've got to know the baseball-cap-wearing sleazeball (meant in a purely affectionate way) a hell of a lot better. Actually, I've got to know the real David too. The guy behind the raucous laughter and endless grubby puns. We've talked horror. We've got drunk together. The guy's a stand-up fella and it's been a frigging blast knowing him.

But going back to our first meeting, if I'm honest, I wasn't entirely sure what to expect from the first *Wind-Up Toy* story when I agreed to review it. Dave's no small bloke. He could easily have jumped in a car and been outside DLS HQ before I had time to pack my shit together, and along with my family, got the hell out of town. So, with this in mind, I was very aware that I'd be giving the book a fair few DLS Skulls. Luckily, as it turned out, such low-level cowardice didn't need to be considered in the final rating.

You see, *Wind-Up Toy* is a veritable masterpiece of extreme horror and unparalleled sleaze. Within a matter of just a handful of pages I was utterly sucked into the perverse world that Dave had lovingly (and let's be honest, quite psychotically) created. The novel stank of unashamed depravity and deviant perversion. Reading about Simone's despicable exploits, I felt like I'd been pushed face-first into the slimy, dirt encrusted filth of a cum-drenched back-alley gutter. Furthermore, you couldn't help but imagine David sitting at his writing desk with a leering grin plastered across his face, no doubt getting some weird perverted kick out of writing this despicable filth. The man clearly has no shame!

But it's not all sleaze and over-the-top violence. Yeah, Dave floods our senses with hard-hitting grit and grime and outlandish degeneracy. But snuggled amongst such lowbrow delights is something else. Something that allows David to step up out of the gutter, if only for a minute or two, and peek above the quagmire of depravity. You see, there's much, much more to the *Wind-Up Toy* tales than just base perversion.

In *Wind-Up Toy,* Dave has created a submissive sexual slave by the name of Simone. This is a man who would quite happily be dragged through the most deplorable pits of hell if his mistress so wished it of him.

He'd quite happily succumb to sadistic beatings, humiliation, torture, degradation and depravation – all for the very meekest of rewards.

Simone is a character who tests our senses. Should we feel sorry for him? Should we be siding with him? Possibly even root for his continued freedom? You see, he's not exactly a saint. He's like the *uber* anti-hero. In fact, Simone's a sociopathic serial killer with more libido than a sex-starved nympho in a free-for-all romp-fest. How the fuck do we side with that?

Through Simone, we the readers are made to juggle a whole host of mismatched and purposefully conflicting emotions. The way in which Simone's projected upon us pushes you to (almost unconsciously) side with him. After all, this mixed-up, handsome, and strangely charming young man has gone through a veritable torrent of abuse. He's the product of a mind-bogglingly dysfunctional upbringing. A warped and unimaginably corrupted individual who's learnt to take pleasure from his own suffering and near-constant humiliation. Because of this, you can't help but feel sorry for him. Pity him as he bears his soul. And then he goes and fucks someone up good and proper and we're slung back in that messed-up quagmire of conflict – wrestling with our confused emotions once again.

A mere month after *Wind-Up Toy* had been unleashed upon the unsuspecting world, Dave followed it up with the short story "Wind-Up Toy: Playtime, Simone". The short was another venture into the dark pits of sexual deviance intermingled with sadistically uncompromising violence – this time in the form of a precursor to the original novel.

Those that had already read *Wind-Up Toy* would be all too familiar with Simone and his dominatrix mistress – the ball-busting sadistic bitch that is Chaos. And so, for this follow-up story Dave turned his attention to what it was that first moulded Simone into the fucked-up perverted killer that he's become.

As with all of the instalments in the *Wind-Up Toy* series, there's always a standout scene that really pushes the boundaries of taste. In this second offering, you've got one that's beyond wrong – it's fucking disturbing. Simone's bat shit crazy, all right. Yeah, we pretty much already knew that. But what we didn't know up until this point is exactly how far gone the psychotic nutjob actually is. And what better way for Dave to demonstrate Simone's craziness than through a bit of show and tell?!

Of course, "Playtime" wasn't going to be the end of the series. A few months later, *Wind-Up Toy: Broken Plaything* reared its ugly head. This included the bonus story "Wind-Up Toy: Happy Birthday, Simone", which was written for the *Madame Movara's Tales of Terror* anthology. Of course, there was still plenty of life left in Simone's and Chaos' sadistic debauchery – and so *Wind-Up Toy: Chaos Rising* followed a mere handful of months later. However, all good things must eventually come to an end. And that, my friends, is exactly what this collected volume marks: The final instalment in Dave's twisted-as-fuck series.

Titled *Wind-Up Toy: Into The Playpen*, the final chapter into Simone's mind-bogglingly perverted world is everything you'd expect it to be. There's more violence and sadistic glee than a spot of bare-knuckle fisticuffs with Charles Bronson. And that's before you've got to the ending. And what a brain-shattering, gut-churning, downright explosive ending it is! For those who have already ventured some way down this series' perverted pathway, trust me on this – you really ain't seen nothing yet!

Don't worry, I'm not going to ruin any of the sick surprises that await you. Although if you've not yet dipped one of your virgin pinkies into the bubbling broth of filth that is one of Dave's *Wind-Up Toy* stories, then you really should be warned – this stuff is sicker than the source material for one of Ed Gein's wet dreams.

As previously touched upon, it's not just filth and extreme horror that make up the *Wind-Up Toy* stories. Hughes isn't just some one-trick-pony, offering cheap thrills and fucked-up shit in order to please his deranged fanbase. If you peel back the smeg-encrusted foreskin of any of his offerings, you'll find a hell of a lot more lurking below the smouldering surface of these charmless tales.

First and foremost, Dave can write. His tales – no matter how long or short – flow with a seemingly effortless ease. Furthermore, his storytelling is one-hundred percent unpretentious. So perfectly geared at getting straight into the thick of the narrative, without the need to dance around the subject matter unnecessarily. Indeed, this is so much the case that at times it can feel like you're reading a Richard Laymon novel, purely from the bounding prose and the author's obvious joy of telling his tale.

Of course, Laymon himself liked to delve into the bubbling pool of eroticism from time to time. Indeed, the vast majority of his tales included some scantily clad saucepot gallivanting around the vicinity, flaunting the wondrous assets that the good lord chose to equip her with. After all, there's no shame in a little sauce on your chips. It adds a dash of zing. A splash of spice. Although, if we continue with this analogy, then I guess what Dave's been serving up is a veritable bucket full of sauce accompanied by just a side garnish of horror-roasted fries.

In fact, although marketed as extreme horror, it has to be said that the *Wind-Up Toy* books aren't exactly your typical fuck-with-your-gut extreme horror. Okay, so there's some absolutely horrific savagery injected into the veins of the tales, along with a whole host of shockingly brutal scenes almost exclusively designed to push the boundaries of taste – but the predominant driving force behind each one of Hughes' instalments is undoubtedly filth. Plain and simple. That's Dave.

Of course, all good things must at some point come to an end. The original *Wind-Up Toy* story was never meant to be anything more than just a single cum-stain on the literary world. But I for one am incredibly glad Dave saw the continued potential in the story, and in doing so, made Simone's world into something so much more.

To know that the *Wind-Up Toy* series has finally come to a close is certainly sad, but on some strange level, weirdly a relief. Each and every chapter in the life of Simone was filled with more sleaze than a hunt through Josef Fritzl's cupboards. But there's only so much that you can take before it just becomes too much. The absolute worst thing that could happen to the series would be for the reader to become desensitised to the filth. For it to lose that slimy, sleazy chill factor. Luckily that's something that's not happened with Dave's series – and never will. If anything, the hardcore filth has got increasingly more extreme. The brutal delivery of each despicable scene, that much more sadistic. That much more gut-wrenching. That much more perverted. You're expecting degradation, debauchery and lashings of sleaze with each instalment. And each time, Dave pushes the filth that little bit further.

Then there's the ending. The final sequence in this journey of unparalleled corruption. The final chapter of Simone's life in the *Wind-Up Toy* series. And (without ruining anything) what a frigging bowel-loosening ending it is! Dave obviously had to pull out all the stoppers for this final explosion in the arse of the literary world. And by Simone's stained undergarments has he done just that. What an ending. What a way to sign off the *Wind-Up Toy* series. What a despicable, deplorable, quite frankly utterly unnerving piece of fucked-up writing it is.

Prepare to be shocked, repulsed, excited and worryingly titillated as you enter the fucked-up world of Chaos and Simone for the final time…

Chris Hall - October 2016

HAPPY BIRTHDAY, SIMONE

Simone lay on his bed and stared at the floor. His mother's words from last night rang in his ears: "*This time four years ago, I was being rushed to the hospital. You were such a precious-looking thing, my special baby boy…*" she'd slurred, tapping a finger gently against his nose. "*You'll be a big boy tomorrow*!"

After a bottle of wine, she regularly got soppy with him.

It was a cute quirk of hers, which helped build a magnificent personality. Not just a personality, but a woman and a mother.

Every year, on the eve of his birthday at around nine o'clock, she would tell Simone of being rushed to the hospital and having to endure nine hours of labour, which ended with a breech birth.

"*Aw, Mammy's special little soldier!*" she'd supposedly cooed on having him placed in her arms.

From that day forth, Simone and his mother had been the best of friends. Sadly, she was his *only* friend. He'd never found it easy to talk to other children. To reach out and connect.

His classmates laughed at him. Mocked his silly accent. Due to him having an Italian father and a Welsh mother, they called him "half-breed", among other childish names. The girls pulled his hair. The teachers forgot about him.

And yet he liked school. Simone never let the little things bother him. He had a good home life, even though his father had left before he was born, along with a great mother and half-sister, Sian, who cherished the ground he walked on.

In Simone's eyes, that was all he needed.

Friends will come. One day…he thought, turning his head to look out his window. The curtains were wide open, which in turn allowed sunlight to filter through, causing him to squint.

His radio alarm clock, which was in the shape of the A-Team's van, burst to life – it pumped out the show's famous soundtrack. Simone sprang from his bed, and commando-rolled along the floor.

"I pity the fool!" he screeched, causing his prepubescent voice to crack.

When the A-Team's intro came to an end, a news broadcaster kicked in, informing him it was nine A.M, June seventh.

"*Ugh*!" Simone said, switching the contraption off.

"Are you up, love?!" his mother called from downstairs.

"Yep!"

"Hurry down, soldier – I have presents and pancakes ready and waiting! Get 'em while they're hot. The presents too," she said, laughing.

"Yes, pancakes!" Pulling his sagging PJ bottoms up, Simone raced through his bedroom door and downstairs. When he got to the entrance of the living room, the smell of buttery goodness caused his flat stomach to rumble.

Licking his lips, he walked into the room and saw the bunting his mother had put up on the walls: balloons, banners and streamers. He made his way into the kitchen, where he found his mother lathering his pancakes in syrup.

"I hope you're hungry!"

"Mmm, I am, I am!" he squealed.

"Do you want to open your presents as you eat?"

"I didn't think I would be allowed to…" he said, his words trailing off.

"It's your birthday, soldier. You can do anything you want!"

"Cool. Then yes, I'll scoff as I open. Where's Sian?"

"She had to go to school, silly!"

"Oh, I thought she may have been allowed to stay home with me…"

"Nope, just you and me, Simone," she said, smiling. After planting a kiss on his forehead, she then gave his nose a honk before pinching his cheek.

"Aw!" He giggled, wiping her wetness from his face.

When his breakfast was plonked down in front of him, he started stuffing large chunks of pancake into his mouth. Syrup trickled down the sides of his mouth and chin, causing some to dribble onto his pyjama top.

"Slow down! You'll choke, unless you're hoping to see the inside of an emergency room on your birthday?!"

Simone snorted a laugh, and chewed lumps of food spattered the table.

"Don't make me laugh!" he garbled.

"*Ew*! Mushy grub!" his mother bellowed, pointing at the debris that had come from inside his mouth. "Disgusting!" She then laughed and gave his bed-hair a tousle. "I'll get your first present."

With that, his mother was gone, leaving him to kick his legs, eat and hum "Happy Birthday to Me."

A silly, lop-sided smile appeared on his face.

"Look what I found!" his mother said, coming back into the room with her arms full of presents.

"*Wow*!" Simone said, spitting food chippings.

"Which one would you like to open first?!"

Looking at the brightly wrapped mountain before him, Simone was immediately drawn to the biggest one. "That one!" He pointed.

"Nuh-uh, soldier. No way. That one's from me and will be the last one you get to open."

"Is there one from Dad this year?"

"Surprisingly, yes! I guess there's a first time for everything."

"Awesome. Can I have that one first?"

She passed him his father's gift. Simone ripped the plain brown packaging off and instantly lost interest in the unwrapped present that sat before him. "Paddington Bear…*Really*?!" he said, looking at his mother, who removed the bear from the table.

"The less said about that the better!" she said. "Here, open this one – it's off Sian."

Eagerly, he tore the paper free from the parcel – his pancakes sat forgotten, the syrup hardening.

"Oh, wow – G.I. Joe action figures!" he said, showing his mother. "This is turning out to be the best birthday ever, Mam."

"I just wish we could have invited a few friends around…" she said.

Her words seemed to catch him off-kilter. All of a sudden, Simone felt like a loser. Did his mother think that? Simone had no mates.

He smiled a sad smile, but she didn't seem to detect it.

When he looked at her closer, he could see she had a sad way about her eyes. Her smile didn't quite fit her mouth.

Simone wanted to say something, to tell her he was fine in life, but words failed him, and as his mouth flapped, she pushed her present under his nose.

One corner was not taped down well enough, so he picked away at that section until a huge strip of paper came free in his hand. With the gift at his mercy, he savaged the rest of the packaging to reveal a massive clown.

The figure of fun bore black, reds and purples for colouring – his hair was huge and floppy. He didn't have a goofy red nose like most clowns. Its eyes looked sinister, its teeth sharp.

Simone was glad the thing was tied to its box.

"Don't you like him?" his mother asked.

"Uh…"

"Oh, I thought you would have loved him, being as you like all things horror and terrifying."

Simone couldn't answer. He was rooted to the spot. The clown's eyes felt as though they were boring through him. They were questioning and seeking out all his childish fears.

The urge to pee came from nowhere.

"He's cool…" Simone managed. His tone sounded shaky.

"Have you seen all the awesome weapons he comes with?" his mother said, pointing out the clown's mini arsenal, which was taped down: chainsaw, knives, hatchet, and axe. "Hey, he could be the leader of the G.I. Joes!"

Her words passed over him.

Finally, he broke the clown's intense stare and read the words arched across the top of the box: *Friends Until the End*! Blood dripped off each letter.

Friends...Simone thought. The word stuck in his head.

"Are you sure you like him?"

"Yes…" he said with caution. *I bet the clown can smell my terror.* Simone could almost hear it laughing as if tickled. "Mr. Tickles," he blurted, and then smiled. As he undid the ties around the toy, his mother cleared the paper away.

"I'm just going to throw this lot in the bin," she said.

"*Friends forever, sir*!" Mr. Tickles said into Simone's ear, which didn't startle the youngster.

"Do you reckon we can whip these G.I.'s into shape?" he asked the clown. "You're going to be my number two."

"*Yes, sir*!"

Picking the packet of G.I. commandos up, Simone eyed their names. "I think we're going to have to rename these men. Give them some sinister sounding names."

"*Agreed, sir!"* the G.I.'s said in unison.

Simone smiled. He finally had a group of friends to play with – his mother would be so proud.

"Who are you talking to, soldier?" his mother called from the kitchen.

"Oh, just my new friends!" he said, and then whispered into the clown's ear.

PLAYTIME, SIMONE

"Well, if it isn't faggot chops!" he heard a voice call from behind him.

Simone knew exactly who it was – Cartwright. First name; Phillip-John – he was the most feared boy at Simone's school, but Simone had taught him and his goons one hell of a lesson last year…*Some people never learn*, he thought.

"Thought it was pretty funny, didn't you, whacking me in the bollocks with a hammer? I spent months in the hospital because of you, you little fuck!" Simone heard the lad crack both sets of knuckles. "Payback is a bitch, right?"

Turning, Simone saw that Cartwright was on his own; he didn't have his two chimps with him like he always did. "Where are your bitches?" Simone asked.

"Gary has a permanent limp, thanks to you smashing his knee in."

"And Ricky?"

"He's lost use of his arm. Again, that's down to you, my friend."

Simone smiled. "Yeah, beating you three was funny – you acted like a bunch of pussies. Fancy three getting taken by one?" Simone said, watching in amusement as Cartwright's face turned a deep shade of red. "I told you never to speak of that day again, or I would make your life a misery…"

"Yeah, well, I'm not about to let some little fuck get away with breaking my balls, Simone. Prepare for the beating of your life!" Cartwright said, stepping forward.

"Are you sure you want to do this?" Simone said, slipping a hand inside his trouser pocket.

"Oh, I'm more than sure!" Cartwright said, stepping in to attack.

He was much taller and weightier than Simone, which made him sluggish. This gave Simone a chance to dig the miniscule squirt bottle out of his pocket and stick it in Cartwright's face.

Without hesitating, Simone squeezed the trigger and filled Cartwright's face with bleach.

"*Argh*!" the boy screamed, as the hot liquid burned and ate at his flesh and eyeballs. He hit the deck and placed his hands over his eyes, which sizzled. "You fucking bastard! What have you done?!"

Simone looked about him. There was nobody around, which was why he always chose the riverside path to walk home from school.

"Yell all you want, Cartwright!" Simone said, circling the fallen boy. "Nobody's going to hear your sissy screams!" He gave him a few hard kicks to the balls. "Manage to fix 'em, did they?"

"Ah, you fuck. Fuck you!"

"Well, keep talking to me like that, and I'm not going to call you an ambulance!" Simone said, smiling.

"I'm sorry, please! Call me one – call *someone*!"

"Call you a what?"

"An ambulance!"

"Are you sure?" Simone mocked.

"Yes, please! It burns," he cried. "I want my mam!" he bleated.

"Looks like you've had an accident!" Simone said, looking at the boy's wet crotch.

"Ugh…" Cartwright wept.

"Okay, okay, what can I do for you?" Simone said, picking up a large stick, which he used to poke the boy with.

"*Ow*! Don't do that, call me an ambulance…"

"Okay, okay…Cartwright is an ambulance, Cartwright is an ambulance…"

"What are you doing, you little fuck?"

"Doing as you asked!" Simone said, before starting to beat Cartwright about his head with the thick stick.

He yelped a few times, as blood poured out of his nose, eyes and ears. Once bored, Simone took to the lad's ribs and stomach. After a few more minutes of pummelling him, Cartwright took his last gasp of breath, before succumbing to death.

"That'll fucking teach you!" Simone said. "Never will you bully me again."

Making sure the boy was dead, Simone rolled him into the water, and watched as the current carried him down stream. He smiled, then giggled, before running off to his safe place…

****

The floorboards creaked as he walked across them as quietly as he could…*She can't possibly hear me*, he thought. *How many times have I done this? Not once has she caught me.*

But deep down, Simone knew she knew.

And even deeper down, he knew she loved it, and she knew he knew that.

It was an endless game of 'Peep'n'Come-Play', which she loved as much as he did.

Did it bother her that he was a lot younger? Did it fuck!

And did it bother him that she was much, much older? Not a fucking chance. Had the boys in school known what he was getting up to with an older woman, he'd be in a coma from all the high-fives he'd receive.

Tits, arse and legs – that's all the guys spoke about at school these days. He supposed they were of that age, not that he was popular among his peers. But Simone didn't care about that, as he had a good home life, and a family that loved and looked after him.

Getting to his destination, Simone put Mr. Tickles on the floor – his toy clown loved this just as much as he did, as he lay on the floor beside him, and then removed one of the floorboards. This, in turn, exposed a hole in the floor, and when looked through, he could see directly into the room below him, which was her dance room.

"If she really doesn't know I'm peeping, then I'll be in for the hiding of my life if she ever finds out!" he whispered to his clown.

"Chill. You know for sure she'd love it. She has guys looking at her body every night of the week. Go with the flow, man," Mr. Tickles said. *"The bitch is hot for it…"*

Simone smiled. "I guess you're right."

"I'm always right. Now, have a good look, because I want a good fucking eyeful too, you little pervert!"

Simone stifled a laugh. "I'm the pervert?" he uttered. "Yeah, right! You were the one who wanted to lick Sian's pussy!"

"And you're telling me you never did?" the clown said, his eyebrows raised.

Simone smiled and tried to hide his blushes. "Well…Oh, come on, you know I did. I liked it when she used to play doctor and nurse with me. She used to make my dick go all hard."

"Well, that's supposed to happen! Don't they teach you anything at school these days?"

"Shh, or she'll hear you!" he whispered. "We'll be able to talk a bit louder once she puts her music on."

"Fair point," the clown said.

"What's taking her so long?"

"She's probably slipping into character…I hope she plays Amber. I love it when she does Amber and puts her stockings on. Makes my cotton cock stiff!"

Again, Simone had to stifle a laugh, as he put his hands over his mouth.

Below, he heard a door bang shut.

"Sounds like our girl has finally come to play…"

"Oh, man!" Simone said, beaming.

The clown beamed back, but before he could speak, heavy rock music started thudding through the ceiling – Alice Cooper started singing "Poison". When this happened, Simone lowered his head, and put his eye to the peephole.

He couldn't see her, just an empty room filled with dance mats and walls covered by mirrors. "I don't see her!" he said in a sulky way, whilst keeping his head where it was.

"Give her a chance!" the clown said.

As Simone was about to complain some more, he noticed the lights dim in the room below. This was followed by flashing lights, which were multi-coloured and piercing to the eye. Before he knew it, she was out in the middle of the dance floor.

"Oh, man!" he muttered again.

"What?" said the clown. *"What?!"*

"You're going to freak out when you see this, Mr. Tickles. Looks like she's Trash tonight!"

"The punk?!"

"The very one," he said, looking down at the woman before him.

Even though the lighting was slightly poor, he could make out every inch of her body and what she wore. She wasn't the tallest of women, but her legs were long; very long, in fact, which matched the length of her black, curly hair. She wore it down tonight; it flanked her pretty face.

As she danced energetically, her hair skipped and thrashed, which drove Simone wild. Sometimes, she wore a headband or scrunchy, which kept her feral hair in place, but not tonight – it was on full display, much like her body.

Even though she wore a bodystocking, it was fishnet, and exposed every contour of her young, tight body. Her nipples could be seen poking through the holes in the flimsy fabric, which, in turn, gave him an erection.

Beneath the fishnet however, she wore nude-coloured tights, which gave her amazing legs a glossy shine. Her feet were bare, making it easier for her to glide across the mats.

"Oh…" he groaned, as he tried to get his face closer to the hole in the ceiling. "This is much better than watching the girls at Bunnies, Mr. Tickles!"

"Let me see, you little pervert!"

"Wait your turn!"

"Did you see her oil her body?"

"No, but maybe she didn't do it tonight."

"True. I just love watching her oil those tiny tits of hers…"

"Her nipples are hard, Mr. Tickles."

"Oh…Come on, let me have a peep, Simone. Please!"

"Just a few more minutes, okay?"

"*Fine*," the clown huffed.

"No need to pout!" Simone said, giggling.

When "Poison" came to an end, the silence weighed heavily. Simone tried not to move, for fear of causing a creak in the boards. With a held breath, he pulled his face away from the hole.

Shh! he mouthed to the clown, putting a finger to his lips.

"*Phew*, that's loosened me up!" came the woman's voice.

Mr. Tickles sniggered at this, causing Simone to smother a laugh.

Putting his head back to the hole, he noticed she was now standing by one of the mirrors, while holding on to one of the bars affixed to it. In one quick movement, she put one leg up on it, and did a few stretches.

Simone's breathing started to come in ragged rips as he watched her rub her leg before putting it down and doing the same with the other. "Break the oil out…" he whispered, but she didn't.

After a few more moments of stretching, another rock song kicked in, causing her to start dancing around again. This song was much slower, so she used the pole that was situated in the centre of the room.

She rubbed against it as she danced flirtatiously, before jumping on it and wrapping her legs around it.

"She can't half move!"

"She's gorgeous…" the clown said.

"I think her routine might be coming to the end."

"Let me get in there, then!"

Thinking they had plenty of time to switch position, Simone rolled out of the way for Mr. Tickles to get in to his place, but the music stopped just before they could complete their task. A few boards creaked, causing Simone to wince.

"*Shit!*" he whispered. "Did she hear us?"

"She's looking around…"

"Oh, fuck – we're so screwed."

"I think we're fine, Simone. She's now towelling her body down."

"Thank God!"

"Oh, no…She's looking up!"

"Let me see!" Simone said, moving the clown out of the way. Sure enough, the dancer was looking up at the ceiling. Her words tore through him, causing his dick to go limp.

"I know you're up there, Simone. I hope you enjoyed the show? If you're a good boy, then maybe I'll take you back to Bunnies. You'd like that, wouldn't you?"

He kept quiet.

"There's no need to be shy. I know what you get up to. Why don't you come down, so we can have a bath together? I'll let you scrub my sweaty back," she said, giggling. "Come on, there's no need to be shy. I'm not mad with you, you know that."

"You promise?" he asked, looking through his peephole.

"I promise, silly. Now come down at once."

"Okay," he said, abandoning his position. *What an interesting day I'm having so far,* he thought. *All this playing and sneaking around…But how am I going to explain all this blood up my arms? I could just tell her. I doubt she'll be mad…*

****

In the bath, they faced one another and looked lovingly into each other's eyes as steam rose between them. It misted the only mirror in the room, along with the small window. He was down by the taps, with Mr. Tickles on the floor beside him.

It's only right that the man should be down by the taps, when you're in the bath with a lady, he thought as foam bobbed and filled the gaps between them. Bubbles flew towards the ceiling as they played footsie beneath the surface.

"And you say that blood belongs to a boy who used to bully you?" she asked.

Dropping his head, he went shy. "Yes. But I needed to put a stop to him once and for all…He would have continued."

"It's okay, Simone. I forgive you, my love…Did you get rid of the body?"

Looking up, he smiled. "I pushed him in the river, and the current carried him away."

"Well done. But my, you're not half a naughty boy," she said, lovingly placing her wrinkling foot in his crotch, her toes played with his shrivelled nut sack. "It's this kind of behaviour that got Sian in so much trouble, you know…"

"Will they ever let her come back?" he asked, then groaned with joy as he instantly stiffened. The tip of his penis jutted from the water like a periscope.

"Maybe. But only if she's good, and you learn to behave, Simone. You're naughty!" she said, wrapping her toes around his cock.

"Who did you say is the naughty one?" he said, and smiled.

"You can never, ever tell anyone about this, Simone…Or I'll end up like Sian. I could never lose you."

"That won't happen."

"Sex with a minor is so very, very wrong."

Following suit, he placed one foot between her legs, causing her to groan as he hit the right spot. Her hair tickled his foot and toes as he burrowed deeper and deeper. This was their favourite of all places to spend time, but never had it been like this before. He knew she loved him, but he never thought she or he would go this far. After all, he was so much younger.

The spying had been innocent compared to this.

Sure, the bedroom was fun and cosy and all those other things, but he'd only ever done sex things with Sian. She had taught him many, many things, and not just in the house, but outdoors, where they were free to roam and take plenty of risks at the same time.

He and Sian had made love and played with each other in many places, to which they had never been caught. He tried to think of the most unusual place they had played, but couldn't, as she slid her foot up and down the length of his shaft. *She's trying to tease me into an orgasm*, he thought. *But no, not yet – I don't want to. I want to make it last.*

Blocking out the intense pleasure, he managed to think about all the places he had enjoyed himself with Sian.

Fucking inside a confessional box at the church had been a good one. Sian had muffled her squeals of delight as the man-of-the-cloth had sat next to her, trying to preach some good into her.

The train ride home from Cardiff had been another good one…Boy, had that been awesome. She'd masturbated him to a climax as they sat opposite a hoity-toity couple from London. *If only they had known what had been going on underneath my jacket at the time*, he thought.

He tried desperately to think of more times with Sian as his mind drifted back to the present…

Suddenly, his mind filled with the day Sian had been taken away from him, which hurt.

Shifting in the bath, he found a more relaxed position as he tried to cast his mind back once more. But nothing except that awful day would come to him, now he'd thought of it.

"Did you enjoy my dance, Simone?"

His eyes burst open. "Yes, I did."

"What about Mr. Tickles?" she asked, causing him to blush. "What's the matter? You don't have to be shy around me, you know. We're close, you know that, don't you?"

"He said you're sexy. Much sexier than the girls you work with at Bunnies. He thinks you're hot, and very fuckable."

"*Simone*!"

"Sorry, but that's what he said!"

"*Tut*, I'll have to wash that clown's mouth out with soap and hot water."

"I'm not sure he'll like that, you know!" Simone said.

"No, he fecking wouldn't!"

"Simone, no swearing!"

"But it was Mr. Tickles!"

She gave him a stern look. "And what do you think? Do you think I look better than the girls I work with?"

"Yes. Your boobs and legs are amazing…"

"Aw, that's sweet of you. But you know, we can't go on like this. It has to stop, and you have to be punished."

"I know," he pouted.

"There's no point in sulking, you know. That won't work with me!"

He looked up at her, his eyes falling on her gleaming tits – her nipples stiff. *What would it be like to suck on them? Sian's tasted so nice…But she's gone. Locked away.* The thought made him sad.

"You're thinking about your sister again, aren't you?" she said.

He nodded.

"They'll never allow her to come back here. You know that, don't you?"

Again, he nodded slowly. "Is it time for my punishment?"

"Yes," she said, a smirk on her face. "It's for your own good, Simone. You can play with the girls at Bunnies, but I'm off limits. This will be your last bit of pleasure from me."

"Okay," he said, resigning himself to the fact.

"I'm also going to padlock the attic, so you won't have your peephole any longer."

"*Aww!*" he whined.

"Simone!" she warned, giving him another stern look. "Hand it over, come on," she demanded whilst snapping her fingers.

He knew it was time – there was no avoiding it any longer. He reached over to the soap dish and picked up the cutthroat that lay there. Her eyes lit-up as he flicked the blade open and clicked it into place.

Handing it to her, she took it in her left hand whilst she held his arm still with her right. She then started running the sharpened steel down various sections of his arm before turning her attention to his other arm.

He clenched his teeth and pulled his lips back over his gums as pain tore through him. His blood trickled and flowed down his arms and into the lukewarm water, where most of the bubbles had now gone. All that remained was crimson suds.

She increased the speed of her strokes at the sight of him touching himself with his free hand – his foot continuing to probe between her legs, making her moan.

They brought themselves to orgasms as water sloshed and swished over the side of the bath in a violent manner, soaking through the mat, which was positioned beside the tub.

Spent, she lay there panting.

He jigged once as a joyous spasm ripped through his body, before lying still; his arms running a river of red.

As the water settled, she spoke.

"Did you enjoy that?"

"Yes, mother, I did," he beamed.

WIND-UP TOY

CHAPTER 1

"Hello?" came the voice. It was soft yet slightly high-pitched, as though it belonged to a schoolgirl. Maybe she did this part-time, or maybe it was a summer job? No matter, he liked it. He was also glad it had been a woman who'd picked up this time.

After all, this was his fifth attempt.

The first three who'd answered had been men and he wasn't a fucking fruit.

The fourth *had* been a woman, but she'd sounded old. Too old. He liked them young. Young and pretty, with thick thighs – not *thunder* thighs – just *thick* thighs. Thighs that looked awesome inside a pair of stockings or tights. Thighs that looked amazing in French knickers, hot pants or short-shorts. Thigh-high boots and little skirts also did the trick.

"Hello?" came that cute little voice again.

He licked his lips. *I wonder if her pussy's bald,* he thought. *I bet her boyfriend likes it that way. I can just imagine this young fuck having some butch bastard as a fella – a fella who only likes to shag doggy-style. I'll bet he's a big dumb fucktard who lacks panache in the sack and who has little to no imagination on how to treat this dirty bitch.*

"There's no need to be shy," she whispered into the phone.

His cock started to stir. It pushed against the cool bars that encaged his privates – a male chastity belt. Chaos never allowed him to leave the house without it. They both loved his restraint.

"Do you want to talk a little first?" she asked.

Fuck, she was cute. Too cute. If he didn't keep his mind straight, he was going to blow his load in his pants, but he didn't want that, even though it had been months since he had been allowed to touch his dick. This had to be controlled…Focused. He wasn't ringing up to get some jollies. No way. He needed to be serious.

"Yes!" he said in a shaky, almost pathetic voice. "Talk," he insisted.

"Well, my name is Lara."

That was a lie right there. The name had come out in an insecure breath and he could tell she was pretty new to this job. *First week? More than likely*, he thought, letting 'Lara' drone on in the background. He kind of liked the name, even if it wasn't her real tag. *Lara*, he mouthed. It sounded nice. Rolled off the tongue with ease.

And I'm pretty sure her pussy would take my tongue with ease, too, he continued to muse.

His dick was now completely stiff. He could feel semen oozing out the tip. He had the urge to rip his trousers off – to expose his caged dick, but no, he couldn't do that. It wasn't the fear of being caught nude, because he was sitting in a dark and secluded spot. Nobody would see him, even though he could hear others close by. No, it was the thought of what he might do if he ripped his trousers off. Who he might hurt…

Shaking his head, he closed his eyes. When he opened them, he looked up. The lights at the fairground had come on. He could see the *Beach Party* ride starting to move; screams and laughter carried on the sea air.

He tried to control his breathing at the thought of the fair and how he liked to ride the *Ghost Train.*

Try to focus on her voice, he told himself.

"I've been working here for little over three years…" she said.

Another lie. *What the fuck is wrong with this bitch? She's trying to put me at ease, that's all. She can probably tell I'm scared. Scared?! I'm not scared. Apprehensive? Yeah, that's a good word. Ap…pre…hens…ive.*

Be honest with me! That's what he wanted to tell her, but he let it slide.

"Would you like to tell me your name?" she asked.

God, your voice is softer than blended chocolate, he thought. He put his hand against his dick, and rubbed it – it helped ease the stiffness. He wished it would go soft as the bars tended to leave indents in his flesh. He'd also heard that if the 'slave' was left in its cage with a hard-on for far too long, it could shorten the penis. The thought excited him, because he knew his mistress would ridicule him for having a short cock.

He tightened his grip on the phone. His heart started to hammer in his chest, causing his hands to shake. He needed to calm down, to keep his horn under control.

He gulped. The wind started to pick up, whipping his body. The sun began to set, which he liked, and the coolness of the evening would help control him. Bending over, he pulled the legs of his jeans up, allowing the chilly wind to ice his crotch.

"Hello?" Lara asked again. "Would you like me to continue?"

"Yes," he rasped. *This conversation can't go on like this,* he told himself. *She'll hang up. No, she won't – she can't do that. She's there to help. She'll keep coaxing me to talk. Lara won't give up on me.*

"Well, I'm not sure there's much more I can talk about," she admitted. "Why don't you tell me a little bit about yourself? Why are you calling this evening?"

He didn't know how to answer that one. There wasn't a straight up reply for it. It would take hours to explain it all. Days, even. Perhaps weeks. All he knew was that he had to speak to someone. Things couldn't go on the way they were. He had to be stopped, and Chaos sure as hell wasn't going to allow him to stop.

He was her pet, and she was his mistress.

"I need help," he said, his voice but a whispery tremble.

"Okay," she said. Her tone had taken on a more serious edge. It was less jovial and strident – the adult in her had taken rule.

"I…I…" he started, but his sentence broke down. It had been years since he'd held a conversation with a woman, besides Chaos.

"Yes?" she pushed, but lightly.

The line went quiet. He tried to think of what to say – to form the words inside his mouth. Why was he so scar…*Apprehensive*? Chaos wasn't going to find out. She was at home, busy cleaning and lining up her tools of play, pain and pleasure.

He gulped. Sweat broke on his brow.

His penis had finally shrivelled.

"Okay, okay…" she said. "Let's start with something simpler. Tell me your name?"

Her soft tone gave him the courage he needed. "Simone," he said. "It's Italian."

"That's a nice name."

He could tell she was smiling – could almost see her face glowing with it.

"Th…thanks."

"How can I help you, Simone?" She sounded genuinely concerned for him.

"I'm scared...*No*, apprehensive," he corrected himself.

"Why are you apprehensive?" Again, the line fell silent. "Simone, are you still there?" Nothing. "There's no reason to be shy around me," Lara pushed. "I'm here to help."

"I want to be a good boy, Lara. Really I do!" he whined. "I don't want to hurt no more – ever," he pleaded. "I'm…" He started to sob.

"Hey, hey," she cooed. "Whatever's going on, we can work this out together."

"You mean that?"

"Of course. I've helped many, many people before now and I'm pretty sure I'll be able to help you too, Simone. Trust me."

"I do," he said. The tears had stopped.

"That's good. Are you calling from home?"

"Yes," he lied.

"It sounds like you're out…"

"I'm having a drink and a fag in my garden – it relaxes me," he lied again.

"I see. Well, that's good. Hopefully it will help you open up too," she said. That sweet and innocent voice was back.

She seems too chipper for her line of work, he thought. *She must be new – soon, they will pick her up on it.*

"Maybe," he said, having difficulty speaking. His throat had become desert dry. He could put up with that now that his dick had deflated and the shakes had gone away. Simone was now under control.

"Would you like to tell me more about why you are calling me this evening?"

"I told you – I'm apprehensive." His shaky tone had now gone and his own smooth and calculated manner kicked in. He had a broad Welsh accent.

"What are you apprehensive about, Simone?"

"Myself."

"What about you?" Lara asked.

She carries off the 'I'm so worried about you' tone perfectly, Simone thought. *I wonder if she rescues animals in her spare time, or goes to the soup kitchens and helps feed the poor.* He fought the urge to grab his cock and snigger.

"I'm fed up with being the way I am. I want it to stop."

"And what way *is* that, Simone?"

"Perverse," he admitted. "I've been like it all my life."

"What do you mean, perverse?"

"That I'm a pervert. It controls my life. It has for as long as I can remember."

"It depresses you?"

"All the time," he said. Tears were close to pouring out of him again.

"Has it caused you big problems?"

"In what way?"

"Relationship wise?"

"No, I have a partner. I've been with her for years."

"Right, okay…"

"She doesn't understand. I want it to stop!"

"Maybe you should be telling her this, Simone?"

"I've tried, but she just gives me the whip. Kicks me around. Locks me in the attic." Now, he was sobbing.

"Hey, calm down. It's okay. We can work this out together," she soothed. When he didn't answer, she spoke again. "Have you tried leaving her?"

"No, she'd kill me!" he blurted.

"Okay. Then talk to her."

"I'm talking to you," he said, gripping the phone tighter. "I just want someone to listen, to hear me out and to help."

"That's what I'm here for, Simone," she said with serenity in her voice.

"Good."

"Why don't we go back to when this all first started? Can you do that?"

"I probably could. Why?"

"Speaking about it will help," she encouraged.

"As though I'd be exorcising my demons?"

"Yes, something like that. It may also give you the courage to stand up to your partner and take control back over your life."

"That makes sense," he said. "Where shall I start?"

"What's your earliest memory of being the way you are, Simone?"

"Erm, probably when I was just a young lad. Nine, maybe ten."

"That's very young!" Lara said, the shock evident in her voice.

"Not in my house," he said.

"Your parents approved of your behaviour?"

"My dad left before I was born."

"He walked out?"

"Yes. He went back to Italy – to directing. My mother wouldn't go, see."

"Her family are here?"

"Uh-huh," he said. "She met my dad when holidaying there – he put her in a few of his movies."

"Wow, that's exciting!" Lara said. "Anything I would know?"

"I wouldn't have thought so. They were mainly horror and soft core porn," he said.

"Oh…I see. And you've seen your parents' movies?" she asked with trepidation.

"Many times as a child," he confessed.

"I see. Why did they move here?"

"My dad wanted to make my mother happy. He also had a fondness for Wales and my grandparents."

"Your mother's parents, I assume you mean?"

"Of course."

"How long before she fell pregnant with you, Simone?"

"Within the first three years of them living here."

"Did they make movies over here?"

"My mother didn't, no. My dad kept his connections in his country. He would fly back and forth. Sometimes, he'd be gone for months."

"That must have put quite the strain on things. What profession did your mother have at the time?"

"She took up modelling and dancing. Dancing mainly."

"Stage dancing?"

"Stripping," he said.

"I see. You're an only child?"

"No, I have a half-sister who is four years older than me. I don't see her anymore."

"What happened to her?"

"She was taken away," Simone said, sorrow in his voice.

"Who took her away?"

"Children's services. They found out about her."

"What do you mean?"

"Never mind that," he said. "I thought you wanted to know about my childhood? A memory?"

"Uh, yes. Yes, of course. You have a memory in mind you said?"

"I do. As I said, it's the earliest one I can remember. I'm around nine years old, and I'm at home."

"Go on," Lara urged.

"I'm doing awful things," he admitted. Lara fell silent. "Not things a normal child would do."

CHAPTER 2

Even though he was in the cellar, her music came thudding through the floorboards from two levels up. Alice Cooper was singing about loving the dead. Simone liked the song, but it didn't half derail his train of thought when it pounded inside his skull.

She was more than likely in her dance room. Getting her "groove on", as she told him.

"*Loving the Dead*"*? No, the single isn't called that.* "*Dead Lover*"*? No, not that, either. Damn it! Why can't I remember?* "She's told me loads of times," he spat, turning around with rage coursing through his body. He faced Paddington Bear, who was laced to a chair by a pair of his mother's stockings.

She would always give him the ripped pairs to play with, or "laddered" ones, as she called them.

Lashing out, he caught the stuffed bear in the face with the hammer he was holding. Even though there was a bare bulb in the room, it didn't do much good in illuminating the space; in the disjointed light, Paddington looked hurt by the blow. The expression on his face seemed to change.

But that was madness – it was just the bad lighting warping things.

"Where are your rebel forces, Bear?!" Simone yelled at the teddy. He wanted to make sure he could be heard over the deafening music. Bear didn't answer. "*Well?!*" Simone yelled at the top of his voice, before pounding Paddington some more. "Talk, *traitor!*"

Turning from the bear, he walked around the back of the chair Paddington was tied to. "Mr. Tickles," Simone addressed the two-foot stuffed clown to his side. "Our pal doesn't want to talk. Maybe we need to make an example out of one of his friends!"

In Simone's mind, the clown nodded. "*I agree, sir – make the rebel filth speak – break his fucking toes with the hammer!*"

"Perhaps a bit much for now," Simone said. "But soon."

Silence.

For a horrid, split second, Simone had thought he'd gone deaf. Never had he felt such crushing peace. But his panic did not last long, as a new track kicked in – this one he didn't know. Alice was now singing about a maniac being in love with you; the lyrics made him smile. He loved all things dark. "Mam has been a great in…flu…ence on me," he said. "No matter what Smelly Sian says," he said to Mr. Tickles.

"*Your sister is a fucking whore – a small titted one at that!*"

Simone smiled at Mr. Tickles' comments. "He-he," escaped him. "You're right – they're not as big as Mam's," he said.

"*You got that fucking right, kid. Now, are we going to finish this little fucker's friends off?*"

Simone turned his attention to the wrestling figures he had on top of the cellar's workbench. A tool rack also lined that wall – the hammer had come from one of the slots there. Mother had said it had all belonged to his dad; that he was free to use it all as he pleased.

And so, he did.

Opening the vice to halfway, he then picked up the first wrestler from the pile he laid a hand on, which happened to be Papa Shango – the figures had been bought for him over the years by various family members.

Holding Shango by his legs with one hand, Simone used his free one to close the vice on the brawler's head. He turned the iron bar until he heard a faint *crack*. Mr. Tickles gave off a light chuckle.

Satisfied, Simone moved away from the vice. He picked the hammer back up. "Now, you are either going to talk or your second in command is going to die!" the youth screamed over the drone of music. "*Well?* Answer me!"

Paddington didn't say a word, as expected.

"He's a tough son-of-a-bitch this one!" Mr. Tickles said.

Screaming, Simone turned and swung the hammer with all his might. The ballpoint smashed through the plastic figure, which exploded into hundreds of tiny pieces. Papa Shango's head remained in the vice.

"Talk!" Simone yelled. "Talk, talk, *talk*!" he repeatedly screamed – his prepubescent voice cracking and squeaking. Without much thought, he picked up another figure, Jake 'the Snake' Roberts, and crushed him in the vice, before wildly smashing up two more figures: Ax and Smash. "Now will you talk?!" he asked Paddington, getting right into the bear's face.

"*Please, don't hurt me. I'll talk,*" Paddington squeaked.

"*The dirty fucker's pissed his pants,*" Mr. Tickles said.

"He's not allowed to clean himself until after he's given us the information we need," Simone said.

"*I'll talk – I swear! Just don't hurt any more of my men…*" Paddington squeaked on.

"I'll do what I want!" the youngster said. Turning, Simone looked up at the G.I. Joe action figures he had placed by the side of Mr. Tickles. Their originals names had been Road Pig and Rock & Roll – but Simone had renamed them Spiked Mace and Rape Charge. "You two – go and see if there are any more of the enemy close by." Picking them up, he put them into the pockets of his jeans, thus giving the illusion of them having gone to follow orders. "Good," he said, nodding his head before turning to address the other three G.I. Joe figures standing behind the vice.

Their names had also been replaced from Gristle, Hotwire and Overload to Neck Snap, Incest and Cumslot. "You three! Go and help the others. I need to make sure this *bear* hasn't got support near. Go! And make sure you don't spare any prisoners. They *die*!"

All three G.I.'s nodded in unison.

Turning back to Paddington, Simone got close to the soft, furry face of his prisoner. "Something to tell me?" he whispered.

Paddington had once again retreated to silence.

"I see," Simone said. "I guess we will continue to press your lieutenants."

"*Do as you wish, cunt! When I get out of here, I'm going to rip your guts out. His, too,*" Paddington said, indicating Mr. Tickles with a flick of his head. "*And when I'm done with you pair, I'm going to rape your mother – fuck her in the arse and spurt my jism on her tits…*"

Simone smiled as he back-handed the bear across the face. "Mr. Tickles, would you hand me Stanley, please?"

"*Nooo, not that – anything but that. Please! I beg you – not my stuffing*!"

"Yes, the stuffing! Unless you're willing to talk?"

"*Never*!"

"I was hoping you would say that, Paddington," Simone said – his boyish smile was wide, matching Mr. Tickles'.

Picking up the Stanley knife, Simone closed in on his fluffy target's chest. He smiled when he saw Bear turn his head away and whimper.

"*Please…I beg you…*"

"We're past begging, I'm sorry."

"*Cut the pig traitor open!*" Mr. Tickles said. "*It ends today.*"

Moving his aim from the bear's chest, Simone grabbed a fluffy ear, and pulled on it as hard as he could. "Think I'll take this first!" he said to nobody in particular.

"*Argh*!" Paddington squealed.

The clown clapped his hands together as loudly as he could. He did this repeatedly, making Simone think of thunder. He hated thunder. And lightning. It scared him – made him wet the bed. But that hadn't happened in a long time.

Mam says I'm getting to be a big boy, he thought.

On that note, his mother's pounding music stopped, which caused him to let Paddington's ear go. He listened with pricked ears. She was starting to move around in her dance room – it was her favourite room in the house; his too. He loved how she looked in all the mirrors which surrounded the space.

All the walls and ceiling were covered in them. She'd had them specially made, along with the guardrails that ran the length of the walls. Simone had been told they were used for dance moves. He'd seen her using them, of course, many times, even though she had told him to stay away from the room when she was dancing.

He couldn't resist – he loved watching her; loved seeing her buttocks and slender legs move beneath her tight jogging trousers. Sometimes, she danced naked. Let everything out. She'd never caught him spying on her naked, as he'd cut a peephole into the ceiling above her room.

She'd thrash me but good if she ever caught me, he thought.

Thinking about his crawlspace and peephole at the top of the house, and hearing his mother move around, Simone's face flushed.

"I wonder if she'll take me to the club tonight, Mr. Tickles," he said.

"*Can I come if she does*?" the clown asked, breaking out a big, fat cigar.

"Of course – I couldn't very well leave my second in command behind."

"*Thanks, boss*."

Simone smiled at this. He liked the fact that his men called him 'boss', or 'gang leader', depending on the game they were playing. He'd always wanted to be in a gang. A street gang, of sort. Their way of life puzzled him – intrigued him, much like the gypsies and fairground hands that crawled through his home town of Porthcawl during off-seasons. He'd heard whispers that they met up and held fights outside the fairground at witching hour.

He relished the thought of them beating the crap out of each other close to the sea as the moon shone down on them. He thought of how cool some of them looked – wearing bandanas, scruffy torn jeans and T-shirts with dirty logos on them; that some probably had scars and eye patches. They had 'Mum' tattoos on their muscular forearms…

The sound of rushing feet on the stairs above brought him out of his thoughts. "You'll keep!" he told Paddington as the door to the cellar opened.

"Simone?" his mother called down the stairs. Even her voice stirred excitement in him. He loved her so much.

"Yes, Mam?" he said, his voice squeaking.

"I'm heading off to Bunnies soon – I've left something for you to eat in the microwave, love."

Her scent wafted down the cellar steps – it stuffed his nostrils. "You smell nice, Mam."

"Aw, thanks, love."

"Aren't you going to come down to see me before you go?"

"I wasn't going to. I have my heels on. Hang on, I'll come down. I want to give my big, strong boy a kiss before I go," she said, making her way down the steps.

"Can't I come with you tonight? You always take me to your shows, Mam."

"Not tonight, love. We've got one of the big managers in this evening."

"Who's going to look after me, then?"

"Sian well be here in ten-minutes," she said, her form finally appearing in the gloom.

"Wow, you look pretty, Mam," he said.

"*Look at the fucking tits on that!*" Mr. Tickles said.

Simone wanted to scold his second in command for saying such a thing, especially in his mother's presence. But he couldn't – because he spoke the truth. She looked amazing in her very short cheerleader skirt and top to match, which showed off a lot of her cleavage and midriff. Her long black hair flanked her pretty face, which was scant of make-up.

"Thanks, love."

"And I definitely can't come tonight?"

"Not tonight, sorry. But I'll give Crystal your love?" she said, teasing him about his crush on one of her colleagues.

"*Mam!*"

"Oh, come on – I know you like her," she said, giving him a wink.

His face flushed. "Stop it!" he said in a low and coy way.

"You're a young, normal lad. You should be having such feelings and urges. The girls at Bunnies love you like you're their own, Simone, you little heartbreaker," she said, hugging him and then turning to go back up the stairs. This gave Mr. Tickles a fine view of her shapely arse.

Simone knew his clown was looking. It didn't bother him.

"Don't forget your dinner in the micro, love. And share some with Sian. I'll be home around five in the morning. Bye!"

"*Bye!*" he called up the stairs after her. Her smell lingered in the dank, squalid room.

Lowering his head, Simone felt sad. He hated it when she left home without him. He wanted her around all the time.

"*Hey, boss – there's no need to be sad,*" Mr. Tickles said.

"Why?"

"*Because we have Sian coming around, and you just know she's going to want to play doctor with you!*"

The thought brightened him. "Good point. Best we round the guys up, and head to HQ," Simone said, meaning his bedroom.

"*Uh-huh,*" the clown said, putting his cigar out.

"Neck Snap, Rape Charge, Spiked Mace, Cumslot and Incest," he called. "Fall in, men."

Standing the G.I.'s on either side of Mr. Tickles, he stood back and looked at them. Admired them. First in line was Neck Snap: he looked mean as sin, with bared teeth and long red hair, which he had tied into a ponytail. He also wore dark shades, so his eyes couldn't be seen. He was Simone's best scout. Next to him was Incest – the ninja of the group. His combat armour and helmet made him look a little like a cyborg, which he wasn't. On one hand, he had a massive set of steel claws, making him look a lot like Wolverine. Simone had even given Incest the comic book hero's catchphrase: "*I'm the best there is at what I do, but what I do best isn't very nice.*"

Beside Incest was Cumslot – the plainest of the bunch. The only thing that stood out about him was his white tech coat and black gloves. He was the mad experimenter of Simone's gang. Then there was Mr. Tickles, the leader of the men. His garish purple and black make-up would have scared the living shit out of any nine-year-old, but Simone thought he was cool. His look helped instil fear into the men. It kept them trained and focused. Nobody would dare laugh at his freaky eyes or floppy shoes. Simone had seen the outcome to such a thing.

Standing as rigid as a poker the other side of the clown was Spiked Mace. He was Mr. Tickles' right-hand man – the enforcer. He wore no T-shirt, exposing a massive cobra tattoo on his chest. His eyes were straight and staring, making him look even more intimidating, along with his flat-top haircut. The cobra tattoo was a mark of his clan – the Cobra clan. The other three G.I.'s wore the same mark on their uniforms, unlike Rape Charge, who didn't belong. He had once been a good guy, but had defected. He now fought with Simone and the rest, which he was glad of, as Rape Charge was one of his favourites. He liked how he wore a bandana and two bandoliers of bullets over his upper body.

They were indeed impressive. They were his men – his gang of Krulls, and Simone was the leader. Krulls. *Where have I heard that before?* he thought. In a film? Then it came to him. Sian had told him all about this cool book she had been reading about a band of killers named the Krulls. She'd promised to read it to him, but never had.

But that didn't matter. She'd told him enough about the killer gang and their ways. Enough so that he could recreate his own gang of murderous Krulls. *What a funny word,* he thought. *It sounds like Skulls. Maybe I could draw mini skulls on them?*

"*Awesome!*" he shouted.

"*Sir?*" Mr. Tickles said.

"Oh, erm, yes, right. Now that I have you all here, I want you to regroup in HQ. We'll leave the prisoner tied down here for the night."

"*You heard him, dirt bags!*" Spiked Mace said. "*Let's move the fuck out.*"

Just as Simone pocketed all his figures and grabbed Mr. Tickles, he heard Sian upstairs.

"Simone, where are you?"

"Down here, Sian."

"Well come on up here," she said.

"I was going to go to my room."

"Aw, don't you want to keep me company?"

That thought stirred him. "Yes," he said. His face flushed. "Can we play games?"

"Uh-huh," she said – playfulness in her voice.

"*Let's have her!*" Mr. Tickles said. "*Make her* play *with us, like she often does.*"

Simone's heart raced. He nodded. "Good idea…" he said, letting his words trail off as he headed upstairs to greet his sister.

CHAPTER 3

When Simone had stopped talking, there was no response. He knew Lara was there, because he could hear her breathing. His little memory had either shocked her into silence, or she was thinking of something to say – of how to react. Surely she'd heard worse? She was a Samaritan, for Christ's sake.

As he waited for a reply, he looked over to the fair once again. The sun had now gone away completely, leaving the sky peppered with stars. The glow of pretty, glimmering lights from the fairground called like a beacon. If he had time, he would definitely head on over there – maybe ride the *Ghost Train*.

But won't Chaos wonder where I am? he thought, looking at his watch. No, it was still very early. She knew, once she let him out for a 'scavenge', that he wouldn't return until midnight. Later, even. It wasn't unusual for him to be out until four or five in the morning.

A solid minute must have passed since he'd stopped talking. He was beginning to wonder if Lara had suffered a heart attack. "I have finished," he said, making sure she knew that.

"Oh…I…"

"I know how it must sound."

"I'm sorry, I didn't mean to come across rude…"

"Huh, it's fine."

"How old are you, Simone, if you don't mind me asking?"

"I'll be twenty-six this summer. You?"

"Er…"

"It's only a number – it's not like you're telling me your personal *phone* number."

"Nineteen"

"You're at university, aren't you?"

"Simone, this should be…"

"You are, aren't you?"

"Yes," she conceded.

"So, this is just a summer job – a part-time thing?"

"How…"

"So, what's your real name?"

"I told…"

"I know what you told me, which was a lie. If I can't trust you, I can't fully open up to you."

She sighed. "It's Toni, with an I."

"As in Antonia?"

"No, just Toni."

"Very nice. What are you studying, Toni with an I?"

"English Literature."

"Nice."

The line fell silent. He was making this about her, which is what he didn't want. He wasn't trying to pick her up. To lure her back to his home. He wanted to confess to her. Tell her everything. *This was meant to be the end to my whole sordid ways*, he thought. *I knew talking to a woman was no good. It should have been a man, as first planned. It's going to happen all over again.*

No. He could never talk to a man about such things. Never. He loved interacting with women. To flirt with them. He'd always found it easy to pick them up. Always.

Change direction, he told himself. *Now.*

"Yes…"

"I'm fucked in the head, aren't I?" he blurted.

"Oh, Simone, don't say that about yourself. Everyone has problems to deal with. We're not all perfect, you know?!"

"*Huh*!" he huffed.

"It's true. You shouldn't feel bad. At least you are trying to get help now. Tell me more about your sister."

"What do you want to know?"

"You said she…played with you. Doctor, was it?"

"That's right. It went on for years. When it first started, which was two years prior to that memory I just gave you, I didn't really know what was going on. I mean, she was my sister. Touching and kissing seemed normal."

"It would seem it, I guess. Kissing and touching the people we love *is* normal...I thought playing harshly with your toys was your oldest memory?"

"Except she was my sister. I knew no better," he said, ignoring her question.

"Well, yes...But you know what I mean."

"Of course."

"How was she caught? How old were you?"

"I believe I was eleven years old."

"So, by this point you knew exactly what was right and wrong – that what she had been doing, and was still doing, was completely unorthodox. That she had abused your and your mam's trust."

"Huh," he said.

"Who caught you?"

"Our mother. She had Sian taken away. I was crushed."

"What did your mother do to you?"

"Nothing. She saw it all as Sian's fault. People suggested therapy, but my mother would have none of it."

"She loved you very much, didn't she?"

"My mother? Very much so."

"Before we talk about your mother some more, do you want to tell me about the night you were caught with your sister?"

****

Electric blue rain splashed across his bedroom window as lightning lit up the night sky. A clap of thunder made him turn his head to look, but the fear of storms had left him long ago. No more wet nights.

"*Fucking thunder,*" Mr. Tickles said. More lightning raked across the sky. The azure flash splashed across the doll's face, making him look otherworldly, especially as Mr. Tickles had his mouth wide open, exposing a mouth filled with tiny, razor-sharp teeth. "*But lightning is beautiful, boss.*"

"I agree – but the fucking thunder is annoying," Simone said, facing his TV again. Grabbing the remote, he hiked the volume up. The film playing was one of his favourites – *The Texas Chainsaw Massacre.* He'd seen it a thousand times now. He'd first watched it with his mother, when he was much younger.

Mr. Tickles had wanted to watch one of Simone's mother's films, but he hadn't wanted to. He'd seen them too many times, and it was starting to spoil the sexy image he had of his mother. But not Mr. Tickles.

No way. He loved looking at her tits every opportunity he got. *The naughty clown*, he thought, taking a sneaky glance over at his playmate. His second in command. He smiled then carried on watching his film.

Leatherface was so cool. Simone had asked for the action figure for Christmas, along with Jason Voorhees and Michael Myers. If he was lucky enough to get any of them, they would become new members of his Krull gang. *But only if they can pass their initiation,* he thought. *I wonder if they come with weapons, like the G.I.'s do? They must.*

"*Oo, I love this bit of the film,*" Mr. Tickles said. "*I just wished the old man in the chair could grasp the hammer, and smash Sally's brains out!*"

"I don't understand why Leatherface or Chop-Top doesn't do it for him? The guy is clearly dead."

"*Remember caving Paddington's head in with the hammer?*"

"How could I forget that? It was amazing. Especially when you and the rest of the guys helped me pull his arms and legs off!"

"*Ha-ha!*" the clown chuckled. His voice had grown deeper. More sinister over the years. Simone loved that. "*Dancing around in his spilt fur was pretty funny.*"

"He-he-he!" Simone blurted. "Smashing all his men to smithereens with the hammer was also great."

"*Yeah, it was smash…ing!*"

They both erupted with laughter at that one, which drowned out the buzz of Leatherface's impressive chainsaw. "Nice one!" Simone said. "I wish we could go back and play that game again," Simone confessed.

"*Torturing that fucking twerp of a bear was fun. Killing off all his men was fun, too.*"

"Too true."

"*Do you think Mam knows we killed Izzy?*"

"No. I heard her talking on the phone to Auntie Claire the other day. She thinks our cat ran away."

"*Good. So much blood for such a tiny animal!*"

"I knew we shouldn't have used a drill on its face straightaway – we could have drawn that one out."

"*I don't know – Spiked Mace had told me that Izzy had been informing the Power Rangers of what we were doing, you know?*"

"About the spying on Mam? She can never find out, you know. What if they tell on us?"

"*We need to silence them, just like we silenced Bear.*"

"Agreed. First thing tomorrow morning, you, me and the rest of the guys are going to storm the toy chest – smoke 'em out, if we have to!"

Mr. Tickles clapped his hands together wildly, but stopped when there was a knock at the bedroom door.

"Mam?"

"No, it's Sian."

"Is Mam home yet?"

"No, it's only midnight – she won't be back for a while yet. Can I come in?"

"Can't you sleep?" he asked.

"No, the storm is scaring me. Can I sleep with you?"

"Of course."

Simone looked at Mr. Tickles, who winked. Picking up his remote, Simone turned the TV down. He knew Sian wouldn't want to watch it with him. She hated horror films. They scared her. She'd once told him that her dad used to tie her up, and make her watch them. That was one of many cruel things he used to do to her, which went on for years. It wasn't until Mam found out what he'd been doing to her that she got up and left him.

His door edged open. "Are you decent?" she asked.

"Yeah, come on in," he said, beckoning her with his hand.

His eyes automatically drew to her legs, as the nightshirt she wore was short. The caption on the front depicted Care Bears with magical unicorns and colourful rainbows. As hard as he tried, he couldn't look away from her lightly tanned legs. They were mesmerising. They had him caught somewhere between heaven and hell, and thoughts of his mother's legs in the fishnet stockings that she sometimes wore in her dance room.

Even though Sian was only fifteen, she had started to develop quickly. Her body was becoming a woman's. Her breasts had become much bigger over the last few months.

"What are you looking at?" she said, playfully.

"Uh, nothing!" His face heated. "*Nothing*!" he whined, lowering his head slightly.

Sian smiled. "Okay, if you say so," she said, turning to look at the TV. "Can you put something else on? You know I hate horror films." Her face suddenly lost its colour.

"Sorry," he said, switching the channel. "What would you like on?"

"Anything."

"Not much on at this hour," he complained.

She pulled the covers back and he noticed she was looking at his boxers. Then he saw her blush. He found it amusing since she'd seen him completely naked many times.

"That's okay. We can just cuddle up and listen to the rain."

"Sounds good."

"*Ew*!" she squealed. "What's *he* doing so close to the bed?!"

"Who?"

"That…that *clown*!"

"It's only Mr. Tickles," he protested.

"I hate him. Please put him in the wardrobe or somewhere else. He scares me!"

Simone smiled and got out of bed. "Sorry, pal," he told his second in command. "I've got to put you away."

"*Keep the cupboard door open a crack, boss. You know I like to watch. She has a fine little arse on her*!" he said.

This caused Simone to giggle.

"He-he, what's so funny?" Sian asked.

"Nothing."

"*Something's* tickled you?"

"You, being scared of Mr. Tickles – the funniest clown in the *wooooorld*!" Simone said, placing his friend in his wardrobe. He left the door open a sliver for his right-hand man. "There you go, friend," he whispered.

"Are you talking to that clown?" Sian said, stifling a laugh.

"He's my friend."

"I think you're funny in the head. Maybe nurse Sian can help you out?"

Simone turned, and saw that his sister's nightgown had rucked up around her midriff. She wasn't wearing any knickers. A heat stirred in his boxers. "Sian…" he started, but his words caught in his throat as he spied her privates. Not an ounce of hair could be seen on her soft, almost womanly parts.

"What?" she asked, putting her hand down there. She started to finger herself – to ply the skin.

His jaw fell slack. They'd done *things* before, but she'd never showed him her…her… *pussy*, as he'd heard it called in films. He'd seen his mother's, on screen and off. He'd seen plenty of them at the club his mother worked at – tits, too. But this was Sian's.

"You want to touch it, don't you?!" she said, almost pouting. "You have before. And put your willy in it!"

Simone could only nod. Seeing it was a lot different to blindly touching it with his penis and fingers

"Then why don't you come closer? I won't hurt you."

He hesitated. There was no need to worry – Mam wouldn't be back for hours.

"Fucking bastards," she muttered, closing the door behind her. Her bunny ears fell to the floor as she unzipped her thigh-high boots and kicked them off. "They could have told me they didn't want me this evening," she continued to grumble.

Looking down at her legs, she noticed she'd snagged her fishnets here and there. The gaping holes on the left helped expose the massive tattoo of a female jester she had there. It had been done some ten years ago, but the colour was still impressively vivid. The naked clown, sporting ample breasts and macabre face and body paint, held in her one hand the four aces, whilst in the other she had a magic eight-ball.

Simone loved the ink.

Noticing the living room lights were out, Carla moved in there and switched them on. The TV was off. So too were the kitchen lights. "Not like them to be in bed so early on a Friday night. They're normally vegged out in front of the box down here."

Shrugging, she moved to the kitchen. Her hair was plastered to her skull and back from the heavy rain outside. "God, I need to dry my mop," she said, ruffling her lank strands of jet black hair. Putting the kettle on, she used the toilet as it boiled. Finished, she poured herself a mug of black coffee before taking it upstairs to her room.

With the landing light off, she could see that Simone's room was lit up due to a glow coming from under his closed door. Before heading over to his room, she first went to her own. She placed her mug of coffee on her bedside table, then closed her door to ajar. Carla proceeded to slip out of her jumpsuit first, and then sat on her bed to peel her fishnets off. Once they were free from her body, she rolled them into a ball and threw them into the wastepaper bin by the side of her dressing table.

Naked, she stepped up to the back of her bedroom door and unhooked the bathrobe that hung there. She closed the oversized garment around her and snuggled into it before picking up her mug and heading out the door.

As she started to cross the landing, she noticed Sian's door was wide open. The light was on inside. *How didn't I notice this?* she wondered. Stopping there first, she poked her head inside, expecting to find her daughter crashed out in front of her TV as usual.

But that wasn't the case.

The TV was in fact playing, but Sian wasn't there. Her duvet lay in a rumpled heap on top of her bed, suggesting she *had* been there. Carla couldn't help but smile on seeing the boy band posters on Sian's walls among many pink and fluffy articles. "She certainly doesn't follow me," she whispered. *You've definitely got more of* his *personality in you, you poor thing.*

She hadn't thought about her ex-husband in years. Why tonight? She should have seen and known what he had been up to with her. Shaking her head, she cleared her mind. "She must be in the bathroom," Carla surmised, which was across the hall from where she stood.

Not bothering to check the toilet for her daughter, Carla crossed to Simone's room. Before she entered however, a strange, gasping-giggling sound came from within, stopping her.

The TV? she thought. *No, it didn't sound like…*

"Oh, Simone!" Carla heard her daughter gasp. "Not like that. I've showed you once!" Sian said, giggling.

"What the hell?!" Carla whispered, putting her hand on the door handle. She plunged it downward without another thought and threw the door wide. The mug seemed to fall from her hand in slow-motion. It hit the carpeted floor and spewed its contents.

On the bed, in a lovers' knot, were her son and daughter. Her children. Her *babies.* They were engaged in a sexual activity. "S…S…Sian, what the *hell* are you doing to him?!" Carla screamed. "He's your brother! He's only eleven years old!" she seethed, going to her daughter and pulling her off Simone by grabbing her by her upper-arm. With her free hand, Carla slapped her daughter about the head. "You stupid, stupid child! How could you – after everything we've been through?!"

"Mam, stop it!" Simone screamed from the bed. "You're hurting her!"

"Do you have any idea of how wrong that is!" she yelled at them, continuing to hit Sian. "Get some clothes on, Simone. Now!"

"What are you going to do with Sian?" he asked, watching his mother drag his naked sister out of his room. Sian wailed as her shoulder popped out of its socket, but that didn't stop Carla, who seemed to drag the girl along even harder.

"I knew having you here would end up being a mistake. You'll burn in hell like your father!" Carla screamed at her daughter.

****

"I've only ever told that story to one other person, and that's Chaos. She knows all about me," Simone said. *But I'll never tell anyone about killing the cat. That's my secret.*

"God, it's *awful*!" Toni said. "What happened after that?"

"Mam beat her some more, before calling the authorities."

"Your sister was taken that *night*?!" Toni asked, sounding astounded.

"Yes, that very night. My mother blamed it all on her. She said that I had been the victim."

"That's terrible."

"I was as much to blame, but my mother would have none of it, saying I was too young to understand any of what happened."

"It must have been a dreadful time, Simone."

"It was. We were the talk of the town. People gave us black looks, which never went away. It never forced us out, though. We dug our heels in."

"Brave," Toni said.

"Yes. I've carried the guilt of my sister around for years. Talking about it helps."

"That's what I'm here for. I won't judge you, Simone. I'm just here to listen and help."

"It's good to know. I think you're right. Talking about my problems and my past is going to help me change my ways."

"You're feeling a little better?"

"A bit, yes."

"There's probably a lot more you need to get off your chest, Simone. Maybe you should start seeing a doctor, too?"

"Maybe, but I've tried before. I think I'll keep talking to you for now, if that's okay?"

"Of course. You can ring at anytime," she said, giving Simone her extension number. "Do you want to talk more now…?"

"Not now. I have to go. It's getting late, and Chaos is going to expect me home soon."

"Right, okay. Well, you have my number, so ring when you feel like it," she said.

****

Simone disconnected the call before saying, "Bye." He felt slightly irritated. The bitch seemed to condemn Sian without even knowing her. *No, that's not true,* he argued with himself. *She was only trying to help – to get the full picture. She told me herself that she would not judge, only listen.*

Pocketing his phone, he took a deep breath. Holding it in, he let it out when his lungs started to hurt. The night had finally settled in. The moon hung low over the shores of Porthcawl – casting its milky glow over the calm sea.

Looking to his left, Simone took in the sound and sight of the fair; the coloured bulbs called to him, along with the excited screams and laughter. Excitement started creeping back in. His hands started to shake.

Closing his eyes, he put his head back and took in a few more gulps of air before stalking off towards the fair. "Let's see if I can hook me a prize," he said, giggling as he disappeared into the gloom.

CHAPTER 4

"Simone?" Toni said. "Simone, have you gone?" *Damn*, she thought. *I should have tried to get him to hang on longer. There's no saying he'll ring back, or, if he does, he might start chatting to someone else.*

Do I really care? That was my first conversation with the guy. He's also a major pervert. Yeah, but there was something soft about him, she told herself. *Something gentle. He sounded so hurt and lost.*

"Long, hard call, Toni?" Stuart asked. He sat in the cubicle beside her.

"Huh, you can say that again," she said, removing her headset. "Your phone is quiet?"

"Yes, which is a good thing. It's Friday, and I'm ready to party!" he said. "I'm busting to get out of here."

"You're going to Metal-Land again, Stu?"

"Damn right. It is buy one get one free on Friday nights. You should come. Let your hair down!"

"I can't. I don't finish until eleven, and then I have a pile of Uni work to do when I get home."

"Toni, it's the beginning of summer, love. Take some time off. Live a little. Rock that body of yours!" he said, getting off his chair to do a little jig of his own.

Smiling, she removed her headset. "I don't think I'm in the mood for beer, joints and metal music tonight. I have work to do," she said, placing her headset down. "I need a coffee. Fancy a cuppa?" she asked him.

"Are you making?"

"Of course," she said, smiling.

"Then, yes. I will."

"Two sugars?" she asked.

"As always."

"Cool. See you in a bit," she said.

Before Stuart could answer, his phone started ringing. "Hello, Samaritans?" He waved her off as she gestured to leave.

She smiled, and then headed to the kitchen at the back of the office. The building was small. It only comprised one floor for fifty staff. Tonight, most of the others had gone home. Oddly, it never seemed that busy over the weekends. *You'd think that's when people were the loneliest*, she thought. Apparently not. Monday through to Thursday was crazy busy. The phones barely stopped ringing at the start of the week.

"Hiya, Mike," she said, passing one of the older guys she knew. Mike was a veteran. Had been with the job almost twenty years. Like her, Mike worked the afternoons through to the evening.

He was on the phone, unable to answer back, so she mouthed the words, "Fancy a coffee?" and made a drinking motion with her hand. He gave her a thumbs up in return.

A hubbub rippled through the mostly deserted office, which was kind of nice. She'd only been doing the job for the past four weeks, and she loved it. Even though it was only a part-time job to help her through Uni, she was seriously considering taking it up full-time when she finished education. Helping people gave her a real buzz. A sense of purpose.

Pushing the kitchen door open, the sudden darkness took her by surprise. A harsh chill swirled the air inside and prickled the skin on her arms. The hairs at the back of her neck instantly raised. "Hello?" she said, feeling silly. "Too many scary books, Toni!" she said, fumbling for the light switch.

She couldn't find it.

Then she heard an intense flapping sound coming from behind her. "Who's there?" she said, her voice almost breaking. "Simone?" *Simone*?! *What the hell are you saying?* she thought. Had that conversation startled her? She finally found the light switch and flicked it on.

Straightaway, Toni could see it was the window blinds making the noise. A window had been left open, causing them to flutter. *No wonder the room is so cold*, she thought. Going to it, she pulled it closed. "Probably been open all day. It has been nice out," she muttered to herself.

Taking the milk out of the fridge, she turned to put the kettle on.

"Where's that cuppa?" a voice boomed behind her.

With a shriek, Toni jumped and dropped the bottle of milk. It smashed on impact with the tiled ground, sending white liquid everywhere.

"*Stu*!"

"Oh, shit! Sorry, I didn't mean to make you jump. I was only coming in to give you a hand. Why are you so spooked?"

"Huh? Oh, I don't know," she said. "I came in here and the lights were off…"

"Was that last call of yours a bad one? They can rattle me at times," he confessed.

"No…Well," she said, bending down to pick up some of the bigger shards of shattered glass.

"Hey, no, don't do that – we have a dustpan and brush under the sink," he said, going for the cupboard doors. "Here, out of the way. This is my fault," he told her.

Toni looked down at him and smiled. She now wished she could go out and have a drink with him. "So, are you heading down to Porthcawl tonight?" she asked, knowing the answer and that she couldn't go.

"Having second thoughts?" he asked, not looking up.

"Possibly."

He let out a huff.

"What?" she asked.

"Oh, nothing. Hey, fancy getting the mop out of the walk-in cupboard behind you?"

"Uh, yeah, sure." Turning, Toni pulled open the door which was directly behind her. Locating the mop, she pulled it out along with the bucket. Placing the red plastic pail under the hot tap, she filled it with water and cleaning fluid.

Stopping the water when the bucket was just under half-full, Toni took it from under the tap and placed it on the floor. After dunking the mop, she rang it, then started to dab at the milk. "Have you got it all?" she asked.

"All the big bits, yes. But I'm sure there's still plenty of particles," he said.

"I wouldn't worry, as long as the worst of it's up."

"I'm so sorry. I really shouldn't have crept up on you like that. Silly."

"*Tut*, don't apologise. You weren't to know I'd act like a little bitch," she said, winking at him.

Looking up, he smiled, before going back to the sweeping.

God, you look sooooo cute, she thought. He had the whole surfer image going on: the shaggy, long blond hair. He wore a rope necklace with a shark tooth for a pendant. On his right wrist, he wore lots of different bands – some depicted gigs he'd been to; others were of charities he supported and helped. On his left forearm, leading up to his neck, was a sleeve tattoo of various sea creatures, skulls, pirates and old ships.

Mother's worst nightmare for a boyfriend, she told herself. But she didn't live with her mother any longer. Toni lived with a student flatmate in Bridgend. Suzanne was a great person to live with – clean and tidy. She kept her stuff organised, which Toni loved, since that's what she was like: a clean freak with a splash of OCD. Had she been sharing a place with someone who was the complete opposite, they probably would have ended up killing each other.

This way, everybody was happy. And alive. Plus, she and Suzanne studied the same course, which meant they were reading the same material and taking on similar topics for essays. It really was a great situation, as the first semester had proven.

Maybe one drink with Stu wouldn't harm…

"What do you think?" he asked.

"*Hmm*?" she asked, her face flushed.

"Ha-ha, that interesting, am I?" he ribbed.

"Oh, no, I, er…*Sorry*!" she agonised, scrunching up her face.

"Stop apologising. I was only teasing, Toni."

"What were you saying?"

"I was wondering if you'd changed your mind about tonight. Would you like to come for a beer? A few guys are having a small party down on the beach. Close to the point," he said.

"By the *Hi-Tide*?"

"Yep, that's right."

"Sounds lovely. Can I bring Suzanne?"

His smile widened. "Of course. Is she single? If not, she can bring her fella. You, too." he said, lowering his gaze.

"Oh, no, neither of us is seeing anyone," she blurted.

"Cool," he said. "Then it's a date…"

Surprise lit her face.

"You know what I mean," he said, and blushed.

"Yeah, it's a *date*," she teased.

"Behave," he said, giggling. "Shall I pick you both up?"

"If you want. You sure you don't mind coming from Porthcawl to get us?" she asked.

"Not at all. You finish at eleven?"

She nodded.

"Okay, cool. The guys aren't getting the party going until twelve-ish. You want to come just before then? I'll swing by around ten-to, if that's fine by you?"

"Sounds good," she said, mopping the last of the milk up. "We'll be ready for you."

"You're sure your flatmate will want to come?"

"Suzanne? *Pfft*, you must be kidding – anything for a drink in the company of a group of fellas."

He let out a huff-laugh as he stood up and emptied the contents of the dustpan into the bin. "Now, shall we make the cuppas?"

"Okay," she said.

Once the coffees had been made for Stu, Mike and herself, Toni once again sat at her desk. The phone had gone quiet. For now. And with Stu on a call, she had nobody to speak with. So, she picked up that day's newspaper from an empty, neighbouring desk and started flicking through it.

Death, destruction, murder, war and terrorism. That's all the news reports were these days. Either that, or there were stories about dumb, Z-list celebrities who liked nothing more than mouthing off about each other. And why? Just so they could have five minutes of fame in a shitty magazine or low-key newspaper. *Sad*, she thought.

The sound of Stu's solemn voice made her look up. He always tried to sound so positive on the phone. Although she couldn't see him, as all the desks were closed off for privacy, she couldn't help but look over at his cubicle. He sounded pained.

It was understandable, as some of the people who called in were very upset. Unhinged, too, at times. In the short time Toni had been here, she'd had five suicide calls. One woman who'd had her children taken off her due to her decline after her husband had left her, had told Toni that she was going to start swallowing pills until she "went to sleep."

That had been one of her very first calls. It had startled her. Left her shaken and afraid to take another. Her manager had sent her home early that night. She'd planned to never return. But she had. It had made her stronger.

Maybe Stu was on such a call.

They could be very regular at times.

When a call came through to her, Toni jumped. Again, she'd gone into her own little world. She laughed as she put a hand to her chest. Her heart thundered beneath her ribs. *What on earth is wrong with me tonight?* she wondered.

Closing and folding the paper, she placed it to one side and answered her call. The line was silent. Crackly, but silent. At first, she thought it was Simone. Had he rung back? "Hello?" she asked. "Anyone there?"

She waited a bit longer.

"Blood…Everywhere. It's on the sand…in my hair…on my body…"

The line went dead.

"What the hell was that?!" she said out loud. A chill snaked its way down her body and settled in the pit of her gut. Her neck hair stood on end. Although the line had been bad, with the signal cutting in and out, she had distinctly heard the words 'blood' and 'everywhere'. The voice, however, had not been distinguishable.

A prank? she wondered. They often had a lot of them. *More than likely*, she tried to reassure herself. *Could it have been him*? Toni questioned. *No, it couldn't have been. He was harmless. Slightly perverted, but not a…killer. Killer*? *What are you talking about – you don't even know if what you heard is correct.*

Her phone rang again.

She hesitated.

"Hello?" she said, picking the phone up quickly, before her nerve got the better of her.

"Hi," a female voice said. "I need someone to talk to."

Toni let out a massive breath. She hadn't even realised she'd been holding it.

"Hello?" the voice said again. It belonged to a very blue person. "Have you gone?"

"No, I'm still here – sorry. I'm having connection problems," she lied. But it gave her enough time to recover. "How can I help this evening?"

The woman didn't need much encouragement to start speaking. She told Toni how her life had spiralled out of control the last five months after losing her job. The loss had come after losing her parents and brother in a car smash last year. Her whole life had crumbled.

Instead of trying to pull herself back together, she had turned to the bottle; had lived at the bottom of one every day for the past three months. She was barely sober. Tonight, knowing she was going to try and ring for help, she had stayed away from the booze. She had wanted to keep a clear mind.

Just like with Simone, Toni told the woman her name was Lara, and that she had been doing the job awhile. She didn't like people knowing her real name, and she certainly didn't want people to think they were talking to someone brand new. Someone inexperienced; a mere *child* who had no sort of street cred or life experience.

For a woman who had crawled out of a bottle, she spoke calmly and clearly. She was obviously an educated woman, who had been a teacher before her troubles first started.

The call lasted an hour-and-a-half, which took Toni past her finishing time at eleven o'clock. Stu came over to wave her a goodbye and leave a message on her desk. Until she closed the call, she hadn't looked at it.

Huffing, Toni took her headset off and slouched in her chair. She was glad the call had ended, even though it had been very positive. She'd managed to soothe the distressed woman, who had promised to stay away from alcohol for the next twenty-four hours. She'd also promised she would call Toni back tomorrow evening for another chat.

Sitting up, Toni looked at the note. It had Stu's phone number on it, along with '*call me after you finish.*'

"All finished, Toni?" Mike called from his pod.

"Yes, Mike. Thankfully. You?"

"Sure as shit," he said. "Home for a beer and a soak in the tub. You?"

"A beer, for definite," she said, taking her coat off the back of her chair and putting it on.

"Want me to walk you out to your car?" Mike asked.

"And they say chivalry is dead!"

"Shows what they know."

"It does. And yes, I'd like that, Mike. Thanks."

"No worries. I just need to use the loo first."

"That's fine. I need to get my things from my locker anyway."

"I'll be right back," he said

Looking around her, Toni noticed only one person left taking calls. It was their supervisor, who often helped out. Toni gave her a wave, and received one back. Most of the lights were now off in the building, as they were only open until eleven-thirty. Mandy, the super, would be last out the building.

Heading over to the bank of lockers, she put the key into hers and took her bag and car keys out.

"Ready to go?" Mike asked, approaching her.

"Yes."

"Let's roll," he said.

As she was about to walk out the door behind Mike, her work phone started ringing. Stepping back, she noticed the red light on the phone – it was blinking wildly. She couldn't possibly know who it was, but something told her it was Simone.

CHAPTER 5

As he walked along the seafront towards the fair, Simone looked out across the water. Ship lights could be seen out in the distance. "*Ugh*!" he shuddered. He hated the sea. Never had liked it; would never swim in it as a child. *You never know what lies beneath the murky depths*, he thought.

He remembered once, as a child, going into the sea for the very first time. He had pissed his trunks when a piece of seaweed had brushed past his leg. He'd run out of the water screaming and crying for his mother. People had laughed and pointed, along with older children and children he'd known from school. It had taken him a few years to live that one down, but he had.

Humiliation had become his friend over the years. He'd found solace and pleasure in it. Chaos would often put him down, which, to this day, still turned him on. Got him all fired up and going. She knew exactly what to do, and that was why he would find it hard to break away from her, even though he knew it was the right thing to do if he was to end his ways.

If he didn't, he was worried he was going to seriously hurt someone like he had once before. And when he had, he'd paid dearly for it. They had taken him away from his mother, house and gang. But he didn't like to think or to talk about it.

Putting his hand to his crotch, he could feel the weighty cage wrapped around his cock. He felt for the miniature padlock. It was still in place; that would never fail on him or Chaos, as it was made from steel. At the beginning, he'd loved the cage, and had fantasies of being locked up and dominated, to which Chaos had more than accommodated.

She had loved him. Would have done anything for him. She knew all his dirty, dark secrets and desires. But now it was time to stop. The problem was, Chaos had put her life and soul into the part of dominatrix. She would find it hard to break character – to come back to reality, and she had lost that love for him.

Things had to change. Life couldn't go on for either of them this way. Neither of them had a job. They were living in a house that was bequeathed to her by a family member, along with a pile of money. The life he had been leading the past six years was starting to scare him. His grip on reality was starting to slip. He'd never been that tethered to reality or sanity if truth be told. He was a loose cannon. A cannon that, if fired, could cause unspeakable damage.

Releasing his stare on the sea, he walked on. The jeans he wore were rather tight, which hurt his crotch. Every now and then, he had to readjust; to try and wriggle into a comfortable position. It was starting to become a bind. Not only that. Chaos had made him keep it on the last four months without a release.

That wasn't like her, as he performed all her tasks and commands. Not only that, but he did them to the very best of his ability. Last night, he had licked her *Fuck-Me-Boots* clean from heel to toe. He'd even wrapped his tongue around the impressive heels and lapped them clean. They'd shone once he'd finished.

He was sure that would have earned him a release, even if she had just taken his cage off and stroked him to full erection. That would have done, even though it would have been like a hair-trigger, but no. She had beat him and ordered Simone into his dog's cage for the night.

Simone pushed the thoughts to the back of his mind. He was wound up enough as it was. He didn't want to go off in his trousers. If he did, and Chaos found out, she would beat and whip him to the point of unconsciousness. Sometimes, she had little mercy or respect for him, especially of late.

When she'd seen how good a job he had done on her boots, she had slapped him and ordered him to perform oral sex on her. He *should* have been grateful for this privilege, as it was a sign of how appreciative she was. But still…He'd wanted his.

The cruelty was a game.

She loved it. Loved to watch him and his cock suffer. She loved how it bulged against the steel trap – the bars cutting into flesh.

He'd also loved it at the start – the teasing and torturing. But lately, his mind had gone to much darker places.

Getting closer to the fair, Simone left his crotch alone. He was starting to mix in with the crowds as they came and went. The sounds coming from around him were deafening: roller coasters *whooshed*; teenagers screamed and yelled; buzzers, hooters and bells rung and sang out; small children ran about the park drenched in multiple colours. It was a psychedelic war zone that drowned out his wicked, perverted thinking.

Walking through the twelve-foot-high, wrought iron gates with Coney Island written across them, Simone was in awe of it all. It had been a very long time since he'd been allowed to come to this part of town. He only came here if he was in his own company. Chaos would not allow such entertainment. The *only* fun Simone was allowed was that which Chaos granted and provided him.

Again, if she found out he'd been here this evening, she would whip him half dead, and it wouldn't be with the tame, limp whips she liked to use to tease either. No, one of the barbed or steel ones would be used to cut his skin open.

He shivered at the thought of the gashes in his flesh those fuckers made. She could tear a limb off him if she put her full effort into it.

Simone looked up and saw the *Beach Party* ride rip through the air above him. As it swung, it rotated and did a loop. It made him smile, seeing all those upside-down smiles and teeth-exposing grins. Their screams of terror were cut short by the immense G-force.

Stepping through the gates, Simone ambled along. He first walked the length of the stalls to his left. All types of games were available to win a prize at, such as hooking a duck, darts, knocking bottles or cans down via a softball, a shooting gallery, basketball, strongman competitions, and so on.

Combined with the frantic music from various rides, Simone felt giddy with excitement and freedom. It had been seven months since Chaos had last taken his collar and leash off. Seven months since he'd been allowed to leave the confines of the house.

He felt drunk.

He searched his pockets, relieved to realise he'd picked his wallet up. Of course he had. *Remember the whole fuss of getting it out of the house?* he reminded himself. She was bound to see that missing. His phone, too. Either way, he was in for a punishing. A leathering of the first order.

So what? She can break a fucking Kendo stick over my back tonight for all I care, he thought. *Tonight is my night, and I plan to go wild. I plan to make the most of it. To earn my thrashing and every filthy, gratuitous lash she can dole out.*

Simone removed his wallet from his back pocket and opened it. There was eighty-pound inside, which was made up of four twenty-pound notes. A small, girl-like titter escaped him. That was plenty to play with. He would go on some rides, play in the arcades, eat greasy food and drink beer… *That money has probably been in my wallet for years*! he thought.

"*Such places are a waste of money, Slave*!" he could hear her say. "*Money that could be spent on your precious Madam. Your Mistress.*"

"Fuck you!" he screamed at the top of his voice, causing adults and children close by to look at him. Even some of the stall workers gave him a glare. Smiling, he held his hands up. "Sorry," he said, then giggled.

After spending the best part of an hour playing games at the stalls, Simone moved on. He went into an arcade close by and played a few fruit machines before pumping money into gun games like *Time Crisis*, *Rambo* and *Terminator*. After this, he went to the next amusement. *This one is much better*, he thought.

It was called Retro-Land. It housed button-bashers from the late eighties through to the late nineties. It was like strolling down memory lane. It took him back to when he used to play on his home consoles with Mr. Tickles and the rest of the gang. While meandering through the noise of old beat 'em-ups, shooters and platforms, Simone came across a few of his old favourites – *Sunset Riders*, *Rolling Thunder*, *Mortal Kombat*, *Lethal Enforcers*, *N.A.R.C*, *Mad Dog McCree*, *Tetris*, *Columns*, *Splatterhouse*, *Final Fight*…They were all here.

He was like a child in that proverbial shop. Before he knew it, Simone had used up fifteen-pound, then managed to drag himself out of there. Taking a deep breath to calm his giggles and boyish excitement, Simone found he was hungry. Ravenous, actually.

Spotting a burger van close by, he went to it and ordered the biggest cheeseburger he could, along with a side of chips and two cans of Coke. Within ten minutes, he'd wolfed the lot. "Time for a ride!" he squealed, releasing a monster burp that could have caused a rip in time. "*Beach Party* first? Why the hell not. It's the scariest and biggest ride here," he said aloud.

When he got off the ride, Simone had a hard time walking a straight line. His legs felt like pillars of jelly. He thought his kneecaps were going to blow apart. Zigzagging his way through the crowd, he thought, *If I don't look green, I sure as hell feel it.* He clutched his flip-flopping guts.

Shaking his head to clear the dizziness, Simone ventured on to the next ride he could find, which happened to be the *Spook House*. From behind the creaky, wooden walls and hiss of pyro machines, Simone could hear shrieks of terror and joy. It made him giggle while he waited in line.

This brought a few looks his way, but he just rocked back and forth on his legs and grinned like a sinner.

She watched him from the side-lines and laughed. His actions made him look like a fruitcake, but that didn't bother her. *Nobody* that *good-looking could be as crazy as the Mad Hatter*, she thought, giving her friend a nudge with her elbow. "Have you seen him over there, Sara?" she said, tittering.

"Yeah, he looks like a freak, Michelle. Hot, though!" she admitted.

"I know, right?"

"You moist for him, or something?" Sara asked.

"Maybe!" she said. "Don't you think he's fuckable?" Michelle asked.

"Yeah, but he looks a bit mental for me. Plus, I think he's a lot older than us."

"And?"

"And nothing. Don't you think it's weird a guy of his age wanting to ride the *Spook House*?"

"Nah, I think it just shows he has an *out there* personality," Michelle said.

"Maybe we can get him to buy us a few drinks in *The Buccaneer*!"

"True. I never thought of that, like."

"Shall we try picking him up after or before his ride?"

"After, I think," Sara said. "Oo, he just looked over at me and smiled!"

"The dirty dog – he just winked at me!" Michelle said.

"Perhaps that's his thing – two at a time."

They both laughed. Being only sixteen and seventeen, neither girl had much experience with boys. Sure, they'd messed about with guys their own age in school. Kisses and feel-ups around the back of the bike shed, but nothing heavy. Sara, being the oldest, had told Michelle she'd only seen one dick. Michelle had never seen or touched one.

"I think he keeps looking at my legs," Michelle said.

"Well, you do have a very short skirt on!"

"He-he, I know. My dad played hell with me. I had to sneak out with it on in the end!"

"Ha-ha!" Sara said. "My parents don't care that I wear slutty clothes."

"They did when the school sent a letter to your house!"

"*Oops*, yeah – my dad called me a *tramp* for taking my skirt up three inches," Sara said, laughing, causing Michelle to cackle.

"You had some dirty looks that day."

"Aye, even that dirty prick Daniels had a good perv."

"Our head?"

"Yeah, Mrs. Daniels can't be giving him any!"

Again, both girls giggled.

The pair had been best friends all their school days, and had been there for each other at moments of crisis and happiness. There wasn't a thing they didn't know about each other and the problems they had at home. Both had wanted to leave their families, but, without money, they couldn't. Plus, school kept them tied in place too.

Michelle and Sara had awkward dads. Michelle's was an out-of-work, drunken bum, whereas Sara's was a womaniser. He stayed out all hours, only to come home and beat his wife. It was sad, yet true. They didn't really give a shit about how their daughters dressed. Or how they acted. Or even where they went – they just liked acting the big man. The big 'I Am.'

"Ew, have you seen her?"

"Mrs. Daniels?" Sara asked.

"Yeah."

"No, why?"

"She's a wrinkly old bag!" Michelle said, with glee in her tone.

"Ha-ha! That explains a lot."

"Hey, look, he's coming." Michelle gave Sara a few digs with her elbow. "How are we going to play this?"

"I say we follow him for a bit and see what he does. Maybe we can get a convo going with him, you know?"

"Sounds like a plan!" Michelle said.

****

He knew they were interested and were following him. How? Because he had seen it all over the dirty little fuckers' faces back by the *Spook House*. He was not a stranger to women approaching him. He was also no stranger to being picked up or indeed doing the picking up.

Sex drove him more than anything.

The pair currently trailing him stank of pureness. Their seals had not been broken. He could and would change that. Maybe not this evening, depending on how pliable they were, but he would have them baying for more. Much, much more.

Like them, Simone was captivated. They were young. Much younger than him. The smaller of them had caught his eye first – the way she wore her long blonde hair in a ponytail and the tight jeans she sported along with a flimsy T-shirt that was transparent drove him wild. Through her top, Simone had seen her peach-coloured bra. It had stood out among the lively colours of the fair like a fuck-beacon.

His cock stirred into a semi-hard state.

Even though it had been the blonde one that had caught his eye, with her peach bra and small tits, the dark-haired girl was just as fit. He probably fancied her more. It wasn't that she had a better face or body; it was because of her legs. They were on display. She was wearing a very tight, above-the-knee skirt with tights. Black tights with a good denier. Her thighs were amazing and had that perfect amount of meat on them. Not too fat, and not too skinny. If he didn't stop thinking about them right now, he would come in his pants.

Oh, if only I had those girls in my cave at home, he thought. *The fun I would have...I'd have them bleeding and crying.*

Out in the open, it wouldn't be as wild, but it'd still be fun.

He grinned as he walked slowly through the crowds of people. He could hear them right on his shoulder. They were giggling. Whispering. They were probably wondering how they were going to get his attention. Or how they were going to get a conversation started.

They needn't worry, Simone thought. *I'll be taking that concern out of their delicate little hands, and sooner than they think.*

Stopping at a coconut shy, Simone knew this would give them their best opportunity to talk to him.

"Fancy a shot, do ya?" the bloke behind the stall said.

Simone nodded. The girls had gathered at his back.

"A prize for your fancies?" he asked Simone, winking at the girls, who giggled in return.

This made Simone smile. He turned to face the two teenagers. "What do you think? Reckon I can hit one of those coconuts down?" he asked them.

They both reddened.

"Going to show us how strong you are?" the blonde asked.

"Yeah," the dark one chirped, finding confidence in her friend's forwardness.

This only encouraged Simone, who pulled back the right sleeve of his T-shirt to flex his impressive bicep.

"Wow," the blonde said. "Mind if I feel?" she asked, breaking away from her friend.

"If you want," Simone said. When she got close, he could smell her perfume. He could also smell the spicy odour rising from between her legs. His nose had grown acute to it.

When she placed her bony fingers on his muscle and looked into his eyes, the child in her was exposed, and it drove him fucking wild. Instantly, he wanted to rip her top and bra off, so he could suck her tits. He wanted badly to finger her at that moment.

But he smiled and shrugged the urge off.

"Oo, it's solid!" she giggled, then stepped back.

"Want a go?" he asked Blondie's mate, but she tittered and shied away.

"Hey, *douche* – are you going to play or fuck about?" the guy minding the stall asked.

"No need to be rude," Simone told him, turning to pick up the three balls at his fingertips. "They aren't nailed down, are they?" he asked, smiling. The guy's face dropped. Simone thought he was going to start something, but instead lifted the coconuts off their stands to show he was an honest Joe. "Cool," Simone said.

"Now take your shots, *sir*!" the man said. "I do have other customers wanting to play, you know?"

Simone looked at the unshaven, unkempt man who wore a holey beanie and fingerless gloves. He nodded at him. "Sure," he said, taking aim and hurling the first of three balls at the coconuts. It glanced off the side of his intended target, which wobbled the hairy drupe.

His second shot also grazed the side of a coconut, but the third ball ploughed straight into one, taking it clean off its perch. It hit the hay-covered floor with a soft thud.

"We have a winner!" the stall worker called out. This brought attention to his game and Simone. "Congratulations, sir. Here's your prize," he said, handing him the coconut.

"Oo, well done!" Blondie said from behind.

"Yes, that was some awesome throwing," her mate agreed.

"My name's Sara," Blondie said.

"And how old are you, Sara?" Simone asked, giving her mate a wink.

"Nineteen," she said, pushing her boobs out as far as she could.

"Me, too," the dark-haired girl said.

Simone laughed. "Your name?"

"Michelle," she said.

"Fancy taking us for a few drinks?" Sara asked, putting on a cocky tone and look.

"Oh, that sounds like a good idea. But I think I'd get in trouble for buying drinks for underage girls." Their faces sank. The jig was up. "Plus, wouldn't people think I look like a pervert?" he said. He was laughing on the inside, and he knew that if Mr. Tickles was here with him and not at home with Chaos, he would be pissing in his clown trousers with laughter and excitement.

"Come on, just one drink!" Sara pleaded.

"How old are you really?" Simone asked.

"I'm seventeen," Sara said.

"I'm only sixteen," Michelle said.

"Cool, okay," he said.

"So, does that mean you'll take us?" Sara asked. "I think you're *well* fit!" she said, turning to Michelle and giggling.

Simone walked between them and headed towards the back entrance of the fair. He cockily threw the coconut into the air and caught it in one hand – he repeatedly did this. "Maybe," he said, smiling.

They trailed behind him like a couple of love-sick puppies. He fed off the attention. It drove him bananas. But something stopped him from totally thriving off it tonight, which were thoughts of Toni and their conversation.

Suddenly, he longed to speak with her. *Tomorrow*, he told himself.

"Sooo, where are you going?" Sara asked. She was clearly the mouthpiece of the duo.

"You want to party with me, don't you?" he asked.

"Uh-huh," Michelle said, saddling up to his side. Sara followed suit.

"Don't make it too obvious, ladies," he said. "We wouldn't want people getting the wrong idea."

On this note, the girls dropped back a bit, giving Simone room. Once they were out of the park, he turned to them. "I'm going to pop over to that shop first, and then we are going down to the beach. How does that sound?"

"Whatever for?" Michelle said, putting her fingers to the hem of her skirt in a shy manner.

"Yes, what do you have in mind?"

"A private party," he said. "I'm off to get some booze. Wait here," he told them. "I'll be right back."

Behind him, he heard both girls giggle and whisper. They were putty in his hands.

Simone left the shop with a carrier bag clung to his chest and noticed that the girls had gone to sit on a bench close by. They had their phones out, to which he assumed they were texting or updating their Facebook statuses. "Is that all youngsters do these days?" he uttered. "All I had were my toys and Nintendo when I was your age."

On hearing him, Sara was the first to turn and speak. "What's in the bag?" she asked, smiling.

He gave it a rattle. "Cider," he said.

"Bow?" Michelle asked.

Simone nodded.

"How did you know?" Sara asked.

"Isn't it the drink of choice by all boys and girls under the age of eighteen?" he said.

"I guess," Michelle said.

"Where to?" Sara asked.

"I thought we could go and sit under the pier – out of sight, see."

"Sounds good," Michelle said.

"I agree," Sara said. "A private party indeed!"

"You girls were texting your parents to say you were going to be late?"

"*Fuck* no!" Sara said, laughing. "I was playing a game on my phone."

"Do we look that sad?" Michelle said. "I was messing about on Facebook, like!"

"Follow me," he said. Turning his back to them, he walked towards the beach. The tide was out and the sky was clear, exposing an array of bright, blinking stars.

Simone got onto the dry beach and took a left, leading them to an old, broken pier. It had fire damage and was replaced years ago by a more modern creation, which stretched a mile out to sea.

The smell of wet sand and seaweed assaulted his nostrils, which he loved. The moon was also pretty high in the sky, which lit up the patch he had in mind perfectly. *We'll all be able to see what we're doing*, he thought. "How does this spot look to you, girls?" he said, putting his bag down. He leaned it against some rocks as he crawled under the broken pier. Most of the planks and structure had been burned to ashes. What remained was nothing more than charred, chipped and broken timber. "Coming under?" he asked. "It's lovely and cosy. The sand is still pretty warm, too."

Sara laughed, and got to her knees to join Simone. To get her courage up, she popped a can. Not to look like a silly girl, Michelle did the same. Before Simone knew it, the girls were a can-and-a-half in, making them playful.

"Let's play truth or dare!" Sara said.

Michelle giggled, taking another sip of cider.

"Okay," Simone said. "But I get to go first, agreed?"

"I don't know about that," Michelle said. "You could ask anything!"

"But isn't that the fun of it?" Simone grinned.

"I don't care what you ask!" Sara said. The cider was bringing her horse shit bravery to the surface.

She will be easy to break, he thought. *And, knowing she may look like a wimp in front of her friend, Michelle will follow suit.*

"Agreed, Michelle?" he asked.

At first, he thought she was going to run off crying, but she nodded.

"Right, okay," he said. He knew he was barely visible to them in the darkness, so he moved to his right until the moon illuminated him. "What can I ask?"

"I bet it'll be something *dirrrrrrty*!" Sara slurred.

"Okay, I'll choose dare."

"I knew it!" Sara blurted. "Who are you daring?"

"Michelle!" he said. "I dare you to kiss Sara on the lips." The look on her face was priceless. He went for a can of cider himself. This was going to be interesting.

Sara squealed, putting her hands to her mouth to laugh.

"*Ew*! That's fucking gross!" Michelle said.

"Not too chicken shit, are you?" Simone asked. This took Michelle aback. She was clearly soberer than her friend. Had she even been drinking? Or was she pouring it into the sand? Fuck, he hadn't noticed. This may not be as fun as he'd first hoped.

"No, I'm not chicken!" she said.

"Ha-ha-ha, you look it!" Sara piped in, which Simone found totally unexpected. He was sure she was going to side with her friend. "Come and give your old pal a kiss!" Sara continued, leaning over.

All right, Simone thought, smiling as he watched Michelle shuffle closer to her mate. As she leaned in for a smacker, Simone took his chance and put his hand on Michelle's tiny, yet well-formed arse.

"Oi! Cheeky," she said, slapping his hand away. His fingers had managed to stroke her pussy just before she'd battered him away.

He smiled. Her legs were fucking amazing.

Sara laughed, then crashed into Michelle's lips with her own. Simone thought it was going to be a quick peck, but the girls lingered. He was impressed. "I think you should put your hand on her boob, Sara!" Simone encouraged, to which Sara did. He was further amazed by Michelle's lack of protesting.

Finally, Sara pulled away. "That was nice!" she said, winking at her mate.

Michelle kind of shied away. "Yeah, it was cool," she said, pulling her rucked skirt down, much to Simone's displeasure.

"Now it's our turn!" Sara said. "Come here, Michelle."

Simone sipped at his can and watched as the girls huddled close. Even though the lighting was poor, he could still see their nipples pushing at the fabric of their tops. *So young, but not very innocent*, he thought.

When both girls erupted with laughter, he came out of his trance-like state. "Have you thought of something?"

"Yes!" they said in unison.

"But Sara can ask you!" Michelle said.

"Really?!" Sara said.

"There's no need to be shy," Simone said.

"Okay, okay…We choose dare."

"That's fine," he said.

"Well, we want you to…" Sara started, but couldn't finish. She took a few more swigs of her third can. As he suspected, Michelle was disposing of hers into the sand. She was only pretending to drink. *Clever girl.*

"Yes?" he said.

"We want to see *it*!" she blurted.

"My dick?" he asked.

"Uh-huh," Michelle said.

"No problem," he said. Standing, he saw the anticipation on both their faces, which got him excited. But, due to his cage, he couldn't get fully stiff. *This could be weird to explain*, he thought.

When he pulled his trousers and boxers down, Sara shrieked with laughter, causing Michelle to do the same, even though she didn't know why she was laughing.

"What?" he asked. Their laughter sparked a fresh flame of excitement in him.

"What the *fuck* is on your cock, dude?" Sara asked, letting rip with more laughter.

"My mistress makes me wear it," he said. "She likes to keep me under control."

"What?" Michelle said.

"My mistress – she keeps me locked up. And if I don't obey, she beats and punishes me," he said.

"That's fucking weird!" Michelle said. "I'm going."

"No, don't go!" he said. "Come and play with it – show me more of your legs."

"Ew, no – you're weird!" Michelle said. "Sara, let's go."

"She's right. Plus, I'm not being nasty, but you shouldn't go showing that *thing*," Sara said.

"What's that supposed to mean?" he said.

"Dude, your dick is small!" Sara said, smiling. This sparked Michelle into a fit of laughter. "Let's go, Michelle," she said.

"No!" he said. He felt cheated. "I want a fucking release!" he yelled. As both girls crawled out from under the pier, he lunged for them, managing to catch Michelle with an ankle tap. This caused her to trip over herself, sending her to ground. Her head smashed against an exposed rock.

A jolt of pleasure shot through Simone, causing him to come.

"*Michelle*?!" Sara screamed. She looked back at Simone, who was on the sand, shaking. "What the fuck did you do?! You've fucking killed her!" Not realising she hadn't completely cleared the pier, Sara stood up fast, smacking her head on a beam.

As she collapsed to the ground, Simone got to his knees. He put himself decent and then he crawled to her. Straddling her back, he grabbed her head and twisted it as violently to the right as he could. Her neck snapped as easily as a chicken's, but that didn't stop him twisting the neck back the other way. The sound of popping vertebrae got him hard once again.

Getting off Sara, he pulled her back under the pier. Once she was out of sight, he grabbed Michelle, who started to scream – she'd only been temporarily knocked cold. Grabbing the rock she'd initially hit, he fell on her, and then smashed her skull in with it.

It was only after the fifteenth blow he stopped. Blood had spattered his clothes. Had landed in his hair – had decorated his face. "What the fuck have I done?" he whispered, going for his phone in a panic.

Thinking he'd dialled Chaos' number, Simone spoke in a rushed way, not knowing he'd rung the Samaritan's helpline. When he realised, he shut his phone off, panicked that he had raised the alarm. "Shit, shit, shit!" he said. "The line was bad. Nobody that end could have possibly heard a thing I said!"

His panic soon faded. He looked at the dead girls. Now they *were* his, and nobody was around. "I'll just stay here and have some fun. Wait for the tide to start rolling in, before getting rid of them," he said.

A smile spread across his face as he hiked Michelle's skirt up as far as it went, exposing her tights completely. He broke the lock off his cage and then masturbated to the sight of her legs. Simone made sure to come all over the youngster. He didn't care that she was dead.

He then turned his attention to Sara, by ripping her top and peach-coloured bra off. Her tits looked young, underdeveloped, which got him going again. And again, and again…

CHAPTER 6

After leaving work, Mike walked her to her car, which was parked on the fifth floor of the NCP car park around the corner. At night, it could be a little shady, especially on the weekend. On getting to her car, Mike took the stairs to the tenth floor, which was where he'd parked.

Even though she hadn't been doing the job long, people had been very nice to her. They'd been pleasant from day one, which had been a massive relief to Toni. She'd never liked being the new person anywhere – at University or a workplace. But she'd been lucky on both accounts. On her first day at Uni she had bumped into Suzanne, who had put Toni at ease immediately, which was the same for her part-time job as Samaritan – Stu had been awesome to her from the moment she had walked through the door.

Although the Samaritan job was only voluntary work, she loved it. It was definitely something she would love to keep doing after her studies, but a full-time paying job was more important to find. Toni was lucky she had the support of her parents, student loans and accommodation to help her through higher education, so money was not that much of an issue yet.

She got into her car and locked her door, which in turn locked the other three. She then put her key in the ignition, but didn't turn it. She put her bag and coat on the passenger's seat before digging her phone out of her bag, along with Stu's note.

Opening her text messages, Toni started a new one to Stu. '*Hi, thought I'd send you a quick text to say I'm currently leaving work. I should be home in ten minutes or so. I'll give you a buzz then. Speak soon. Toni. X*'

After sending the message, she was unsure of whether or not she should have put a kiss at the end of it. *What will he make of it? After all, he is a bloke, and blokes get all kinds of things into their heads from something as simple as an X at the end of a message*, she thought, smiling.

Don't be silly. Stu's not like that. He's got brains – he's not some moron. He's a little bit older, too. Looking into the rear-view mirror, Toni could see how dark and empty the car park was behind her. Some of the lights were out on this floor, with a few of the others blinking. It gave her the willies.

"*Ugh!*" she said, shivering. It was even more terrifying on occasions, she thought, when the tramps hung around. Toni had nothing against them – she hated seeing people suffer – but she'd heard of them setting on people when they were refused money. She'd even caught one of them defecating in one of the lifts, which had been disturbing.

They were usually found loitering inside and outside the NCP – some had been found sleeping in the stairwells and all sorts.

Starting her car, she put it in reverse, but made sure there was nothing behind her before releasing the handbrake. Pulling out, she straightened the car and turned her music up, before slipping the gear stick into first. Happy, Toni moved forward. She navigated the tight corners on the down ramps slowly – she'd clipped a tyre once, which had popped it.

That night, she had hobbled home on the rim after her dad had told her it would be fine. There had been no way she had been waiting two hours for a member of AA to come and rescue her. The streets of Bridgend at night were uncouth to say the least. She would have been a sitting duck.

After clearing all the ramps, Toni made it to the bottom, where she placed her ticket in a machine. This in turn lifted the barrier, freeing her to go. Once she was on the main road, it took her less than ten minutes to reach her shared flat. Pulling up outside, she noticed Suzanne's bedroom light was glowing.

I sure hope she does want to come tonight, she thought, switching her car's engine off. *Why wouldn't she want to go out? There'll be boys and booze! That's an arm-twister right there.* Looking over at Suzanne's window again, she noticed the light in the room wasn't that strong. *Ah, shite, she's studying. That's the only time she uses her lamp.*

She undid her seatbelt and plucked the keys from the ignition. *I'm sure she can be persuaded to come for a few beers. It is holiday time – we should be taking a break from books and stuff*, she thought, opening her car door. Her stomach suddenly fluttered. *What if I end up having to go on my own?*

That's not going to happen. And, even if it did, Stu will be there. I'm sure he'll look after me. He's into me, after all. Right? Shaking her head, she smiled. *I hope so.*

On opening her front door, she was blasted by pounding music. Suzanne loved her rock music loud. Calling out to her would have been useless. She slipped her shoes off. Walking the length of the dark hallway to the living room, Toni hit the light before entering the kitchen. After putting the kettle and TV on, she jogged upstairs to Suzanne's room.

Not getting a response from a knock and a call, Toni entered. As she'd guessed, her roommate's lamp was the glowing light seen from outside. Suzanne sat at her desk reading, her back to Toni. Her PC was also switched on and ready to go.

"Suzi?" Toni said in a quiet tone.

"Hey," Suzanne said, not turning around. "Give me two – I'm just finishing this chapter."

"I've got the kettle on – fancy a cuppa?"

"Yeah, please."

"Okay, come on down to the kitchen when you finish. I have something to talk to you about."

"Cool. Will do," Suzanne said.

"Awesome. See you in a bit," Toni said, closing her roommate's door. She headed back down to the kitchen where the kettle was coming to its crescendo. As Toni put her hand to it, it clicked off. Lifting it, she poured the hot water into two mugs she had prepped with teabags. As they sat stewing, Toni heard the music go off in Suzanne's room, then heard her coming down the stairs.

"Toni?" Suzanne called.

"In the kitchen – tea is seeping."

"So, what's up?" Suzanne asked, walking into the kitchen.

Clapping her eyes on her, Toni wondered if Suzanne ever had a moment of the day where she didn't look her best? No matter what time it was – day or night – Suzanne always looked good. It didn't matter whether she was just waking up with bad bed hair, or walking through the door after a long shift at the local pub. She always looked stunning.

Toni was pretty sure you could slap a bin bag on the girl, and she'd still look like a million bucks. She had such a pretty face, with high cheekbones. Make-up was not needed, along with designer clothes and fancy shoes. Suzanne was such a down-to-earth, easy-going girl. Her inner personality shone through, giving her exterior its beauty.

"I was wondering if you fancied going to a party?" Toni asked.

"*Now*?!"

"In an hour's time."

"Hell yes!"

Toni smiled. "I haven't given you any details yet!"

"You said *party*. That's enough!"

"Ha-ha, you're wild."

"My parents used to tell me the same thing," she admitted. "They were right, too!"

"Yes, they were."

"So, tell me more – who's party and where? Do I have time for a shower?"

"It's a beach party. A guy I work with invited me."

"Oooo-ooo, getting some action on, hey?! Dirty girl!"

"Stop it!" Toni said, blushing.

"Ha! Don't worry – I have condoms in my room."

Toni's mouth hung slack. "*Suzi*!"

"Relax, you're a student. You're meant to get drunk and have meaningless sex. It's in the contract!"

"Really? I must have missed that part."

"It's in the small print, toots," Suzanne said.

"That would explain it."

"I guess it would. And a shower?"

"Yeah, plenty of time – I'm going to grab one myself."

"Cool. What time are we leaving?"

"I'm going to ring Stu now – he's the guy I work with."

"He's picking us up?"

Toni nodded.

"I'm off to delouse, in that case," Suzanne said, giving Toni a wink.

"Ew, you're a right little piggy!"

"A piggy you love!"

"This is true," Toni said.

"See you in a bit," Suzanne said, taking her tea up to the bathroom.

With Suzanne in the shower, Toni took her tea and mobile phone to her bedroom. She noticed there was a text message awaiting her. Butterflies flapped in her stomach. She was eager to see what he'd responded with. Putting her tea down, she sat on her bed and opened her messages.

It was from Stu. This pleased her. It read: *'Thanks for letting me know. I'll await your call before I let the guys know my movements.'*

"No kiss," she uttered aloud, feeling disappointed. Could she have misread the signals? She was certain he liked her. *Maybe he's playing hard to get?* Not bothering to reply, she rang him.

The phone was answered after the fifth ring. "Hey Stu, I've not long got in."

"Are you still coming tonight?"

"Yes, definitely. My roommate too, if that's okay?"

"Sure. The more the merrier. Pick you up at twelve-ish?" he asked.

She looked at her watch, noting it was going on for eleven forty-five. "Can we make it quarter-past?" she asked. "A bit pushed for time," she admitted.

"No worries – what's your address?" he asked, to which she told him. "Awesome. I'll see you in a bit."

"Coolio," she said. "See you soon. Bye."

"Bye," he said.

She hung up the phone and had a little giggle to herself. "He's so handsome," she muttered.

Hearing the bathroom door open, Toni went to her door and opened it. She saw Suzanne wrapped in a towel on the landing. "All done?" she asked.

"Yeah, go ahead, toots," Suzanne said. "Is Stu picking us up?"

"Yep. Quarter-past.

"Sweet. That gives us plenty of time."

"Yeah, so I best get my backside in the shower," Toni said, grabbing her towel and heading to the bathroom. Inside, she locked the door before using the toilet. Even though Suzanne had left the window open, the box-sized room was still thick with warm mist.

Finished on the loo, Toni stripped and started the shower. Setting it to the right temperature, she got in. The hot spray bombarded her body as she twirled beneath it. "Oo, that's the ticket right there," she said, spitting water as she spoke.

She grabbed the shampoo and gave her scalp a vigorous scrub before moving on to wash her body. Within ten minutes, Toni was finished. As she stepped out of the bath, Suzanne was knocking at the door.

"Done?"

"Almost!" Toni called back. "Just drying."

"Cool. I need to brush my pegs – I can't be kissing any lads with grubby teeth," Suzanne said.

"Yeah, right – they'd kiss you even if you had a ton of spinach wedged between your choppers!"

"What are you trying to say?" Suzanne said, giggling.

"That your boobs are amazing – they could distract anything!"

"Well, they are pretty ginormous!" Suzanne said.

"What did Peter call them?" Toni asked, sniggering.

"Bouncing Buddhas!" she shrieked.

"Ha-ha, he also called them *Wife Material*."

"He-he, he did!"

"He was a funny guy – I miss Peter on campus," Toni said.

"We aren't all cut out for Uni life, toots. Now, hurry up, Stu isn't going to be much longer."

"Okay, okay, I'm coming!" Toni said.

"Not from where I'm standing!"

"Hardy-ha-ha," Toni said, opening the bathroom door. "Go on, in you go, Miss Norks."

This enticed Suzanne to bounce them up and down as she passed Toni and entered the bathroom.

"You could take someone's eye out with those things!" Toni laughed, going to her room and closing the door. Within a few minutes, she was dressed and ready to go, which was a good thing, as a car horn blasted outside.

"He's here!" Suzanne called from downstairs.

"Go out to him – I'll be there in a sec," Toni called back, grabbing her hoodie off the back of her bedroom door. Rushing downstairs, she jammed her feet into her trainers and dashed out the front door. She could see Suzanne smoking a cigarette by Stu's car – she could also hear them passing a few words and having a giggle.

Closing and locking the front door, she joined her friends.

"All set to go?" Stu asked from the driver's seat.

"Yep, let's *paaaarty*!" Suzanne said, getting into the back of the car.

Toni nodded, opening the passenger's door and getting in.

For the first few minutes of the car journey down to Coney Island, nothing was said. It took Toni to break the near unbearable silence.

"Looks like you've picked a good night for it, Stu."

"Yeah. I've spoken with the guys – they're down at the beach setting up."

"I would have brought some booze," Suzanne said, "but it was all a little bit short notice for this party hound! You sure you don't mind me smoking back here?" she asked Stu.

"Nah, you go for it – the guys normally light up back there, so it's no sweat, dude. Honestly."

"Sweet," Suzanne said, lying back in her seat.

"How many friends are waiting?" Toni asked.

"Two," Stu said. "Anthony and Jacob – Jacob's girlfriend is also there. Her name is Jasmine."

"Is Anthony unattached?" Suzanne asked.

Toni snorted a laugh.

Stu looked into the rear-view mirror and smiled. "Why, yes. He is! You're in luck, Suzanne," he said. "He's on the lookout for a nice girl, too."

"*Nice* girl? Ah, that's you outters then, Buddhas!" Toni said, causing Suzanne to shriek with laughter.

"Do you have to refer to my rack as that, and in front of a stranger?!"

"Stu's no stranger," Toni said. "He's a guy I work with!"

"Yeah, but he could still be dangerous!" she said, laughing.

"She's right, you know?" Stu said, smiling. "I may just tickle you both to death!"

"*Nooo*!" Toni said. "At least not my feet – I could pee myself!"

"*Ew*!" Suzanne said.

Stu laughed.

"Man, I'm starting to get a thirst on!" Suzanne said. "How much longer?"

"Not far," he said. "Have you ever been to Coney Island?"

"Nope – I'm from west Wales. I'm just in Bridgend for Uni," Suzanne said. "But, I'm looking forward to this. Toni has told me lots about the place."

"It's really nice, especially when it's in season," Stu said.

"Off-season is brutal, though," Toni chirped in. "It gets so quiet and eerie around, and the fairground people drink in town, making it rough at nights."

"Sounds delightful!" Suzanne said. Stu and Toni both laughed. "Will there be plenty of beer at this little get-together?"

"Oh, definitely. Anthony was doing the beer run – he always comes back with too much!"

"I'm liking him already," Suzanne said.

"What about food, Stu?" Toni asked. "I'm a little bit peckish."

"Yeah, the guys will have food, too. They were preparing a fire when I spoke to them last."

"Sweet," Suzanne said. "I could do with a hotdog or something along those lines."

"Okay, here we go," Stu said, driving down to the front. "I'm not sure we'll find a place to park this close to the beach, so we might have to walk the rest of the way," he continued.

"Look, there's plenty of spaces to park by there," Toni said.

"Awesome," Stu said, pulling his car into an empty bay. After the three of them poured out of the vehicle, he locked it, and then pocketed the keys. "Follow me, guys," he said.

Crossing the deserted road, Stu led the girls past the fair, which was due to close in the next thirty minutes. It was still bouncing with activity – all the rides and stalls were heaving with trade. The noise beyond the park entrance was deafening. Not paying much notice, the trio headed straight down to the sands. In the distance, Stu's friends could be seen huddled around a fire, which was set up close to the new pier.

As Stu got closer, he raised a hand to wave. The three people by the fire waved back. "Looks like they've got the beers on the go!" he told Toni and Suzanne.

"That's what I like to hear," Suzanne said.

When they approached the fire, Toni could feel it burn her face. One of the guys standing closest to the blaze came over and introduced himself as Anthony. "And that's Jacob and his girlfriend Jasmine," he told Toni.

"Nice to meet you," she said, shaking Anthony's hand. He was much bigger than Stu and Jacob – with a thick, chiselled framed. His jaw looked like a block of granite.

"This is Suzanne," Toni told Anthony.

They all said "Hi" in unison.

Stepping from Anthony, Toni went over to Stu, who gave her a beer.

"Hi," Jacob said. He looked very geeky with thick glasses. The same could be said for his girlfriend, who also wore dense eyewear.

President and vice-president of the reading club at Uni? Toni thought, stifling a laugh. She was sure they were very nice, and regretted having thought such a thing of people she didn't even know. "Nice to meet you both," she said, shaking their hands.

"Fancy a nibble?" Stu asked from behind her.

Turning, she saw that he was cooking a burger over the fire. "Mm, yes please," she said, taking a drink of her lager.

"You can have this one," Stu said.

Looking over her shoulder, Toni noticed Suzanne and Anthony were hitting it off – she liked men who played rugby, and, from his frame, he sure looked as though he did.

"Thanks. Are any of your friends still in Uni?" Toni asked Stu.

"Anthony is doing a sports degree, but that's about it."

"He's a big guy – does he play rugby?"

"Yes. He had a call-up for the Cardiff Blues a few months back. He's still going to finish his degree, though. He says it a back-up plan, just in case he gets injured one day."

"Very sensible. You can't be too careful," she said, having a bite of her burger. She washed it down with some more lager. She watched how Suzanne flirted with the big man. *How does she do it so easily? Come on – look at her. She's goddamn gorgeous!* Toni thought.

"Your food okay?" Stu asked.

"Hmm?" she said, turning to look at him as he laughed. "What?"

"You have a blob of red sauce on the end of your nose," he said.

"Gawd! Thanks for saying," she said, wiping it away.

"I was asking you how your food is?"

"It's scrummy!" she said. "I've not had a bite to eat all day."

"Really?"

"Yes, it's been a bit of a crazy one."

"Here, have a second," he said, slapping another burger in a bun.

"But what about you?"

"I'll have the next one," he said.

She smiled.

"How do you like it at the Samaritans?"

"I love it – I'm thinking of doing something along those lines when I leave education."

"Don't you want to teach?"

"I really do, but helping people through their problems is so inspiring."

"It really is," Stu said.

The hubbub of the waves crashing mixed with the dying sound of the fair and fire made her feel relaxed. It was nice being in good company whilst having a few beers and a bite to eat. Before she knew it, Jacob had put some music on, which pumped from a portable CD player.

"Yeah, let's get the party going," Suzanne said.

When Toni looked over at her friend, she noticed she was dirty dancing with Anthony. She shook her head, and laughed.

"I do apologise for my friend's loud behaviour," Toni said.

"Ha! Not at all," Stu said. "It's nice to kick back."

"I don't think you've told me what you do aside from the Samaritans?" she asked him.

"Oh, I work at the 'Three Horseshoes', which is a pub if you hadn't guessed from the name. It's my local."

"Cool," she said. "I'll probably have to get myself a full-time job. I mean, I can't live off fresh air. Maybe I can still do charity work in the evening or weekends?"

"*Phew*, that would be hard work – working close to forty hours a week and then doing charity gigs?" he said. "I guess people do manage it, though."

"Of course. I mean, if I was to stay with the Samaritans, I could do it for a few hours over the weekend, ya know?" she said, swallowing the remainder of her beer.

"Another?" he asked.

"Please," she nodded, draining the dregs.

"Here you go," he said, passing her another can out of a cooler box.

"Thanks," she said.

As the time passed, Toni found herself more relaxed around Stu and his friends. Before she knew it, most of the night had burned out, and it was almost six in the morning.

Most of the beer had been drunk. All the food had been consumed. Jacob and Jasmine had passed out under the pier, along with Anthony and Suzanne. Both couples were in a lovers' embrace.

This left Toni and Stu, who were sat by the fire. They had spent all night chatting to each other, and were still going at it as they watched the sun rise. They drank the last of the cans as they did so.

"Well, I have to thank you for bringing me out here, Stu."

"No worries. We lost the others pretty early, huh?" he quipped.

"Yeah, but it was nice having a chance to chat without interruption," she said, moving closer to him.

He put his arm around her, and pulled her closer. The early morning breeze was starting to kick up, chilling her to the bone.

"Want my jacket?" he asked.

"No, I'm fine like this," she said, looking up at him.

"You want to go?"

"Let's wait until the sun is completely up."

"Agreed."

Before the sun reached its zenith, Toni and Stu's attention was distracted. Close to the water in front of them, a lone figure with a dog ran across their field of vision. He appeared to be in a great rush, as every now and then, he took a tumble in the sand.

He seemed frantic. Wild, almost. Every time he got back up to run on, he looked over his shoulder as though someone was in pursuit of him. But there was nobody there, only the dog.

Toni felt her blood run cold. She was worried the person would run in their direction, but he didn't. Soon the lone figure and his pet disappeared in a cloud of kicked up sand.

"What the hell was that all about?" Stu asked, looking at Toni.

"No idea, but I think we should wake the rest and get the hell out of here. That's pretty much freaked me out!" she admitted.

After waking their friends, they gathered everything and left the beach. Toni managed to persuade Suzanne to take the ride home with her and Stu, but never told her about the lone figure running across the beach, and how much it had startled her. After all, what had that person been running from?

CHAPTER 7

She was restless. Bored. Her toys did nothing for her tedium. *Where in the fuck is my Slave*?! she wondered, lying on her bed naked. *I told him not to be late*! With her curtains wide open, the glow from the moon drenched her in a chalky-creamy colour. Not only did it light her body and bed up, but her entire room.

Chaos liked feeling exposed to the night; to people who may be walking past her window. There had been complaints about her behaviour from neighbours, but she paid little heed. She lived perilously. She lived without thought of what others may or may not think of her.

She was her own woman. And no fucker was going to rule her ways or dictate to her. Her father had tried that, until she'd put him in his place.

"Oh, Slave – where are you?" she uttered, frustration in her voice. Anger was starting to rise. "I should not have let you out tonight. You were too highly charged."

Mammy's going to have to bring you down, she thought. *But only if you're good to Mammy*. Smiling, she rolled about her bed – the sheets were silk, making them soft, cool and slippery. Her skin started to crawl with the coldness, which made it prickle with goose bumps and tease her nipples into an erect state. The hairs at the nape of her neck stood on end. Her pussy moistened.

"*Slave*! I need my fucking Slave," she demanded, thumping her fists against the mattress. She wasn't prone to temper tantrums, but she could get very pissed off. It led to things being smashed and her Slave getting beaten badly. Getting up from her bed, she went to the window.

A few older teens had gathered at the streetlamp on the corner. They knew about her, just like most of the people in the neighbourhood did. She smiled down and gave them a wave. *Titillation: There's nothing like it*, she thought, watching the young lads react.

One, wearing a hat, was first to respond. On seeing Chaos in the window waving, he gave his mate next to him a nudge. He automatically looked up at her window. She gave him a cheeky wink before blowing him a kiss. The third boy, who had his back to Chaos, immediately turned to face her. He was the fat one of the bunch – there was always a fat one with a pair who thought they were cool.

Had the fat one been alone, she may have thrown him a mercy fuck. But she didn't want all three of them up here. Not tonight. Besides, her Slave was not here to watch. This made her grit her teeth, as she looked over the clock on her chest of drawers.

Four minutes after two.

Where was he?

He knows his curfew. That was the rule. And he knows what will happen if he doesn't play by the rules, Chaos thought as she continued to smile down at the boys with tightly drawn lips.

They were encouraging her to press her tits against the glass, to which she obliged. It felt nice against her warm skin. They started whooping and cheering, which only encouraged her to snake her hips. To smooch with the window that in turn misted their view.

By opening it a crack, the night air helped clear the mist from the glass. From the sliver of a gap, she could now hear their whoops and hoots of delight.

"Why don't you let us in!" one shouted up.

"Yeah," the fat one joined in. "I could use a bit of action!"

You need a fucking gym, fat boy, that's what you need, she thought, smiling all the while. Putting the window up further allowed Chaos to poke her head out. "I think you boys should go home to your mammies!" she said, blowing them a kiss.

"Why don't you come down and make us!" Fat Boy said.

"*Yeah*!" the one next to him said.

"Naughty boys!" she yelled down.

"Is that you making all that fucking noise, Charlotte?! For fuck sake!" a new voice said. It belonged to her fuck-head of a neighbour three houses down.

Sticking her head out more, she saw Steven hanging out his window. She'd tangled with him a good few times in the past.

"I'll call the police this time, I swear to God I will!" he bellowed.

"And shouldn't you boys be home at this hour? Not hanging around on street corners!" he growled. "Some of us have fucking jobs to go to in the morning, even if it is a weekend. Now, fuck off!" he told them. "And you!" he said, looking over at Chaos. "What the fucking hell is wrong with you? Hanging your fucking tits out the window at this hour – parading yourself to a bunch of youngsters! Put some bloody clothes on, woman!"

"How's the missus, Steve? Still massively overweight? Giving you a hard time getting it up, is she? No wonder you're so frustrated. Poor boy," Chaos said, closing her window and locking it. The fun was over, even though she could still hear Steven muttering. "Arsehole," she uttered, looking at the clock again.

It was pushing three in the morning.

If Simone doesn't know he is in for a beating, he sure will when he gets home, she thought. But then again, that was probably *why* he was staying out – he knew what was going to happen when he got in, so he may as well stay out as long as he liked. Make the beating worth it.

Well, two can play at that game, she thought, going into the bathroom. Thinking he wouldn't be much longer, she started filling the bath with cold water. She would start him off with an ice down. Nothing hurt more than whips on icy-cold skin. She'd whip him purply-blue, before taking him into the basement, she thought. That's where the real fun and games would begin.

But first, the bath. Which was now half-full with freezing water. Content, she shut the tap off. Walking out of the bathroom, she went back to her bedroom. From the open doorway, she looked at the four-poster bed, which was draped in black and purple bedding. Handcuffs and a ball gag hung from the top-right bedpost.

"Yes, the cuffs and gag will come in handy," she said, unhooking them and throwing them on the twisted sheets. Turning, she faced a wall known as her battery. The wall was lined with all sorts of sex toys and weapons of mass dominatrix: spreader bars, whips, chains, penis gags, bondage hoods and belts, cock rings, corsets, bondage cuffs and mittens…

The list was inexhaustible. Some of the stuff wasn't used any longer.

The cellar was where the bondage furniture was kept. And that's where Simone would find himself later, she thought. Porn bondage was child's play – what Chaos put Simone through was downright dangerous.

Taking one of the whips from her rack, Chaos played it between her hands before giving the bed a taste of its lashes. She'd cut through many bed sheets in the past on the account of missed blows to Simone's back, legs or body.

This whip isn't good enough for that cunt, she thought. *He needs a callous lesson this time around. Soft leather straps are no good for that.* Replacing the whip, which looked a lot like a cat o'nine tails, Chaos removed another. It had just the one strap, which was made of toughened leather, and would hurt more. It also had little studs moulded into it – Simone had tasted this whip many times before.

He enjoyed the pain it inflicted. That was no good.

She wanted him to beg.

To plead for her stop.

She wouldn't get it with this whip, either. He was a tough son-of-a-bitch. Breaking him would not be easy. Safe words did not exist in this relationship. She would beat his fucking brains out. A trip to the hospital had ensued many times.

Not this time. If she hammered him that much, he could suck it up. Tend to his wounds here. She wouldn't be taking him anywhere. The fucker would be paying with his life for such disobedience tonight, she thought.

"Better run and hide, Slave. Mammy is very pissed off," she said, giving the bed a crack with the whip.

Displeased, she put the instrument back on the rack. Next up was a whip made of snaking steel and barb. *Yes*, she thought. *That's it.* It had never been used. Chaos had it specially made a few years ago – Slave had been too nervous to have it used on him.

Well, tonight he would get to taste it.

When she lashed at the bed with this one, the barb caught in many places. On retracting the whip, the sheets tore. This caused her to smile, as she thought of her Slave's skin. How it would break so easily. Without another thought, Chaos lashed the bed again and again and again…Bits of silk clung to the wire teeth that were wrapped around the thick chain.

"Bleed, you bastard!" she yelled, catching a glimpse of herself in the massive wall mirror to her left – she looked wild and dangerous in the moon glow. "You sexy bitch!" she told her image, gnashing her teeth. Turning from the bed, she faced the mirror.

Looking at her short, slight frame made her smile. She knew she was sexy. Knew her Slave knew it, too. Pulling her gaze away from her bald pussy, Chaos looked at the whip. It reminded her of a poem she once wrote, many years ago:

Filthy

It's her lair; you paid to enter –
Demanded the stockings and suspenders;
She don't care – with her long heels
And whip of snaking steel.
She'll lash your skin and graze your chin

With grown claws
That will cost you more. The
Bitch will smile a lucid smile.
But you won't see, with your silk
Covered grin.

Cuffs of stainless steel cage you
For her need; observe her word
For she will spill the foam
From within.

Her sheets of pure satin – are
Made for drinking patrons' matter.
You're just the first of many, throughout
Her filthy day.

Yes, she was pretty sure that's how it went. She hadn't thought of the poem in years, but she could still remember her tutor's comments – "If I were you, Miss Ros, I would place this at the back of a deep, dark drawer, and forget about it! Such nastiness."

Four months later, he'd been expelled for being caught *playing* with some of the younger schoolboys. "Why are men such perverts?" she asked her reflection. "They *all* need keeping in line. Every single one of them." Turning back to her bed, she placed the lethal whip on it, next to the gag and cuffs. "What's a girl to wear?" Chaos said, going to her chest-of-drawers.

Opening the top drawer, she looked inside. It housed her bras, knickers, stockings, hold-ups, suspenders and knee socks. "Hmmm, something colourful? No, definitely not. Something which matches how annoyed and vengeful I feel," she uttered.

Picking out a skimpy red bra and matching panties, Chaos considered them for a moment. The colour certainly looked angry, but it could also mean passion – and the set she was holding was very sexy. Slave would be too happy with the sight, and she couldn't have that.

Putting the red back, she picked out a black/purple/red coloured bra with matching knickers. "Now that's more like it!" she squealed, putting them on the bed. Normally, she would parade around the house nude for Slave, knowing how much that would tease and excite him. But not tonight. *Tonight, he gets nothing.*

I may allow him a look at my legs in some tights, she thought, getting some out of the same drawer. *Yes, that should do.* Putting them with the rest of her attire and toys, Chaos left the room for the kitchen.

Once there, she grabbed her phone, which was on charge. Unplugging the charger, she checked to see if she had any missed calls or text messages. Nothing. The time on her phone read three thirty. Only one other time had he done this. He'd promised never to do it again.

Not after his brutal punishment.

That would be stepped up this time around.

With her phone in hand, she left the kitchen and went to the front door. Undoing the safety chain and unlocking the deadbolts, Chaos edged the door open an inch at a time. She wanted to make sure those boys were not still hanging around before opening up completely.

Stepping onto the doorstep, she could see the boys disappearing around her street corner. Gone. The night air cut her to the bone, but she didn't care. It was nice. She was a freak. Looking the other way, she noticed the street was deserted. There was no sign of her Slave, much to her annoyance.

There was nothing she could do but wait. Closing and locking the door once more, Chaos returned to her bedroom. There, with her phone in hand, she lay on her bed. Her eyes had grown heavy. Setting an alarm for an hour's time, she drifted off to sleep.

Insistent beeping woke her. Rolling over, Chaos saw that it was her mobile phone. "Shit, that hour went fast!" Grabbing the device, she switched the alarm off, noticing it was five in the morning.

"*Slave*!" she called. There wasn't an answer. *Still not home?* she thought. She couldn't believe how defiant he was being. Getting into a sitting position, Chaos checked her phone again. There was a missed call and a text message awaiting her response.

Opening her messages, she saw immediately it was from her Slave: *'Chaos, I've been bad. Very, very bad, which is why I'm late getting home. I hope you can find some mercy for me and my body when I get there. I shouldn't be much longer. Maybe an hour. I love you, Mistress. XX'*

On closing her phone, she noted the text had been sent fifty-two minutes ago. It was time to prepare for his arrival.

Shaking her head, she got off the bed. "Such a fucking bastard! What has he gone and done this time?!" she spat. Throwing her mobile phone to one side, Chaos got into her panties before picking up her tights and sitting on the edge of her bed with them. She placed her right leg into them first, then did the same with her left before slowly inching them up her thick-ish thighs. Oh, how Slave loved them.

Once she was in her tights, which boasted a quality denier, Chaos slipped on her bra. It helped enhance her small cleavage. Dressed, she looked in the mirror. She was satisfied with her look. *Not too sexy for such a dirty, naughty fucking boy*, she thought.

The only thing missing was gloves. *Yes, I want some gloves.* Going to her drawer again, she picked out a pair of lacy ones. After popping her hands into them, Chaos picked her steel whip up. It measured three feet from the base of the handle to the tip.

She cracked it.

The sound it made as it cut through the air caused her knees to weaken.

Her pussy dampened.

She did it once more before settling to await her Slave like a coiled spring… "Come to mama…" she uttered.

CHAPTER 8

He sat in the sand with his knees up to his chin. The sun had started to rise and soon there would be nowhere to hide. Rocking back and forth, with the desire burned out of him, Simone looked at the girls.

Both had their heads caved in.

He'd needed to make sure they were completely dead.

No chances could be taken.

Looking at them now, he couldn't tell which one was which, not even by their bodies. His memory of their names and looks had rushed out of him along with his want and bodily fluid. His desire to come had been strong. Chaos had kept him in his cage for far too long. And, even though he hadn't fucked them, coming over their tits and legs twice had been enough to stem his yearning. For now...

Both girls were naked. Once finished with the peach bra and tights, he'd set them to one side to keep. They would be souvenirs of the event, and would also come in handy for future nights alone. Something to play with, if Chaos allowed it. *I may not even show her the trophies*, he thought, *as she might take them off me and use them for her own gain.*

The girls' faces had been so pretty, he thought, looking from one smashed-in-face to the other. Now they were just a mangle of flesh, blood, shattered veins and bone. Fragments of their teeth and skin decorated the sand. *I could bury them? No, what if a dog comes along and digs them up? People bring their dogs to this part of the beach all the time.*

"*Fuck*!" he spat, finally taking his eyes off the dead bodies. Looking at his clothes, he thought it best to dress, so he did. Once finished, he sat back down. He then noticed the smashed lock from off his cock cage and the device itself. Picking them up, he pocketed them, along with the bra and tights. He also took their panties – the one pair smelled of piss. He could only guess at them belonging to the second girl he'd killed.

I could drag them to the end of this pier – I'm sure the sea comes up this far? he thought. *The tide has started to come in, too, so they'll be dragged out later today. I may have to cover them with a bit of sand, but not too much. I don't want to weight them down.*

Excited, he started moving the girl closest to him. *Is this one Sara?* he wondered, grabbing her by the wrists. *I'm sure it is, looking at her tits.* They were small and pointy. *Yes, I'm pretty sure they were hidden under that spectacular peach bra*, he continued to muse. At first, he couldn't get the body to move. "What the…?" he said in a baffled tone. *She's not that heavy.*

Kneeling at the body, he rolled it over. Sara had been lying on the rock he'd used as a weapon. Before getting back up to start dragging her again, he firstly dug a deep hole, dropping the rock into it. Quickly, he covered it, before standing up as far as he could. What with the pier being low, he couldn't stand to his full height.

With the rock removed from behind Sara, the body was easy to drag. Taking her close to the pier's end, Simone kneeled once again. The sand was wet and the moisture soaked through his jeans. A smile spread across his face. Perfect. The water would come up here, and sweep the bodies out to sea.

Digging a shallow grave, Simone rolled Sara into it. Moving back, he looked at his work. A part of her face was uncovered, along with a few toes and fingers. He covered the exposed bits before going back for Michelle.

Looking down at her, he recalled how amazing her legs had looked in her tights. They had been the most exciting thing about the whole episode. How tight her skirt had been, which now lay in a torn heap next to Sara's clothes.

No need to get upset, he thought. *There are plenty of nice legs out there. Chaos' for a start.* He grabbed Michelle by her ankles and then dragged her down to where he had dumped Sara.

Whilst digging the hole, he thought about how the girls had laughed at his cock. How it had made him feel and how quickly he had squirted his load. He wasn't shocked at having his dick laughed at, not at all, as he had many fantasies involving humiliation.

It was one of his favourite things. He loved it when Chaos ridiculed his dick, even though it wasn't that small. These bitches had giggled through nervousness and on seeing the cock cage. They were young – they knew no better. Still, their ignorance had been his gain.

Stuffing Michelle into the low grave, he started burying her. *Where did the small penis fetish come from? I can never, ever remember being ridiculed in such a manner,* he thought, slowly concealing Michelle. *Had it started long before Chaos? Yes, of course it had. I used to masturbate to such porn and thoughts. Weird, I just don't understand where it started. But then again, I like many forms of sexual fantasies and stuff – I love it. Just like I'm obsessed with lovely thighs and tights. I can't get enough of it. Hell, if this fuck hadn't been wearing such a short skirt with tights, they may both still be alive right now.*

He shrugged and shuffled back to look at both bodies. He'd done a better job with Michelle, as none of her was showing like some of Sara had been. "Great," he said, looking about. The sun was still pretty low, but it was getting there. The beach was also empty, but it wouldn't remain that way for long – people would be out and about walking their dogs.

After all, it was the weekend.

Satisfied with his labour, Simone moved back to where he had killed the girls. He wanted to clean the area – to get it looking the best he could. Before he did anything, he looked to see if he could remember where the stone had been buried, but he couldn't. There were no tell-tale signs, which was perfect. Smiling, he got on his hands and knees, and then started disturbing all the sand that had blood on it.

With that done, Simone gathered the remaining clothing and put them to one side. He then checked to see if he could spy anything else – with the sky getting brighter, it helped his endeavour.

Then, just as he was about to stop searching, he saw an earring in the sand. Moving closer to it, he grinned and picked it up. "Oo, you could have cost me a lot," he said, putting it in his pocket. After another quick scan, he was happy the place was clean.

"What to do with the clothes?" he said aloud. "Shall I just bury them with the girls? Why not. They'll get dragged out to sea, too."

Happy with his idea, he went back to the graves and started digging another shallow patch for the garments. As he busied himself, Simone lost all concentration, and didn't hear the dog until it was at his side. It barked down his ear, thinking Simone had a treat or a stick for him to play with.

The pooch nuzzled its nose into the sand where Simone was digging. It managed to uncover a few fingers as it did so, much to Simone's horror. "Hey, get out of there!" he said, grabbing the dog by its collar. *Collar?* He thought. *Shit, his owner must be close by.*

Simone panicked and scanned the area. He saw a man approaching from the distance. "Fuck!" he uttered. "Get out of here, boy!" he said, trying desperately to shoo the mutt away. Realising it was not working, he looked feverishly for a stick to throw.

He found nothing but a short, heavy lump of wood, causing Simone to give up. He cast his eye over his shoulder once again, seeing the man right on top of him. He had a perplexed look on his face as he slowed his approach.

The jig is up, Simone thought. *I'm going to prison.*

"Hey, what are you doing?" the man said. Simone guessed the bloke was in his late fifties.

I could take him down, Simone thought. *Take the fucker out of the picture. I've already killed twice tonight. A third isn't going to harm… And who would miss an old bastard like him?*

"None of your goddamn business!" Simone snapped. "Now, get your fucking dog out of here!"

At first, the man seemed shocked – wounded, almost. Then his face turned to puzzlement again as he watched his dog uncover the arm of a once living teenaged girl.

"Oh, my God! What are you *doing*?!" the man screeched. "I'm calling the police!" He put a hand to his coat pocket.

"I wouldn't do that if I were you!" Simone said, sliding his hand through the sand to grab a hold of the wood he had disregarded moments ago. Feeling it, he closed his hand around it.

Seeing the man produce a mobile phone from his pocket, Simone pounced off the sand like a cat. He threw all his weight at the man, who jumped back in surprise. That, combined with Simone's mass, was enough to take the bloke off his feet. His phone flew out of his hand and landed in the sand a few feet away.

He had enough time to let out one scream before Simone clubbed him between the eyes six, eight, ten times before stopping. He was breathless. The man's body quivered as though he was having an epileptic fit. *I must have damaged his brain*, Simone thought, getting off the man.

Looking around, he saw nobody. He'd got away with it. When the man finally stopped moving, Simone dug another hole, and rolled him in. The dog did nothing but sit and watch as his owner was being disposed of. "That takes care of him, hey boy?" Simone said, giving the Labrador a stroke on its head.

Finding the man's phone, Simone pocketed it with everything else. "Shall we go home?" Simone asked the dog, which barked in return. "Come on then!" he said, running from the pier.

As he rushed up the beach, Simone kept tripping and slipping in the sand. *Come on, I have to keep it together,* he thought. Then he saw people by the new pier – he couldn't tell if they were men or women, which was a good thing. If he couldn't make them out, then they sure as hell couldn't distinguish him.

Not that it mattered, because soon he was clear of the beach. The streets were deserted, which he had been hoping for. But, not taking any chances, he ducked into an alley. The dog was still on his heel. Leaning against a wall, Simone took a breather. He looked down at himself, and noticed he was plastered in blood. "Shit, anyone could have seen this!" he said. "God, what have I done?!"

Panic washed over him once again. "I need to text Chaos – let her know I'm on my way home; that I've been a naughty boy! Can I tell her I've killed?!"

After contacting Chaos, he'd run the length of the lane he was in and found himself two streets from his house. He tried to keep his worry at bay. *Almost there*, he thought, jumping into another alley, which he followed to the end before joining another.

After exiting the third alley, he was on his street. Ducking behind a car, he searched for his home. He was less than ten doors away. "Almost home and dry," he told the dog. Taking his keys out of his pocket, Simone made sure he had the front door key ready.

He made sure there was nobody in the street, or at their bedroom windows, before moving. He ran the distance between him and his sanctuary. On his doorstep, he slammed the key into the lock and turned it. He ushered the dog in, and then entered himself.

He slammed the door shut and fell back against it. He was out of breath, but he didn't have much time for a break, as Chaos called him from upstairs.

"Up here now, Slave. And I mean fucking *now*!" her voice boomed.

He gulped.

"I…I…I'm coming," he stuttered. Before going upstairs to his Mistress, Simone led the dog to the back door, where he put the animal outside. He then walked back to the passageway on jelly-like legs – a breath hitched in his throat as she yelled down at him again.

"What the fuck are you waiting for, *boy*?!" she asked. This was followed by an intense whip crack.

Putting his foot on the first step, which creaked, Simone almost pissed himself. He could hear her up there, playing with the whip. It was the one she'd never used before – the steel one, which had barbed wire wrapped around it. *I'm in such fucking trouble this time*, he thought, too scared to take another step.

His hand trembled as he placed it on the stair-rail. Without its aid, he wasn't sure he could make it to the top.

"I'm waiting," she spat.

Her chain rattled – the barbs scraped like fingernails down a chalkboard as she dragged it along the wooden flooring.

"I'm on…on…my way u…u…up…" he said, pitifully.

A step groaned underfoot.

His bowels clenched.

"Must you keep me waiting so long? You should be running at the command of your Mistress, Slave!" she bellowed. "I told you to be home early, did I not?!"

"Sorry, Mistress. It's just…"

"It's what?!"

"I'm scared…"

"And so you should be," she said, playfully. "You've been a very bad boy, haven't you?"

"I have," he whimpered. Tears started spilling down his face. His voice cracked. "Extremely bad, Mistress…Please, don't hurt me…"

"Hurt? You're going to be in so much pain that you're going to be begging for the sweet release of fucking death, *cunt*!"

His sniffling intensified. "No…"

"Stop acting like the little sissy you are, Slave, and try being a *man* for once!"

"I…"

"Get up here. *Now*! Or I'll beat you twice as bad."

Moving slightly faster, Simone reached the top of the staircase. Early morning sunlight lit the dark, eerie landing. She couldn't be seen, but her chain could be heard chinking. The barbs grating. He'd be surely made to polish the floor until the scuff marks were no longer visible. But that wouldn't be today.

That chore will wait until I can walk again, he thought. This wasn't going to be a pleasurable whipping. Mistress was intending on being vicious. Venomous, even. She was going to whip him for staying out late. For totally disobeying.

If she finds out I've killed, she'll beat me to death… he thought. *I can never tell.*

He was positive nobody had seen him on the beach; that nobody had seen him running through the streets – the police would never know it was he who had killed those people. *Nobody, not even Chaos, will suspect a thing.*

Another board creaked as he slowly walked the length of the landing.

She would also beat him for breaking his cage. That would displease her the most: She would know he'd pleasured himself. This was a massive no-no – only *she* could allow such an act – an act that had to be completed in her presence, and her presence alone.

"I can hear your pathetic whimpering out there, Slave!" she said. "Get the fuck in here and show yourself."

Edging closer to her bedroom, Simone starting shaking violently. Normally, he liked being punished. But this would be brutal. As he approached the door, which was closed to a sliver, he could see her through the slender opening. She was semi-dressed, which was a bad sign in itself.

If it were a pleasure whipping, which I haven't had in a long time, Mistress would have been naked, he thought.

Putting his quivering hand to the door, he gently pushed it wide. As it swung inwards, exposing more and more of his dominatrix, Simone's fears were realised. It was indeed the whip of steel – a whip he'd dreaded the taste of.

Even though he trembled, he couldn't help but think how amazing she looked. Her body was small and tight – she was only a spit over five-feet tall, yet she struck a fearsome pose in her underwear and tights.

On seeing him, she gasped. "What a naughty boy!" she said. "Do you want a good beating?! I think it's disgraceful, you rolling in here at this hour!"

"N…N…No, Ma'am! Please, don't hurt me."

Walking up to him with her whip dragging slowly behind her, she grabbed him as hard as she could by his ear, twisting it.

Her lace gloves felt good on his skin, but the pain from having his ear wrenched made Simone bend over as she dragged him to the mirror. "Look at yourself!" she bellowed. "You're a fucking perverted disgrace! A late perverted disgrace."

"Yes, Mistress. What would you like me to do?"

"I think you should strip out of those clothes, don't you?"

He nodded. "Yes, Mistress."

"Well, get fucking to it!"

In the mirror, he watched her walk away from him to her bed, where she put the whip down and picked up the crop. Quickly, he pulled his top off and then undid his jeans and slid them down his legs along with his underwear. He instinctively covered his cock with his hands.

Not because he was shy or embarrassed around his Mistress, but because he was hoping to hide the fact his cage was missing.

Instantly, he knew she had noticed. His hands had not been quick enough. Not that she wouldn't have noticed or found out in the end.

"Coy, all of a sudden?" she asked playfully.

"Cold," he said, trying to make his teeth chatter.

"Oh, really," she said, stepping closer to him. She put the tip of the crop to the back of his hands. "Move them," she said. He kept them where they were. "Are you going to make me ask you a second time, Slave?"

His chin wobbled. His lips quivered.

Standing in defiance, he kept his hands where they were.

"Slave, I have told you to remove your hands. Now, do it!"

Without a second's hesitation, she lashed the back of his hands repeatedly. His tolerance for pain had built up over the years and it wasn't until his skin started turning purple did he drop them.

Her mouth sagged.

He took a deep breath on seeing her face change.

"You little fucking shit!" she spat. "Where is it?"

In total insubordination, he said, "What are you talking about, *Chaos*?!"

Answering back and/or being cheeky was one thing. But to actually use her name instead of 'Ma'am' or 'Mistress' was a whipping of the highest order, without already being in so much trouble.

She lashed him across the mouth with the crop.

Simone's head flung to one side. When he faced front again, he smiled at her, leading to three more cracks across the face. This drew tears from him. It also drew blood from his lower lip, which was split and shaking.

"I see you've finally found your balls, Slave!" she said. "Times ahead are going to get interesting, I'm sure." As she spoke, she lowered the crop from his mouth to his chin. She traced it slowly down his chest to his stomach. Once there, she circled his bellybutton.

He shivered.

Smiling, she moved on, until the crop was placed under his semi-erect cock. "The little fella is excited," she stated. "What a naughty, dirty, disgusting and despicable *little* boy you really are, Slave."

"I am," he said, barely being able to smile. It made him wince, exposing his teeth, which were coated in blood; his gums, too.

"Oh, I know you know, I was just stressing the point!" she said. "Now, tell me where your cage has gone, and I may not punish you as badly." His smile faltered – he wasn't expecting any mercy. "I may even let you pleasure me, Slave. You'd like that, wouldn't you?"

He nodded.

"A little bit of ice on that mouth of yours, and you'd soon be able to tongue-fuck me," she said, circling his cock with the tip of the crop.

Groaning, Simone fought to keep his hands by his sides. "Okay, I'll tell," he said, feeling his dick stiffen to its full potential. And so he told her. He told her about the girls. About how they had excited him. About how he had needed a release, etcetera… But not how he had killed them. How he had smashed their heads in and spunked all over them. He told her that he had got rough with them, explaining the blood.

"My, you have been busy. Well, Slave, for being good and telling me that, I won't spare you a thrashing, but I will allow you to pleasure me with that delicious tongue of yours," she said.

This made him smile to the best of his ability.

"But first, I want you to clean yourself up. I can't have you touching or coming near me stinking of stale come!"

He looked down at himself. His pubic hair was matted with the stuff – he was a walking disaster. "Yes, Ma'am," he sulked.

"Good, Slave. I'll have a new cage awaiting you," she said. "There's a nice bath run for you. It'll help you cool off." Smirking, she turned her back to him. "Hurry along, there's a good boy."

Simone shivered as he headed towards the bathroom. He was more than relieved she'd allowed him to take a soak. But when he got to the tub, he didn't see any steam rising. The window was wide open. His stomach sank. *Another cold bath…* he thought

All that's missing is ice cubes, he thought. *But not for long, I'm sure.*

"Are you in, Slave?"

"Getting in now, Mistress," he said, lifting one leg up and dunking it into the freezing cold water. His teeth started chattering on dropping his second leg in. Biting down on a harsh gasp, Simone lowered himself. He dared not shriek. "I…I…I'm…in…" he stuttered. "It's lov…lovely, Mistress…." Huddling himself, Simone tried to think nice thoughts. Of warm water about his skin.

"Oh, good," she said, standing in the doorway. In her hand was a bucket. "Let me freshen the water for you," she said, emptying the icy contents of the pail into the bath.

The ice cubes hit like bombs – their fat bodies exploded cold water into Simone's face as he sat there and winced. He felt like crying, but he didn't buckle. "Thank…thank you!" he managed.

"Good, boy," she said, giving him a pat on the head. "Now, make sure you give yourself a good scrub," she patronised. "I'll be waiting for you. I've also put clean bedding in your kennel too, so make sure you get every smeg of jizz off your body."

"I…I will," he said. His lips started to numb.

"*Good*!" And on that note, she left him to it.

After five minutes of vigorous cleansing, Simone was glad to jump out of the ice-cold water. On searching for a towel, he noticed there were none. He wasn't allowed one.

"Mistress," he called. "I have no towel."

"Shake yourself off the best you can, then come in."

A few minutes of rubbing as much water off himself as he could with his hands, and indeed shaking as instructed, Simone walked into the bedroom. The cold was almost unbearable.

Mistress was on her bed, waiting for him. Her legs spread-eagle – her pussy awaiting his attention. He formed an O shape with his mouth, which was starting to feel much better thanks to the rub he'd given it with the ice cubes.

"Come here and show me how much you appreciate your Mistress," she said.

Slowly, he moved in her direction. When he was at the foot of the bed, he got on his knees. The wooden flooring was cold, but the heat in the room was starting to warm his dead-like flesh.

"You'll have to make your own entry," she said.

Knowing what she meant, he put his head between her legs and nibbled at the moistened crotch of her tights. Soon, a small hole emerged – it was enough for him to get his teeth into. With one fierce bite, he ripped the garment apart, making room for his tongue to probe.

Soon, Mistress was moaning and bunching the torn bed sheets in her hands. *It didn't take much to please Mistress*, he thought, twisting and turning his tongue around her G-spot. He drooled as he did so, which was unavoidable. He lapped at her clit and swallowed the fluids she offered, which mingled with his saliva.

He groaned himself – he could eat her pussy for hours. It tasted amazing. Simone didn't need to fuck her, as simple tasks such as this was enough. All he really wanted was a release now and then, even if it was in the form of oral sex or a hand-job. She rarely sucked his cock, so it was a treat when she did.

Having thought that, a hand-job had not even been performed on him in months. *That led to last night's disaster*, he thought. *It was Mistress' fault, but she will not see it that way.* He hated her. But at the same time, loved to pleasure her. Walking away was not going to be easy – not as easy as that girl on the telephone was trying to make out. Saying he should stand up to Mistress.

Toni? Yes, that was her name. She'd sounded very sexy – a mere squeak of an immature voice. Dare I ring her again? I should try to find out if she heard what I said to her when I rang her by accident. But there was no need to panic. After all, she was a Samaritan. She couldn't divulge information. He knew this, as he'd seen stories in the papers about charity workers knowing about killers and what they had done and what they had threatened to do.

It sounds commonplace, he thought, continuing to pulverise Mistress. He'd become very good at this act – his sister had been quite the tutor when they'd been growing up. Of course, they had just been children. It wasn't until he'd started going with girls his own age that he really mastered the art of oral sex and foreplay.

By the time he was seventeen, he was a master at most sexual acts. Girls his own age bored him. They were mere childish twits – the thought of a boy or man sticking his tongue in their twat made them shriek and whine. But not Mistress – she had found him and had played out all his dark fantasies for him.

But somewhere along the line, hardcore play became reality. Not that it had bothered him, until now. *Because now I've become dangerous*, he thought. And on that thought, he bit Mistress' clit, making her howl and jump up.

"What the *fuck*?!" she said, grabbing the crop from by her side.

He smiled up at her, leaving his face open for attack. She cracked him as hard as she could around the head, causing him to slump to one side. Holding his temple with one hand, Simone begged for forgiveness; that he hadn't meant to nip her, which was a complete and utter lie.

"You fucking bastard!" she said, spitting on him. He crawled towards his kennel, which was a cage especially made for his frame. "I was going to spare you, and this is how you repay me?"

"Please…" he begged, getting to his knees.

Without hesitation, she hit him in the same spot again, causing Simone to buckle once again. "I let you pleasure me, and this is what you do?" She spat on him again, and then slipped into her heels and kicked him in the side four, five, six times.

A bone broke.

She smiled.

He collapsed into a ball of agony.

"I was going to show kindness, mercy, to my poor Slave. But not now."

Rolling onto his stomach, Simone crawled towards his kennel – if he could make it in there, then he would be safe from her attack. Then he screamed in ecstasy and pain as his Mistress walked over his back and stamped on both of his hands. When he continued to move, she kicked him in the face. One eye instantly blackened and bulged – it was still weak from the previous attack.

Had he not been so turned on, he would have fought back this time. But he was his own body's weakness. He was pathetic.

"I continue to see a change in you, Slave. You're becoming bold. And it's too brazen for my liking. I'm going to have to stomp it out of you! Break you once and for all."

"I'll behave!" he blubbered. His lips had started to swell from the cruelty he had suffered earlier.

"I'm not sure I believe you," she said, putting the crop down and picking up the steel whip. She lashed him so hard, a second rib cracked. Some of his skin was also removed by the barbs, which clung to the lethal whip and dripped blood. "Oh," she gasped as an orgasm shook her body. "Time to pay, Simone. Time to pay in full!" she uttered.

The second crack of the whip was as intense as the first, but she didn't stop there. Mistress continued to beat and stomp her Slave until nothing but a bloody, bruised and quivering wreck adorned her bedroom floor.

Once out of breath and energy, she sat on the bed, spent. Her Slave didn't move. He lay in a heap, pissing blood and moaning. Showing no mercy, she rolled him onto his bed before giving him one final kick in the face for good measure.

Content, she went and took a shower. She whistled merrily as she scrubbed herself clean, knowing she had taught her Slave a good lesson; a lesson she would teach him again if he should step out of line once more.

CHAPTER 9

She tried to concentrate on *Macbeth*, but it wasn't happening. Frustrated, she closed the book and pushed it to one side. It wasn't as if it needed to be read just yet – she had the whole summer ahead of her. University work could wait until the new term started.

But, Toni being Toni, she liked to get ahead. Her reading list was the length of her arm, and so the time off would be a good opportunity to eat away at it – especially some of the classics. She'd already ploughed through *Wuthering Heights*, *The Great Gatsby* and *The Duchess of Malfi*. Toni had also made notes on all three books, making sure her bases were covered.

Her tutors were impressed with her. They were keen on seeing her excel and had advised her to work hard over the summer, to have an edge over the others when she returned in the autumn. She'd been told that her marks so far were impressive. But today, like yesterday, and the rest of the week, Toni couldn't concentrate.

She'd become scared. Terrified, even. Stu had asked her to go out with him on a number of occasions since the night at the beach but she'd refused. She'd even missed a few nights of work, having feigned sickness. She'd confided in Suzanne, but she had thought Toni was being paranoid; had convinced her that there was nothing to be worried about.

"People go missing all the time," she'd said.

"But what about the dead guy?" Toni had replied. "It's possible the girls could also have been murdered."

"You're overreacting, toots – you'll see."

That had been three weeks ago. Just two nights after the beach party. At first, the papers had been quiet – reports on missing school girls from the Porthcawl area: one sixteen, the other seventeen. Their pictures had been on the news every day since. A few days after their story, a report of a third missing person hit – one of a middle-aged man. He'd been out walking his dog and never returned.

Two weeks after that, the search for the man had come to an end. His body had been found on the beach. It had been lying in a shallow, watery grave, just under the old pier. *That hadn't been far from where we'd been partying*, Toni thought, getting up from her chair. She walked about her room, unable to settle on anything.

Looking at her clock, she saw it was a little after three P.M. Work didn't start until seven, which gave her plenty of time to do whatever she wanted. But with Suzanne out with Anthony, she had little option. "I could go upstairs and see if Karen and Amy are in," she said aloud, and then remembered they were away until the end of the week.

That's a shame, she thought. *Karen and Amy are always good for a laugh, what with them also being students. Suzanne and I will have to arrange a games night with them some time soon.* She flopped down onto her bed. She could still see the guy's face – the one who had gone missing. She'd actually stroked his dog – a big, fluffy, playful Labrador.

Apparently, when they'd found the guy's body, it seemed it had been ravished by fish and crabs. Reports found online had said he'd been *'picked at'* – that his carcass was water-logged. This in turn had caused his remains to bloat and split his skin in many places. Some sick person had leaked images of the body online.

The things some do for money, she thought, shivering. But, having bumped into the John Doe, she nor Stu had reported seeing him. That had played on her mind the most – they'd been too scared. What if the person they'd seen dashing across the beach had been the killer? If it had been, and he or she had recognised her or Stu, then going public with it may have been the worst thing to do.

Hell, that person could be looking for them. To make sure they stayed silent. This is what she'd relayed to Suzanne, who had pooh-poohed it and said that Toni was worrying for nothing.

But Toni was not sure – it was easy to find and trace people in this day and age. *What if he'd recognised any of us?* Knew *us?* It could easily have been someone they knew. *Now that is being silly – the chances are very much against that*, she thought.

Besides, Toni couldn't make out if the person had been a man or woman – the distance had been too great, not to mention the poor lighting. Also, it had now been close to a month since the incident. Enough time had passed. Taking a week off work and staying in up until now had been wise, though.

Stu had understood, even if Suzanne and Anthony hadn't. Not that they would have been spotted by the person, anyway. Switching the TV on, Toni tried to push the thoughts from her mind. It was time to move on – life couldn't stand still. Yes, she'd made a mistake by not going to the police, but there was nothing she could do about that now.

Apart from go to the police! she thought. *It isn't too late. But then they'd ask why it took me so long to come forward. I could say I was too scared – that I was worried the person had recognised…No! Forget it. I'm not endangering myself, or Stu. I'm sure the police can figure it out.*

Flicking through the channels, Toni stayed away from the news – she couldn't cope with seeing or hearing more about it. Then, just like that, her mind flicked to Simone. How strange it was, that she had not heard from him since the beach incident.

Why on earth would he pop into my mind? With all the calls I've taken and people I've spoken to, he comes to mind. Could he be connected to what happened? That's madness! The guy is a pervert, not a killer. Why hasn't he called me? I was sure he would have...

As much as she hated to admit it, she'd been hooked by his story – it was something different. Most people had family, job or money problems, not sexually explicit ones. *Maybe he'll ring tonight? Or, maybe he has been ringing, but has been speaking to someone else. He may not have liked chatting to me*, she thought.

Frowning, she continued to speed through the channels until she found a quiz show to watch. She loved such shows. Keeping the sound down, she proceeded to think about things. Her mind was racing, as it had been since that night with Stu.

Her phone beeped, which startled her into giving a yelp. Grabbing it, she opened her messages – it was from Stu. *'Hey, what time are you working?'* She texted back, telling him that she would be there for six-thirty. Five minutes later, a second text came through from Stu – *'Cool, I'll see you there. I'm working from six-thirty to eleven. X'*

The X made her smile. Even though they'd only spoken and kissed a couple of times, it felt like the real deal to Toni. When she'd taken the week off after the death of the dog walker, Stu had texted and rung her every day – he'd made sure she was okay. He'd sympathised with her. They'd not officially said they were boyfriend and girlfriend, but Toni hoped that's where it was heading.

They'd shared secrets and evenings together at both their places over the last few weeks, which had been nice. He'd even promised to take her to the fair this coming weekend, to which she'd agreed. She'd suggested going with Anthony and Suzanne, to which he'd approved.

She texted him back – *'I'm looking forward to seeing you! X'* A smiley face was a reply, along with a kiss. This made her smile widen. It pushed her jitters to one side. Suzanne was right – she *was* being too paranoid. Nobody was out there to get her. Maybe a few days away from studying would be good. Go out and have some fun with Stu, who clearly wanted that.

Beaming, she shut the TV off and sprung from her bed. Time was now moving on for five, and she thought it best to grab a bite to eat and a shower.

Shortly after six o'clock, Toni made her way outside to her car, which was parked a stone's throw from her home. With it being summer, the afternoons had started to stretch out, with the sun still pretty high in the sky. She was thankful for this, as she hated going and returning to work in gloom.

Just before getting to her vehicle, Toni used the electronic locking system on her key fob to unlock the car. It made a *beep-beep* sound as the head and sidelights flashed the once – this indicated her action.

Opening her door, she stepped in and turned the key. Before moving off, she put her seatbelt on and produced sunglasses from the glove compartment. Ready, she set off. It took her less than fifteen minutes to get to work, which was good for a Thursday evening.

Coming home, it would take less than ten.

With the music at a respectable level, Toni sang along. Thoughts of Stu and the summer ahead of her made her feel good. Today was going to end well. She could sense it in her waters. *When I get to work, I'm going to ask Stu if he would like to do something tonight – maybe go to the cinema*, she thought.

Happy with that idea, she started singing along to the music with gusto. She turned the volume up an extra few clicks. The rear-view mirror started to vibrate due to the *boom-boom* coming from the speakers. Winding her window down, Toni smiled as she passed people on the streets who looked at her because of her 'noise pollution'.

When she got to the NCP car park around the corner from work, she lowered the music as she approached the ticket machine. Pressing the appropriate button, a thin card was spat at her – she would need to use it to pay her parking fee later that evening. Accepting it, she steered her car onto the first floor.

Being this late in the day, she doubted very much that she would find a space on the ground floor, which she was right about. Heading up, Toni found there was nothing on the next four floors either.

Reaching the twelfth and final floor, Toni found the rooftop to be deserted. Sighing, as she knew she'd hate coming back here later, she parked. *Oh, hang on*, she thought. *Stu is finishing at the same time, so maybe he'll bring me up – he's bound to be parked in here.*

Smiling, she turned the key in the ignition, which killed the engine. Getting out, she made sure she had her parking ticket safe, and then locked the car. Satisfied, Toni headed over to the stairwell. When she opened the door, her nose wrinkled. It stank of piss, weed and shit.

To her shock, she noticed someone had defecated in the corner. Ignoring the sight and smell the best she could, Toni made her way down to the next floor. Her stomach did summersaults when she heard a few crass voices echoing up the concrete passageway.

There were homeless – four of them – gathered at the turn down to the tenth floor. Thinking she should turn back and use the lift, she hesitated. The four men parted. This made room for her to pass. Tentatively, she made her way down. As she walked through the middle of them, one belched in her face, causing two others to laugh.

"Any spare change?" one asked, baring his broken, yellow teeth. His breath reeked of cheap whiskey and tobacco.

"No, sorry," she said.

"Come on, you must have some money – you've just parked, bitch!"

The harshness of their words took her aback. She'd heard others in the office say that the homeless had got rather abusive lately. "*So many brush-offs, probably*," Mike had said. "*I tend not to give in to them – it's expensive enough to park, let alone dole your change out every night to them.*"

"I'm sorry, I haven't got any to spare," she said, starting down the next flight of steps.

"Show us the inside of your purse, 'en?!" one said, making a grab for her handbag.

"*Huh*!" Toni gasped, feeling coarse hands on her. "Hey!" she said, managing to pull away. Her feet tangled, causing her to slip down a few of the steps. Her heart caught in her throat.

They laughed, making her run down the remaining steps. *I should have taken the lift*, she thought, wiping tears from her eyes. She could hear their vicious cackles bounding off the walls.

"We'll be waiting for you, girlie-girly!" one of them called down after her, which was followed by a thunder-clap of a burp.

The threat made Toni whimper as she rushed down the remaining few steps and exited the cold, dank building. Stepping into a sun-drenched afternoon, Toni took a minute. She placed her hand against a wall and leaned. Taking a few breaths, she managed to calm herself and stop her legs from trembling. Her heart rate also steadied.

"Calm down, it's over. Nothing really happened," she tried telling herself. *Are you crazy? They almost caused you to fall down the steps by making a snatch for your bag*, she thought.

Breathing slightly better, she started walking. *I hope to God I can get one of the guys to walk me up there later*, she thought. *There's no way I'm going up there alone.*

By the time she got to her office block, Toni had managed to stop shaking completely. At the door, she took one last deep, calming breath before walking in. The place was near deserted, from what she could see. Her supervisor, in her usual spot, gave a wave as she walked towards her own desk.

Mike, who was also working, gave her a smile as she walked by. It was pretty much all the older guy could do, as he was on the phone. Approaching her own desk, Toni could see that Stu was also on a call – he too flashed her a smile, which lit up his entire face.

She felt a flutter in her stomach as she sat down. It helped drive away the horrible experience in the car park. Putting her bag down by her side, Toni dug her mug out of it, along with a book and crossword puzzle, just in case the phones should go quiet. When they did, it was like a ghost town, and things got boring, fast.

Once her bag was empty, Toni took it to her locker. She then went and made herself a cuppa before plonking herself at her desk once again. Stu had finished his call, freeing him up for a chat.

"You're early?" he said.

"Traffic was much lighter than I thought," she said. *I'm not going to tell him about the car park*, she thought. *I don't want him worrying.* "Fancy going out tonight?"

He beamed. "I'd love to – we could catch a film, seeing as we both finish so late?"

"That's what I was thinking. Or bowling? It's student night tonight," she said.

"Oh, man – it is! We could grab something to eat and hit the arcade, too?"

"Sounds like a plan. Straight after work?"

"Def…" He was derailed as another call come through. "Hello, you're through to Stuart, how can I help?" he said, turning away from Toni. He disappeared back behind his partition.

Sighing, Toni set her phone up. It was fifteen minutes-to, so she decided to get things going early. *No point in hanging around*, she thought. *Let's crack on.* As soon as she went in to the system, her phone rang. "Good afternoon, you're speaking to Emma, how can I help?"

Even after Simone had worked out she was lying about her name, Toni still disguised her real one – the thought of giving strangers that kind of personal information chilled her.

The voice that spoke back sounded like a familiar one. At first, she thought it was him. Simone. But it wasn't. After her ears attuned themselves, Toni could hear it was a woman's voice – it was disguised by a gruff, hung-over tone. Now she was pretty sure she hadn't spoken to this person.

As the call proceeded, Toni discovered the woman was swallowing pills along with copious amounts of Brandy. "It's happened again," she said. "He promised it wouldn't. I believed him," the voice hissed down the phone.

Trying to find out what had happened was proving difficult. All Toni could do was sit and listen as the woman spoke in riddles. "Now he'll never do it again."

When the line went silent, Toni stepped in. She asked the woman who 'he' was, and what had 'he' done? After ten minutes of chasing her tail, Toni finally managed to get the woman to open up.

"My husband, love. The fucking bastard has been fucking other women behind my back. When I confronted him about it, he beat me. Like he always does."

Toni swallowed hard as the woman's story continued to unfold. "I caught him with my sister last night. After he beat me, he promised he wouldn't do it again. I didn't believe him, so I made sure of it…"

Pressing, Toni got the woman to confess to the murder of her husband, which had taken place an hour before this phone call. After he'd passed out blind drunk on booze she'd spiked with date rape drugs, she'd plugged the clothes iron in and placed it on his face – it had taken less than forty minutes for it to burn through his face.

"Now I'm going to end my life. I just needed to tell someone this before I moved on to the next life…"

The line went dead.

"*Hello*?" Toni called down the phone. "Are you still there?" A sizzle of dead air spat back.

"Are you okay?" Stu asked. "You've gone chalk white!"

"I…I…just had…" Then she stopped herself from talking. She remembered about not being able to say anything to anyone about her calls. Shaking her head, she fought bile back down her throat. She could just imagine the guy's face being aggressively corroded by searing heat – too drunk and incapacitated to do anything about it. "Nothing, just a bad one," she said.

"Oh, I am sorry," he said. "It's never easy when it's the first one of the night."

Putting herself on 'hold', she grabbed her mug and went to the kitchen. After being so bouncy and full of life in the car, her evening was turning into a nightmare. *Should I tell a member of management about that call? That woman is killing herself. She's already murdered her husband*, she thought. *But she could also have been bluffing – and if I say something, then I would be breaching confidentiality.*

After making herself a brew, Toni sat back at her desk. "Okay, let's do this," she said, taking her phone off 'hold'. The phone rang immediately. The person on the line had called her a couple of nights ago. He was young – roughly her age. He'd lost his mother to cancer, which he was having a hard time coping with.

Their conversation lasted over an hour-and-a-half, which ended with a few chuckles and a positive note – he also said he'd like to talk to Toni again, and so she'd given him her extension number.

Putting the phone down, she again put herself on 'hold'. Stu did the same as he came off his call.

"Pretty busy tonight!" he stated.

"Yeah. That was a long call, but it ended well."

"Are we still on for tonight?"

"Definitely, why?"

"I thought you might have changed your mind after starting with a negative call."

"Don't be silly – I'm really looking forward to it!" She smiled.

"Great. Me, too."

"Best we get back to it."

"Yeah," he said.

Turning back to her phone, Toni took herself off 'hold'. It didn't ring immediately, which she was grateful for, and didn't look like it was going to any time soon, so she picked her crossword book up. She merrily flicked through it as she waited for another call. That's if another one came through.

She'd done many shifts in the past having only ever taken one or two calls. It's how it went. Some calls could last hours, too, which made it impossible to take more than one or two.

Stu, on the other hand, had not been as lucky – he'd been practically straight in.

After a forty-minute wait, her phone finally rang. Toni had started to think she'd go the rest of her shift without another. *Wishful thinking*, she thought, smiling. "Hello, you're through to Elaine, how can I help?" she said.

"Toni?" the voice said. Her skin crawled. Gooseflesh climbed her arms – the hairs on the back of her neck stood on end. "It's Simone. Long-time no speak," he said.

CHAPTER 10

The first few times he'd rung, Simone had been told that Toni was not working until later that day, yet nobody could tell him when. He'd been encouraged to keep trying, if indeed he wanted to speak to her.

"Other helpers are at hand, if the matter is urgent?"

He'd told them each and every time that he would prefer to speak with Toni, as she knew his worries.

The last time he'd rung, which had been a little over forty minutes ago, a young guy by the name of Stuart had told him that Toni was due to start at seven. With that knowledge, Simone hung up and waited for the time to pass.

It was currently six-thirty.

Maybe a trip to the loo? he thought. *That will take me a few minutes, what with my ribs.*

Thinking about it, he decided against it. It could keep. He wasn't desperate. Besides, the thought of moving at that moment made him wince. This was his fourth week of being laid-up. Healing time would have been quicker, but Mistress had slowed it down by giving him regular beatings.

Beatings out of frustration.

With her Slave down, she had to do everything herself, such as the shopping and cleaning. Also, as he was in no fit state to pleasure her, she had been going out constantly to find herself a toy for the night, which was where she was now – out, giving Simone chance to speak with Toni.

He'd desperately wanted – *needed* – to speak with her over the last few weeks, but he'd been in no fit state. After the initial whooping he'd taken off Chaos, she had kept him in his kennel for the first week. He'd been left to fester in his own piss and shit, as he was unable to move, let alone get up and walk about.

She'd beat him within an inch of his life with her barbed whip. Skin about his body had been flayed – deep gashes lashed into his flesh with joy. He'd lost quite a lot of blood, which she hadn't bothered stemming. It was lucky that the inflicted injuries had not been fatal.

He'd been left weak. For the first day or so, she hadn't even bothered giving him food or water. When her anger subsided a tad, Chaos had found it in her to nourish him; to let him drink.

After that first week, she dragged him out of his kennel, stitched his wounds and placed him in the spare room. She'd put him in the bed there after bathing him. Sometimes, she could be a very good Mistress. However, on this occasion, it probably came down to not wanting too much of a mess.

Once in the spare bed, he was able to recuperate. Except for the occasional whipping, she left him alone. With luck, the clothes he had been wearing the night he'd come home from the beach had been placed in his room, enabling him access to his phone and trophies.

All items currently resided under the mattress within his reach.

He'd sniffed and played with the panties many times over the last few weeks, which had been his only enjoyment, after life came back to his fingers. Luckily, Chaos' auntie had been a nurse, and she had learned how to do some basic first aid – she'd dressed his wounds and made some splints. It had taken a short while for the bones in his fingers to heal.

They still ached, but they were much better, just like his ribs. Within a few days, he would be completely healed.

Yet, this didn't stop Chaos from bringing other men home. He'd hear her being fucked and yelling insults across the hall, knowing Simone was listening. He had to admit – he got off on it. Even though he couldn't play with his cock, due to it being caged, it didn't stop him from getting hard-ons.

Once, she'd even brought a man into the spare room to have at it, right in front of Simone. She'd wanted to show him her Slave – to show him how she had to lock his pathetic cock up. She also wanted her Slave to see a real man fuck her.

Humiliating, but oh so pleasurable and fun.

This, Mistress knew, and knew only too well.

What she didn't know, was that he didn't care about her any longer. His longing to please and cherish her was over. It was over the night he'd taken that first step in seeking help. And, for the past month, all he could think about was Toni. He needed to speak with her.

Looking at the clock by the side of his bed, he saw it was a few minutes to seven. *There would be no point in calling yet*, he thought. Putting his hands flat against the mattress, Simone pushed himself up into a sitting position. Sweat poured down his face from the effort and strain the movement caused his sore ribs and fingers.

Picking up his phone, Simone readied the number. It was now seven-fifteen. Her extension number was busy. "Damn it!" he yelled, slamming his phone down on the mattress. "I knew I should have rung at seven. Seven, damn it – *seven*!"

Every few minutes, Simone tried the Samaritans again, but every time he entered Toni's extension number, he got the same engaged tone. Frustrated, he decided to give it a little bit longer. There was plenty of time – Chaos wasn't going to be home for some time. She normally crawled in during the wee hours, blind drunk and lusting over some arsehole.

Simone drummed his fingers and decided to get up and go for a piss. He was glad he didn't have to use the bottle any more – that had been so humiliating. It had been supplied by Chaos, knowing he couldn't get up to go. She'd also made him wear a nappy before getting him into the bed.

She could cope with emptying his piss bottle, but not scraping shit off his sheets. His nappy had been changed every day, when she could be bothered.

On making it to the bathroom, Simone took an agonising piss. It was a relief to see it back to a bright, yellow colour. At the start of his recovery, his urine had been red.

When he was finished, he shuffled over to the sink as slowly as he could whilst clutching his ribs. "Fuck, still stings like a motherfuck," he spat from behind clenched teeth. Looking up, he saw the damage to his face. This had been the first time in weeks he'd seen his image.

The one eye was now slightly bruised, whereas the other was back open. It was banged up, but looking much better. Thankfully, Mistress had not caught him in the face with the barbs, so apart from bruising and a split lip, there wasn't anything major.

"*Time we took that fucking twat down*," a voice said from behind him. "*She was fun to begin with, but now she's getting to be a right fucking bore*!"

In the top corner of the mirror, Simone saw Mr. Tickles. "So that's where she stuffed you!" he said, turning around. His toy clown had been placed on top of the airing cupboard. "Why didn't you call me before now?"

The clown shrugged.

"Let's get you down from there!" Simone said, reaching up tentatively. "Oh, fuck…my ribs!" he said, grabbing his toy.

"*Sir, that bitch is going to kill you if we don't strike first.*"

"Are you the only one left?"

"*No, sir. A couple of the men are in hiding. She found and smashed the others, sir. She said she would, remember?*"

Simone nodded. "Where are the others?"

"*Here, in my pouch.*"

Digging his hand into the pocket at the front of the clown's trousers, Simone found Spiked Mace and Rape Charge. "Good to see you men survived. It's going to be just the four of us these days," he said.

"*Yes, sir!*" both G.I.'s said, saluting their leader.

Grabbing them all, Simone hobbled back to his bedroom.

After a light struggle, Simone was back under the covers. He'd placed Mr. Tickles and the commandos at his side, and now picked up his phone to try Toni's number again. This time he got straight through to her. He gasped on hearing her voice.

"Yes, it's been a long time," she said. "Where have you been?"

"Unwell," he said.

"Flu?"

"No," he said, looking at Mr. Tickles. He felt ashamed. Tears started to slip down his face. "She beat me. She beat me black and blue!" he admitted.

"Your girlfriend?"

"Mistress, yes. Chaos, that's her name. I'm sure I told you?"

"Yes, I think you did. Are you all right?"

"Just about."

"Why did she beat you?"

"Because I came home very late the night I spoke with you. She was furious. She whipped me until she broke bones and blackened my eyes. I've not been able to move my fingers or body. It still hurts."

"You poor thing! You need to leave her, Simone."

"I want to. I'm definitely going to do it this time. Only one person has ever beaten me this bad, and I made them pay for that, along with Mr. Tickles and the rest of my gang," he said, realising he'd parted with too much information. It was too late to try and cover his tracks, as Toni was straight onto it.

"Oh?" she said. "Would you like to tell me about that, Simone?"

"I..."

"Anything you tell me will be held in the strictest confidence, I can promise you that," she said.

He could hear the compassion in her voice – it was driving him lust-crazy for her. *She genuinely cares for me*, he thought. *Yeah, and for all the other fucking losers that call her.* No, she seemed to be truly interested and concerned for his welfare. "Are you wearing a skirt, Toni?" he asked.

Fuck, he thought, tearing the phone away from the side of his face. Why in the fuck had he asked her that? *You stupid, stupid fucker!*

"Er...No, why?" she asked.

"Nothing, forget I asked," he backtracked. "The last time someone hurt me in such a way was when I was thirteen."

"Who did it?"

"School bullies," he said, remembering back to that day.

****

Standing at the school gates, Simone looked both ways. Phillip-John Cartwright and his two goons were nowhere to be seen. For the last couple of years, since entering comprehensive school, they had bullied him non-stop.

Rumours surrounding his sister had surfaced. People talked. Children were cruel. When Cartwright found out about it, he was quick to start his shit with Simone, who absorbed the abuse day in, day out. Week in, week out. Month in, month out.

After all, it was only words.

Sticks and stones, and all that bollocks.

They never hit him; pounded him for it. They just found the rumours to be hilarious. After all – they were just rumours; tittle-tattle formed by narrow-minded people who acted like old washer women. 'Apple Pickers', his mother used to call arseholes like that.

Some people may have known the truth – about why his sister had been taken away, but nobody could prove it. It wasn't just the gossip about Sian, either. The bullies loved picking on him about his stripper mother. About how she would take random men home every night and fuck them right in front of him and his sister. Of course, they were lies. The stripping bit wasn't, but the fucking of strangers was. He never told his mother, either. Or the teachers. Or anyone of authority.

Simone took it.

It didn't bother him.

It was just words.

He loved his mother and sister. No matter what.

The fucks in school knew no different.

But then, just like that, Cartwright overstepped the mark.

Seeing that the bullies weren't in sight, Simone started his walk home from school. The previous summer had been kind to him – his body had started taking shape. He'd grown a few inches in height and added bulk to his once scrawny frame. His genitals had also started forming, and Simone had taken to masturbating. His mother had caught him doing it a few times, and had told him it was normal – that every boy his age did it.

She hadn't told the women down at Bunnies, mercifully, who may have said some really embarrassing shit to him. Mind you, if they had, Simone probably would have loved it. He'd felt kind of weird when his mother had caught him at it the first time. He felt excited about it too. He couldn't quite put his finger on it.

It was as if he wanted to be caught, but without knowing it.

And that's the reason she used to catch him at it – he wanted it.

Of course, he never told her that.

Once he was out of his school's street, Simone made a left, which took him down a backstreet. This was a shortcut that only he knew about – Cartwright and his flunkies lived the opposite side of town, so there was no way that they could know about this route.

He couldn't wait to get home. His mother had bought him a couple of new games for his Sega Mega Drive: *Streets of Rage* one & two. They were his new favourite beat 'em-up games, alongside *Final Fight* and *Mortal Kombat.* They were ones he'd either played in the arcades down on the seafront or at a friend's house. That was one of the best things about living in a seaside town – the arcades.

Mam is great – she always gives me pockets full of change and lets me go nuts, he thought, heading down the backstreet. *At night,* he thought, *I bet it's creepy as hell. All the monsters come out at night and play, like werewolves, vampires, zombies, Freddy, Jason…*

"*Hey*, sister toucher!"

Shit! Simone thought. He knew the voice belonged to Cartwright without having to turn around.

"Been slipping your sister the finger lately?" he mocked.

"Nah, the slag has been put away!" one of his cronies piped up.

"True, that," Cartwright bellowed, and then laughed as hard as he could.

Fat piece of shit, Simone thought, picking up his pace. *If I can just reach the next turn, I'll be back out in the open.*

"Where are you running off to?" Cartwright yelled. "We're not finished talking to you, arsehole."

"He's probably off to see his mother at Bunnies!" the second goon said.

They all burst out laughing.

"Fucking dogs, my dad calls them – he's been down there. They're filth, he says."

Again, they all burst out laughing.

"Flea-bitten pussies!" Cartwright said.

He's a fine one to talk, Simone thought. *His mother is a right fat tub of lard that does fuck all every day. A right down-and-out. A pathetic piece of shit. An oxygen thief*, he thought, smiling. *She's so fat she has to wash herself with a rag on a stick.*

A titter escaped him.

"He thinks it's funny!" Goon One said.

"Ha-ha!" Goon Two snorted.

"Let's show him how funny we think it is!" Cartwright said.

Not liking the sound of that, Simone went to make a break for it, but tripped on his shoelaces.

"*Simone, make sure you keep them tied tight at all times*!" his mother's words echoed.

As he went sprawling over his own feet, Simone's mouth fell open. Hitting the deck, he slid into a huge mud-puddle. Some of it went into his mouth as he glided through the murky water. He could hear an eruption of laughter behind him as his body came to a stop.

He coughed and wheezed as he sat up. Clumps of mud stuck to his school uniform, coat and hair.

"Enjoy your trip?" Goon One asked.

"Send us a postcard next time, loser!" Goon Two said.

Cartwright pushed past his helpers and grabbed Simone by his jumper. Being such a lump of a lad, he was able to pull Simone up into a standing position. "That's what you get, when you're ignorant!" he said. "Karma gives you a big, fat kick in the arse, dickhead."

Simone couldn't understand what he had done to deserve such harsh treatment. He'd done nothing to these bastards. Why didn't they just leave him alone? "*Fight back, sir*!" he heard Mr. Tickles say from his schoolbag, but he was outnumbered and dazed.

He knew what was coming and took it. There wouldn't be a next time, he thought, as he took a robust punch to the jaw off Cartwright. It took the bigger boy six more attempts before he managed to knock Simone off his skinny legs.

"Tough fucker, isn't he?!" Goon One said, laying into Simone's ribs with heavy blows. This encouraged Goon Two to join in with the kicking.

That left Cartwright to stamp on him like a sissy bitch. Simone was fine with the pain. He liked it. Pain was his friend.

After a beating that felt as if it lasted a lifetime, Simone dragged himself home. His mother had tried getting the truth from him, but he lied. And when she knew he was lying, he said he would never tell.

Which he didn't.

That night, Simone and the rest of his Krulls made up a devious plan.

After spending the next week off school, Simone struck back when the bullies least expected it.

Having mapped out *their* route home through spying on them, Simone made his move when they hit a part of their path that was deserted. Now, he could have killed the fuckers if he'd wanted to, but that wasn't what it was about. It was concerning pain. Harsh, brutal and devilish pain.

Pain they would never forget.

Armed with implements from his dad's workbench, Simone set out. He crept in the bastards' shadows. Watched them from behind parked cars and bushes. He got so close to them at certain points, that he could hear their breathing.

He was under no illusion – he was probably going to get hurt. After all, there were three of them. Surprise was everything. It would ensure the damage to himself was minimal.

Once the boys hit the spot Simone wanted them, he pounced. After drawing a hammer from the work belt he wore, Simone smashed out the knee of Goon Two before he knew what the fuck was going on. He hit the deck like a sack o'shit – blubbering like an infant, and rolling about on the ground holding his shattered kneecap.

"Ahh, it hurts, it *hurts*!" he bleated.

On turning and seeing his mate down, Goon One wet himself, much to Simone's amusement. Cartwright seemed welded to the spot, and could only watch as Simone drew the hammer back and smacked Goon One in the face. His jaw came clean off its hinges – bits of teeth were sent flying. His nose crumpled under the attack.

He collapsed like a house of cards.

Cartwright held his hands up. "Please! We were just messing about, that's all. We didn't mean to hurt you like we did," he pleaded.

Simone was shocked that he'd managed to round on the three of them with such ease. "Oh, so you're sorry. Sorry for making my mother out to be a whore? Sorry for tarnishing my sister's name? My family name? Sorry for beating the crap out of me? Sorry for making my life hell for the last two years? Why? So I don't hurt you like these shitheads, is it?" Simone said.

Cartwright did a sort of nod-shake of the head, as though he didn't know which way to go with it. He was scared witless. His troops continued to blubber on the ground – crying for their 'mammies'. Simone giggled. "What a tough pair you've got on your side – not like Mr. Tickles and the rest of my crew, who think you should all be gutted like fish," he said.

Goon One put his hand up and pulled on Simone's trouser leg. For some reason, this annoyed the hell out of him. Prying the boy's fingers free, Simone pinned his hand to the ground and smashed his elbow in with the hammer. This caused the lad to roll away. "Now he has two sore spots," Simone said, looking from Cartwright to Goon Two, who was still holding his collapsed knee. "Not sure he'll walk again, and I'm not sure you'll ever father children," he said, swinging the hammer up hard and fast.

Simone could almost hear Cartwright's nuts crack like walnuts. He let out a horrendous squeal – a bit like a pig when it has its throat cut. He dropped to his knees hard; it sounded as though he'd blown one out.

With all three down, Simone circled them. Goon One had taken enough punishment, he decided, so he went to him first. He stripped him – not caring that he hurt him more as he did so. Once he was done, Simone moved to Goon Two. With only one knee gone, Simone pulverised the boy's hands before stripping him.

Lastly, he went to Cartwright, who was still howling in pain. "You've smashed my balls!" he wailed.

"Yeah, I know. I'm going to tell you something, and I'm only going to say it once. If you tell anyone about this, about what I've done here, I'll make the rest of your life a complete misery. I'll stalk and hound you for the rest of your days. The way I see this, you were attacked by much older children. There must have been at least four or five of them. You keep these two in line, or I'll get you. I'll get you so bad, you'll pray for death," Simone told Cartwright, before stripping the fat lad of his clothes, too.

Taking their uniforms, Simone made a run for it, and looked back over his shoulder. It was funny seeing them lying there, bollock naked for the whole world to see.

Once the bullies had recovered after months of care and surgery, nothing was said. Simone went through the rest of his school days without so much as a bad look placed his way. Word in the schoolyard was that Simone had dealt with the three bullies, but nothing was ever proven.

****

"Bloody hell, Simone!" Toni said. "And you were never caught? They never told?"

"Never. It's a code bullies live by, I guess. I was never picked on or abused ever again. I wanted them to feel the same embarrassment I felt – going home to my mother all beaten and bruised was shameful," he said.

"But she was your mother – I'm sure she understood."

"She did, but it was still awful. I didn't want to seem like a weakling in front of her. I loved her. I wanted her to feel safe around me," he said.

"What happened to your mother, Simone? You've not told me much about her apart from her filmmaking and dancing."

"It's not something I'm ready to open up about just yet, Toni. You're a great listener, by the way," he said. He could tell his comment had made her blush – the silence spoke volumes.

"Oh, thanks," she said. "I understand you not wanting to talk about your mother. You tell me what you feel you need to."

"Thanks."

"Can I ask, though – is that the only time you've ever hurt someone?" she asked. "From what you've told me, you seem to like being dominated," she said.

There's that silent blush again, Simone thought. "No. I've hurt someone else, too."

"In a bad way?" she asked.

"Yes, in a very bad way."

"Oh…" she said.

"That time, I was older – fifteen or sixteen."

"Do you want to tell me about it?" she asked.

"Not tonight. How about tomorrow night?"

"You want to chat to me again?" she asked.

Was that excitement or fear in her voice? he wondered. "I'd very much like to, if you don't mind chatting to me at length again?"

"Not at all – I like listening to and helping people."

"Good. Then I'll ring you tomorrow. Same time?"

"Yes, I keep the same hours."

"Okay, I'll ring then. Bye," he said, hanging the phone up. The loss of her voice was almost too much for Simone to take, but he knew he couldn't spend all his time speaking to her, even though it was a free phone number.

Looking at his clock, he realised he'd spent the last hour-and-a-half speaking with Toni. His stomach started to rumble. If he was going to eat, then he would have to go down to the kitchen and make it himself. There was no way that bitchy Mistress of his was going to make him any food when she got in, and that was more than likely hours away.

Gritting his teeth, Simone swung his legs over the edge of his bed. With his feet planted on the floor, he made the effort to stand. Taking a deep breath, he walked on shaking legs. Once out of the bedroom, he felt a little better – the dizziness had gone; so too had the shakes in his hands.

The pain in his ribs still hurt when he breathed and walked, but he'd learned to cope with it. To deal with it, much like he dealt with other pains that he found satisfying.

Making it to the top step of the stairs, Simone put one shaky leg on the next step down. This would be the first time for him to negotiate the stairway since Chaos' brutal attack on him. *If the bitch had left me food, like normal, then I wouldn't have to do this. She must think her Slave is now capable.*

"Fucking *whore*!" he raged, taking the second, third and fourth step without much of a problem. By the time he'd reached the bottom, Simone was breathing and sweating hard. "Jesus!" he uttered.

Holding on to the banister, Simone took a few deep, painstaking breaths before moving through the lounge to the kitchen. When he got there, he put the kettle to boil and made himself a sandwich, which he ate with a packet of crisps. He didn't have the energy or desire to make himself a hot meal.

Once finished, he washed the plate and put it back. He sought out a few biscuits to go with his tea, which he drank in the kitchen. He made sure to clean his cup, too, then placed it back in the cupboard with the other mugs and china.

Leaving the kitchen, he turned the lights off as he went. When he got to the passageway once again, he was startled by a loud knock at the front door. His heart started to quicken its beats – had the police finally cottoned on to him as being the man who had killed that dog walker a month ago?

The bodies of the girls were never recovered and they were now pegged as runaways, but not the man, obviously. At first, the police had thought it an accident; that the man had fallen and hit his head. But deeper investigation found that he'd been beaten.

Another knock.

He couldn't move.

If it was the police, surely they would have identified themselves by now?

"Who is it?" Simone called.

"Er, could I have a few minutes of your time, please?" the voice called back.

"Who are you?" Simone wanted to know.

"My name is Stephanie," she said. "I'm here on behalf of our Lord and saviour."

Simone was baffled. "What?!" he sounded rude.

"I'm a Jehovah's Witness. I'd like to speak with you."

"At *this* hour?!"

"The Lord's work is never…" she started, but was startled into jumping back slightly when Simone opened the door sharply. "Hello," she said, smiling. She couldn't have been more than twenty-three, twenty-four, Simone thought. For a Witness, she was remarkably pretty. "You're the first one to open their door to me," she said, handing him a pamphlet.

Not to be rude, he took it. As he pretended to look at it, he peeked over the top of it. She was wearing a knee-length skirt with blue tights underneath. His heart rate started to increase by the second. *So pretty*, he thought, licking his lips.

"Not much luck out there, hey?" he asked.

"No, not really."

"I thought you came in pairs?

"We do – Gray, the chap with me, is in the street opposite," she said.

Such big tits for a God worshipping whore, he thought. *But, then again, that's the kindness our Lord dishes out to all the good little boys and girls. Dirty fuck just wants to get it on with big-titted whores in the Kingdom of Heaven.*

"Why are you smiling?" she asked. "This is a serious cause."

"Oh, I wasn't trying to be rude," he lied. He hadn't even realised he *was* smiling. "I just find it odd, how I was just thinking about converting, and here you are! It's a miracle." His smile widened.

She smiled back. "Well, I can leave that with you and come back. I know time is getting on, and I wouldn't want to…"

"No, not at all. Please, come in," he said, stepping out of her way. Once she was standing in the hallway, he looked out onto the street. Nobody appeared to be around or at their window.

"What's the matter?" she asked.

"I was just checking to see if my partner was anywhere to be seen. I'm expecting her at any minute," he lied.

It was hard keeping the enormous grin off his face as he closed and locked the door. *Welcome to my parlour, said the spider to the fly*, he thought, turning to usher her into the living room.

CHAPTER 11

After Simone disconnected the call, Toni had put herself on 'hold'. With only a few minutes of her shift left, she didn't want to go over – not tonight. She felt exhausted from having spoken with him.

As crazy as he sounded, Toni couldn't help but feel something. As soon as she knew it was him calling, an excitement cramped her guts. She wanted to know about him – about his past and what was truly going on with his life right now.

He hurt those boys, though, she thought. *And look what he got up to with his sister! Not forgetting, I still don't know what the story is with his mother and he just confessed to hurting others on a greater scale.*

What if he was behind the abduction of those school girls? The killing of that dog walker? No, that's insane. They were local. So is he. What's so insane about it? He's already confessed to hurting others. With such a chequered past, he could quite easily be the number one suspect.

His voice is so nice. I could fall asleep listening to it. What are you saying? Madness! she continued to muse, unaware that Stuart had been trying to get her attention for the past couple of minutes. It wasn't until she bit down too hard on a fingernail that she noticed his hand movements.

"Hello?!" he said, smiling. "Anybody home?!"

"Very funny!" she said, doubling over in mock laughter. "You're killing me."

He smiled. She winked.

"Are you all finished?" he asked.

"Yes. I just need to grab my stuff. Why?"

He looked wounded. "I thought…"

"Oh, yeah – bowling!"

"That's right. You still fancy it, yeah?"

Thoughts of Simone danced in her head – she didn't, no. All she wanted to do was go home, soak in the tub, and think about her last conversation. *God, what is it about him*? He was getting into her head. "Of course!" she said. "Ignore me. I went into my own little dream world. It happens."

"A blonde moment?" He smiled.

"*Cheek*! Just for that, I'm going to give you a drubbing at bowling."

"Fat chance, missy! Five-time county champion, right here," he said, poking himself in the chest with his thumb.

"Ha! If you say so. I just need to get my bag from my locker," she said, picking up her coat and mug.

"Cool. I'll wait outside for you. I have to go to the toilet before we leave."

"Okay, see you in a few minutes," she said. "I think I'll go, too."

They parted company at the lockers after waving a goodbye to Mike, who was still on the phone. Opening her locker, Toni removed her bag. Inside were her car keys. She got them ready. Locking the door, Toni headed to the toilet. There was no sign of Stu.

After leaving the bathroom, Toni slipped her coat on before moving to the outside. Even though summer was in the air, it was chilly. The wind had picked up, which was now biting at her face.

"Nippy!" Stu said, appearing from behind the corner.

"Jesus! You almost gave me a heart attack, Stu!" she said, putting her hands to her chest.

"Oops, sorry."

"It's okay. Why on Earth were you lurking around the corner? Couldn't you have stayed in sight?" she asked, smiling.

He shrugged and then giggled. "Sorry," he repeated.

"It's okay, and yes, it is cold!" Toni flipped her coat collars up. "It was so lovely earlier, too."

He nodded. "Where are you parked?"

"Top floor of the NCP."

"I'm one down," he said. "I'll take you up." Smiling, he took hold of her hand.

She wasn't sure she was comfortable with that, but she went along with it. She did very much like Stu, but they still hadn't really said they were 'going' together.

As they walked and talked, she found herself liking the hand holding more. She'd managed to stop thinking about Simone, even though he was lurking at the back of her mind. She couldn't fathom what it was about him and his sick ways that fascinated her.

There had been plenty of weirdos over the last few weeks.

What was so special about this one?

It was his voice, she decided. It was hypnotic. She found it sensitive; found *him* sensitive.

Crazy.

Not really – she wanted to try and help him. To help him get rid of his demons. He sounded so sad on the phone this time, just like the last time. *I really do hope he calls me again tomorrow. I should have given him my mobile number,* she thought.

You can't do that, she scolded herself. *If anyone were to find out, it would mean my job. Maybe more. Come on, it's my life.* My *phone number. I do what I want.*

"Have you been listening?" Stu asked, forcing a thin smile.

"Huh?" She sounded baffled. "I'm sorry – it's been a long day. What did you say?"

"I asked if you'd like me to ride the lift to the top with you, or are you okay? After all, chivalry is dead, right?" A laugh escaped him.

The memories of the vagrants came flooding back. Even though it sounded quiet inside the concrete building, up top could be packed with them.

"Yes, please. I'd like that very much." Toni completely missed his attempt at humour.

When the lift reached them, the door slid open to reveal an empty carriage. *So far, so good,* she thought, stepping inside with Stu.

"Are you sure you're up for tonight? You seem a little…"

"A little what?"

"Distracted…"

"I'm sorry," she said, exhaling. "It's just been a strange day. The last couple of calls I had were a bit stressful," she lied.

"Yeah, I know what you mean. Few people make it past the first few weeks. The stress and whatnot takes it out of them."

"And you?"

"I learned to deal with it quickly. I never talk about the call or callers, either. I put it all out of my mind as soon as I leave there."

That's where I'm going wrong, she thought. *I'm letting Simone into my head – I should be closing him out. But why just him? Why not others? Because you find him interesting. Mesmerizing, even.* Toni had been with a couple of boys sexually, but nothing intense. Simone's world seemed to offer danger and difference.

As much as she hated to admit it, she was highly-sexed, but managed to keep it contained.

Until now.

Stop it. Enjoy Stu's company, silly. He's so interested in you, she thought, looking over at him. He smiled at her, just as the lift came to a halt. As the door slid open, she heard voices in the stairwell. *They're still here. Oh, God.* Swallowing hard, she stepped out of the lift alongside Stu. *At least he's here with me.* She grabbed hold of his hand.

I'm going to try and make this as quick as I can, she thought, taking the lead.

"What's the rush?!" he said, bemused.

"Nothing. Well, it's this place – it gives me the creeps at night." She pushed through a door that led to the stairs. Toni almost burst out laughing with relief when she saw it was a couple of their colleagues standing by the exit to the top floor.

It was them I heard chatting.

Bidding them a goodnight, Stu escorted Toni to her car. "Do you want to follow me or the other way around?"

"Well, seeing as I'm at my car first, how about I take the lead? I know the way."

"Okay," he nodded. "Give me a few minutes to get to mine, then head on down to the next floor."

"Cool." She closed her door. By the time she'd fired up her engine, Stu had vanished. She was shocked at how fast he was. With the car running, the CD player kicked in and she lowered the volume so she could concentrate on reversing out of the gap and then straightening up.

After driving down to the next level, Toni saw Stu in his car. She passed him and then applied the brakes until he was out of his parking spot and able to follow. It didn't take them long to reach the exit.

Soon they were on the open road, with Stu's car visible in her rear-view mirror. Smiling, she turned her music up. She was looking forward to doing something fun with Stu. It was nice when he came over to watch movies and chill, but that's all they had done.

But that wasn't entirely down to them.

It had been her fears. She was still worried that the person had recognised them. But slowly, as time passed, she was letting go of it. Tonight would be a good tester for her.

She loved being out on the roads when it was like this. Often, after hours of studying, Toni would either go on long midnight walks or take the car out. It helped clear her mind. It also helped her digest the knowledge she had taken in from the reading.

She'd even given herself mental tests whilst being out alone. Suzanne thought she was crazy for doing it, even though she would sometimes tag along for the ride. That was cool too, but Toni preferred the solitude. She was weird, but could deal with that. She was down with being an oddball, which made her standout. Made her unique.

Toni could only thank her parents for the way she was. They didn't try to smother her with protection or encouragement. They were just there, nudging her in the right direction every so often. They didn't judge her for the clothes she wore, the friends she hung with, the music and games she played. They let her explore life.

And when she told them that she wanted to be a teacher, even though they had hoped she would want to go into medicine, they backed her. At first, she thought they were going to be on the phone to her every day – worried that their little girl was out in the big wide world.

But no. Just like when she had been growing up, they were in the background. There for when she needed them. For that, she thanked them. Respected them. In return, she never got too drunk, too high, too loud, too moody or too rebellious.

Toni got on with life, thinking herself a sensible girl.

If I'm that sensible, she thought, *what am I doing thinking about giving a mad person my number? Now that, I don't have an answer for.*

She pulled her car into the car park of the bowling complex, and found a space immediately. Toni killed the engine and undid her belt, but she didn't get out. Instead, she firstly watched as Stu sourced a spot and parked.

Once in the fresh air, she walked over to meet him at the front of his car. Hand in hand, they walked over to the bowling complex, which comprised of an amusement arcade, food court and cinema.

"Fancy grabbing something to eat before we bowl?" he asked.

"Erm… Maybe after, if that's okay?"

"Yeah, sounds good to me."

"Cool," she said, walking up to the counter belonging to the bowling range.

"Five games for two people, please," Stu told the man working the till, who took his money and gave them the required shoes to play in.

"Thanks," they told the man in unison.

"You're welcome. Enjoy!" He smiled.

The first game went to Stu. *He's fairly good*, she thought, watching him re-enter their details into the machine for the second game. *But he's not five-time county champion good*! She held her laugh in. *I have gone easy on him, mind. It takes a couple of games to get the swing of it – no pun intended.*

"What are you smiling at?" he giggled.

"Just thinking how much of a schooling I'm about to give you!"

"Oh, really? Well, you lost the last one by forty pins!" he stated.

"I was getting my eye in!"

"Ha! Lucky me, hey?"

"Very," she said, picking up the ball for her first shot. With the precision of a missile locked onto its target, her ball thundered down the lane and hit a strike. "Very lucky indeed," she continued, turning to face him. His mouth hung slightly open. "Oo, burned!"

"What…How did you do that?!" he asked, bafflement on his face.

"Not sure." She acted dumb by putting a finger to her mouth.

"Knock it off," he laughed. "Right, prepare to be annihilated!" He launched his ball, coming away with nine pins after his spare.

Toni went on to take the game, along with the third. She wasn't bothered about winning or losing – it was about the crack; the banter. All through their matches they chatted about general stuff and work, but never the call or callers. She found herself liking him more by the second, but couldn't shake the nagging thoughts of Simone.

She wished she could speak with him after bowling. Or text him, at least. *What am I going to do*? She'd thought this evening with Stu would help her forget about things; about Simone – but it wasn't working. At least she wasn't being rude to Stu any longer by not listening to him.

He was such a nice guy, and she didn't mean to offend him in any way at all. It was just…Simone. The weeks leading up to this evening's call were almost painstaking. She'd wanted him to call. Urged him. As the days and weeks passed without a word from him, she'd assumed he'd either been calling someone else, given up, or had become happy with his life and situation.

The woman he lives with – Chaos? *Sounds like a right bitch*, she thought, as she lined up to take another shot.

After the last game, which Toni also won, they ate at the Burger King situated in the food court. Once they'd finished, Stu walked Toni to her car.

"I've had a lovely evening," he said. "Are you working tomorrow?"

"Me, too. Yes, same time."

"Yeah? Me, too. Maybe we could do something tomorrow evening?"

"Sounds good," she said, smiling. But deep down, she didn't want to. She had something else in mind, if all went to plan.

"Great!" he said, trying his best to conceal his excitement.

She smiled. *Maybe I should be honest with him – or tell him I have studying to do or that I promised Suzanne I'd do something with her. No, don't lie to the poor boy*, she thought. As she was about to speak, he leaned in for a kiss. It was totally unexpected.

It wasn't unwelcome, she thought, letting herself get caught up in the lingering smooch. *It's just I'm not sure I want to proceed with Stu. I have to get my head straight with Simone. I need to know his full story – I need to know everything about him.*

It was becoming an obsession.

It's disgusting and disturbing, she thought.

"Erm…" she said, pulling away from Stu. "*Phew*… That was nice, but I have to go."

He looked a little crushed. "Shall I text you later?"

"Yeah, cool." She was fine with that.

"Okay. I'll drop you a line when I get in – make sure you got home safe," he said.

She smiled. He was so sweet. *I could be really happy with him*, she thought. *Then claim him, numb nuts*! *No, not until I get these stupid thoughts and feelings about Simone out of my head.*

"Goodnight," she told him.

"Night," he said, giving her a wink. "Next time, you're going down, matey!"

"I think not, baby puppy!" she said, using a Russian voice.

"*Cats & Dogs*?"

Smiling, she wished him a goodnight once again. She then watched him as he walked over to his car. Once he was out of sight, Toni got into her own. She waited for Stu to pull out and leave before starting her car. When she looked in her rear-view mirror, she stared at herself.

"Are you really going to do it?" she asked herself.

Huffing, she didn't know. *The heat I could bring down on myself would be unbearable. Yeah, or he may not even be interested*, she thought. *Either way, I have to find out. I need to know more.* She gave herself a little smile. *I guess my mind is made up. Tomorrow night, when Simone rings, I'm going to give him my mobile number. Invite him to ring or text me whenever he feels he needs to. After all, I'm really concerned about him. He needs help to break the chains that confine him.*

Happy with her decision, Toni reversed her car out of her parking spot and made for home.

CHAPTER 12

She'd grown to hate these types of places.

After meeting Slave on the scene six years ago, Chaos thought that was the last she'd ever have to come to such a joint. The travelling was bad enough – there wasn't a dominatrix underground in Porthcawl or Bridgend. The closest place was Cardiff, which meant she had to drive there. It was a pain in the arse, but if she was going to get her thrills while Slave was down, then she needed to go through it.

Chaos had arrived at the city centre at around six o'clock, after leaving Slave at five. She hated him being in the house alone. She preferred keeping an eye on him. But, knowing he had his cage in place, he couldn't get up to much.

He can't even masturbate, she thought, smiling.

When he'd come home a few weeks ago with it broken, doubts had set in. If he'd smashed it off once, then he could do it again.

No, he wouldn't dare – not after the beating he took, she thought, eyeing the bar full of men dying to be dominated by a powerful woman. Out of all the sex clubs in Cardiff, *Whips & Chains* was by far the best. It was clean, along with the punters. So far, Chaos hadn't bought a single drink. The slave-hungry men about her had plied her with all the alcohol she wanted. *Men, they're pathetic. Just like that little-dicked sissy Slave of mine*, she thought, viewing her prey from a darkened corner.

If I get home tonight and find he has tampered with his cage, I'm likely to kill him. But she didn't think she had anything to worry about. He hadn't attempted anything so far, even though he had started to recover. He was a horny fuck – damaged bones would never stop him.

I could castrate him? I bet he'd love that, she thought, giggling. *No, I do love that fat cock of his. It might be short, but it's fat – fat enough for me. When I want it, of course.* She toyed with the whip in her hand.

That was another plus for *Whips & Chains* – they had changing rooms at the back of their establishment, used by punters to change into something more…pleasing.

Once she'd arrived at the club, Chaos had changed into the all-in-one leather dress she now wore, with matching whip. Her plain clothes were locked inside a locker. It was perfect. Safe, too.

Not that she was ashamed of wearing such things. Had there been no such option available within the club, Chaos would have simply dressed in her attire. Hell, if she didn't find what she was looking for here, she would move on to another place. And, if that were to happen, she would remain in her dominatrix gear.

Fuck society, she thought, taking a sip of her cocktail.

She wasn't that fussed with cocktails – they tended to be too fruity and juicy. When at home, she liked slugging Brandy, but not out in the open. It got her hammered too fast, and that would never do. Beer and the like weren't for her. She hated the taste, so it had to be cocktails if she wanted a boozy buzz.

All those years ago, when she'd met Slave here, he'd been all over her. Her exposed, tight-clad legs had drawn him from the pack. "*I've always had a hard-on for legs in stockings or tights*," he'd told her. "*It drives me nuts. You have the perfect thighs. The most perfect I've seen in a long time,*" he'd drawled.

He'd hooked her with his boyish good looks and smooth-sounding voice. It was like silk. She had no doubt in her mind that Slave could have had any woman he'd wanted to. But he'd chosen her.

Had Slave been into dominating, he probably could have buckled her rather easily. It had been the first time a man had ever had her hypnotised by their voice and sight alone. Her pussy had gone instantly damp. That moment she had his cock locked up and he was ready and willing to be whipped by a dominating woman, Chaos thought she was going to orgasm on the spot.

Luckily, she had controlled it.

God, if only it had gone the other way, she thought, continuing to eye her prey. *He would have had me under his spell. Would have had me cuffed to his bed day in, day out. Would have only fed me his dick when he'd wanted.* The thoughts were making her moist. She'd need to find someone, and soon. It had been far too long since her pussy had taken a pounding.

The last few slaves she had taken home had only pleased her orally. She needed fucking. If Slave hadn't been laid up, she may have welcomed him. She was almost sorry she had punished him so brutally.

Once healed, she would be good to him for a while. Give him plenty of release and sexy chores to do around the house. He'd like that. *I'm sure he's not going to hold such a beating against me, even though he's been a little insubordinate of late. I have been rather harsh on him. Maybe it's time I changed my ways? After all, he's such a good boy.*

Out of the crowd came a man dressed in leather. She couldn't see his face – it was hidden beneath a gimp mask. He was tall. Giant-tall, compared to her miniscule stature. He must have been pushing six-foot-six, maybe more. He wasn't quite her type – he was too scrawny.

His coyness was almost too much for her. Pushing the bigger ones around was more fun than the average-sized slave. He was almost too shy to get within ten feet of her. There was no way she was going to coax him. *He's going to have to do it all by himself*, she thought, smiling at him.

Watching him take baby steps was hilarious. A turn-on, too. Her Slave was much bolder than this one. Brazenness would get this new one nowhere. She had that at home. *A new Slave would be nice after all*, she thought, watching this one's cumbersome movements. *Like a puppy learning to walk for the first time.* Getting rid of her current Slave would be no big deal. *I'll hurl him out. Tell him I'm fed up with him. I'll order him gone. He'll have to go. Every slave has a sell-by date. New blood will be nice. And look how angelic this one seems – I've not seen such a shy one in a long time.*

A bit of gentle encouragement won't be harmful, she decided, pushing off the wall she'd been leaning against. *After all, it's not like he'll get too big for his boots. If he does, a beat-down will ensue.*

She beckoned him forward with a gloved finger. The leather creaked. This was her favourite outfit. Chaos loved how it clung to her big arse, making it look that much curvier.

On her summon, the lanky slave moved closer. Then closer still. He was making a meal of it. If he over-played it, he would lose her interest. At current, he had her – her knickers were damp from his apprehension. But she didn't want him knowing that. Oh, no.

If he behaved, then she would let him fuck her pussy with his tongue, but *only* if he behaved and controlled himself.

"Come on," she purred. "Closer. This Mistress won't hurt you…" she lied.

This seemed to stop him in his tracks. Scared him? On the inside she was laughing. Laughing at how pathetic and helpless he looked. But then he started his shuffle towards her again. "Good boy," she said. *You're playing the game well, my friend.*

When he was standing directly in front of her, he towered over Chaos. "My, you are a big boy," she said. "I'll allow you to slide the zip across on your mask, Slave. You may speak to me." Slowly, he lifted one trembling hand to the zipper. When he opened it, it revealed pink, pouting lips. *Oh, my, this one likes to wear make-up.* "Do you like being a sissy bitch?"

He nodded.

"Answer me!" She showed him the whip. The lashes were studded.

"Yes," he said.

Even his voice sounded girly. God, he was more than pathetic. "You really are a wretched soul, aren't you, Slavette!"

"Yes," he quivered.

"Are you wearing panties?" she asked him. He lowered his head, giving her the answer. But that wasn't enough. "Well?" He kept his head bowed and muttered something inaudible. "I will not ask you again, Sissy!" she bellowed. This caused a few people to look over. She glared at those who looked in her direction. "Fuck off!" she barked. "This is between me and this pathetic piece of shit!" She gave the man in front of her a smack around the side of his head.

"*Oww*!" he howled. "Yes! I'm wearing panties. Pink ones! Please, Ma'am, don't hit me again."

"Then I suggest you answer when you're spoken to, boy. Don't just stand there like a sorry sack of shit, shouting like a two-year-old! Do you have any balls in that sack of yours?" She grabbed his privates.

He stood on tippy-toes, and sucked in a harsh breath. "Ma'am…*Please*…" he whined.

"I think you mean 'Mistress', if you plan on coming home with me, *Dog*," she said, applying more pressure to his bollocks.

"Yes, Mistress," he said. The way his lips were pulled back, exposing his teeth, made her laugh. His tongue flapped as it protruded from his mouth.

"Good, Dog. Now, go and get Mistress another drink. Show Mistress how good a doggy you can be," she said, releasing his nuts. As he bent over to clasp himself, Chaos gave his head a rub. "Good boy, good boy." She couldn't help but titter at his whimpers. What a gigantic softy. Handing him her glass, she told him what she wanted.

Like the little lapdog she would train him to be, he was off, limping through the crowd. "My, my, what delicious fun I'm going to have with him. I remember a time when Simone was that good. He's such a wicked boy these days. *Tut-tut*," she said.

He's taken his Mistress for granted. No, allowing him any pleasure is a no-no. Not now. No way. He's become too unruly. He can forget me being nice to him ever again. I will continue to try and break him. If not, then I will order him to go, she thought, watching her over-sized Dog limp back through the crowd. He had two drinks – she assumed the other was for him.

"There you go, *Mistress*."

Bless him. He's already seeking my approval. This is too easy. He's going to be a splendid doggy. He has so much respect. She took her drink off him and placed it down by her side. Turning sharply, she smacked his drink out of his hand. He watched as it flew through the air, turning end-over-end, spilling its golden content as it went.

"Did I tell you to get *yourself* a drink?!" she snapped. He shook his hand from where it had been slapped. He'd also drawn in a sharp breath on her harsh contact. "*Well*? Did I?!"

"No…" he said, distracted.

She backhanded him across the face. "No, *what*?!"

"*Mistress*. No, *Mistress*!"

"I'm disappointed in you, Dog. I was hoping you had the makings of a good doggy, but I think I may have been wrong."

"*Please*, Mistress. I can prove myself," he said, getting down to his knees. He placed his hands to her feet as he grovelled. "Please, please!" he begged.

Lovely, she thought, smiling. A fuzzy feeling burned in the pit of her guts. He did play the game well. He could have taught Simone a few things. *Oh well, that pathetic worm will be taken care of. We'll see how funny it is to be disobedient then, won't we?* she thought.

"You can get up, Dog. I'll give you another chance," she told him. "From now on, you'll respond solely to 'Dog' or 'Slave.' They are your new names."

Slowly, he got to his feet. His frame towered over her.

The slightest touch and Chaos knew she would come – would orgasm two or three times. She wanted his tongue. She *needed* it inside her. She wasn't even sure she could make it back to the house.

"Do you have a car, Dog?"

"No, Mistress."

"Fine. Okay. Right, once I finish my drink, I want you to walk me back to my car. I will give you a lift back to your new home," she said. "We can work everything else out once we get there. Understand?"

"Yes, Mistress."

"Good boy," she said. "You catch on fast. Not like the Slave I have at home currently."

His eyes said it all. Disappointment.

"Don't worry about him. He'll be gone tomorrow. You may have some fun with him first, if you'd like, Dog?"

"That would be very nice of you, Mistress."

"Good." Taking her drink, she downed it in one. Looking at her watch, she saw it was just past midnight. This would be the earliest she'd gone home in some time. Slave would probably be sleeping when she got back. *Well, he's in for a rude awakening,* she thought.

"Don't worry about changing into your normal clothes, Dog. I'm only parked around the corner." Putting her empty glass down, Chaos led her new Slave to the backrooms. Once there, she cleared her locker out. She then waited for him to do the same. When he was ready, she led him outside.

The streets of Cardiff were dead. Most of the younger party-goers would be in nightclubs at this hour. They did pass a few drunken dickheads who made a few comments, but nothing she couldn't deal with.

When they arrived at the car park, Chaos led them to the third floor, where her vehicle was parked in a corner space. Before she unlocked the doors, she ordered Dog to unzip her jumpsuit.

She felt his hands at the zipper, which was located between her shoulder blades. It made an awful scratchy sound as it was drawn down slowly. Removing his hands, the suit slid from her body and gathered at her feet. Turning, she unlocked the doors and sat in the driver's seat and parted her legs.

"Don't stop until your mouth goes numb, Dog!" she said, watching as he slowly got to his knees.

After spending a half-an-hour in the car park, Chaos had ordered her new playmate to stop, as she couldn't take any more of his attention. With a flushed face, she dressed and bundled herself behind the steering wheel.

Her Slave sat in the passenger seat.

"Such a good doggy!" she told him as she drove for home. "You're certainly a good catch, aren't you?"

"Thank you, Mistress."

"No slave has ever made me come quite so hard. Or as much. My, my, I am impressed," she said.

"Thank you, Mistress," he repeated.

"Good boy." Chaos then fell silent. She couldn't stop thinking about Simone and how she was going to go about getting rid of him. It excited her. She couldn't wait to see how crushed he'd look. *Then again, I could go to the police? I'll tell them that I'm a victim of abuse? I could get Slave to beat me? Give me bruises?* A titter escaped her. Dog said nothing.

At first light, I'll go straight to the police station, she thought, parking her car outside her house. When she killed the engine, she noticed the lights appeared to be off inside. She'd been right – her ex-Slave was in bed. Sleeping. *If I do go to the police, then they will see his marks… Hmmm, maybe that's not the best of ideas. I think asking him to get out is the best way after all.*

This is going to be very interesting, she thought. Even though she'd taken men home before, this was going to be different. She would tell him it was over; that the new Dog had overthrown him. But he could spend the night and be played with, if he wanted.

Laughing again, she led the way. She unlocked the front door, with Dog on her heels. Entering the house, Chaos knew something was off-kilter straightaway. The kitchen light was on. So too was the living room's. Turning to her new friend, Chaos put a finger to her lips, indicating for him to be quiet.

She crept towards the lounge door and popped her head around it. Slave was nowhere to be seen. Edging into the room, Chaos headed towards the kitchen. It was also empty.

"What the hell?" she muttered. He knew better than to leave lights on.

Turning, she saw the hulking mass of Dog. She shooed him out with her hands. "He must be upstairs," she whispered. "Be very quiet. I don't want to wake him yet!"

His lips turned into a smile.

She liked this – he was enjoying the game as much as she was.

Going to the stairs, Chaos started to climb, but a noise from below her caused her to stop. It sounded like a muffled scream. Was someone crying? She couldn't tell.

Stepping off the step, she pushed by Dog and walked to the door that led to the cellar. She placed her ear to the cool wood. The barely audible sounds were coming from down there. *Don't tell me he's down there playing with his fucking toys. I've told him about that. God, he's in for such a whooping…*Her thoughts came apart when she heard a scream. It was a woman's, which sounded suffocated, as though she was choking on her tears and snot.

What the…?

Then there was silence.

Footfalls could be heard coming up the steps.

Snapping her fingers, she ordered Dog to her side.

"Stand in front of me," she whispered, hearing the footsteps coming closer.

What's he been doing down there? she wondered, stepping from her new toy.

"When he comes out of there, Dog, smack him!" she whispered. He whimpered, but nodded. "You make sure you level him. Mistress will have a nice treat for you if you do."

She watched as her massive gimp readied himself: His fists were balled and he was breathing hard. He psyched himself up for combat, and stepped back from the door, making it so he could get a punch in.

The sound of footsteps stopped.

At the bottom of the door, a shadow could be seen. Her Slave was right there.

A creaking sound pierced the silence as the handle to the cellar door was pushed down. *Why is he taking his time? Had he heard us?* Chaos wondered.

Dog didn't wait. He grabbed the handle, plunged it down fully, and ripped the door open.

He gasped, along with Chaos. Her Slave was standing on the other side, naked. He was drenched in blood. It gelled his hair. Flecks could be seen on his teeth and framed his piercing eyes.

"Simone…" she whispered.

"Hello, dear. I wasn't expecting you home so early?!" he said.

"Hit him!" she screamed.

Dog was too cumbersome. Simone punched the scalpel he'd been holding into the throat of the giant man. Blood jetted from a torn vein. Before Simone could retract the surgeon's tool, the gimp collapsed forward, forcing Simone to jump out of the way.

Chaos watched in shock as the man crumpled to his knees. His huge hands were clamped to his spurting neck as he tried to stem the gush. He choked and gargled on his blood as he hit the wall behind Simone. After head-butting it, he fell sideways, taking a thundering crash down the cellar steps.

"Simone, what have you done?" Chaos said.

"I think our fun and games are over," he said, closing in on her. Grabbing Chaos by the hair, he yanked her down into the cellar as hard as he could. She yelped and screamed to be released – that the pain tearing through her scalp was too much.

When they got to the lower level, Dog was seen doing a nifty jig in a lake of blood gathered at his back. Simone and Chaos watched, until the man was lifeless.

"Oh, I was enjoying that!" Simone said.

Chaos screamed until she thought her lungs would burst.

CHAPTER 13

Stephanie, he thought. That's what she'd said her name was. He watched her while she drank the tea he had made her. His was on the table in front of him. "I find it most strange that you come knocking so late," he said. "Strange, yet very endearing. I have to admit, I'm rather envious."

She smiled. *How innocent and child-like she looks*, he thought.

"Why envious?" she asked.

"You clearly have a passion for what you do. You have something you like to spend time doing. You try helping others. I wish I had such a thing," he lied.

"Well, you can convert. Come to our rallies and meetings?"

"I would love that!" *Not a fucking chance*, he thought. *I'd rather eat a handful of rusted nails.*

Again, she smiled. "Would you like me to tell you a little bit about what we do and believe in?" she asked. "That's why you invited me in, right?"

"Of course!" he said, trying to sound as convincing as he could. When she set off on a rant, he couldn't help but focus on her legs. Her skirt had risen slightly, revealing outstanding thighs. He wasn't that keen on the blue tights, but he could work with them.

She's clearly unaware of what I'm up to, he thought, rubbing his chin and nodding every so often. The pretence was working. *How can I get her into the cellar? I don't want to startle her. I wonder if Chaos has any Chloroform left? She usually keeps it upstairs in her bedside drawer. I should know – the fucking cunt has used it on me enough. I could empty a few drops onto a rag…She won't know what's hit her.* He tried his best to keep a smile off his face. Butterflies fluttered in his guts. *I'm turning into a monster. Yeah, but it's great fucking fun. I'm finally living the dream – we always knew it would get to this stage. We?* he thought. *Who's 'we'?*

"*Me, sir!*" Mr. Tickles' voice boomed in his head.

Of course, how could I forget you.

"*All the training has led to this point in your life, sir,*" the clown said. "*You always pick the ones with the best legs!*"

"Is everything okay?" Stephanie asked.

"Hmm?" Simone asked, looking up.

"You seem a bit…distracted," she said, finally realising her skirt had ridden up her legs. Red-faced, she pulled it down.

"Oh, I was just taking it all in," he lied. "My mother was a Witness for many years. She tried her best to convert me, but never could. I'm sorry now, what with all the years I've missed out on."

"You shouldn't feel like that. Our Lord forgives all his children. He has a special place in his heart for those who seek forgiveness."

He smiled. *What a crock of shit,* he thought. "Thanks – I find that very reassuring. Please, continue," he told her.

"Well, with the rallies and meetings…"

He tuned back out.

How much longer was he going to let her prattle on before taking her down*? I need to excuse myself and get upstairs. Get the good stuff,* he thought. "I'm sorry," he interrupted her. "Would you mind giving me a few minutes? I have to dash to the toilet."

"Oh… Em." She looked at her watch. "I really should be going…"

"I won't be long, promise. I'd like to discuss with you some more."

She gave him a thin smile. "Erm, okay – but I really don't have much more time. I didn't realise it was so late…"

I'm sure you fucking didn't, bitch, he thought, all the while smiling at her. "I won't be long, promise," he said, leaving the room.

"Okay." Stephanie flashed him another weak smile.

He moved up the stairs as fast as his injured ribs allowed. He pushed the pain to the back of his mind. Simone wasn't going to let it get in his way. At the second floor, he first went to grab Mr. Tickles and the G.I.'s. Pocketing the commandos, Simone put the clown under his arm and then hobbled to his Mistress' bedroom. Once there, he went to her bedside drawer. Opening it, he found what he was looking for. Picking it up, he noticed the bottle was a little under half-full. "That will do," he uttered.

When he turned around, he noticed handcuffs in her arsenal. He grabbed them, too. He put them in his pocket, along with the Chloroform.

"Is that everything?" he asked himself. Nodding, he hobbled back to the stairs. He could hear Stephanie moving around.

His heart quickened.

"That's better," he said, making his way back downstairs. "I'm sorry about that – it came over me all of a sudden." As he approached the last step, he placed Mr. Tickles down.

"It's okay," she called to him.

As he entered the room, he saw her by the mantelpiece, her back to him. She was looking at the photos there. Looking over her shoulder, she asked, "Who's the woman in this photo?"

"That's my partner, Cha…Rebecca," he lied, making up a name for Chaos.

"She's very pretty. You're a lucky man, Simone. Right, I best be on my way," she said. "Thanks for the tea. I very much appreciate it," she said, moving past him.

"Won't you stay a little longer?" he asked. "I've found the conversation rather refreshing. It gets a bit lonely here on my own of an evening."

"Oh? Where's your partner?"

"She's gone visiting family. Won't be back until late next week." He found telling lies easy – making up stories was fun.

"Well, I really should get going. I wanted to go to other houses, but it doesn't look like I'll be able to now…Five more minutes?" she said.

"That would be great. Can I offer you another drink?"

"No, thanks," she said, sitting down again.

"Okay," he said, smiling. "I'll just take these out to the kitchen," he said, picking up the used cups.

"Would you like a hand?"

"Yes, please."

Stephanie lifted her cup up and followed Simone into the kitchen. Once there, he put both cups and saucers into the sink. When she turned away, he grabbed a tea towel.

"Please, go and sit down. I'll be there shortly."

"Okay," she said, going back to her seat.

When she was out of view, Simone folded the towel down to a manageable size and then laced it with the liquid from the bottle, which he then left by the side of the sink. Hobbling to her with the rag by his side, Simone jumped on Stephanie. His weight overpowered her, but it didn't stop her from wriggling.

Before she could scream, he clamped the rag over her mouth.

She continued to buck, but it was useless. Within seconds, she was out cold.

Simone cursed the air blue as he got off her – she'd managed to catch him in the ribs with a couple of stray blows. "Bitch!" he yelled in her face.

His eyes latched on to her skirt. It had been pushed all the way up to her waist in the struggle, revealing her thighs in their entirety. Kneeling, he put his hands to them. His dick went instantly hard.

Simone could feel his sperm rush. The need for release was great, once again. With his cock straining against the cage, he could feel the bars digging into his flesh. Undoing the buttons of his pyjama bottoms, Simone tried to pull his caged manhood out.

He wanted to touch it; to stroke it, but couldn't – the restraint was too tight. "Fucking bitch, Chaos," he said, pulling at the device.

Going out to the kitchen, Simone grabbed the meat hammer. Taking it back into the living room, he started laying into the padlock. It didn't take much for the hard metal head to break the padlock, which cracked open after the fifth hard wallop. Grabbing it, he pulled it off and threw it to one side.

Simone began stroking his cock to its maximum stiffness.
Once fully hard, he left his manhood alone and picked up the hammer. He smashed away at the cage until it was a twisted, useless wreck. Later, he would do the same to the ones upstairs.

No longer would Chaos keep him under her control.

It was over.

Content the cage was crippled beyond use, Simone got close to the unconscious girl and started stroking his cock as fast as he could. His attempt to come was furious. His passion collided with his rage. "You fucking whore!" he screamed at the girl who couldn't hear a thing. "I'm going to fuck you up!" he continued, feeling his orgasm nearing.

He continuously looked at her legs, spying her white panties beneath the skin-tight tights. "Fucking blue – they should be black. *Black*!" he continued to yell, taking his hand off himself so he could punch her in the face twice, before going back to masturbating.

Blood trickled out of her nose.

"Come on, come on!" he urged himself. "The last fucking thing I want is Chaos walking in on me."

Stephanie started to stir.

Shit! he thought, unable to stop himself as he moved closer to climaxing. *The punching must have roused her.* He watched her face twist this way and that. *She's in agony. Fuck, I couldn't have used enough Chloroform.*

He didn't stop. *Couldn't.* Tears of frustration welled at the corners of his eyes. Simone tried his best to focus on her thick thighs. "Please, come. Come!" *I should have fucking tied her up. I should have*, his mind screamed.

Then she started crying with her eyes closed. Slowly, her hands rose to her nose. "*Ow!*" she blubbered. "*Ugh…*" she groaned. Her eyes fluttered. "Where…what…what happened…" she said, breathlessly. Her eyes continued to flutter.

Simone carried on.

His breathing came in ragged rips as he gasped for air. Panted like a dog.

"Blood?!" she gasped, trying her best to open her laden eyes. "What happened? *Blood?!*" she repeated. "*Blood!*"

Startled, she appeared to force her eyes open.

Simone gasped, reaching his climax. A thin stream of come spurted from him and splashed her legs.

Stephanie screamed as she tried to get up, but her legs buckled. In that frantic moment, Simone lost control of his body. His legs turned to jelly and he crashed to the floor. He could only watch, breathlessly, as Stephanie made a crawl for the lounge door.

"No, come back!" Simone screeched, kicking off his trousers, which were gathered at his ankles.

"Leave me alone!" she screamed. "Help! *Help*! Someone, please help me."

"Be quiet!" he insisted, getting to his knees. He frantically looked about. *Where is it? Where is it?*! he thought. *There*, his mind screamed, his eyes falling on the hammer.

Stephanie had almost made it out the living room door. Soon she would be at the front door. "*No!*" he called, watching her get to her knees in a cumbersome way. *The drug has not fully worn off*, he thought, seeing her crash against the doorframe.

He dove for her, but came up short, landing on the lower half of her legs.

A snap ensued, causing her to scream. "Please, let me go! I won't tell…I *promise!*"

Simone desperately climbed up the backs of her legs. He grunted as he did so. The effort was great, because she tried to wriggle free – he could feel his dick rubbing at her tights. He left a snail-like trail of sperm as he went. "Stop moving!" he screamed.

"*Noooo*!" she begged.

He straddled her back. Without hesitation, he raised the hammer as high as he could, bringing it down hard and fast. It made a harsh sound as it tore through the air. The spiked side of the hammer connected with her back – it hammered the air out of her. She gagged on a scream. The area between her shoulder blades instantly blossomed with a bright purple colour.

This didn't stop Simone. He clubbed her head. Once, twice, three times…He stopped after he heard a sickening *crack*. Blood pooled about her smashed cranium.

A hiss of air escaped her parted lips.

Her eyes didn't move.

Gasping, Simone rolled off her. "*Whoooo*!" he screamed as an immense thrill tore through him. "*Whoooooooooooo*! What a fucking *rush*!" he bellowed, repeatedly smashing his balled fists against the floor.

The smell of blood mingled with semen got him hard once again. Simone got to his feet and looked down at the battered body of Stephanie. In the struggle, he'd laddered her tights. "*Fuck*!" he yelled, slamming his fist against the lounge door. "Never mind, I'm sure they're fine on the front."

He grabbed and dragged her out of the room. He headed towards the cellar door, which was situated under the stairs. He opened it. A flight of steps led to the dark depths below.

"*Nice kill, sir*," the clown said from the hallway.

"Thanks," Simone grunted, hoisting the dead girl off the floor and onto his shoulder. "You want to come down?"

"*Yes, please.*"

"I'll come back and get you," Simone gasped, and then headed into the cellar. When he got to the bottom, he put his hand out for the light switch which was on the wall to his side. When it burst to light, the room was drenched in a red glow. This was Chaos' 'Playroom'.

He threw the carcass down onto a padded table. It boasted stirrups, along with leather wrist straps and a ball gag. *They won't be needed*, he thought, looking at the woman. *She's beautiful.* He traced a finger down her face. *In another world, I could have seen myself with such a woman – a shy, nervous type. Someone I could relate to. Why aren't I normal?* Sometimes, at night, he wished for normality – to love like a normal man.

However, Simone loved his perverted ways too much. His dark, undiluted personality – it was all he knew. All he truly wanted to be. And now he'd killed, he felt free for the first time.

He pulled his eyes off her face and jogged upstairs. In the hallway again, he grabbed Mr. Tickles and took him down to the basement.

"*She looks good in the red light,*" the clown said.

"You don't think it's a bit too much?"

The clown shook his head. The bells on his hat rattled.

Simone smiled. After all these years, Mr. Tickles' costume and paint still looked pretty damn good. He'd been meaning to do a bit of maintenance work on him.

"*Where are the others?*" Mr. Tickles asked.

"Oo, I'd forgotten about that pair," Simone confessed, running back upstairs to get them. "They were in my trousers pocket," he told the clown when he returned and placed the action figures next to Mr. Tickles. "It's nice being around the gang again," Simone said to nobody in particular.

His soldiers grunted in response.

Going to Stephanie, Simone started peeling her tights down her legs. His semen had dried into the material, but he could still smell it when he pressed them to his nose. On sniffing the crotch, he could smell a hint of her juices. *Something had fired her engine*, he thought, putting the garments to one side.

With the tights out of sight, he was able to remove her slightly damp knickers. He sniffed them, too.

"*Pissy?*" the clown asked.

"No, but there's a whiff of womanly excitement in them, just like there was in the tights," he said.

"*Nice,*" one of the G.I.'s said.

"Very," Simone agreed, undoing the button and zipper on her skirt. He pulled that off, too. With her privates exposed, Simone became aroused. *Would it be going too far if I penetrated her?* he thought.

"*Not a chance,*" the clown answered. "*We've come this far, sir. We may as well see the job through to the end.*"

"True," he said. Close at hand was his toolbox. Inside, he found his Stanley blade. Going to her throat, Simone ran the knife across it – a couple of squirts of blood splashed his face and chest. "I just want to make sure she's dead," he told the others.

"*Very wise,*" Rape Charge said.

"*No harm in taking precautions,*" Spiked Mace chirped in.

Once she was completely drained of blood, Simone got on top of her, and that's when he heard the movement above him. His penis shrivelled. He listened with pricked ears. Whoever it was, they were trying to make as little noise as possible.

"It can only be that bitch Chaos!" he uttered.

"*Shh, boss – she may hear you!*" Mr. Tickles said.

"I don't care. Let's give her something to think about," he said, letting out a pitiful whimper, followed by a faint scream. Going to his toolbox, he picked out the scalpel. "Time to take the fucking pig down!" he told his troops.

He moved to the cellar steps and started to climb them slowly. Surprise would be everything…

CHAPTER 14

By the time she got home, Suzanne was already in bed. Toni had thought the girl would still be up, as she often burnt the midnight oil. *Never mind, I'm sure I'll get a grilling off her tomorrow morning*, she thought. Suzanne was bound to want to know the ins and outs of where she had been this evening. *She probably guessed I was out with Stu,* Toni thought, smiling.

When she'd finally made it home, she'd taken a long, hot lingering bath. She'd thought about Stu, and Simone. There had been a text awaiting her response from Stu when she'd checked her mobile, but she hadn't responded immediately. Toni had let him sweat until she'd run her bath and poured herself a glass of wine. Just before popping into the tub, she'd replied to his message. She'd then put her phone on charge.

Now, as she lay on her bed, Toni wondered how to respond to the text that had come through to her whilst she'd been in the bath. '*I really like you, and I'd like to make US official, xx*' it read.

Toni had re-read it a dozen times, thinking what to reply with. Looking at the time, she thought it may have been a bit too late to message him back, as it was past two.

No, I'm sure he's awake, awaiting a response. God, what's wrong with me? This is a simple situation. He likes me, I like him. I should be telling him that I want him. But it wasn't that easy. She needed more time. *Just a week or so – by then, I'll know all of Simone's backstory. But what if someone else intriguing comes along? No, that won't happen. I just need to get this one out of my system. He's the only person to have got to me*, she thought. *That doesn't help me with this text though, does it?* Looking at his words, she decided to write back. '*I very much like you, too, but I'm not quite ready to commit yet. I want to take it slowly. Make sure it's right, you know? Xx*'

Without giving it another thought, she sent it. *I'm a bitch,* she thought. *What a shitty thing to have said to him. I'm sure he'll be cool with it.* After waiting a full twenty minutes for a response, Toni began to think he was hating her right now. Who would blame him?

Her mind liked playing paranoia games with her, especially late at night.

After thirty minutes of waiting, she turned her lamp off. She'd given up. *Facing him at work tomorrow will be awkward*, she thought. Then her phone buzzed. Picking it up, she opened the message.

It was from Dominos. They were offering her great discount on pizzas. "*Ugh*!" she groaned, snapping her phone shut. "He may have fallen asleep," she tried to convince herself. "Or he could be thinking of a response?" *Fat chance.*

Not bothering to put the light back on, Toni settled down. *It's not my fault if he can't be bothered to play the waiting game. What if I really did want to take things slowly? This is not the type of reaction I would have liked.*

Her phone jangled again.

Hesitantly, Toni rolled over and grabbed her mobile off her night table. She kept the light out. *Probably Dominos again*, she thought, opening her phone. But it wasn't – the message was from Stu. *'I completely understand – it was foolish of me to say such a thing so early. Sorry for the late reply – my phone died!!! I didn't want you thinking I was pouting. ☺ xx'.*

Seeing his words made her smile. Whether the bit about his phone dying was true or not, she didn't care – his text seemed chirpy enough. She decided to text back, knowing there was nothing to get up for in the morning. She didn't need to be all bright-eyed and bushy-tailed.

'I'm so glad you feel like that – I really do like you, Stu. I want things to be perfect. I don't want it going wrong, and that's what I'm worried will happen if we push things, okay? In other news – fancy going to the cinema tomorrow night after work? Xx'

He replied with a simple 'Yes', along with another smiley face and a couple of kisses. This prompted her to respond with 'Goodnight', followed with kisses. Closing her phone, she settled down and drifted off to sleep.

At seven o'clock her alarm started screaming at her. Having forgotten to turn it off last night, Toni rolled over and killed the buzzer. "*Ugh*!" she huffed. "Stupid alarm!" That was it. Once she was disturbed from sleep, she couldn't go back.

She rolled onto her back and stared up at the ceiling. *How many hours did I manage – three? Four? Not sure, but I need coffee. I might as well try and get a bit of reading done before work,* she thought. "*Ugh*!" she groaned again, throwing the bed covers to one side. "Why me?" she grumbled, slipping her feet into her Garfield sleepers. "I bet Suzanne is out for count!"

Opening her bedroom door, Toni went across to the bathroom – facing the mirror, she pulled a scary face. "*Rawr*!" she growled at her reflection, laughing. Turning, she locked the door and started the shower. After lingering under the hot spray for fifteen minutes, Toni washed and got out.

Before leaving the misty room, she brushed her teeth and hair, and then went back to her room to dress. Once presentable, Toni headed for the kitchen.

On the landing, she stopped, listened and adjusted to the sounds within the house. Suzanne could be heard moving around.

Going to her door, she tapped on it lightly. "Are you decent?" Toni asked.

"Aye, come on in!" Suzanne called.

"Morning," Toni said, poking her head around the door. "Did I disturb you?"

"I heard the shower going but I was already awake." She stretched, followed by yawning. "You're traipsing the boards fairly early, toots?!"

"Stupid alarm woke me up." Toni laughed.

"Something amusing?"

"Your hair – it's wild!"

"Like, jungle wild?"

"Like, wild, *wild*! Looks like you've jammed your fingers into a plug socket."

"Cheers for that!" Suzanne said, winking. "Are you sticking the pot on?"

"Of course. Fancy some bacon and eggs?"

"Oo, yes! And I want all the goss on your disappearance last night, young lady!" She gave Toni a wink.

"Anything you say, El Capitano!" Toni said, closing the door. Shaking her head and smiling, Toni trotted downstairs. Considering the time she was up, and with what she had said to Stu via text last night, she felt pretty good. Excited, even. She couldn't put her finger on it, but felt upbeat. Getting to the kitchen, she put the kettle to boil after lighting the stove. As she rustled up the pans, bacon and eggs, Toni whistled as she worked.

While the food sizzled, she threw teabags into two mugs and filled them with hot water, letting them stew. She then began plating the food. She also cut fresh bread and poured orange juice into two long glasses.

"Come and get it!" Toni called.

"I'm coming!"

"Are you sure it's not just the way you're standing?"

"Oh, ha-ha!" Suzanne boomed. "Aren't we the stand-up this morning?!" she said, entering the kitchen. Toni placed her friend's food and drinks on the table in front of her. "Looks good, toots!"

When Toni placed her food down, she was greeted by Suzanne stuffing a load of grub into her mouth. "It's like feeding time at the zoo!" she commented.

"Now that you mention it, you do remind me of an orangutan. Hairier, though!"

"Cheek!" Toni said, whipping Suzanne on the arm with the tea towel.

"Hey, watch – you almost knocked my bacon and egg sandwich out of my hand."

"That's okay. I'm sure your arse could do with a calorie break!" Toni giggled.

"The boys love the jiggle!" Suzanne said, stuffing more of her sandwich into her mouth. Brown sauce dripped out the sides of her mouth. A dollop splashed her pyjama top, which depicted a sunny field with bunnies hopping around.

She's a right girlie-girl, Toni thought. "Feeding your boobies, too?" she asked.

"*Hmm*?" Suzanne looked down at her top. "Damn," she said, spitting crumbs free of her overloaded mouth.

"Classy!" Toni said, cutting her food with a knife and fork. Stopping, she took a few gulps of her cooling tea. "What are your plans today?"

After swallowing, Suzanne spoke. "Not sure yet – I was thinking of doing a bit more studying. The day looks like it might be nice, so I'm going to play it by ear. You?"

"Hmm, I'm not sure. I have work later, so there's not much I can do."

"I see. So, tell me about last night – where did you get to? I was expecting you home early." Toni told Suzanne about her 'date' with Stu and what had been said via text after it. "You should ring his bell, toots. Live life. Have fun!"

"I don't want to come across slutty," Toni said.

"*Pfft*, please – dropping your knickers for one guy you like isn't going to turn you into a whore!"

"I know. It's just…"

"Just what? Come on, go and have fun."

Toni wanted to tell her about Simone, but she didn't know how to approach that subject. She certainly couldn't tell her he was someone she speaks to on the phone. That he was someone who was screwed in the head. No, saying that about him was unfair. "There might be someone else…" she said, wincing.

Suzanne looked up and stopped chewing. Before she spoke, she made sure her mouth was empty. "You dirty little dog! You sure kept that quiet, toots."

"I know. I feel bad for Stu, though."

"Guys do it *all* the time."

"Maybe. But Stu is different, you know? He's sweet. He doesn't deserve me messing him about."

"Look, you've told him you want to take it slow. You've not committed to anything, so you're not messing anyone around."

"That makes sense, I suppose."

"So?"

"So what?" Toni asked.

"*Tut*," Suzanne said, rolling her eyes. "Who is he?!"

"Oh, nobody you'd know…" she said, trying to stall the conversation. *What am I going to say?* she thought.

"Okay. Well, if he was in Uni, I'm guessing I would have seen you with him, right?"

"I actually work with him," she blurted.

"Another one you work with? Bloody hell, you are one lucky girl! Especially if he's as fit as Stu!" she said.

Toni made an O shape with her mouth, and then laughed. "*Shh*, you!"

"Well, you snooze you lose," Suzanne said.

"Ha! How old are you again? Anyway, Stu is smitten."

"Well, whatever you decide to do, let me know," she said, getting up to put her plate in the sink. "I'll take my tea up with me. I'm going to do a bit of reading."

"Okay."

"Give me a shout before you head off to work."

"Will do," Toni said, watching Suzanne leave the kitchen. "Your pound knickers have fifty pence worth stuck up your arse," she called after her friend.

"Thanks for the heads up," Suzanne called back. This was followed by the sound of snapping. "No wonder I was feeling a bit uncomfy! Thanks for breakfast, toots."

Toni laughed as she placed the last bit of her food into her mouth. She flushed it down with her juice. Like Suzanne, she took her tea to her bedroom. When she got there, she decided to hit the books, as she had over eight hours before having to head to work

When the clock clicked over to five-twenty, Toni decided it was time to make a move. Rushing was horrible; she hated it. Her mother would always tell her to leave in plenty of time for an engagement; that she shouldn't be driving around in a hurry. By the time she got into her car, it was a little after half-past six.

Starting the engine, Toni checked her blind spot before moving off. After a short journey, she was at the NCP. She prayed for a parking spot close to the bottom level, but had to settle for one on the sixth floor.

Having no trouble inside the parking garage today, Toni was able to walk into work happy, and not agitated. Going straight to her desk, she waved at Stu, who was on the phone. Unzipping her bag, she took her mug out before heading off to her locker.

Mike didn't appear to be in today. It wasn't like him. *He's normally here every evening. Oh well*, she thought with a shrug. Once she'd stuffed her belongings into her tiny locker and locked it, Toni went to the kitchen to make a cup of tea before heading back to her desk.

Stu was still on the phone. He appeared to be in deep concentration. Sitting down, Toni set her tea to one side. She then started setting her phone up by plugging her headphones in. At a few minutes-to, she entered the system. She liked to show she was eager.

Thirty seconds before her shift was due to officially start, her phone rang.

It was Simone.

He sounded in agony.

CHAPTER 15

Throwing Chaos up against the table Stephanie lay on, he barked at her, "Push her off!"

Chaos, who had tears streaming down her face, blubbered, "Please, Simone…If this is about the beatings…I'm sorry…I went too far at times…"

"Roll her *fucking* off!" he bellowed. "*Now*!" His voice box hurt from the vicious yelling. "I won't tell you again, you fucking whore – get that dead bitch off there!" he demanded.

"Okay, okay!" she said, holding her hands up. Turning, Chaos grizzled as she put her weight against the dead girl and pushed. She huffed with the effort – the youngster was heavier than she appeared.

"Put some fucking oomph into it!" Simone said.

Chaos turned on him. She had that fire in her eyes. "Stop fucking shouting at me, you pathetic cunt! I'm not going to protect you over this, you sack of shit."

"*Cut the fucking slut's throat!*" Mr. Tickles chirped in.

Simone smiled.

"This is no laughing matter, Simone. You've killed people! They'll never release you. But I can protect you. I can guard my Slave," she said, putting her arms out to show him that she wanted to hold him. "We can stop this right now, Simone. Start fresh. I can see now I've pushed you too far." He stepped into her arms. She closed them around him. "There," she said, soothingly.

Backing out of her arms, he put the tip of the scalpel to her chin. "Thanks for the pep talk. Now, get that fucking body off the table, you stupid bitch!"

"*Fucking right*," Mr Tickles said. "*Cut her eyes out. Cut her tits off!*"

"Not a bad idea, Mr. Tickles," Simone said.

"Simone, the clown isn't real!" she screamed in his face. "It's all in your head!"

"I told you to get that body off the table. Now, do it! Or I'll cut your throat," he said.

Huffing, Chaos turned around and began shoving at Stephanie again. Simone couldn't help but admire his ex-Mistress' arse – the way in which it protruded. The tight leather made it look amazing. He put his hand out to grab it, but she batted it away.

"No! You never get to touch it ever again," she said, turning on him.

He slapped her across the chops the hardest he could. She yelped, her head flying to one side. "You don't get to tell me anymore, *bitch*. Now, move that fucking body or the next one will be much worse!"

"Okay!" she yelled. Fresh tears trickled down her face and she stamped her foot. Simone had to stop himself from laughing. This was the first time he'd ever had her against the ropes, and he wasn't about to lose his advantage. "She's too heavy," Chaos said, grunting.

"Better put your back into it, then!"

Chaos continued to push with all her might, and Stephanie's body started to move. Once it was on its side, gravity took over. The carcass hit the deck with a wet slap. "*Ugh*!" Chaos said, turning from it.

"Good. Now get up on that table and lie down. I want your legs in the stirrups, too."

"Not a chance," she said, whirling around to face him. He nicked her across her left cheek with the razor-sharp surgeon tool. "*Ow*, you bastard!" she raged, raising her hand to strike him across his face. But he was too quick, and slashed her other cheek. "*Argh*!" she cried, backing off.

"Don't make me spoil your good looks, Charlotte," Simone said.

"How…"

"Did I know your real name?"

She nodded, holding both cheeks. "I've never told you my real name."

"Ha-ha," he chirped.

"I have nothing laying around with my name on it – you weren't allowed near the letters when they arrived. You…"

He wiggled the scalpel at her. "No, I wasn't, was I? You kept me in my kennel all the time. You *thought* I was a good Slave. I was – until you started beating me black and blue all the time and then started leaving at nights to go prowling." She lowered her gaze. "While you were out having fun, I was nursing wounds – awaiting you to come back to fuck a stranger."

"I'm sorry…" she mumbled.

"Don't be – because while you've been out the last few times, I've been rummaging around in your things. Finding shit out about you. Now, get on that fucking table, cunt!" he roared, getting in her face.

She backed away. "Don't…" she said, hopping up on the table. Without hesitation, she lay down.

"How does it feel to be powerless?" He put the scalpel to her throat. "I could end you…" His words were cut short when her hand darted up and clutched his balls. She squeezed.

He let out a high-pitched screech as she tried crushing them. "*Huh*!" he gasped, her hand closing around his bollocks tighter. Out of sheer agony, the scalpel fell from his grip. It made a rattling sound as it hit the floor.

"I should rip 'em off!" she growled, sitting up. "You didn't honestly think your pathetic scare tactics were working, did you?!"

"*Ugh*, let me go! I…I…was only play…playing…you…*Argh*!" he wheezed.

"Maybe I'll just cut them off? Your maggot, too!" she said, getting off the table and picking up the blade Simone had dropped.

"*Huh*!" he panted, seeing the shiny implement in her clutches. "No…"

"Not so fucking funny now, is it?!" she said, baring her gritted teeth.

In his mind, Simone felt his nuts turn to slush. He'd read plenty of stories online about Mistresses emasculating their men and slaves in such ways. About how they would crush their balls with their bare hands or use other such implements. Some would employ suppressing drugs – kill off their man's horniness. Make their dick permanently limp.

If she did manage to turn his balls to sludge, that would be the end to his dirty, naughty fun and games. He'd never be able to satisfy himself again – he'd be trapped in a perverse hell.

He felt her fingers dig in harder, making vomit rush up his throat. There was nothing he could do to stop it – Simone spewed down his chest. His body started to convulse. His knees weakened.

Another wave of sickness came over him as more vomit poured out of him. A smelly pool gathered at his feet. His eyes rolled. The pain that coursed through him was like nothing he'd ever felt. She'd punished his balls with pegs and spiked rollers before, but nothing this extreme.

"*Peace*!" he pleaded.

She got close to his ear. "Safety words are not going to work tonight, Slave," she said, feeling one of his balls start to soften in her intense grip.

One thing he had forgotten about Chaos was the fact that she liked training her grip every day. Never was she seen without metal grips or stress balls. She often bragged that she could rupture an apple.

He'd never seen it, but he was feeling the truth behind it now – one of his testicles broke down to mush.

Simone felt blood trickle out of his mouth and nose.

His body started slipping into shock.

Before long, he would fall unconscious. *I need to make a move,* his mind screamed at him.

Finding a scrap of energy, Simone put all he had into a backhand across her face. Chaos, being the Mistress – the one who constantly dished out the beating – was not used to pain herself.

His smack was enough to get her to loosen her grip and stagger backwards. Simone held his ruined ball sack, and collapsed against the wall. "You bitch!" he wept. "What the *fuck* have you done to me?!"

Seeing her struggle to her feet, Simone searched about him. Nothing came to hand. Chaos dove on him. She had hold of the scalpel. She raised it into the air and brought it down. Simone was quick enough to stop the tool from punching into his throat.

They grappled about the floor as one tried getting the better of the other. They rolled until Simone managed to push Chaos off him, but not before she slashed the blade across his bare shoulder. The wound spat crimson.

Simone hissed. "*Fuck*!"

"There's more where that came from!" she said, pushing herself off the floor and going for Simone again. He jumped to one side, avoiding her attack. The wall closest to him had a rack on it filled with various whips. He took one down and lashed her.

The leather strap caught her across the face, instantly opening up a bloody slit across her chin. Not stopping, he caught her twice more in the face, causing her to fall away. The scalpel hit the floor.

When he saw it, he jumped for it.

So did Chaos.

They both got a hand to it, but it was Simone who had the better grip this time, wrenching it from her. "No!" she gasped. "Please! I'll be good. I'm sorry for hurting you."

I must be crazy, he thought, standing. *I should just kill her!* "Get on the table and cuff your hand down," he told her, throwing her the steel bracelets that were hanging on the wall with the whips.

"Don't kill me, Simone. Please!"

"If I was going to kill you, I would have by now," he snapped. "I want some…fun. Now, on the table." He winced. The pain in his groin was beyond anything he'd ever felt.

Once on the table and lying down, Chaos cuffed her one hand whilst Simone secured her other. "Right, now I have you helpless, I can relax," he said, putting the scalpel down.

Chaos released a clutched breath.

"I told you I wasn't going to hurt you," he said, looking at his balls. "Which is more than I can say about you!"

"You should go to the hospital. You have me locked up – I'm not going anywhere."

"That is true, but I know how slippery you are. I don't trust you!" he snarled at her. "I had the oddest feeling that you might have been trying to get rid of me," he said.

Her face lost its colour.

"I'm not far off the truth, am I?"

"Don't…Don't be silly…" she said. Her voice quivered.

"Silly?" he said, limping around the room.

The red light made the situation creepier. "Yes. You're overreacting, Simone. Why would I want to get rid of you?"

Hobbling over to the dead gimp, Simone gave the carcass a stiff kick. "You've been bringing shit like this home for the past two weeks. What's a Slave supposed to think? Especially a murderous one."

"I would never turn you over to the police!"

"Who said anything about you turning me over to the police?"

"But…"

"I said you were trying to get rid of me. To break me. I didn't say you were going to turn me in, did I?" he said, smiling. "Was that your plan? Keep bringing dickheads like this home in the hope it would break me?" She looked horrified. *I'm either spot on, or she's shocked I would think such a thing*, he mused.

"How dare you!" she said. He could tell straightaway that she was lying. There was something in her eyes that gave her away. "Why would you say such a thing, Simone? I've done nothing but loved you. Kept you safe!"

"Why?"

"Because I love you – I just told you!"

"Please! You don't know the meaning of the word. No, you haven't found a suitable fuck-buddy, have you?"

"No…I…What?"

"Cut out the dramatics. I don't believe a fucking word of it."

"I'm telling…"

"Shutty!" he said, stuffing a rag in her mouth. Before she could spit it out, he wrapped tape around her head several times before cutting it.

"Mmm-mmm!" she cried, frantically pulling at the cuffs, which violently rattled.

"Now, be a good girl. I'm just popping upstairs," he told her. Simone tried to focus. The pain shooting up from his scrotum was so intense, that he was finding it difficult to stand up. *Shit, I need to sit down*, he thought.

When he reached the top of the cellar, he made for the living room. Once there, he flopped onto the sofa. He didn't have a clue what time it was, but dawn had started breaking. Natural light had begun to flood the lounge.

He lay on his back and put his hands to his testicles. Simone felt for the ruptured one. To his surprise, it was okay. It was swollen, not ruined.

He let out a clutched breath.

Sweat poured out of him.

"Thank fuck for that!" he bellowed. However, knowing there was no damage did nothing for the pain. Yet he was relieved there was no lasting injury. "I need to get some ice."

Trying to sit up was a challenge in itself, as shots of pain raced into his stomach. He fell back down, unable to move. "Come on, come on…I have to get the swelling down. I need to fully check that bitch hasn't damaged anything."

He took a few shaky breaths; Simone pushed himself off the sofa and into a standing position. He let out a yelp as another wave of intense throbbing raced from his groin. "*Fuck*!"

In all his years, he'd never felt such torture. Chaos had squeezed his balls before, but never to this point. The extremity had reached another level. Hobbling out of the room, he made his way to the kitchen. As he passed the cellar door, he could hear her raging.

He smiled. "Sleep tight, bitch!" He closed the cellar door. "I'll deal with you later. Promise." Stumbling into the kitchen, Simone went to the freezer and took out a bag of frozen peas. He then went to the sink, where he filled a glass with water. "Tablets. Where does she keep them?" he muttered to himself.

He pulled drawers out frantically, searching for painkillers. Then he remembered – Chaos kept them by the bread bin. Finding a box of pills, he took them with him along with the water and peas.

Back on the sofa, he gently placed the icy veg to his privates and swallowed four tablets with a few gulps of water. He put the glass on the table and lay back. His head had started to pound through lack of sleep.

She'll be safe down there, he thought, feeling his eyes close. *She can't get out. She's well cuffed down and there's nothing she can use to help her escape. God, if she does, mind you, she'll kill me. I should get up and lock the cellar door...*But he drifted off into sleep before he could motivate himself.

He woke with a start, causing him to sit bolt upright. Sweat poured down his face. "Where...Where...?!" he gasped, swallowing hard. He reached for the near empty glass of water and slugged it. Panting, he lay back down. "Shit, shit, shit..." he said. His nightmares had always been bad.

Always.

The room had become dark. Dusk had settled.

"I've slept all day!" he uttered between pants. Then he suddenly realised he had a wet patch between his legs. "I've pissed myself!" he blurted, putting his hand between his legs. He laughed when he saw the bag of peas had melted.

Removing it, he felt his balls. The swelling had gone down. The pain had also eased. After ten minutes of feeling around and examining, Simone was happy there was no lasting damage. "I thought you had me there, you fucking cunt. You're going to pay for that little stunt," he whispered.

Swinging his legs off the sofa, Simone sat up. He grabbed the tablets off the table and popped four more into his mouth. He swallowed them dry. "*Ugh*! Bloody foul," he said.

There was still a bit of stabbing pain in his scrotum, but not like it had been. His ribs still hurt, too, which he had forgotten about until now. Moving gradually, Simone went to the cellar door. He couldn't hear Chaos moving around, not that it meant anything.

I should check, he told himself. *Just to be on the safe side*. Gingerly, he walked down the steps. By the time he got to the bottom, he was sweating again. Looking at Chaos, he could see she had her head turned from him.

The room stunk of piss.

He moved closer to her and noticed she wasn't moving or breathing. "Chaos?" he said, putting his hand out. He shook her shoulder. "Are you sleeping…?"

Her face flew at his. She screamed beneath her gag. This caused Simone to jump back. As he did so, his legs tangled. He hit the deck with a hard thump, but laughed. "Shit, you scared the fuck out of me!" he said.

Looking at her, he could tell she'd been crying.

He got to his feet and told her to be still, but she didn't listen. "If you settle down, I'll take the gag off, okay?" Her eyes were crazy-wild, yet she seemed to listen to him this time. "Good girl," he mocked.

True to his word, he removed her gag, roughly.

"Why the fuck did you leave me down here for so long, bastard?! I've pissed myself!"

He laughed. "Yeah, the joys of being helpless," he told her. "Not nice, is it? I should have supplied you with a bottle – repaid the favour."

"*Cunt!*"

"Shh, or I'll put the gag back on. Would you like something to eat and drink?"

He could see her struggling to bite her tongue. "Yes, please!" she forced.

"Okay, I'll get you something." He put the rag back in her mouth and taped it.

"Mmmm-mmmm!" she muffled.

He started getting aroused by it, but knew he couldn't do anything. Not with all the pain his body was currently dealing with. "I'll bring you something down in a bit," he promised.

Simone knocked the cellar light out and proceeded up the steps in the dark. Once at the top, he closed and locked the door. Satisfied, he went and made himself a bite to eat.

After finishing food, he'd thought about feeding and watering Chaos. If he was going to have his fun with her, he would need to keep her strength up. "Nah, fuck it – she can wait a little bit longer," he said to himself.

Noting it was almost seven o'clock, he decided to give Toni a call. After all, he had promised to ring again this evening.

At a minute-to, he rang her number and got straight through. "Hello. I'm really happy I managed to get you so quickly," he said with a smile on his face.

CHAPTER 16

"So, what would you like to talk about tonight, Simone?" Toni asked.

"Well, I believe you asked me if I'd ever hurt anyone apart from the bullies?"

"Yes, that's right – you said you had?"

"I've killed."

"*Excuse* me?!" She hadn't meant to sound shocked. She knew he'd probably hurt others in a bad way, especially after what he had done to his school bullies. "I'm sorry, I didn't mean for that to sound so rude…"

He chuckled. "It's okay – I've learned to deal with it over the years."

"You spent time in prison for it?" This time, she did manage to disguise her astonishment.

"A young offenders home. It happened a few years after the bullying incident."

"Oh…" she said.

"Yes," he sighed. "I only served a couple of years, as it was seen as self-defence."

"I see," she said, taking a deep breath. She was glad. Slightly happier, as though the 'self-defence' bit made his actions seem fine'n'dandy. He was still a killer, no matter how you looked at it. *But still,* she argued with her mind, *it's not like he planned the murder or anything…* "Do you want to tell me about it?" she carefully asked.

"Just so you know, I've not told this story to anyone. I guess I trust you," he said.

She smiled.

"It's okay – whatever you tell me, stays with me, Simone. Please, go on."

"I hadn't long started my teenage years."

****

Legs. Women's legs. Damn. Can't seem to get them out of my head tonight. Short legs, long legs, legs in stockings, tights, shorts, blah, blah, blah…The ones that could wrap around a guy's neck and pop his fucking head off like a bottle cap. Yeah – Boa-like legs. Maybe I should just get my fill on Stocking-Tease and be done with it? Maybe. Nah, not tonight.

Not enough time to get the PC on and warmed up. And why would I, he thought? *Because tonight, tonight I have Jill right across the street from me, and in about thirty seconds, those legs she's hiding under that robe of hers will be revealed.*

He knocked the light off in his room, picked up his binoculars, and raced to the window from his computer desk. She hadn't been looking his way and wouldn't have noticed his light go dead.

Her bulb was burning, her curtains open.

Dirrrrty girl. She must know what she's doing. I'm sure she's caught me with my prick in my hand a few times as I've spied on her, stroking it to a crescendo of mind-numbing pleasure.

Twenty…nineteen…eighteen…God, they are long legs. Long and curved right down to her toenails. The ultimate pair of cock-teasing pins that would be TNT in a pair of pull-ups. He shivered. His dick faltered, but remained a solid, thick five inches of throbbing flesh. She had a Hispanic look about her.

Jill, whatever-the-fuck her surname was, had moved in opposite to Simone's mother's house almost three months ago. MILF. That's the term he had used for her – *Mam I'd Love to Fuck*. Even though she wasn't a mam, she sure seemed old enough to be one. She was fucking dynamite without the fuse.

Look at her, would you? Prancing around her room with next to nothing on. The robe fell to the floor – four seconds shy of time – and showed her to be wearing a pair of red thongs and matching bra. Dribbles came out the end of his pulsating hardness, instantly gluing his boxers to him. His grip intensified on the binoculars.

"Tart," he whispered as he watched Jill unwrap her hair from inside her towel and propel it above her like something out of a shampoo advert. "She must know I'm watching. That she's turning a fifteen-year-old school boy on?"

Jill started to rub her hair vigorously as she stood, legs apart, in front of her window – the towel cut his view off as she did so.

Simone took his chance and removed his cock. He took his eyes off the glorious view for a split second before turning back to Jill, finding she had stopped rubbing her hair and was now running a brush through her long, brunette shocks.

"Magnificent," he said with a shaky breath. "Wait until I tell the guys at school. They may like me once I do. I could get *photos*!"

He'd never thought of that before. Even though he'd pleaded with the bullies that he had pictures, and that he would show them, he never did. He didn't have the steel in his guts to take them. Or the means. This had been long before Jill had moved in, and long before Nadoleg, too. It was at a time when May was living there – the seventy-year-old grandmother had moved out in a wooden box and carted off in a black limo marked by death.

"*Ugh*." Seeing her naked had haunted his dreams many a time – but so long ago. Now, now he had a sexy, full-bodied neighbour – and not an oldie, or a fatty like Nadoleg. And a phone. A mobile phone that could take pictures. It was a purchase out of his pay as a part-time paperboy. An item he had asked for on more than one occasion for birthdays and Christmases, only for his mother to deny him every time, *knowing* what he was like.

Especially after catching him with his dirty books.

"Well, I have a phone now," he said, snatching it out of his pocket.

Simone resumed his peeping.

Jill had finished brushing, and was now sitting on her bed. She fluffed her hair, then started to pull a stocking, which had a red top, up one leg. Simone couldn't believe his luck. She was dressing up. *Her bloke must be coming round*, he thought.

She pulled the stocking up ever so slowly, slipping it past her knee-joint like a pro. Once it was to the top of her thigh, she smoothed the creases out of the silky garment, and then proceeded to slip the other on, taking as much time and care as the first.

Simone stopped masturbating, fearing he would come too soon. He didn't want this show to end in a terse way. Jill stood up, and eyed herself in her full-length mirror. "She's smokin' hot." He gritted his teeth.

Jill strutted around her room like a catwalk model, working her legs and wiggling her tight arse. The thong looked as if it was painted on her golden body. Then she stopped and went to her window. She leant out and looked down at the guy who was standing at her door. Simone ducked down slightly, fearing he'd get caught.

In Simone's excitement, he hadn't noticed Jill's new boyfriend pull up in his car and pound at her front door.

"I'll be there in a jiffy, Chris," she called down to him. Her voice had an echoing, distant sound to Simone, who still had his head down until he heard Jill's door open and then thump shut.

He popped his head up and saw them standing in the middle of her room. *Fuck – she answered her door in her undercrackers?* Simone thought. *She's dirty, or a whore, as Mam would call her.*

He seems rather plain for Jill, Simone thought. *He's all gangly and skinny, with a pockmarked face. Ugh. How can she kiss him?* Then her hands were unzipping his trousers and unbuckling his belt, before pulling them down to his ankles. Her face was now level with Chris' solid dick. She took it into her mouth, and settled on her knees.

"*Mm*," Simone groaned, stroking himself slowly. "She's like those sluts on that DVD I have," he said aloud. "But this is much better viewing. *Much* better!"

Chris had his head thrown back, his balled hands clutching tufts of Jill's hair. He aided her in the moving back and forth of her head.

"I wish that was me," Simone said. "Lucky bastard. How does an ugly guy like him get a woman like Jill?"

She got to her feet, her head level with his chest, and looked up at him. He peered down and their lips fused. Her fingers raked his back and he pulled her close, trying to make her part of his body. Her tits squashed flat against him.

Simone felt himself about to come, but managed to stop wanking before it was too late. "That was almost the vinegar stroke," he said, letting out a small chuckle. He'd heard the older boys at school refer to coming as just that.

Then Simone's face lost its smile as he witnessed Jill knee Chris in his balls. He doubled over and rested his head against her shoulder, holding his privates. She heaved his body sideways, and he collapsed onto her bed with a spring-like effect.

He rolled around on her mattress as she slipped a stocking down her left leg and pulled it taut between her fists like a garrotte.

"She's going to strangle him!" Simone uttered, and then lowered his binoculars before putting them back to his eyes.

She was now on her bed, and had the leg garment around Chris' throat. Jill pulled backwards hard, like she was controlling reins. She had one knee firmly planted at the base of Chris' back.

"Oh, fuck, fuck, fuck…" Simone said. He now had both hands on his binoculars, the horn taken out of him as he watched on in disbelief. This was a woman he had spied on many times before. She seemed to like nothing more than skipping around the place in next to nothing as she sunbathed in her garden, lounged in front of her TV, or sat in her bedroom. *A happy-go-lucky kind of girl*, Simone thought as he watched Chris flail his arms and Jill jig and bounce around like a wild cavewoman as she throttled him.

"I have to call the police!"

He started to lower his binoculars when he noticed Chris go for the bedside lamp in a last-ditch effort to get Jill off him. He swung it, but couldn't get his arm back far enough to hit her with it. So, he smashed it against the table and picked out a shard of glass.

But he was weakened from her attack.

Jill's grunting and writhing came to a halt. She got off the half-dead Chris, and rolled him onto his back so she could take the large piece of glass out of his hand.

Simone licked his dry, cracking lips. *I wish Mr. Tickles and the guys were here with me, and not down in the basement*, he thought.

"No," he whispered as he watched Jill plough the jagged instrument into the side of Chris' neck time and again, ripping flesh and plastering her midriff in blood. Gore found its way into her hair and onto her wall behind the bed as she kept stabbing long after Chris stopped bucking.

She turned to face the window, her teeth beaming white from behind her drawn-back lips. Her hair wild, her face dripping crimson.

"*Shit!*" Simone yelled, flying out of sight as Jill looked straight at him. "Bollocks, she saw me. She fucking *saw* me!" He tried to calm his racing heart by taking deep breaths. He threw his binoculars to one side. "Damn it." He slammed his fist against the wall. "She *killed* him. It was coldblooded. Fuck... She couldn't have seen me – my room's in darkness. Unless the lens of the binoculars caught a reflection or something?"

"Fuck." He popped his head over the windowsill slowly. Her lights were off, her curtains still open. "Phew! She didn't see me." He collapsed against his wall again. "Best I call the police." Simone dug his mobile out of his pocket and started to key in 999 when his front door started receiving hard *thump*, *thump*, *thump* sounds.

"Oh. My. *God*." He almost pissed himself. "She's at my door!"

More banging sounds. He visualised the door shaking in its jamb. He looked about him and saw a large pair of scissors lying on his chest of drawers. He got up and grabbed them. They felt heavy in his hand.

"You won't get me, bitch!" he said, racing down the stairs to the front door, which *was* rattling. "Go away!" he yelled.

"Let me in, you little *shit*," Jill yelled. "Now!"

Simone held the scissors tight in his grip, opened the door, and then plunged the snipping implement deep into the woman's stomach. Blood raced up his arm and pattered across his face. He retracted the weapon, which made a sloppy sound, and let it fall to the floor.

He watched as Jill clutched her wound and collapsed to the floor. It took her less than five minutes to die.

****

"That's all I remember," Simone said.

There was a brief moment of silence before Toni spoke. "What did your mother do?"

"I was lucky, really – she got home just before the police arrived."

"What happened?"

"I told them what I'd seen, and that I thought she was coming to kill me. My mother was a wreck, because they took me away. Even though it was self-defence, the judge found my actions as 'staged'."

"What?"

"Yeah, he seemed to think I was laying in wait – that I could have avoided killing her and called the police. That I took matters into my own hands; I was sentenced to two years."

"And your mother?" she asked.

"It changed her. She was a different woman after that – four years after my release, I found her dead in her dance room. She'd hanged herself."

"Aw, Simone…I'm sorry."

"She'd left a letter, apologising to me for how I had turned out. She blamed herself for everything. Even Sian. I took it pretty hard."

"I'm not surprised."

"After that, I pretty much became a recluse until I found the courage to move on with my life. Not long after that, I met Chaos."

"You poor thing," Toni said. Tears formed at the corner of her eyes.

"My mother was my world. After Sian was taken, we became closer."

"Would you like to tell me about your relationship with your mother? You haven't really elaborated…" Toni said.

"I would, but not tonight, if that's okay with you?"

"That's perfectly fine. Are you going now?" she asked.

"I was going to, yes. I'm in a fair bit of pain, due to another beating from my Mistress."

"You need to get out of there, Simone!"

"One day," he said. "I'll ring you tomorrow."

"Wait, before you go."

"Yes?"

"This is very much against the rules, but I'd like to give you my mobile number…" Her face flushed. Heat rose up her neck.

"That's very nice of you," he said.

"I thought it would be easier to keep in touch. This way, you won't have to wait until I start my shift," she said. It sounded like a brainless idea, but still she went ahead and supplied a convicted killer with her number.

"That's great – I've written it down. I'll text you later!" He then hung up.

She felt instantly gutted. Simone hadn't been on the phone more than forty minutes. Normally, he kept her online for well over an hour. He seemed rushed, as though something had distracted him.

Maybe his Mistress was walking through the door? she thought. *No, it wasn't that. It was the story he told me. It's saddened him. I hope he texts me later. I'll cheer him up. God, if I told anyone about what I've done, they'll lock* me *up*! Her wandering mind caused her to lose track of what she was doing, as another call came through. It took eleven rings before Toni realised it was her phone going crazy.

"*Shit*," she said, pressing the answer button.

When she started talking, and then listening, her mind drifted back to Simone and whether or not he would contact her. *Maybe after this call, I should go to my locker and check my phone?*

"Hello?" the sad voice on the other end of her phone said. "Have you gone?"

"No, I'm still here. Sorry. I was listening to what you were saying. Please, go on."

"I was just wondering what you thought I should do?"

To Toni's horror, the man had already finished talking. "I…Ummm… You should try and be brave…" she said, winging it.

"I thought you might say that. It's hard though, you know? The say time is a great healer, but I'm not so sure. It's been two years today since she died. My wife was my world…"

Relieved, Toni now had information she could use. "I know, but we must stay strong for the others around us."

"Yes, you're right. I've managed to stay sober for the past two days, which is a good thing. Around the anniversary, I tend to drink heavily."

"Have you tried attending AA meetings? I've heard they can help. A lot of people who go there drink for a reason," Toni said.

"I've thought about it…"

"I had a lovely young woman on the phone last night who told me she had been attending AA. She also said she'd made friends with some of the other attendees who drank because they'd lost a loved one."

"Something to consider, then."

"Most definitely," Toni said. "And we're always here to talk to, too."

"Yes, that's true."

After twenty minutes of talking, the person hung up. Huffing, Toni rolled her seat back and got up. With Stu still on the phone, which was a relief, Toni headed to the toilet.

Even though that call started shaky, I managed to pull it back, she thought. *Jesus, I can't get Simone out of my mind – it's driving me crazy!*

Once finished in the toilet, Toni looked at herself in the mirror as she washed her hands. *What have I done? Come on, it's not a crime. If Simone starts getting weird, I'll change my number. No big deal.*

Leaving the bathroom, Toni went to her locker. Opening it, she pulled her phone out and checked to see if there were any messages. There weren't. *See, if he was that much of a creepy weirdo, he would have left me messages and voicemails by now*, she reasoned. *The chances are, he won't even bother. Don't forget, he has a very strict girlfriend, too.*

Putting her mobile back in her locker, Toni grabbed her mug off her table and headed for the kitchen. By the time she returned to her desk, Stu was ending a call. "Hello!" he said. "We've not had a chance to chat yet."

"Oh, I know – it's madness this afternoon."

"Are we still on for…" he started, but an incoming phone call pulled him away.

Thank God for that, she thought. How was she going to tell him she didn't feel like going out tonight? It hadn't been her intention to let Stu down. But now Simone had her number, she wanted to spend the evening either texting or speaking with him, should he make contact.

Before Toni received another call, Stu had finished his. "That was nice and quick," he said. "Has it gone quiet?"

"Yeah, I've been waiting for at least twenty minutes. Was that someone you've spoken to before?"

He nodded. "So, I was about to ask, are we still on for tonight? There's a couple of good films at the cinema at the moment." His face lit up.

How was she going to let him down? *God, here goes.*

"*Ah*, I'm going to have to let you down tonight, sorry," she said. Having lied, she cringed on the inside.

"Oh?" he said. He looked wounded.

"Yeah, I promised Suzanne we'd have a girly night tonight. Another time, though?" she asked, trying to put her best smile on. *I'm a total bitch!* she thought.

"Yeah," he muttered, and then turned back to his desk. Putting his headset to one side, he got up to leave. "Bathroom break," he said.

Even though he tried to hide his disappointment, she could see it. *Did he know I was lying? No, he couldn't have possibly known that. Don't be silly. Suzanne is right – I am Paranoid Pete!*

Despite her playing off that something was wrong, Stu seemed to avoid Toni for the rest of the shift. And, when it came to an end, he rushed out the door without so much as a goodbye.

Slightly wounded, Toni walked to her car alone. *I should have gone out with him this evening – he's clearly hurt. I shouldn't be messing him about. "Tut,* idiot!" she scolded herself as she unlocked her car and got in.

Huffing, she started the engine. *I'll send him a text later. Make amends – maybe ask about going out tomorrow night. Yeah, he'll like that.* As she was about to pull off, Toni's mobile beeped.

Digging it out of her bag, she opened it. She saw a message from an unknown number. Opening her texts, she read it. '*Hello, Toni. I thought I'd text you now, knowing this is around the time you finish work. I hope to speak with you soon. Simone. X*'

A breath hitched in her throat. She couldn't believe it.

Not being able to wait until she got home, Toni fired a quick message back. '*I'm glad you contacted. I was starting to think you weren't going to…Just about to drive home. Speak soon. X*'

CHAPTER 17

When a text came back, Simone smiled. He had her. She was hooked – he could tell. Hanging up on her early had not been his plan, but Chaos had started making far too much noise in the cellar. He'd been worried that Toni would hear something.

On inspecting Chaos, he found she had managed to kick a few things over with her legs, which hadn't been tied down tight enough. After he'd secured her pins in the stirrups, he'd made them something to eat.

That had been a few hours ago.

He now sat in the dark with a glass of wine in one hand, and his mobile in the other. The fireplace in the lounge was lit, which threw Simone's shadow across the walls in an eerie manner.

After he fed her, Chaos had gone quiet.

This left Simone with his thoughts.

And now Toni.

How am I going to play this? he wondered while looking at her text. It had been roughly ten minutes since she'd texted to say she was leaving work. *I'll give it a few more minutes before I reply.*

Taking a sip of wine, Simone tapped his finger against the glass as he thought things through. "What do you think, Mr. Tickles?" he asked the clown. The toy sat in the middle of the room and faced the fire. The glow from the flames intensified his creepy make-up.

"*Have our fun, and then get rid.*"

"I was thinking the exact same thing," Simone said, taking another a sip of wine.

"*She knows too much about us. She'd have to go!*"

"I fully agree. Do you think we should try to get a few dates out of her first – get close to her?"

"Seems like a good idea – make her completely trust you. That way, she won't suspect a thing!"

"I love how evil you are!" Simone said, watching a smile appear on the clown's face.

"You helped create me, boss – you should be proud of yourself!"

"Yes, I did, didn't I?" Simone said, smiling. Looking at the clock, he saw enough time had now slipped by. Taking a gulp of wine, he sent Toni a new text: *'Hiya again, not sure if you're home yet, but I was wondering if you would maybe like to give me a call later on this evening? Or maybe I could call you?'*

Re-reading it, Simone sent it.

"Don't push too much too soon, boss. We don't want to spook her."

"True. Do we tell her about Chaos?"

"Tell her what about Chaos?"

"That's she's no longer in the picture. That I'm now free of her tyranny?"

"Tyranny," Mr. Tickles said. *"That's a funny word, isn't it? Almost sounds like tranny!"*

They both laughed at that. "Yes, it does!"

"I think you can tell Toni about Chaos – it'll help get you closer. From what I've heard about her so far, she seems very impressionable. I think it'll be easy to dupe her into either coming here or meeting you somewhere."

"Do you think she's pretty, with a good body and legs?"

"Pretty hard to tell from a voice and what you've told me – either way, she has to go!"

"Oh, I know that. But I want to have my fun with her first."

"Agreed. Has she contacted again?"

"Nothing – maybe I should ring her? Or send another text?"

"No, sir. That would be a bad move. You don't want to go scaring the girl."

"*Ugh*, the waiting is killing me!"

"Patience, boss. She's hooked on you – you know that. You've played it cool with her so far. No point in letting it slip now!"

"I know. You're right. What do we do with Chaos and the bodies downstairs? They're going to start rotting before long."

"Yeah, and we can't have that. Let's wait to see what Toni comes back with first. See if she wants to chat. If not, we'll do something about those bodies, sir."

"Okay."

After another fifteen minutes of waiting, Simone started to get impatient once again. With his glass empty, he decided to refill it. "Why doesn't she answer?!" he blurted, getting up to leave for the kitchen.

"She will – she might not have finished driving. Or, if she is home, maybe she's taking a shower. Or eating! Give her a chance. Get another wine. Chill out."

Refilling his glass, Simone went back to his seat. He liked sitting around nude – the feel of leather against his flesh was cooling. Putting his glass of wine down by his side, he picked his phone up. Nothing.

"Nope, I don't think we will hear from her tonight, Mr. Tickles."

"Hmm, it is starting to get a little late, I have to admit. And yet, she seemed so keen! I mean, she was the one who gave her number out…"

"I know! I don't get it, either."

"Okay, so what shall we do with the bodies and Chaos?"

"I think we should make Chaos suffer – I plan to keep her locked up down there until she dies."

"That could take years!" Mr Tickles said.

"It won't take that long. I don't plan on feeding or watering her that often," he said, smiling.

"Oo, you cold machine!"

Grinning, Simone took a big gulp of wine. "After what that bitch did to my nuts, she's lucky I didn't fucking kill her outright. I think making her suffer will be more fun. Don't you think?"

"Definitely. Isn't there a way we could starve her of oxygen? Fuck her brain up?"

"That's some nice thinking. We could torture her, I suppose. Cut her air off and on. Push it too far, and she could end up with brain damage!"

"Yeah, turn her into a cabbage. We could keep her in a wheelchair! Fuck and play with her whenever we wanted."

"Hmm, maybe killing her is the wrong way to go about it. As you say, if we find a way to subdue her, she could be our sex toy for years."

"Until we get bored!"

Excited, Simone picked his wine up and took a few more gulps. "I like that idea. We could cut her hands and feet off? That would really fuck her up!"

"Yes! Pull her teeth out, too."

"Cut the bitch's tongue off."

"Yeah, that way she'll never be able to tell on us. She'll be our prisoner."

"Mm, devious. I love it…I think we should give it a few days though. Have some fun first."

"We need to get shot of those bodies first."

"Any ideas?"

"Plenty. And if we're going to do it, then I suggest we do it tonight, before they start stinking up the place."

"Okay, so what do we do?"

"We chop 'em up and take them down to the beach."

"Let the tide take them out?"

"Yeah, just like it did the girls. I think you were unlucky with the guy."

"Brilliant idea. And if we do it now, we can bag the parts and take them down to the sea in the early hours."

"Well, I think we should spread it out. Maybe do it over two or three nights. Carrying chopped-up bodies would be heavy."

"Good thinking. I'll make my first run tonight. Take a load of the smaller parts – hands, feet, etc…"

Mr. Tickles nodded. Simone drained his second glass of wine. "I need more."

"Not too much, sir. You're going to need a clear head."

"I know. I just need to get my courage up…" He was interrupted by his mobile beeping. A text had come through. "Took your sweet time," he muttered to himself. "I could have fucking hung myself through depression by now."

Opening his messages, he saw it was off Toni. *'Hiya, sorry for taking so long to reply – I grabbed a bite to eat and a shower. I didn't think you would contact so soon. Not sure about a phone call tonight, as I am shattered. I'm happy to text, though? XX'*

"*Oo*, two kisses!" Simone mocked, showing the message to Mr. Tickles.

"She's definitely hot for your cock, sir."

"Yes, I'm beginning to think so myself. Okay, so we won't be chatting to her this evening. We may as well go and get started downstairs?"

The clown nodded.

Before Simone texted back, he grabbed Mr. Tickles and his wine, and then headed down to the cellar. Once there, he fired a message back to Toni as Chaos screamed and thrashed on the table. "*Shh*!" Simone mocked. "I'm trying to concentrate here." Before sending his message, he reread it – *'That's okay, maybe we can chat on the phone tomorrow morning? I'm always up early. Yep, I'm cool to keep texting. How was the rest of your shift? XX'*

Putting his phone to one side, he looked at Chaos. Her eyes were rimmed with redness. It made her look wild. Dangerous, even. "Well, I'm sure you'll be glad to know you didn't bust a nut. Just badly bruised it," he told her.

She growled and snarled beneath her gag, which tickled Simone. "You're going to enjoy this," he told her, grabbing the gimp by his legs. Simone dragged the big man over to another table in the room and then picked him up. "Phew, he's a lump!" he gasped.

Going back to Chaos, he violently ripped her gag off, causing her to scream. Her top lip was raw from where a patch of skin had torn free. Her lips were chapped and cracked. "Thirsty?" he asked, and then smiled. "I'll try to remember to water you!"

"You fucking *cunt*!" she bellowed. "*Help*!" she screamed. "*Help*!"

He joined in. "*Heeeeeeeeelp*!" he screeched. "*Heeeeeeeelp*!" Mr. Tickles sniggered.

"You're fucking crazy! You'll never get away with any of this. You hear? *Never*!"

"I've already got away with it. Do you see anyone coming to your rescue?" She shrunk away from him. "Also, knock the screaming off – you know full well this room is padded, dear."

"You, you…"

"Yes?"

"Fuck you, Simone!"

"No, thanks. I'm moving on to sweeter pastures," he said, wiggling his mobile at her. "I've outgrown you, bitch!" he said, getting up-close-and-personal. He grabbed her hair and yanked her head back. She screamed. "You're going to be my Slave now, Chaos!"

"*Never*!"

"Huh," he said, grinning. "I guess we'll see about that. I'm sure you'll be surprised at what you'll do for food and water…"

"You wouldn't?!"

He didn't answer. "Hey, I have a treat in store for you!" he told her. "You're going to love this."

"What…What are you going to do?!"

"You'll see," he said, running upstairs. When he returned, he had a roll of black bags in his hand, which were the large ones for wheelie bins.

"Oh, Jesus…" she gasped.

Going to the gimp, Simone sized the man up. "Big fella, ain't he?!"

Chaos whimpered as she watched Simone strip her Dog. He hadn't been lying about the panties, which Simone found amusing. "Nothing you haven't done!" she bit.

"Oh, I know. I just find it amusing, you know. Such a big guy…"

"Hardly a small chap yourself!" she said.

"True. But still...*Phew*! Make-up, too," he said, peeling the mask off. "*Wow*, you picked a bit of an ugly bastard, mind. No wonder he wears this thing!"

"He seemed like fun. Obedient, too. Which is more than can be said about you!"

"You sure do like to cut deep, don't you? Well, I've found someone much sexier. Someone who understands the real Simone." He went to his toolbox, which was kept in the cellar. Opening it, he dug his saw out.

"Simone, no!"

"What?" he said, turning to face Chaos.

"Please, don't do this!"

"Aw, it's a bit late for that," he said, placing the saw to the gimp's neck. "I hope you don't have a weak stomach!" He then proceeded to slowly run the saw back and forth, back and forth, back and forth.

The crunching, grinding noise was sickening. Simone didn't mind the sight of mangled flesh or blood. *I've seen plenty of it lately*, he thought, continuing to cut through the man's neck.

Chaos screamed in sync to Simone's saw action.

It amused him.

He even giggled.

Once the head rolled off, he picked it up by the hair and threw it into a readied bin bag, which already had the guy's clothes in. Satisfied, he then cut off the man's hands, feet and legs. He quartered the limbs so they would fit in the bag. "Right, I think that's enough," he said, tying the bag. "Not too heavy, either."

Going to the cellar steps, he put his hand on the light switch.

"Please, let me go..." Chaos whispered.

"I can't do that. But if you are good, I'll bring you something to eat and drink."

She said nothing, just wept. He couldn't help but snigger as he knocked the light off.

Upstairs, Simone put the black bag by the door. Before heading out, he'd need to shower and text Toni, who had replied to him over half-an-hour ago. Grabbing his mobile, he noticed she'd replied twice. "Shit!" he muttered. He read the first one – '*I'm glad I gave you my number. I was hoping you would contact me. I love chatting to you. I haven't been able to stop thinking about our conversations since we first spoke. XX*'

He reread the message.

His dick started to rise. He loved the thought of her thinking about it. Her second text was a simple one – *'I guess you've fallen asleep. I'll ring you tomorrow. Goodnight. XX'*

"Damn it, I've missed her." He sent her a message quickly, in case she was still awake. *'Sorry, I didn't hear the phone. If we don't speak now, I'll look forward to chatting in the morning. XX'* He sent it. Putting his phone to one side, Simone rushed upstairs to the bathroom.

There, he showered and dressed.

It was now going on for three A.M., and so he decided it was late enough.

He picked the black bag up and left, slamming the door behind him. The street was quiet. *Perfect*, he thought, slinking from his door and then darting across the road. At the corner, he dashed down an alley.

A few of the houses had their lights on, but that didn't bother him, as he crept in the shadows. Because he was taking so much caution in being quiet and avoiding brightly lit areas, it took him almost thirty minutes to get down to the front. Normally, ten minutes would have been plenty of time.

When he passed the closed fair, he couldn't help but think how lovely it looked. Most people would have seen it as eerie, he was sure, but not him. It was peaceful, with the multi-coloured bulbs out and the rides at a standstill. All he could hear was the sea; the waves crashed against the rocks.

Come on, I can't afford to just stand here. Get moving, he told himself. He soon found he was standing at the old pier once again. He double-checked to make sure nobody was around before he unloaded the body parts.

Kneeling in the wet sand, Simone dug a few shallow graves and presented them with the bits he'd cut off the gimp. Before he finished, the water started swishing around him. Once the head was in the ground, Simone stood up. He had to wait for the water to recede before he could check his handiwork.

A smile twitched across his lips. There was nothing to see. By morning, the tide would have washed everything out. Nobody would ever know about the gimp or the girl. Tomorrow night, he would bring more body parts for the sea to gobble up.

Simone grabbed the empty black bag and started walking up the beach as fast as he could. When he arrived back at the fair, he made sure the road was devoid of traffic, and then sprinted for the backstreets.

When he was in the shadows, Simone took a five-minute breather before sprinting the rest of the way home.

CHAPTER 18

With pricked ears, Chaos had listened for the sound of the front door crashing shut. Simone had never been one for closing it lightly. And, as she'd hoped, he hadn't this time, even though he was trying to be sneaky.

What an idiot, she thought.

Once she'd heard it, Chaos had started working at her handcuffs.

Because she had small wrists, she was able to pop her hands out of the bracelets with a bit of effort – but they'd been snapped on a little too tight this time. There was no freeing her left hand, but there was hope for the right.

The bastard's not going to snuff me out, she thought, pulling at the right cuff. She couldn't quite get her thumb bone through the steel, but it would go eventually. She was confident of that, even if it took skin, which it was more than likely going to. *Simone thinks he's going to get away with it.* She grunted. Tears welled in her eyes as the cuff started biting into her skin.

"Come on, come on, you bastard!" she hissed, continuing to yank at her hand. She could feel it beginning to slip free. "Almost…" She let out a cry of agony as her thumb snapped under the pressure she applied. "*Fuck*!"

Tears rained down her cheeks. Her bottom lip quivered, but she didn't stop. With a vicious scream, she pulled harder. When Chaos' hand flew out of the bracelet, she yelled with triumph.

"*Ha*! I fucking got you now, Simone!"

With her one hand loose, she was able to release her ankles, which Simone had only tied into the stirrups. With her legs now free, Chaos rolled off the table and stood up. She groaned as she did so, as her knees and back clicked into place.

She reeked of piss.

Looking down at her other hand, Chaos wondered how she was going to free it. The table could not be moved, as it was bolted to the floor. With a bit of light now in the room, due to dawn breaking, she was able to see Simone's toolbox.

"Maybe if I can get close to the floor, I'll be able to get my fingers to it," she uttered.

On her knees, Chaos tried to get her body as far down to the ground as possible, and then stretched her arm and hand out. Her fingertips brushed the toolbox. "Please…" she strained.

Blood and flesh caught in her vision, which made her gag. "Keep your eye on the prize," she told herself, hooking her fingertips over the toolbox. "Got ya!" As she pulled her hand back, it slipped off the heavy-duty box. "*Shit!*"

Out of frustration, she hammered the floor, causing a bolt of pain to race up her arm – she'd forgotten about her thumb. "Oh, fuck…" she groaned. Rocking back and forth, Chaos cradled her hurt hand to her chest. "I'm going to fucking kill him!"

Stretching her hand out again, she made another play for the toolbox, but again could only get her fingertips to it. By extending herself that little bit more, Chaos' cuffed hand screamed in agony as a harsh pressure was applied to her wrist.

"Almost…*Please…*" she gasped, fresh tears rolling down her face. Getting the best grip she could hope for, she pulled slowly. "*Yes!*" she yelled, seeing the box move.

The near unbearable force on her wrist eased as she shuffled backwards. When the toolbox was closer, Chaos managed a much better hold on it, causing her to draw it towards her much faster.

Once she had it at her side, she found a screwdriver inside. Getting to her feet, she jammed the end of the DIY tool into the bracelet and tried to pop it free. The steel didn't budge, causing her to throw the tool to one side.

Eying the hammer, she decided to give that a try. Positioning the cuff on the table, Chaos started to batter it. The steel started to buckle and yield, but didn't give. "For fuck sake!" she bellowed, and then resorted to trying to yank her hand free.

When that didn't work, she looked in the toolbox for something else. She found a small screwdriver and picked it up. Examining the end, she thought she might be able to pick or pop the lock with it.

Ramming it into the keyhole, Chaos worked the implement back and forth. "Open you bastard!" she pleaded. "Come on, come on," she coaxed.

Then her heart leapt into her throat. The front door slammed. *Shit, he's home.* Flustered, she worked harder at the lock, and almost dropped the tool, hearing his laboured footfalls on the cellar steps.

"Please!" she cried. "Open, open now!"

Keeping her eye on the stairs, she saw his legs come into view. Then his hips.

"I hope you've been a good girl?" he said, reaching the bottom. "What the fuck?! Give me that screwdriver!" He walked towards her. Just then, her cuff popped, causing him to stop dead in his tracks. "*Bollocks*!"

"Don't you fucking come near me!" she screeched, holding the small driver up in front of her face. "I'll rip your fucking eyes out if you do! I swear to God, I will!"

"Calm down!" he said, putting his hands in the air. "I wasn't going to kill you!"

"You fucking locked me up, you bastard – practically starved me, too!"

"That's going a bit far. You haven't even been down here that long. And I *have* fed you!"

"I heard you talking to that fucking doll of yours – the plans you were making. The things you were thinking of doing to me. You bastard!"

"Oh, I was messing around. Come on. You know I love you!"

Just then, his mobile phone bleeped.

"Is that your new fancy woman?"

"It's not like that, Chaos. Besides, you're a fine one to talk."

"Look what you've done to these people!" she said, indicating the half-hacked-up body of the gimp. "You've turned it into an abattoir down here, you sick fuck."

"I have to get rid of the evidence somehow."

"There would be no evidence if you could control yourself."

"It's your fault entirely – all of it, you fucking bitch."

"*Mine*?! How the fuck do you work that out?" She swiped the screwdriver at him.

"You...You kept me in that fucking cage for far too long. Teased me too much. I wanted out of the relationship, but those girls got in the way. It wouldn't have happened, had you let me out to play more often. I began to hate that."

"Don't you fucking dare blame me!" she yelled, lunging at him. She stabbed the work tool through his shoulder and tore it downward.

"*Aargh*!" he cried, falling backward. He hit the deck and she followed. When she landed on top of him, she drove her knee into his balls. His air rushed from him, giving her time to retract the screwdriver from his shoulder.

"You're fucking with the wrong woman!" She held the driver above her head. As she brought it down, aimed at his chest, his hand sprang out. He buried his fist in her throat. "*Ugh*!" she gagged, dropping her weapon. Both her hands grasped her hurt, and she fell off Simone.

Laying on her back, Chaos could only watch as Simone got to his feet and grabbed the claw hammer. He was holding his nuts with his free hand, but didn't seem too concerned about his shoulder.

"That's the last time you're going to hurt me!" he bellowed. He brought the hammer down on her face.

She had little time to gasp.

When the blows started to sound soggy, Simone stopped. He fell off Chaos and sat on the floor, with his back pressed against a wall. He looked at the crater he'd made in her face.

It didn't sicken him.

Instead, he burst out laughing. "I'm finally free! *Freeeeee*! I beat you!" He pointed at Chaos. Tears of joy and frustration poured out of him. "I beat you!"

Come on, get a hold of yourself, Simone! he told himself. *We have to clean this shithole up. Get these bodies out of here.* Wiping his eyes dry with the back of his hands, Simone stood up. He winced as his shoulder barked in pain. "Ah, *shit*!"

Grabbing Chaos by her hair, he dragged her over to the bench occupied by the remains of the gimp. "Looks like you're for the chop too!" he said, smiling down at her. "*Oo*, phone!" he blurted, digging his mobile out of his pocket.

The message was from Toni.

'*Good morning. I'm free to chat whenever you are,*' it read. Smiling, he replied. '*Give me an hour – I have a few errands to run first, and then I'll be free to call you. I'm looking forward to it!*'

He didn't wait for a response. Instead, Simone took to the saw he had used earlier and finished cutting the gimp up. He placed all the remaining parts into a black bag, and then placed the Witness onto the table next.

As with the gimp, he proceeded to cut off and bag her hands, feet, legs and head. Once done, he placed all those bits into another bag. Simone then chopped the rest of her up.

When he was finished, he decided to leave Chaos until tomorrow. Her body was still fresh. "I could have some fun with her before I get rid…"

"*You don't need to have any fun with her, sir,*" Mr. Tickles said from the steps. "*We have Toni now, sir…*"

Simone stood and thought about it for a moment. "Yes, you're right." He picked Chaos up and slammed her down on the table before him. Grabbing the saw, he set about cutting her into sections.

He took his time, relishing the destruction of her body.

Simone cut every finger and toe off before removing her hands and feet. He even plucked all her teeth out and shaved her head. Before sawing her head off, he punched a screwdriver through her eyes and cut off her nose.

After disfiguring her, he chopped her into as many pieces as he could, and then filed her away in a black bag.

When he'd finished with the bodies, Simone spent time scrubbing, cleaning and hoovering the room. Once done, he took all five black bags upstairs and put them by the door. *I'll take two out tonight. Three if I can manage it*, he thought.

Satisfied, he jogged upstairs to the bathroom. He took his shirt off and inspected his wound. "Ah, it's not that deep," he told himself. Stripping completely, he got into the shower and scrubbed himself clean.

He got out and grabbed some gauze, bandage and painkillers from the first aid box. After pouring himself a large wine, he went and sat in the living room. With his phone at hand, he dialled Toni's mobile number.

His heart lurched.

Excitement gripped him.

He suddenly realised he was ringing her personal number.

"What a lucky boy I am!" he told himself.

His breath caught in his throat when she answered. "Hello," he said.

"Hey!" she responded in a chirpy way. "How are you feeling today? You sound a little tense."

"*Ugh*, just coming around. I had a bit of a late one last night."

"Oh, how come?"

"I finally did it…"

"What?"

Is there a hint of excitement in her voice? he thought. "I *cut* her loose," he said, smiling at his little joke. "I got rid of my girlfriend. It turns out she was seeing another bloke behind my back."

"Oh, I'm sorry…"

Yeah, you sound it. "I felt relieved, to tell you the truth. It's over. Maybe I can start living a normal life. Try to put the sex games and compulsion behind me. Move forward."

"Well, I'm here to help you."

"Thanks, Toni." He was genuinely smiling, something he felt he hadn't done in years.

"Did you have to move out?"

"Yes, I'm in my own place now," he lied. *After all, Toni wouldn't know whose house was whose. That's if she ever gets to see the place,* he thought.

"It's probably for the best."

"Oh, definitely. She was planning on leaving town with him anyway. I'm glad – it means I won't be seeing her face around as a constant reminder, as I try to move on and rehabilitate myself."

"That's very true. So, what do you plan on doing today? It's a lovely day."

"I thought of going out later this evening. Maybe take a stroll down to the fair. Wait for it to cool down first, ya know?"

"Sounds lovely!"

"I suppose you'll be working later?"

"No, I actually have the weekend off," she said. "I normally get one in four off, which is nice. I was going to use the time to study."

"Very wise, too."

There was a moment's silence before Toni spoke.

"What would you like to talk to me about, Simone?"

"Mother?"

"Oh…Okay"

"I'm not sure what I can tell you, mind. I've told you a fair bit."

"Yes, but you haven't gone into full detail. I know she worked on horror films with your dad and did dancing."

"That's right, and that we were very close."

"Tell me about the closeness. Let's start there, unless you don't want to?"

"No, that's fine. I'd like to – even though it makes me sad thinking about her, we need to remember those we love. To keep their memory fresh in our minds."

"Definitely!"

"We were close before I lost my sister. But after Sian was taken away, my mother and I became tighter. She never left me in the house alone, and always took me to Bunnies with her."

"Didn't she used to take you there all the time anyway?"

"Well, she occasionally took me – it depended on whether Sian was around to babysit or not. With Sian gone, mother used to take me to work every evening."

"Did school suffer?"

"Not at all – I kept ahead with my work. Not only that, I would take naps at Bunnies. It was very cool. The girls there loved me. Treated me like I was their own. All of them."

"Looking back at it now, do you think it was the right environment to be brought up in?" Toni asked.

The line went silent.

"Probably not. But at that age, I loved it. I got to see the girls strip, not that it was a big deal, as I used to hang out in their changing rooms all the time."

"Your mother approved?"

"Of course," he stated. "You think that's weird as hell, don't you?"

"I would never judge you, your mother, or anyone else, Simone. I'm here to listen."

"But I'm asking you – do *you* think it's weird?"

"Er…Maybe a little strange…But you've grown up to be a perfectly functioning human being, so it couldn't have been that wrong. A little strange, maybe, but that's about it."

"You don't think me being a huge pervert has stemmed from that?"

"Possibly. But aren't all men a little perverted? Most blokes constantly think about sex, so I don't think you're *that* abnormal. Maybe you just think you are?"

"Maybe."

"It's not like you've hurt anyone. I mean, the school bullies are understandable – the murder was self-defence, so…"

"They would throw me birthday parties every year. I have countless photos of being surrounded by topless women. Christmas was also a great time," he said.

"The girls would spoil you?"

"Very much so, yes. They thought I was 'cute' and 'handsome'. My mother was very proud. I dreamed of working there. But after what happened to my mother, the dream vanished."

Not to dwell on the matter, Toni took him away from the subject of his mother. "I seem to recall you mentioning one of the girls in particular? Carrie or Caroline?"

"Carrie?" he muttered… "Oh, you mean Crystal?"

"That's it, Crystal. Who was she?"

"She was very special indeed."

"I take it she was one of the dancers – one of the showgirls?"

"Yes, that's right. But she wasn't just a stripper," Simone said. "She was a very talented woman."

"Okay, so what did she do? She didn't fire ping-pong balls out of her lady garden, did she?" Toni joked.

"Ha-ha!" Simone blurted. "Not quite, no. She was a trained ventriloquist. She had this most amazing doll named Harry. When she didn't work at Bunnies, she worked the pubs, clubs, hotels and Pavilion in Porthcawl. She used to do a stint down at the fair, too."

"Why was she so special?"

"She was gorgeous. Crystal was very much a mystery, too. Nobody knew much about her or where she came from."

"Did she ever…strip for you?"

"Oh, yes. On many occasions. I had a major crush on her…"

"What happened to her? Don't you see her anymore?"

"No, not since the death of my mother. Besides, they tore Bunnies down about two years ago. I have no idea where all the girls moved on to. I heard rumours that Crystal had headed west – Carmarthenshire or Swansea."

"Never heard from again?"

"Nope, never."

"Aw, bless you. You've had a fair bit of heartache, haven't you?"

"Yes – a lot of people have come and gone in my life, even though I'm still young. I have no family to speak of. No friends. No partner…"

"Well, you have me, you know?" Toni said.

"That's true, but you're only a voice on the end of the phone."

"I'll always be here to chat to."

"Thanks," he said. "My mother and I would always cuddle up on the sofa and watch horror films together on her days off. She'd buy a load of crap to eat: ice cream, chocolate and crisps. We'd pig out and watch the cheesiest movies with the curtains drawn."

"That sounds nice. Did you always watch her dance?"

"At work?"

"At work and in her dance room."

"Always. I think she knew I used to watch her through my peephole, but she never said," he lied.

"Perhaps she didn't want to shame you?" Toni offered.

"More than likely. Sometimes she knew I watched her at the club. I don't think she much cared about me seeing her nude on stage – after all, it was only her boobs she showed."

"It was never full frontal?"

"No – the girls would always keep their thongs on."

"Okay, I see. I know girls in Uni who do such jobs to pay for their books, fees, and nights out. Some girls even escort."

"I can't say I blame them. There's so much money to be made in the industry."

"There is. But I could never do something like it – take my clothes off for money or escort men on dates. Not that I think there's *anything* wrong with it!"

"Ha-ha, it's okay – you won't offend me."

"I think this is the most I've heard you laugh, Simone. You sound happy."

"I'll admit, talking to you does perk me up, Toni. I found it shocking, yet pleasing, when you gave me your number. I didn't expect you to text back. I thought you may have come to your senses, or changed your mind."

"No, not at all. I'm not like that. If I say something, then I mean it."

"That's good. Not many people are like that."

"I just realised something – we've been on the phone for over an hour! Your bill will be through the roof!"

"Oh, it's fine – I get free evening and weekend calls."

"Ha-ha, that's okay then! I wouldn't want you to have to sell a kidney to pay a bill!" she jested.

"If it came to that, I'd have to, I guess!"

She laughed again. "Oh, you're funny! I'm glad your spirits have lifted. I really hope I can help you get over your demons, Simone."

"Yes, you certainly are, Toni. You're a breath of fresh air to talk to," he said.

"Aw, thanks."

"Listen, would you like to come down to the fair with me tonight? I know this might seem a little bold of me to ask. I just thought we could chat in person…"

"I thought you'd never ask!" she said.

"*Really*?!"

"Yes, really! I'd love to hook up, Simone. What did you have in mind?"

"Well, I haven't thought that bit through, I guess. I didn't think you'd say yes!"

"You know what they say – if you don't ask, you don't get!"

"Very true. You're going to have to tell me where you live, so I can pick you up? Or would you prefer to meet me there? Which is easiest for you?"

"I think it would be better if I met you there, Simone. Not that I don't trust you, of course. I just think it would be best. I drive, so it's easy for me."

"Okay, cool. What time shall we say?"

"Make it eight o'clock?"

"Sounds good to me. By the fairground gates?"

"Seems like the best place."

"Oh, wait – how will we recognise each other?"

"Good question. I know, I'll wear a peaked hat," he said. "I'll have jeans and a T-shirt on, too."

"Right, okay. I'll keep that in mind," she said. "I'll find you, don't worry."

He could almost hear her smile down the phone. "Great. Until then!"

"Yeah, okay. And if you want, you can text me throughout the day – I'm not going to be busy," she told him.

"Excellent. I'll see you later. Bye, Toni."

"Bye."

When he cut the call, he punched the air. "Yes!"

"*Well done, sir!*" Mr. Tickles said.

"Thank you," Simone said, taking a bow. "Tonight is going to be a right laugh!" He smiled at his clown.

CHAPTER 19

When she hung up, the butterflies were back in her stomach. At first, she'd wondered if taking his messages and calls on her private number had been a good idea. But now she had spoken to him, she knew it had been the right thing to do.

"Oh, he sounds so sexy. And cute – very cute!" she said, looking at herself in her mirror. "What am I going to wear?"

"Knock-knock!" Suzanne said, walking into Toni's bedroom. "Dare I ask who you were just talking to?!"

"Oh, er…It was Stu..." Toni said, feeling her face flush.

"Oh, really?"

"Yep…" Toni couldn't hold eye contact with her friend.

"I thought I heard the name 'Simone' mentioned…"

"Oh…"

"You sneaky little devil! You go, toots."

"Stop it! He's a friend."

"A doinking friend, no doubt!" Suzanne ribbed, winking and thrusting her hips.

"You're disgusting! Is that all you ever think about? Simone is a mate."

"So, you're admitting now it wasn't Stu?" She winked.

"*Huh*," Toni said. "Yes, it was Simone, my friend. Happy?"

"Nope, I want *all* the details…"

"Really?"

"Yep. Don't worry, I won't rat on you to Stu or tell Anthony."

"I should think you wouldn't!" Toni said, raising her eyebrows.

"Spill."

Toni's mood turned from jokey to serious. "You have to promise me to keep this quiet."

Suzanne looked perplexed. "Shit, you're not in trouble or anything, are you? I'm sure Anthony would help sort out some creep…"

"No, no! It's nothing like that, I promise. But I have done something a little naughty…"

"This is either going to be extremely funny or deadly serious!"

"And what's that supposed to mean?"

"Come on, toots – it's not like you'd know how to be seriously naughty!" Suzanne grinned. "So, come on. Spill!"

She told Suzanne everything there was to tell about Simone: his sex antics, his mother, his sister, the story about the bullies, how he played with his toys, about how she had given him her number and that she was meeting him and how sexy he sounded… Toni spilt her guts. However, she left out the part about Simone being imprisoned for murder.

"Are you *crazy*?!" Suzanne blurted. "He could be dangerous!"

"*Tut*, that's the type of reaction I'd expect from my mother, not you."

"Yeah, but come on. He could be anyone."

"I've spoken to him loads. He sounds so hot, Suzanne. He's funny, too."

"I can't believe I'm hearing this."

"Come on, just be pleased for me. I'm meeting him later – in a crowded area, before you say anything."

"And what about poor Stu?"

"Oh, so it's *poor* Stu now, is it?" Toni said, smiling.

"Huh," Suzanne sighed. "You know what I mean…"

"I know, and I feel bad…It's just Simone…It's dangerous, yet I can't help myself. We seem to get on so well."

"I could come with you tonight. Maybe bring Anthony?"

"No, it would look odd, me turning up with a couple of mates."

"I suppose you're right. *Hey*! What we could do, is come along but hang back – keep an eye on you?"

"Hmm, I don't know. Sounds a little creepy."

"What? Why?! You know Anthony and *me*!"

"I know. I just wouldn't be able to relax, knowing I'm being watched."

"Okay, fine. Play it your way. Do you have a rape alarm? Or Mace?" Suzanne asked.

"*No*!" Toni said, letting a giggle slip.

"Ugh, you can tell you've never lived in a city. I'll give you my rape alarm, but not my Mace. I'd feel very vulnerable without some form of protection."

"What about Anthony? He looks as though he could wrestle a grizzly bear and win."

"True, but he's not always with me."

"Okay, I'll take your alarm," Toni said, shaking her head and muttering. Then she suddenly remembered about the homeless in the car park, and how easily they had jarred her. *It wouldn't have taken them much to get me to ground. To hurt me. To beat or rape me*, she thought.

"Are you okay?" Suzanne asked.

"Hm?! Oh, yeah, fine. I was just wondering what I was going to wear."

"Ah, okay. I'll be right back. Just get you that alarm." Suzanne left the room. When she came back she gave Toni the small piece of technology, which looked lost in the palm of her hand. "Put it in your handbag. Hopefully, you'll *never* need it!"

"*Hopefully*…Anyway, what were you doing listening outside my door?"

"What do you mean?"

"You must have been pretty close to the door to know what I was saying on the phone."

"Huh? Oh, yeah…Of course!" Suzanne slapped her head. "*Dur*! Karen and Amy are home – they've invited us up for drinks and Mexican food."

"Oh, man – an all-day thing?"

"Well, from around three-ish."

"Damn! Can't they have it tomorrow night instead?"

"Ha-ha, I'll ask them to put it on hold just because you have a fire in your panties!" she said, winking at Toni.

"*Suzanne*!"

"Truth, isn't it? Besides, I'm sure there will be plenty of time to eat crap and get drunk with our bitches upstairs."

"Damn right! Tell them I'm sorry for not making it."

"Will do," Suzanne said, looking at her watch. "Oo, I better get my arse in gear. I have a few things to do before I can get upstairs to them."

"Okay."

"Do you mind if I use the shower first?"

"No, not at all. I'm not meeting Simone until eight, so I won't start getting ready until you've gone," Toni said.

"Cool."

"You wouldn't have been able to look after me tonight, anyway…" Toni said, sounding a little wounded.

"Hell, I would have told them no had you wanted me to go with you, toots. Since you don't, I'm off to get blasted!" Suzanne winked at her and left the room.

After her conversation with Suzanne, Toni had gone downstairs to make herself something to eat before heading back to her room to hit the books. Finally getting tired of reading, Toni flopped onto her bed to watch a bit of crap TV.

Throughout the day, Suzanne had popped back and forth to chat until she eventually left for the evening at ten-to-three. Once the flat was empty, Toni decided to make a shift herself. She'd decided she was going to make herself look amazing for Simone. At first, she'd thought about throwing on a pair of jeans and a T-shirt. *After all, that's what Simone had said he would be wearing. Why be different?*

But as the day had worn on, Toni had decided against it. She was going to dress smart for him. *Maybe give him a little thrill*, she thought, giggling.

As she got up to go to the bathroom, her phone buzzed. It was Simone. *'I'm very much looking forward to meeting with you later.'*

This made her smile. *'I feel the exact same way, Simone. It's going to be a laugh!'* she replied.

Putting her mobile back on the bed, Toni left for the bathroom. Once there, she started the bath and used the toilet. Going back to her bedroom, she stripped and removed her towel from off the radiator. She also grabbed her mobile and took it with her.

Knocking the hot tap off, she turned the cold to a trickle. "Suzanne?!" she called, making sure the flat was empty before she ran downstairs to pour herself a glass of chilled wine. Taking it to the bathroom, she locked the door. Putting the glass down by the side of the bath, along with her phone, Toni stepped into the soapy water. After sitting, she leaned against the back of the bath and slid under the water. "Ahh!" she gasped.

After finishing her wine, completing a volley of texts with Simone, and washing, Toni decided it was time to get out of the bath. Her skin had wrinkled. "I look like a prune!" she laughed.

She wrapped her oversized towel around her glistening body and then stepped up to the mirror. She wiped the mist off the glass with the back of her hand. "Ah, gorgeous," she told herself. Her steel coloured eyes examined her lightly toned skin – her long black hair dangled in ringlets. "Such an innocent face!"

Turning from the mirror, she exited the room, which was engulfed in mist. Reaching her room, she towelled off and looked at her naked form in her full-length mirror. She'd never liked her body. She felt she was too thick around the legs and hips. That her bottom poked out too much for her stature.

Toni disliked her boobs, too. They were small. Too small for her liking. Even though she joked with Suzanne about her bust, Toni secretly envied her friend's breasts and figure.

"We've got what we've got, I suppose," she uttered to herself. *I could never go under the knife*, she thought. *Never.* The mere thought of it made her skin crawl. Beauty should be natural. *God, I hope Simone doesn't think I'm ugly…Or fat. Tut, what a thing to think! And if he does, he can do one. Stu obviously thinks there's something sexy about me.*

Turning from the mirror, Toni went to her chest-of-drawers and picked out clean underwear. Whilst there, she spotted her tights. *I bet Simone would love to see my legs in those,* she thought, taking them out of the drawer. After this, she picked a summer dress from the wardrobe, along with her leather jacket and a pair of boots.

Her phone buzzed again. Excitedly, she picked it up – it was a text from Stu: *'Hiya, I'm finishing early tonight and was wondering if you would like to do something?'*

"*Shit!*" she blurted. Toni had not planned on hearing from Stu this weekend. *What do I do? He knows I'm off…* So she typed, *'Hiya, Stu! I would love to do something today, but I'm not going to be around this weekend, sorry. I'm heading to my parents'. Maybe something in the week?'*

Before she could feel too guilty, Toni fired the message off. Putting her phone down, she started dressing. With her dress and tights on, Toni inspected herself in the mirror. "Does it show too much thigh?" she asked herself.

The butterflies were back.

"Sod it," she said, picking up her bag. She placed her phone inside before applying a few squirts of perfume to her neck and dress. With one more look in the mirror, she was satisfied, and so headed downstairs and out the front door.

After getting in her car, she drove the short drive to Porthcawl and parked along the front. It was ten minutes to eight o'clock. "Perfect," she said, getting out of her vehicle and locking it. As she crossed the road to get to the fairground, Toni couldn't quite get over just how busy it was. She knew it was going to be fairly active, what with it being the height of the season, but this was crazy.

The beach was full of families with small children. People could still be seen swimming in the sea, even though the light of day was fading fast. Packs of drunken men were gathered at the pub based at the foot of the beach. It was called The Cabin Bar; the type of place where you wiped your feet on the way out.

Making her way through the crowds, she felt threatened. Peak-season could be a right hassle. Often fights broke out due to too much sun and booze. A few men wolf-whistled and made a grab for her as she passed the Cabin Bar.

When the gates to the fair came into sight, she felt relieved. *I hope he's not going to stand me up*, she thought as she looked about for a man in a peaked hat, jeans and T-shirt. Nobody by the gates seemed to fit the description. *Hell, nobody in the area fits the description*, she thought, standing in front of the gates.

She looked at her watch. It was a couple of minutes-to. *I am early*, she thought. *But you really shouldn't keep a woman waiting – not a good start, Simone. Not a good start at all.*

Men were giving her looks as she stood and tried to wait for him patiently. The smell of popcorn, frying onions and burgers, sweets and ice cream filled her nostrils. This in turn made her tummy rumble. *Where are you, Simone? You're not coming, are you!*

"Hiya, love!"

Looking up, Toni was met by a gangly man. He had two friends with him – one of which was wearing a peaked hat, jeans and T-shirt. *Shit, I've walked into a trap*, she thought. Alarms bells started to sound. *Why has he done this to me?* "Simone?" she blurted. This caused the three youths to look at each other. They seem confused. *No, he can't be Simone.*

"What's your name 'en? Beautiful, is it?" Hat Boy barked.

"Sorry, look, I'm waiting for someone. I don't mean to be rude."

"Aw, oh cute – she doesn't mean to be *rude*, boys." This was uttered by the guy standing next to Hat Boy. He was disgusting, shirtless, and tattooed on his left pectoral muscle was a huge Swastika. When he smiled, Toni could see that half of his teeth were missing; what remained were yellow, chipped and broken. *A class act*, she thought.

"Well?" the lead guy asked. *He's the cutest of them all*, she thought wryly, with his black eye and crooked nose. His breath stank of onions and garlic.

"Well, what?"

"What's your name, cutie?" Black Eye said.

"Toni," she stammered.

"Woohoo!" Hat Boy piped in.

"Hell of a set of titties on her," Smashed Teeth said.

"Look, I told you – I'm waiting for someone," she said, trying to make her tone sound as strong as possible.

"A fella?" Black Eye asked.

She gulped. "Yes, my boyfriend."

"Oo," Smashed Teeth mocked. "I'm rattling like a bunch of leaves!"

"Ha-ha!" Hat Boy said. "Shouldn't that be *shaking* like a bunch of leaves?"

"Fuck-up, you pair!" Black Eye said. "So, where is this guy of yours? It's not nice, a man leaving his woman on her own. Anything could happen." He put his hand under her skirt.

"*Hey*!" she snapped, smacking his hand away. She couldn't believe how nobody was coming to her rescue. The men in the area ignored the scene. *What the hell?* she thought. *These lowlifes could be trying to rape me, and nobody would help…Rape! The alarm…*

"Oo, *feisty*!" Smashed Teeth said. "I like it when they stand their ground."

"Look, guys. Please! I'm not after trouble, okay. I'm just here to have a nice time with my boyfriend."

Black Eye leaned in closer. He belched his onion breath on her. "I think we should stick around. Meet the lucky fella. How about it, boys?"

"Yeah!" Hat Boy said. "We can give him a hardy handshake."

"Yeah, and a punch in the guts!" Smashed Teeth said.

"Sounds like the fellas want to stick around, *Toni*!"

"But…"

"But what?" Smashed Teeth said. "He'll kick our arses?"

"Let me guess, the come stain is a black belt in Karate?" Hat Boy said. "Maybe he'll do the Five-Fingered-Death-Punch on us all!"

"That's 'Five-Point-Palm-Exploding-Heart-Technique, dipshit!" Black Eye said. "Fucking dickheads, aye. But not like you, pretty girl." He brushed some of Toni's hair out of her face. "Precious," he uttered.

"Problem, guys?!" a new voice said.

It came from somewhere behind the three thugs standing in front of her, so Toni couldn't see who it was. The voice sounded familiar. It was smooth, and sexy.

She watched Hat Boy turn to face the new person. Smashed Teeth followed suit. Black Eye kept his beady eyes on her. "Not at all, pal!" Hat Boy said.

"Good," the new voice said, pushing his way through the goons.

God, he looks so handsome! Toni thought as Simone stepped around Black Eye and grabbed her hand. "And you are?" Simone asked Black Eye. He pretty much towered over the three yobs who, all of a sudden, shrank away.

"Ugh, we were just chatting to your lady!" he said. "Keeping her company until you arrived, like!"

Toni thought Black Eye was going to cry.

"That was very thoughtful of you boys," Simone said. "You can all fuck off now!"

They didn't need much encouragement to turn and leave. "Hi," he said, looking down at her. Her hand felt sweaty in his.

"Hi," she said, her face flushed. *This was definitely the right thing to do,* she reassured herself. *He's bloody gorgeous. And brave. What a white knight.*

"I'm so sorry for running late – the bus was behind schedule. It would have been quicker if I'd walked!"

"Late?" she said, totally oblivious to everything. "Oh, yeah…Don't worry about it! It's a nightmare here when the season's at its peak."

"Yes, too right. Would you like a bite to eat first? I'm rather peckish," he said.

"Oh, er…Yeah, I could go for something to nibble. Definitely. Maybe not too much, though. Especially if we plan to go on rides?"

"Rides? Yeah, too right. I love it down here. What would you like – hotdog? A beef burger?"

"I'd love a burger," she said, catching him looking at her legs. A tingle erupted through her pussy.

"Okay, cool. Come on, there's a cracking burger van inside the fairground."

She let herself be led as he pushed through the crowds of teenagers and parents with their children. Before she knew it, she was standing in front of the fast food van – its griddle smoked and spit as discs of meat bubbled and boiled on it. The smell was incredible. Her tummy groaned.

"Sounds like someone's hungry!" he said, chuckling.

"Gosh, I am sorry!"

"Don't be silly. It's cute." He turned to the man on the truck. "Two quarter-pounders and cheese, please. Would you like a drink and chips?" he asked her.

"Oh, just a drink, please. There's no need to pay…"

"*Sh*! This is my treat. Here," he said, handing Toni one of the burgers. "Bon appetit!"

"Thanks!" she said, taking the food and drink off him. As she tucked in, she made sure to take her time. She didn't want to come across piggish.

"How is it?" he asked.

"Mm, it's delicious!" she said, putting her hand to her mouth.

"Good. Would you like to ride the *Ghost Train* first? It's one of my favourites, I have to admit."

"I'd love to!" She grinned from ear-to-ear.

"Cool." He took hold of her hand once again.

She loved how confident he was, and how he knew what she wanted by holding her hand – but how did he know? The tingle in her pussy was back. She felt wetness inside her knickers. *God, I have to control myself!* she thought, being led into the queue for the *Ghost Train.*

"The last time I rode this ride was the night we spoke for the first time," he said, smiling.

"Do you want to talk about anything, Simone?"

"Not tonight. I want to forget and have fun. To let my hair down and go nuts," he said, arching his back and holding his hands to the sky.

She smiled, and then spied the bulge in his trousers. *Oh, my God!* she thought, stopping herself from gasping. *What is he doing to me? He's so charming and enthralling. I've never felt so attracted to a man so quickly.*

"Are you okay?" he asked. There was real concern in his eyes.

"Yes, of course. I was just thinking about the last time I was here. It's been a while."

"Next two, please!" the man running the *Ghost Train* yelled. "Come on, love birds!" he told Simone and Toni. "In ya get – I've not got all night, ya know!" he snapped.

They giggled as they boarded the small cart. It was shaped like a coffin. Without hesitation, he put his arm around her; drew her close to his chest. She allowed herself to be moulded like she was his play clay. Testing her luck, she pushed her knee against his.

She saw him look down, even though the sun was burning out of the sky. In the gloom, she could see the muscles in his jaw reacting. He liked it. *He likes it very much. You know you can touch me if you want*, she thought, not daring to say it aloud. *Maybe you're waiting for the darkness to engulf us?*

When the ride's worker pushed a button, it sent them on their way. Buzzers and beepers sounded as their cart pushed through a pair of black doors marked with a bio-hazard sign. Pyro machines burped cold air and smoke in their faces as they went. This caused Toni to shriek and laugh at the same time. She felt his grip tighten around her shoulders.

Soon enough, his other hand was on her knee. As their cart led them around the spooky maze, skeletons dropped from the ceiling, along with spiders, cob-webs and bugs. Water machines lightly squirted them, causing her to scream again.

He laughed.

When she felt his hand start to rise up to her thigh, she had no intention of stopping him.

Their cart pushed through the exit doors; day had turned to night. The colourful lights inside the fairground lit the sky, which was a backdrop to the howls, screams and screeches coming from the *Ghost Train* and other rides.

After the *Ghost Train*, Toni decided she wanted to ride the *Bumper Cars*, which was followed by the *Go-Karts* and *Magic Carpet*.

"Okay, my turn!" Simone said, feeling a bit giddy. "I say we ride *Beach Party* next!"

"Let's do it!" she said, winking at him. She couldn't remember the last time she'd had so much fun with a man. Stu was a great guy, but Simone was able to kick it up a few notches. He knew how to charm a woman. What to say. What to do.

After *Beach Party*, they decided to go for a drink. Whilst at a snack stand, Simone bought Toni some candyfloss. "Thanks, but you should let me pay for something, you know!"

"Honestly, it's fine. I'm feeling happy. I'm free, Toni. She no longer has a hold over me."

She smiled, and watched him dance with an invisible partner. "You're crazy!" she said.

"Maybe. Do you like that?"

She nodded. "What would you like to do next?"

"We could go to the arcades? See if I can win you something?"

"Yeah, okay. After that, how about a stroll down to the beach?" she asked, biting her lower lip. The wind flapped the hem of her skirt, causing it to reveal more thigh than a good girl should be willing to show.

It caught his attention. "Sounds good to me," he said.

Going over to the stalls, Simone tried his luck at shooting, darts, and throwing balls at tin cans. Nothing came up trumps. "Not got my eye in tonight!"

"Ha! Don't worry about it," she said, locking arms with him. "Take me to see the sea, Simone," she said, looking up at him.

"Okay," he said, smiling.

They watched from behind a couple of stalls. As soon as they saw them go over the dunes and down to the beach, Black Eye and his goons followed. "Come on boys – let's go and teach that fuck a harsh lesson in manners."

CHAPTER 20

When they got down to the sand, Toni was in awe of the moon – it looked massive in the cloudless sky. Its glow lit the whole beach. "Wow, it seems so close!"

"Do you really think there's a man on the moon?" Simone asked, smiling.

This caused her to giggle. "Of course!"

"Ha-ha! indeed there is.... Which way shall we walk?"

"Shall we stroll up to the old pier?" A look of panic seemed to wash over him. "Are you okay, Simone?"

"Huh?! Yeah, of course." His tone turned sharp.

"Are you sure?" she asked, gingerly.

"Yes. It's just that Chaos and I used to go up there. It's no big deal."

"Sure?"

"Of course."

"Good."

He caught her hand and strolled up the beach with her. "It's so relaxing, hearing the waves crash against the sand, rocks and each other. It's so calming."

"Agreed. But it's pretty creepy what happened here a few weeks ago, right?"

"The dog walker?" he asked.

"Yeah – plus, they still haven't found those girls…"

He shook his head. "Poor things."

"I'm sure you'll protect me, though?" she said, locking her arms around his.

"Of course!" he beamed.

As they approached the old pier, Toni suggested they sit on the rocks. "Come on, let's have a chat." Taking a seat, he asked her what she'd like to talk about. "How about us? Leave all the unhappiness out of this one!" she said.

"Sounds good to me. So, what about 'us'?"

"Well, we've been pretty close all night – holding hands and so on…"

"Yeah, we have."

"Come on, don't go all shy on me now!" She laughed.

"I'm not, honestly."

"So, what do we have? Are you just stringing me along, or do you want us to go somewhere? I have to admit, I was so scared about meeting you. After all, I don't really know anything about you. You could have tried hurting me. But I'm glad I took the risk. I really like you, Simone."

He smiled. "And I really like you, Toni. I definitely don't want this to be the first and last time we see each other!"

"Oh, I don't think that's going to happen," she said, leaning in to kiss him. When their lips locked, she felt his big hand on her knee. It slowly rose up her leg, between her thighs. There, his fingertips brushed her crotch.

She couldn't stop him – didn't want to. His heavy breathing down her ear got her hot, causing her to start gasping as their tongues collided into knots. Lovers' knots.

Following suit, she put her hand between his legs and slid it up the length of his inside leg. When she reached his bulge, a slight moan escaped her. A beat of electricity skipped through her G-spot.

"*Jesus*!" she gasped. Toni felt her face flush. Her body tensed as an immense orgasm tore through her.

"Am I hurting you?" he whispered.

"No!"

They continued kissing. She tugged at his belt and lowered his zipper. She felt the rub of his fingers against her crotch increase in speed. She cursed having put her tights on now, for he wouldn't be able to slip his fingers inside her, which she wanted.

"Wait!" She stopped him.

"What. Did I do something wrong?"

"No," she said, standing up. Just as she was about to take her boots off, someone yelled from behind them.

"Oi, lover boy!" Black Eye bellowed over the rolling waves. He walked out of the gloom, his dogs in tow.

"Oh, shit!" Toni said. "Come on, let's get out of here!"

"*Huh*?!" Simone said, turning to see the three thugs from earlier.

"Quick, come on!" she said.

"Oh, not leaving on our account?" Smashed Teeth asked.

"I think he's shit himself!" Hat Boy laughed. "He ain't so tough in the shadows."

"You got that right," Black Eye said, and pushed Simone as hard as he could in his chest.

This sent him tumbling backwards. His feet tangled in the sand, causing him to go to ground. Hat Boy and Smashed Teeth were on him like attack dogs – they rained punch after kick onto him.

Toni screamed.

Simone managed to roll onto his stomach and started crawling out of harm's way. The pain he could cope with. It was the cowardly three-on-one that pissed him off. It especially annoyed him when he saw the ringleader slap Toni across the face.

Then his hand grasped something in the sand.

On closer inspection, he saw it was a lump of driftwood – one end was stained red. *No, it can't be the same piece of wood?* he thought. *Unbelievable.* Stopping where he was, his fingers worked at the sand. They dug the timber free. When it was clutched tight in his hand, Simone flipped onto his back.

This caused Hat Boy and Smashed Teeth to stop. They looked down at Simone in shock.

"My fucking turn!" he growled. Crimson spittle flew from his bloodied mouth. In two swift moves, Simone smacked both guys in their ankles. They screamed in agony and hit the deck.

Simone pounced to his feet and clubbed them both about their heads, legs, arms, and bodies. When they started crying, he hit them harder, and worse still when their blood started spewing into the air.

"What the fuck are you *doing*?" Black Eye yelled.

When the goons on the sand were nothing more than a pile of moaning, writhing shapes, Simone turned his attention on the leader. "I'm not so tough in the shadows, huh?" he said, breathing in pulsating rips.

"I never said that!" Black Eye squeaked.

"Well, whichever one of you shitbags said it couldn't have been more wrong!" he said. "I thrive in the fucking shadows."

Black Eye put a hand down his boot and brought up a flick knife. The blade snapped into position. "Stay away or I'll open your throat!" he warned.

"What a fucking coward!" Simone threw the timber at the unsuspecting boy.

"*Argh*!" Black Eye squealed as the wood struck him in the face. He fell backwards, the knife sailing out of his hand.

Taking his chance, Simone lunged onto the downed man. He viciously head-butted Black Eye five, six, seven times, before digging his thumbs into his eyeballs.

"*Argh*! Please, get off me…Stop…" He bucked and thrashed beneath Simone, who felt the lad's crotch soak through.

Seeing the eyes bleed from their corners, Simone stopped. If he didn't, he'd kill him. Getting up, he gave Black Eye a few swift, yet very hard, kicks to his ribs.

"Touch her again and you're fucking dead. *Dead*!" he spat. Managing to stop himself, Simone bent over and put his hands to his knees. He tried to control his breathing.

"Jesus, Simone!" Toni said.

Slowly, he turned, and she pounced on him. They fell on top of Black Eye, who wasn't moving.

Feverishly, she undid his belt and pulled her tights down. Straddling him, Toni felt his cock push into her. Within minutes, a second orgasm ripped through her body, causing her to quiver, but she didn't stop. She continued to grind against him, causing not only Simone to moan but Black Eye too, as hers and Simone's weight crushed him to the sand. When she came for the third time, Simone also released his orgasm.

Exhausted, she collapsed onto his chest. "That was amazing," she panted.

All he could do was wheeze – it had been a very long time since anyone had fucked him like that. Rolling off him, Toni got to her feet. She couldn't understand how she didn't feel guilty or dirty. Had this been someone else, she would have called them a slut or dirty bitch. Not only that, but they had just fucked on top of a man who'd had the crap kicked out of him!

Had the situation been different, Toni would have laughed until her sides busted. But she didn't, because for all she knew Simone could have killed the three of them. None of them were moving. But she didn't care – she felt good. Alive, even. For as long as she could remember, all she had ever done was study and stay in. Had been a good girl. Had listened and not acted too recklessly.

It was Toni's moment to have a little fun, and time to stop thinking what others thought – she was going to be proud of her new man. She looked down at Simone, who was getting to his knees.

"I think we should get the hell out of here!" Simone said, giggling.

"What about these losers?!"

"Fuck 'em! And if they don't hurry up and shift their arses, then the tide will roll in and claim them. Do you hear me?" he yelled at the battered trio. He gave Hat Boy and Smashed Teeth a few kicks to their sides. Both groaned in response.

As they headed down the beach, Toni glanced back. She saw two shapes grab hold of the third. Hat Boy and Smashed Teeth were dragging their mate off the sands. She smiled. *My white knight*, she thought. *He's one in a million.*

CHAPTER 21

'*Hiya, Stu! I would love to have done something today, but I'm not going to be around this weekend, sorry. I'm heading to my parents'. Maybe something in the week?*' Looking at the text now, it made him angry.

Stu didn't believe a word of it. She was giving him the run-around, and he was on to her. *Visiting your parents? What a fucking lie!* he thought. He'd known something wasn't right at work. She'd been giving him the cold shoulder. The brush off.

You can tell when someone's being funny with you. A bit distant, he thought. *Besides, Anthony spilled his guts like a good mate, after Suzanne told him Toni was out seeing another guy tonight.* She'd also told Anthony to keep it quiet, but he'd gone straight to Stu.

Suzanne wasn't going to be too happy with Anthony when she found out, but like Anthony had said, "*She's a loose tart, only good for one thing: fucking.*"

He was a good friend.

He wouldn't let some sneaky little bitch fuck Stu around.

Make him look like a fool.

Now, sitting outside Toni's place, Stu had wished Anthony had come along. Together, they could have pulverised the fuck Toni had snuck out to see tonight.

Stu smiled.

Nah, I won't need him, he thought, putting his hands on the steering lock he had on his lap. *I'll break his jaw with this. See, if she had just been honest with me from the start, then none of this would be happening right now. Rejection I can take; being lied to I can't.*

And how many other times? She'd pushed away his advances a few times of late. *What a bitch*, he thought, looking out his window. No lights could be seen in the windows of Toni's and Suzanne's flat, but the flat above was aglow. *Getting drunk and having pillow fights, no doubt.* Anthony had told him that Suzanne had blown him out tonight, too, as she was going to a party in the flat above. "Women can be such cunts," he uttered.

Looking at his watch, he saw it was getting on for midnight, and still there was no sign of Toni. He couldn't have missed her, that's for sure. He'd been sitting outside her block of flats for almost three hours. *Where are you?*

Wait, what if she's decided to stay at that guy's house? No, no way, he convinced himself. She was too bashful for that kind of thing. But a voice at the back of Stu's head wouldn't leave the suggestion alone. She could have been lying about that, too.

Did she ever tell me if she was a virgin or not? Didn't she say she'd been with guys? He couldn't remember. The way she acted suggested she had not been with many men. If any.

Again, that could have been an act.

Look, when she gets here I'll have it out with her. Maybe let her date go home before tackling her? Yeah, that might be a good idea. I don't want to come across as psycho. Or jealous. No, I won't let it happen. I won't let a woman turn me into something I'm not. Once I've called her out on lying and messing me about, it's going to make her look small. Hopefully, she'll feel so bad she'll leave the job, too. There'll be no going back after this, he thought, gripping the wheel lock that had Halfords written across it. Loosening his hand from around the bar, Stu put it on the passenger seat by his side. There was no way he could hurt Toni.

I'm just going to sit and wait for her and her fella to part company before challenging her. It's definitely the best way to go about things. With his hand free, he picked his mobile up. He opened his messages and went to hers: '*Hiya, Stu! I would love to have done something today, but I'm not going to be around this weekend, sorry. I'm heading to my parents'. Maybe something in the week?*'

"Bitch! *Why*?" he spat. *I would have treated you like a queen, had you given me the chance.* He wiped his wet eyes – fat tears rolled down his cheeks. *No, she's not worth it.* He decided to respond to her text: '*Hey, sorry it's taken me so long to reply – no problem. Maybe we can do something next week? How does that sound?*'

Without a second thought, he fired the message off. *Let's see if she responds*, he thought, looking out the window again. He noticed the lights in the flat above go out. Then one came on in the flat below.

Party must be over, he thought, watching as more lights burst to life in that flat. *I could go up there? See what Suzanne has to say about it all – I could tell her I know. Or, try and get on her – make Toni jealous?*

He was about to get out of his car when his phone bleeped. *Oo, now that is a surprise*, he thought, picking his mobile up. The message was off Toni. *'Hey, I'm not really sure about next week, as I have a lot of Uni work to catch up on. Plus, I promised Suzanne I'd have a night out with her somewhere along the line. Sorry. See you at work on Monday?'*

"*Damn*!" he said, thumping the steering wheel. *Fuck this, man. I should just tell her I know she's out with another guy, and that it's no big deal. What am I doing, sneaking around? I'm like some sort of saddo. It's not like we were even an item.*

Throwing his phone onto the passenger seat, which bounced off the wheel lock, Stu put his car key into the ignition. The engine kicked to life with one turn. As he adjusted the rear-view mirror, he saw two figures emerge from the shadows behind. From their shapes and sizes, he guessed one was a man. The other, who was much smaller, had to be a girl.

He killed the engine and slithered down his seat. Stu was pretty sure he couldn't be seen – he'd parked on the opposite side of the street to her flat, and there was no reason for her to cross the road.

As long as he remained ducked out of sight, then he would be fine.

When their voices and laughter grew closer, Stu risked a peek. It was definitely Toni and her fella. *He looks like a right creep*, he thought, putting his hand out to touch the wheel lock. *No, I won't need that. Although, I doubt I could take him if things got hairy*, he admitted. *A big bastard.*

When their shadows passed his car, Stu slid up in his seat. He wound his window down slightly to find out if he could pick up on any of their conversation, as they were talking rather loud.

"I had a wonderful evening, Simone," Toni said. "Will I get to see you again?"

"I was rather hoping you would come to mine tomorrow night – I was going to cook for you."

"Oh, that sounds great!"

"Lovely. So it's a date?"

"Definitely," she said. "I hope you don't think badly of me after what happened down on the sand. I don't normally do *things* like that, only having known someone a short amount of time."

"Hey, there's no need to worry about it, Toni. I have to admit, I really like you. I'm not sure I've ever felt so strongly about a woman before.

This is pretty special. From that first time we spoke on the phone, I knew I liked you. A lot. It might sound crazy, but it's true."

"Oh, Simone! You're so sweet. And, if I'm going to be totally upfront and honest with you, and myself, then I felt the same. I haven't been able to get you out of my head, Simone. Not at all."

When it fell silent, Stu peeped over the steering wheel and felt his blood reach boiling point – he watched them kiss outside the door to her flat.

"She's nothing but a tramp!" he uttered. *Let's just get the hell out of here. Leave whilst I still have some dignity.* But he couldn't. He felt compelled to watch on. Then it struck him – *On the phone? She met him over the phone at work*?! *Oh, fuck. She's in such shit,* he thought. He then scooted back down to listen as they started talking again.

"I'm glad you feel that way, too."

"Are you sure you won't come in for a coffee?" she asked.

"No, I need to restrain myself!"

"How about a lift? I hate the thought of you catching one of the late buses home, Simone."

"You don't have to worry about me. Besides, look at how far you've had to park from your flat. No, I won't drag you out again."

"Okay, if you're sure."

"I am. Besides, you'll see me tomorrow. I'll come by early and pick you up, okay?"

"Sounds good!"

"Great! Now, go inside," he told her.

When it fell quiet again, Stu poked his head up. He watched as Toni went indoors and waved her fella off. After the new guy had walked by his car, Stu got out and went to Toni's front door.

He knocked four times before it was answered.

"Forget something?" she asked, opening the door.

He smiled as her face turned. "What, no smiles for *me*?" he asked.

"Oh, God – *Stu*!"

"The one and only!"

"What are you doing here?"

"Funny, I could ask you the same thing?!"

"But…I told you I was away."

"That's right, you did, didn't you? Well, Suzanne told Anthony what your real plans were this evening, who then came back and told me."

"Oh, Suzanne!" she blasted.

"You can't blame her for this, Toni! I thought you liked me. I didn't realise you were giving me the run-around."

"Stu, I'm sorry – I didn't mean for this to happen. I honestly didn't…"

Before she could finish, he called her out on Simone. "You met that guy over the phone at work? You know that's against the policy – you'll never work on the phone for such an organisation ever again."

"Oh, Stu – you can't go telling anyone. Please. I'm begging you!"

"Why? You've pretty much made me look like an idiot. Anthony probably thinks I'm a fool, too!"

"I'm sure he doesn't. And I told you, I didn't mean for this to happen – it's not like you and I were seeing each other, Stu!"

"*Huh*!" he huffed, shaking his head. "I thought you really liked me, Toni, you know? I felt like shit, hearing you'd gone out with someone else."

"I'm sorry. I should have been honest. Really, I'm *sorry*!"

"It's okay. I'm acting like a love-sick puppy."

"Look, why don't you come in for a bit. Have a cuppa?" she said, giving his arm a rub.

He looked up at her. "I'd like that."

"Okay. We can talk things through."

"Sounds good."

"Come here," she said, giving him a hug. "I didn't mean to hurt you." Releasing him, she stepped aside and let him cross the threshold. Before she closed the door, she looked up and down the street. It was deserted.

From the shadows, Simone watched. The muscles in his jaw ached. His hands balled into fists. A twitch developed in his left eye, and the veins in his neck throbbed and protruded.

"*Motherfuckers*!" he yelled. "So, it's like that, is it? Another woman with a hungry fucking pussy. She's no better than Chaos. Well, I'm going to fucking fix this fucking problem too." Turning, he rushed down the street and hopped on a bus that was pulling in.

On the ride home, all he could think about was 'fixing' them.

CHAPTER 22

When he arrived at his house, Simone flipped out. He walked into the kitchen and swiped all the dishes, cups and glasses off the draining board with relish. The sound of breaking china fuelled his rage and destruction.

He yanked cupboard doors and drawers open, only to hurl the contents across the kitchen. More china broke – cutlery clattered to the floor in copious amounts. "Fucking *bastards*! I'll *fucking* murder them!" he bellowed while flinging stuff across the room.

Finished in the kitchen, he stalked into the living room and put his booted foot through the TV screen, and then upended the coffee table – he snapped the legs off it and used one to club the walls, furniture, ornaments and anything else he laid his eyes on.

"*Argh*!" he raged, stomping into the hallway. There, he put the table leg through the huge mirror that clung to the wall. After one smack, it caved, causing a shower of glass to rain down onto the carpet.

He passed the hallway phone on his way to the stairs and clubbed it to smithereens. He laughed as particles of plastic bounced off his face and nicked his flesh. "Bastards, bastards, *bastards*!" he yelled as he did it.

Simone ran upstairs and let rip on Chaos' bedroom furniture, before shredding all her clothes and destroying her arsenal. Spent, he collapsed onto the bed. His breathing came in jarring rips as he tried to regain control over himself.

"What do I do?" he screamed.

"*Come on, sir – we all know what you have to do!*" Mr. Tickles said.

Sitting up, Simone looked for his clown. "Where are you?"

"*I'm downstairs, sir. In the living room.*"

Simone rolled off the bed and ran downstairs. His clown was sitting on one of the living room chairs. "I never saw you there."

"You were pretty pissed, sir?"

"She broke my heart, Mr. Tickles. She lied. She's a filthy, dirty fucking whore! I was having thoughts of sparing her, but not now. *Never.*"

"What did the cunt do?"

"As soon as my back was turned, she had another cock in her house."

"Ah, the dirty fuck! Well, she's going to have to go the way of Chaos..."

"Either that, or..." Simone said, thinking things through in his head. He then whispered in the clown's ear. "What do you think?"

"I think I just shot in my pants – it's a brilliant idea!"

Simone smiled. "I'm going to go and prepare myself. I need to get out of here in the next hour if I'm going to pull it off, Mr. Tickles."

"Agreed. I'm looking forward to this one!"

"Me, too..." Simone said, letting his words trail off. Walking out of the living room, Simone headed upstairs to shower.

After thirty minutes of prepping, Simone was ready to leave the house. He checked the time. It was gone two. "Perfect. They should all be sleeping by now," he uttered.

He dressed in a pair of black jeans with matching T-shirt. On his back was a holdall in which he put Mr. Tickles. "I'll let you out once we get there."

"Okay, sir."

Simone stepped out of the house and made sure the street was deserted before he started walking. With no buses or trains running at this hour, Simone was forced to walk the six miles to Toni's flat. He was more than sure he could find her street again. After all, he'd memorised the name and location.

He knew he'd be returning, but didn't think it would be this soon.

Simone was careful to take back roads and lanes where he could. The fewer people who spotted him the better. He had thought about hailing a taxi at one point, but realised it would be a dangerous thing to do, as the driver would know his face.

No mistakes could be made.

Simone had to be calculated, not to mention ruthless.

The weight in his backpack made him smile.

It took him just under two hours to make it back to her flat. Like his street, hers was empty. It pleased him. The lights were out in the flats.

"Excellent," he muttered, sneaking around to the back of the students' accommodation. He made sure nobody had their eyes on him. Once at the rear of the building, Simone walked up to the back door and tried the handle. It was locked.

He smiled and took his bag off his back and unzipped it. Putting his hand inside, he dug out his balaclava along with the utility belt he had removed from his tool kit. He slipped both items on.

He then removed a cordless drill, the battery pack full. Simone put the slender drill bit to the door's lock and started the tool, which made a minimum amount of noise. Once he'd drilled through it, the handle came apart. He heard it hit the floor on the other side of the door with a faint thud. He then replaced the power tool and carried his bag into the house.

Simone took the small torch off his belt and lit it. He was in the kitchen. He swept his beam around the room and found keys on the table. He went and pocketed them. They were Toni's. He recognised the Samaritans fob dangling from one of the rings.

"Brilliant," he whispered. "They're going to come in handy." Even though Simone didn't own a car or driver's licence, he could drive. He carefully made his way into the living room and found the bloke he'd seen Toni with sleeping on the sofa.

Not yet, he told himself.

He went to the stairs and made his way up. There were three rooms on this floor. He could see one was a bathroom, as the door stood open. Walking along the landing, Simone made his way to the second flight of stairs that led to the flats above.

When he came to a locked door, Simone again used his drill to break the lock. He snuck in and found a long passageway that led to a kitchen and living room – there was another set of steps. He took them. When he reached the top, he was faced with three doors. He went to the first that was slightly ajar. Edging it open as quietly as he could, Simone peeked inside.

It was a bedroom.

He stepped in and quietly closed the door. Using his light on a dim setting, he saw someone sleeping in their bed. Killing the torch, he put it back on his belt and removed the hammer. With stealth, he walked up to the person and pummelled their head with the heavy-duty tool. They didn't as much squeak. Breathless, he pulled his balaclava off and put the hammer back on his belt. He then straddled the person and put his hands around their neck to squeeze any remaining life from them. After a few minutes, he got off them.

Simone was panting like a dog as he reached for the lamp in the room and switched it on. Turning, he saw the girl for the first time. He'd caved her head in. She didn't move.

Her blonde hair was plastered in blood – her skull had come apart like an Easter egg. Bone and brain matter had sprayed her walls, headboard and bed sheets. Without an ounce of remorse, Simone threw her bedding to one side.

She was naked.

This instantly turned him on – had he not been in a rush, he would have had his fun with her cooling body. But he couldn't. Not only that, he didn't want to leave any form of DNA.

Instead, he took a lock of her hair.

Bagging it, he knocked the lamp off and left the room. He closed the door behind him. Walking across the landing, Simone went to the next door along that was also ajar. Pushing it wide, he saw a bathroom lay beyond.

Leaving it behind, he went to the next door, which was closed. Opening it, he stepped inside and put his light on. The girl in the bed stirred. Before she had chance to open her eyes, Simone caved her head in with his hammer and then strangled her, too.

This one doesn't look as cute, he thought.

Nevertheless, he took a lock of her hair also.

Before stepping into the kitchen downstairs, Simone had made sure to wear gloves.

After checking the rest of this flat, Simone was satisfied that it was empty, and could move on. He felt pleased with himself as he headed back downstairs. Once again, he was in Toni's flat. As he stood in the hallway, he heard a noise coming from the bathroom. "*Shit*," he muttered. When he heard the toilet flush, Simone walked back up the stairs he had come down.

The hallway light flicked on. His heart raced.

"Shit," he muttered again.

The light went out.

He gave it ten minutes, and then appeared on the landing again. The bathroom door was now open. Crossing to it, he made sure there was nobody inside. Then he heard the guy downstairs as he settled himself back on the sofa. Simone smiled and crept downstairs. *Taking him out next makes sense*, he thought. *Eliminate the biggest threat. Let's go and introduce ourselves, Mr. Tickles…* The clown remained within the backpack.

Peeping through the banisters, Simone could see the guy – he seemed to be still. He stood and waited on the stairs. He gave it as long as possible before creeping down the remaining stairs.

Simone towered over the sleeping man and felt a rush of power. Taking his hammer and torch off his belt, he shone his light in the guy's face, causing him to wake instantly.

"What the fuck?!" he gasped.

"Mess with my girl, will you?!" Simone said, bringing the hammer down on Stu's face – blood sprayed him. Bits of teeth and bone pinged off his face, floor and walls. Simone sniggered as he repeatedly hammered away. He didn't stop until the smacking sounds became wet and sloppy. Looking at his handiwork, Simone felt the urge to pull his cock out and masturbate. *How nice would it be to jizz into that bloody, pulpy crater*? he thought.

"Stu?" a voice called from upstairs. A light popped on.

Rapidly, Simone put his balaclava back on and rushed out into the kitchen. He heard footfalls on the steps. "Stu?" the voice came again. "Did I hear you?!"

Gripping the hammer tight in his hand, Simone readied himself.

"*Stu*?!" The living room light exploded to life. "Stu?" the girl said – it sounded quizzical to Simone. He smiled and peeped around the kitchen door. Simone could see Toni's roommate standing by the back of the sofa.

Her hands covered her mouth. "Oh, God…" she whispered.

Before she could yell to Toni, Simone rushed her. She turned and saw him coming, but failed to scream in time. He rugby tackled her, his shoulder ploughing hard into her guts. All her air whooshed out of her.

They crashed to the floor, and Simone put his hands around her neck. His thumbs pressed against her windpipe. She thrashed against him, his cock getting hard. As life drained from her, come filled his pants, causing him to buck.

When she was still, Simone drew his hammer.

He needed to make sure the job was complete.

Suzanne's head was split apart like a sliced-open Christmas turkey. The sight pleased Simone, who left the dead girl to go and claim his prize. Outside Toni's bedroom door, he took his backpack off. He removed a cloth and the bottle of chloroform. He drenched the rag in knockout juice, and then entered Toni's room.

She was sleeping.

Taking no chance he rushed to her and clamped the cloth to her face. "Shh-shh!" Simone said as she struggled and fought. Soon enough, she succumbed to the chloroform.

After loading Toni into her car and taking a trophy from Suzanne, he set the flats ablaze. Simone jumped into Toni's car and headed for home.

When she came around, Toni's vision was blurred. She tried to sit up, but realized she was strapped to a table, her legs tied to stirrups. Her hands cuffed. "Help..." she panted, not able to muster the energy to shout. "What..." she slurred. She felt light-headed. "Where...Hello...?" Her voice was barely a whisper. "Anyone...Help...Please..."

Putting her head back down, she found it helped the dizzying feeling. Then something caught the corner of her eye. When she turned her head, she saw a clown sitting atop a workbench. By its side were two action figures. They looked like G.I. Joe soldiers. Panic washed over her.

"Simone..." she whispered. "*Simone*?" she called, her voice gathering strength. "What have you done?!"

Listening, she heard nothing. *Where is he*? she thought. Tears gathered at the corners of her eyes. Then his voice boomed.

"I thought you wanted me?"

"Wha...*What*?!"

"As soon as I turned my back, you had another man in your arms; in your flat. What was I supposed to think?" he roared.

"No, that's a friend. Stu is a *friend*. Where *are* my friends?!" she gasped.

"Oh, they're just fine..." he lied.

"Where are you, Simone? Please, let me up. We have something *special*!"

"Well, we did!"

"Please, Stu is just a friend. Nothing else!"

"*Cut her fucking head off!*" Mr. Tickles said.

"*Chop the bitch up for fish food*," one of the G.I.'s said.

"You cut me deep, Toni."

"But...?"

"There'll be no buts here," he said, stepping out of the gloom. He stood over her, naked. Her lungs almost tore asunder when she realised he was wearing Suzanne's face as a mask – his tongue rolled around the lips.

"Fuck, fuck, *fuck*..." she gasped.

“Yes. Fun, isn’t it?” he said, picking up his saw. “Time to add you to my collection, Toni.”

“Oh…” she gasped, seeing the blood-spattered cutting tool.

“What’s the matter? Don’t you want to play?”

“Please…” she whined.

He put the saw to her right ankle. “Don’t worry. I’m not going to kill you. I just don’t want my new plaything running away. My new wind-up toy,” he said, starting to hack through her foot…

CHAOS RISING

Men: childish, whiny fucks that need constant attention and are only able to think with their dicks. Their small, miserable dicks at that – even if they do have an ample supply of inches between their legs, it's still not good enough. In the grand scheme of things, their love-truncheon is a minuscule, man-made sex tool that's only good for being cut off and consumed by a Big. Rabid. Dog.

They are a weak, pathetic species that need constant reassurance. Just like a dog with its owner, a man will look for praise. To see if they have pleased you, their woman. If they possessed a tail, they would tuck it between their legs and cover their nuts when they knew they were in the wrong.

But not women. We are proud, strong and able to fend for ourselves. We don't need comfort. We are feline, and can survive anything life throws at us.

We don't break like little China dolls.

Our emotions are strong. Firm.

"Please…" came his plea, breaking her chain of thought as she stood over him, watching him cry. His body shook.

We may weep, us women, but we never let them *see us. We never show our weakness.*

Not like men, or this pathetic piece of shit before me…All he *wants is love. To be respected as a man, lover and slave.*

Well, fuck that!

And fuck him!

Looking down, she eyed the shoes she wore – high-heels. However, they weren't your average pair of heels. These had been designed for her, with steel toecaps.

They gleamed.

Chaos liked the way the bedroom light glinted off them.

So pretty.

"*Arrgh*!" she screamed without warning, lashing out – her toes connected with the jaw of the man who had been sniffling at her feet. He reeled. Flecks of blood splattered her 'pretty' shoes.

Droplets also splashed up her legs, which were clad in white stockings – the type of stockings that needed no support from a suspender belt. The stockings clung to her legs and stopped beneath her arse cheeks.

Her nipples hardened at her sudden outburst.

She *click-clacked* a few steps forward, and gave her Slave another kick. This time, her toes punched into his soft, fleshy throat. A choking sound ensued. He collapsed to the floor. Both of his hands wrapped around his neck, as if holding the hurt would ease it.

"You made a mess of my pretty shoes and stockings, *pig*!" she yelled. She waited for her 'pig' to get to all fours before planting a robust kick between his legs.

She giggled on hearing him gasp, then howl, before slamming against the floor again. Stepping closer, she placed one spiked heel on his back and raked it down to his buttocks.

He screamed, but didn't ask her to stop.

Filthy cunt, she thought, smiling. Placing a hand to her pussy, she could feel how wet she was; juice dripped from her folds. Shivering, she clamped her teeth together as hard as she could. *I bet he's dying to stick his tongue in there. Well, he's not going to get the chance. Not now, not ever.*

He's blown his fucking opportunity with me. I'll break him so hard, he won't be fit for anyone else!

He rolled onto his back and she stamped on his nuts once, twice, three times – she smiled as he tucked himself into a protective ball.

"Please, Mistress…*Enough*!"

"Are you back-chatting me, pig?!"

Before he could reply, she kicked him half-a-dozen times in his ribs, before circling him like a vulture. In her hand, she had a length of chain. It rattled along the floor behind her as she stalked him.

"No…" he finally gasped.

Her face contorted into rage as she flicked her wrist, sending the chain whistling through the air. When it struck his flesh, he straightened like a poker, exposing the rest of his body to her wrath.

Without rest, she continued to whip his body until chunks of flesh came away with the chain. Where his skin remained intact, bruised lumps raised immediately from the brutal impacts.

Blood spewed from gashes and painted the chain links red. Some even splattered her naked body and made-up face. Blood even managed to coat her teeth.

When she stopped her frenzied beating to catch her breath, she ran her tongue over her teeth and savoured the metallic taste. "Mm-mm!" she groaned, letting her free hand slip between her legs. Chaos inserted a finger into her pussy. "You taste divine, dear!" she said, letting out an almost maniacal laugh.

As she stood there, enjoying the feel of her fingers, her Slave started to drag himself away from her. "There's no safe zone, dear!" she warbled, unable to stop pleasuring herself as she watched him continue to drag his bloody body into a dark corner.

"Are you trying to find your cage?" she said between clenched teeth. Chaos could feel an orgasm building rapidly. "You're heading in the wrong direction if…" Unable to finish her sentence due to a bout of gasps, Chaos kept rubbing a finger against her G-spot.

She bit her lip as her body quivered.

The chain fell from her gloved hand.

"Oh, God!" she screamed, collapsing to her bed. Lifting her head, she kept an eye on him. Not only did she want to make sure he didn't turn on her when she was unable to defend herself, but she liked seeing his broken, bloodied body. It aided in her orgasms, which came in waves.

With her free hand, she gripped the bedding and bunched it in her fist. Her face and neck flushed.

Chaos kept her eyes open – her Slave had managed to get into a corner, where he sat watching. She could see the whites of his eyes. The rest of him was a mere silhouette, but she knew he was stroking his cock due to his short, raspy breathing.

"You like this, don't you, pig-bastard?!"

She heard him groan, causing her to smile. Another orgasm washed over her, keeping her pinned to her bed. When she could take no more, her legs began to tremble, and she removed her hand.

Chaos kept still, but never took her eyes off him. "You stay there and be a good boy!" she said in the most condescending of tones before smiling and winking at him.

The control she had over him, and any man she came into contact with, was beyond exhilarating. They were her little playthings. She wasn't interested in giving them any pleasure, or allowing them to milk their cocks via her cunt. No. They did all the providing, whether it was with their tongue, fingers, or by being a punching bag for her whips, chains and other toys of pain.

It was fun.

They lived to serve her pleasure.

It was as plain and simple as that. And when she got bored, she got rid of them.

But not this Slave, no…You've been at my heel for a number of years now, haven't you! she thought, squinting at him.

The strong tremors that had rocked her body so strongly only moments before were now subsiding. Her legs, arms and hands had stopped shaking, and she could talk without a warble in her throat.

"Why do you stay, Slave? It's not like it used to be! You've outlasted your purpose."

Silence.

Slave was too busy wanking and keeping a watchful eye over her.

"Leave it alone and answer me!" she demanded.

"I love you, Mistress…I have for a long time," he confessed from the shadows.

"*Love*?!" she screamed, rolling off the bed and springing to her feet, cat-like. Turning, she searched the floor frantically. When her eyes fell on the chain, she snatched it up and lurched over to him. "Love, you say?! You fucking pathetic piece of shit! If that's the case, I can strongly confirm that it's always been one-way traffic, slave-maggot!"

Chaos retracted the chain and again started to thrash her Slave. Only this time, she caught him about the head and face until it was unrecognisable from blood and bruising.

"I will break you, Simone. And if I don't, I will end up killing you from beatings! You will never, ever be allowed near this body ever again. You're lower than low to me, pig," she yelled until her throat burned. "Do you hear me?!"

"What did I ever do to you but be a good, loving slave?!" he asked. Bloodied saliva drooled from his mouth and pooled on the floor.

"Nothing!" she said, laughing. "I've just become bored. Bored of how happy and eager you always are. That you seem rather content on going on satisfying me without begging for any attention – you could have changed me, possibly, had you been a bit more forceful. Had you been more of a man with me. Maybe I too could have loved you, but not now, worm." Her tone was pure vehemence.

As she screamed words at him, Chaos continued to beat him like a dog, until he fell unconscious.

"Get up! You can't quit on me until I say so, you fuck! Up!" she bellowed, fearing she would tear something in her throat. When he didn't move, she reverted to kicking him in his ribs, arms and legs.

Finally, breathless, Chaos collapsed back onto her bed. "Fucking worm!" she gasped, holding her sides. Taking deep breaths, she tried to regain control over her breathing. "Easy. Take it easy," she wheezed. It had been a long time since she'd beaten him so badly.

The fucking bastard deserved it, she thought, not daring to try and speak until she was breathing normally. *I mean it, I will kill the cunt if he doesn't break, and fuck off soon. Why won't he just go?! I could always throw him out. It's my house…No, I can't. That would be too easy. Also, it would be a sign of weakness, and I can't allow that. No man has ever pushed me to my limit, damn it.*

When she heard him groan, she sat bolt upright.

"Impossible!" she said, looking over to Simone. His head was moving; so too were his limbs. "I beat him cold…"

Her words trailed off as she watched in awe.

Shit, I can't beat him any harder! He's beyond human…No man has ever managed to shrug off my brutality before.

When Simone rolled onto his back, she noticed his cock was semi-hard – it couldn't grow to its full potential, as he was wearing his male chastity device. She seldom allowed him out of it these days.

When he 'wanked', as he had been doing a few moments ago, he had to flop it from side to side in order to get any form of pleasure. It never resulted in an orgasm.

His bollocks must weigh a ton with all that come he's stored!

Chaos rolled onto her side and got off her bed. All the while, she kept her eye trained on his pleading erection.

"Oh, poor baby!" she giggled.

Before going to him, Chaos walked to the other side of the room and opened the door to his cage – it had been specially built and resembled a doghouse with a door.

Inside, he had a bed, blanket and bowl for water.

In all the years they had been together, she had only recently started using the home.

She also had an actual dog bed for him, which she kept by the radiator in her room. But he had not been allowed to use that in quite some time. That was for when he was a good boy, or when she was pleased with him. He may have been a good boy, always had been, but she was not pleased with him. She despised him.

"If you're awake and moving, I suggest you crawl into your home before I beat you some more. Once you've recovered, I'll be unleashing more torture on you, Slave. Mistress has a lot of nasty little surprises up her sleeve for her eager pet."

"*Ugh*…!" he groaned, getting to all fours. His caged cock pin-balled between his thighs as he began his slow crawl towards her. Thick liquorice strings of bloody saliva dribbled from him and dragged along the floor as he went.

"You're making a mess on my floor!" she screeched, and marched over to him. She kicked his arms from under him. His face connecting with the floor in a sickening way caused a smile to briefly flicker over her face. "Lick it up!"

"But…"

"Now, you worthless piece of fucking dog shit!" she said, putting a foot to the back of his head and forcing his face down as far as she could. "Come on, where's that tongue of yours, Slave?"

"Please…Mistress, I beg…."

"Lick, damn you!"

Simone presented his tongue and started lapping at the crimson saliva about him.

"Good, good. Oops, you missed a bit. There, look – there!" she demanded, pointing behind him. "Get every last bit up."

Happy with him, Chaos let him continue his slow crawl to his cage. It was pitiful to watch.

"Can't you move faster?" She walked to her bed and picked up the barbed crop that lay on her bedside table. *This will get him shuffling!*

Returning to Simone, she positioned herself behind him and swung the crop like a golf club.

"*Move*!" She cut the short, stiff whip through the air, which smacked him across the left arse cheek. The barbs clung to his flesh and created shallow culverts that bubbled red when ripped out.

"*Argh*!" he screamed.

"I said move!" She cracked him across the same buttock again – the barbs almost homed in on the same spot.

"Please, Mistress…I'm crawling as fast as I…"

His words were cut short as she whacked him again and again in the same spot – his semi-hard cock had all but shrivelled, like a tortoise retracting into its shell.

"You're not going quick enough, you fucking worm." She again attacked him, causing him to shriek in pain.

As he approached the entrance to his cage, Simone collapsed once again.

"For fuck's sake, get up! Some of us want to get to sleep tonight."

"I…I…Can't!" he gasped. "My body…"

"I don't give a flying fuck! You get in there this instant, or God help me I will kick you about this room. Do you hear me?!" she asked, stepping on his hand with her heel.

"*Ugh*! Yes…" he grizzled, again getting to all fours.

When his head disappeared into the cage, she put a foot to his abused arse cheek, and pushed him forward.

"In!" she bellowed, throwing the door closed behind him. Bending over, she looked at him through the bars. He barely had enough room to turn over, and standing was impossible. If he wanted to, Simone could get to his knees, but he would have to stoop. "Comfy, dog?!" she asked, smiling and then laughing.

"What's the matter, cat got your tongue?" she asked, watching his unmoving form.

"No, Mistress…"

"Does it hurt, does it hurt?" she mocked.

"No, Mistress. Thanks for the beating and attention – I hope you'll come back and play with me soon."

His words enraged her. "You fucking cunt, Slave! You're going to be sorry you were ever born, when you are able to take more punishment."

"Thank you, Mistress."

"*Argh*!" she screamed, giving the bars on his cage door a whack with her crop. "You're going to pay, you fucking maggot. *Pay*!"

Simone didn't answer, but she thought she heard him laugh.

Deciding to let it go, she got to her feet and clicked the padlock into place. The key was on a chain around her neck. Next to that key was another for his cock cage.

"Sleep well, worm," she said. Her words were met by his soft snores. She gave the cage a kick before moving to her bed and slipping her shoes off. Sitting down, she rubbed her feet before removing her bloody stockings.

Chaos flopped onto her back and let her mind twist.

He is so fucking insubordinate these days. He knows, that's why. He knows I will never kick him out. That I will have to break him first. That's never going to happen. I've never seen a man take such punishment.

"Where did it all go wrong for me?" she whispered. "Could he have really changed me, had he been more of a man?"

Very possible…No, I doubt it. I've always loved having power over men. It's the only thing that gets me off and keeps me going in life. If I didn't have such an appetite for sex and dominance, then what would be the point?

Rolling onto her side, Chaos looked over at his cage.

If only…He's very attentive. He'd make a great lover and father…But no, it can never be, sadly. The bitch in me would never allow it, nor would I want it to. No. He has to go! I like men I can bend, mould and snap.

But why?

It's always been there…At least my childhood is not a sad cliché. I was born with a silver spoon in my mouth. My parents loved me, especially my father.

My father. Yes. God, I haven't thought of him in years. Being the cause of his death gave me the biggest orgasm of my life, and I was only thirteen…

****

From the moment she was born she was the apple of her father's eye. To say he loved her more than life itself would have been an understatement – he worshipped the ground she crawled, then later walked, upon.

Her father's love didn't go unnoticed or unreciprocated, as Chaos, christened Charlotte Ros, thought the world of him – or did, until she discovered his secrets. These things helped to change her view and feelings about her dad from a young age.

Gregory Ros, married to Katherine, was an astute, powerful and rich man with a lot of clout in both the business and political worlds. Born into poverty, Gregory left home when he was just twelve years old and made himself a fortune by the time he was twenty-five.

He bought and sold anything and everything until he'd made enough money to start investing in property. Before becoming rich, he'd told young Charlotte of how he used to sleep on the streets and pick waste food from bins, just to save a few pounds.

"Money's hard to come by – look after it, and it will look after you!" had been his words to her on a regular basis.

By the time he was thirty, Gregory's property retail company was the biggest in the country. He'd even started branching out abroad, with offices popping up in France, Spain, Germany, Greece and Italy.

The fortune he'd amassed by his thirty-fifth birthday was so huge that he could buy and sell pieces of land for fun. It was said that he had enough money in his bank account to buy a small to medium-sized country.

It was no lie, as Charlotte came to realise later in life.

She wanted for nothing as she grew up, and had spent a lot of her time moving around the country before her mother and father had settled in south Wales. When Charlotte turned seven, her father started involving her in his business, wanting her to follow in his footsteps.

At first, she'd been uninterested, but had been a bright girl and soon took a liking to the number-crunching and politics that went with buying and selling. She also took a shine to the power of being a boss, and having people work for her.

"Can I be there when you sack people today, Daddy?!" she'd asked Gregory one day.

He'd laughed and tousled her hair. "No, sweetie – that wouldn't make me a very good father!"

It disappointed her, but she'd got over it.

She wasn't like other girls growing up – she didn't play with dollies or skipping ropes or hula-hoops or prams or silly games. Charlotte was a proper daddy's girl, and loved being around him, his work, and his office.

"Don't you think it's unhealthy for her, Gregory?!" her mother had tackled him one day.

"Nonsense! I'm teaching the young lady economics, business and staff management," had been his argument.

Her mother had wanted a princess. A little girl she could bake cakes with and teach respectability to, and how to keep a home. However, she didn't fight her husband on it. After all, he was instilling in her a solid work ethic and numeracy skills. For her age, her arithmetic was beyond excellent, as were her social skills and vocabulary.

"I want her to have a better start at life than I did, Katherine!" Charlotte once heard him tell her mother.

As she got older, her father allowed her to watch him in action with his staff – how he would scorn and roast them before her, if the figures he wanted were not met every quarter.

"You're supposed to by my hit-team – my number ones. What the fuck am I paying you bunch of over-priced dickheads for?!" he would rant, which had firstly scared little Charlotte, but she soon found having power over people thrilling.

At first, she didn't know what it meant. The feeling gave her butterflies in her stomach. So too did the realisation of how much she liked to see people squirm under a watchful, dutiful eye like her dad's.

Every quarter, he'd fire someone just for the hell of it, which he turned into a sport by notifying his staff that someone would be going. He didn't care if they hadn't done anything wrong or not, or whether he got rid of someone loyal and hardworking.

He bought and sold people, just like he did property.

"The looks on their faces are priceless, Charlotte. I especially love it when they beg for their employment. 'But sir, I have three children and a wife to look after. I need this job!' Hysterical."

People around his office would call him a 'cunt' or 'money-grabbing tosser,' not knowing Charlotte's little ears were here, there and everywhere.

When she did hear people talking about her father, she would inform on them, and then watch as he ridiculed them before showing them the door. He may have enjoyed their grovelling and facial expressions, but Charlotte especially enjoyed the fear in their eyes.

It spoke volumes to her.

It was especially great watching a weak man react to her father's powerful outbursts – they would shrink away from his flailing arms, whereas his female employees would break down crying.

"Never, ever let someone expose your weak side, Charlotte. If someone has you against the ropes in an argument or any other kind of situation, never show emotion. Never cry. Never cower. Give better than you're getting! Lash out with words that cut deep. Never be scared of wounding or ripping someone open, especially in business, baby girl."

Her father's words had resonated in her, as they always did.

He had been her hero, right up until the moment she had discovered his dirty little secret. It was strange, because it wasn't what he was getting up to that upset her the most – it was how much his actions had destroyed her mother. It had driven her to suicide.

To this day, she could still remember the look on her father's face when she caught him doing things he shouldn't have been.

"Charlotte, I'm off out!" her mother called from downstairs. "I'll be a few hours, so if you need anything, go to your father – he's in his office."

She put her book down and got off her bed, going to her bedroom door to open it. Charlotte ducked her head out and called to her mother, "Okay, Mum. But seriously, I'm eleven years old. I don't need babying any longer."

Katherine chuckled. "I know, sweetness. I'm off now. Oh, and check in on your father – you know what he's like when he's working from home! The man forgets to eat, drink and rest."

"I will, Mummy. Have a nice morning."

"Are you sure you won't come with me?"

"No, Mummy. Thanks."

"Okay, fine. Bye."

When Charlotte heard the front door bang shut, she stood and listened to the deep silence within the house. When she had been younger, the large family home had terrified her beyond belief, but not now. She found the silence within the six-bedroom building soothing.

They didn't *need* a house so big – it was a display of stature, power, wealth and showiness. Nothing more. There was only one maid and a cook, but they weren't live-ins. Her father didn't like 'strangers' living under his roof.

"Why don't you have quarters built for them, dear?" her mother had once tackled him.

"No, they can commute like other decent, working folk. Build them quarters? Good God, woman – you'll be hounding me to take in all the waifs and strays off our streets next!"

Bored with listening to the silence, Charlotte returned to her bed and began reading again. It wasn't long before her mind started to wander to thoughts of what her father was up to in his office. Of how busy he must be.

Her mother was right. Once he was locked away, nobody saw him for days on end. He only came out at meal times.

I'll finish this chapter and head down to his office. He might like a cup of tea or coffee. Maybe I can make him a bite to eat.

Charlotte became engrossed more and more in the story that was unfolding before her, and forgot all about popping along to see if her father needed anything. It wasn't until she heard the front door slam again that she managed to tear her attention from her book.

God, surely Mum isn't back already! she thought, looking over at the clock on her bedside table. *No, it's too early. But if it is, she'll be so angry that I haven't checked in with Dad.*

Charlotte made a move to get off the bed but was stopped by muffled voices. It confused her. There was nobody in the house apart from herself and her father, and he certainly wouldn't be talking to anyone.

She pricked her ears and squinted as she tried to make out what was being said below. Unable to, Charlotte very carefully got off her bed and tip-toed to her door. Luckily, she had not closed it tight, so she was able to open it without making a noise.

"…And you're sure nobody saw you coming?" she heard her father say.

"Yes," a second voice said. It was male.

"Excellent. These meetings are very risky for me, you understand?"

"Yes."

"Like the others, I'll pay you well. Just keep it between us, okay?!"

"Okay."

"Promise?"

"Yes, I promise. Where's your wife?"

"Out shopping with my daughter. Now, come on. We don't have much time – I was hoping you'd be here sooner. You did get my message, didn't you?"

"I did but I couldn't slip away."

"Never mind, just come with me. I have an office where we can be alone."

Charlotte heard her father's voice fade into the distance, followed by the other person's. She didn't understand what was going on. Did her father have a friend over? Why was he worried about her mother returning home?

Gradually, she opened the door inch by inch, making sure she was not detected. Her heart raced as she stepped from her room and onto the landing. She risked a quick duck of her head over the banister, and saw the coast was clear.

If he doesn't see me, he'll surely hear my beating heart! she thought, listening to the way in which it hammered out the beats per-minute. *Who is that person with Dad?*

Charlotte crept over to the top of the stairs and placed her foot on the step below. Bending, she looked through the spindles and into the hallway. They had definitely gone. She started her slow and steady descent. When she reached the bottom step, she peeped around the balustrade. Nobody. From where she stood, she could see into the kitchen and beyond.

Right, come on. I have to find out what's going on. But if Dad is busy or with a client, he'll kill me. No, he won't – he loves me being involved in his work.

Undeterred, Charlotte made her way through the kitchen and to the rooms on the other side. She didn't spend much time in this section of the house. It was her dad's area – there was a billiards/games room, office and his relaxing room, which was a small sitting room with a sofa, TV and music system.

As she neared the office, she heard voices again.

There's three people now!

Putting her ear to the cool wood, she tried to make out what was being said in the room beyond.

"You'll be back later today?" she heard her dad say.

"Yes," answered the man she had heard earlier. His tone sounded gruffer now that she was closer to him – it was the type of voice that belonged to a thug, she thought.

Her heart quickened.

The danger was exhilarating.

She felt like she had so many times in her dad's office, when he was berating his staff.

"Do you have more like this for sale?" her dad spoke.

"As many as you can handle," Thug said.

"Good. You're new to me, so I'm going to have to gain your trust."

"Of course. But know one thing," said Thug. "You best pay me what you owe on time, every time. I'm not as soft as Richard."

"Ha!" her father bellowed. "You don't have to worry about money – I could buy the whole world if I wanted to."

"That's what I like to hear. Am I to bring the goods here every time?"

"No. I have a little place not far from here – it's buried in the woods just outside of Porthcawl. Do you know Meadow Lake?"

"Yeah, I do. You own a property there?"

"I do. Number six Oak Drive. You can't miss it."

"Okay. So when do you want the goods dropping there?"

"Once or twice a month – Richard used to make the drop on a Wednesday and Friday."

"Fine, that can be arranged. Same time as this?"

"Please," her father said.

"Shall I take this package away and drop it at Oak Drive?"

"No, I'll take this one now, but come back and collect in an hour or so."

"Fine. When I return, I want my money!"

"I'll be paying you for the whole year, and not just for today," her father said. "That's the arrangement I had with Richard."

There was a brief moment of silence.

"Right, I can work with that. I'll be back in an hour," said Thug.

When Charlotte heard approaching footsteps, she rushed from the door and hid in the billiards/games room. Once there, she closed the door to a crack and peered through. From her position, she could see a man standing outside her father's office.

"Don't forget, have the money waiting!"

"You don't have to worry about it – I'm good for it."

"I hope so, because I really wouldn't want to have to bring the boys around here and smash this beautiful home up and divulge all your nasty secrets to your wife and daughter…"

"Hey! Now, there's no need for those kind of threats. I told you, I'm more than good for it. Richard and I had a great trading relationship. Don't go spoiling it, Peter, or I'll go elsewhere!"

The office door was closed on the man, who then tapped on the wood. "Don't forget, one hour!" Peter said, turning to walk away. As he did, Charlotte slowly opened the door she was hiding behind.

I was right about Peter! she thought, watching the man walk to the front door. *All those tattoos and shaven head – he looks like a biker-type. I wonder if he's carrying a gun or knife? Why is Dad doing business with a man like that? The men and women he usually deals with wear sophisticated business suits and nice shoes…*

Muffled sounds from her father's office grabbed her attention. Fully opening her door, she snuck out into the hallway and up to his office.

She placed her ear to the office door.

Nobody was talking.

All she could hear were moans and gasps.

God, he's hurt! she thought, putting her hand to the door handle.

"Don't stop!" Charlotte suddenly heard her father shout.

What is going on…

Taking her hand off the handle, she bent over and tried to look through the keyhole, but the key blocked her view.

Damn! Come on, just go in. He's not going to be mad. If he is busy working with someone, then I can always make some form of excuse…

Plunging the door handle down, Charlotte threw the door open.

She stood on the threshold in shock. She could feel her jaw sagging.

Her father hadn't noticed her. His eyes were closed, his head thrown back. He stood before his desk with his trousers around his ankles. Kneeling before him was a lad of no more than twelve or thirteen – he had her father's penis, which was engorged and veined, in his mouth.

He too didn't notice Charlotte standing there.

On closer inspection, she noticed the boy had his index finger up her father's anus.

Covering her mouth, she stopped a laugh from escaping her. She scrunched her eyes and puffed her cheeks. *Oh, my God!*

She'd seen certain things on TV and had heard some of her friends talking about boys in school, but this had been the first sexual act she had seen in the flesh.

No matter how hard she tried to stop herself from giggling, she couldn't hold it back any longer, especially when her dad started raking his hands through the youngster's hair – Charlotte erupted into a fit of laughter. She pointed at her father and the lad before her, who turned and looked at her, stunned.

Her dad pushed the boy away and scrabbled for his trousers.

"Oh, God…Princess…I…It's not what it looks like. Oh, Jesus!"

"Daddy, what have you been getting up to?!"

His face flushed. His words were stammered.

"It's…Please. Oh, dear God…"

Tears started to form at the corners of his eyes. "Get out!" he yelled at the boy, who scrambled to his feet and ran for the door.

"Peter will want paying – he'll beat me if I don't…"

"Here!" her father yelled, pulling money from his wallet and stuffing it into the boy's hands. "Get out. Now!"

The lad didn't take telling a third time. He hightailed it through the door.

"Charlotte! I…He…He was just helping Daddy out, that's all!"

"Daddy, I know exactly what he was doing! I know more than you think."

"Please, don't tell Mum. This is our little secret, right?!"

She looked down at his exposed privates.

"Yes, *little* secret!" she said, smiling.

His mouth sagged. "Charlotte! How dare you…"

"I don't think you're in a position to be 'how daring' me, Daddy. What will Mum say?" she said, smiling.

His flustered ways excited her in a way she hadn't felt before – there were butterflies in her stomach.

"No! You can't…"

"Oh, but I can, and I will!"

"I'm your father – you're supposed to love me unconditionally, not to mention respect me!"

"I did. Right up until this moment. Besides, you've taught me so much about the business, Daddy. You've become obsolete to me. Outlasted your use. Now I can play with you like you play with your employees. What fun we will have!"

His look was one of pure aghast, but something told her he liked it, deep down.

"Look, Daddy, your secret – it's getting bigger! Do you like being teased?" She covered her mouth and giggled.

He raised his hand, but couldn't follow through with striking her.

"Go ahead, Daddy. Would that make you feel better?! Just know, if you do, I'll destroy you, just like your dirty secret will destroy Mum."

He whipped his trousers up and collapsed into his chair.

"My God, you're a monster!"

"One you created, Daddy. I'll tell you what, I'll keep what you're doing from Mum, but you will dance to my tune."

"Wha…what?!"

"I'll be twelve in a few days, and there's a list of things I would like. I'd also like you to open up a bank account for me. You'll be depositing a large amount of money into it," she said, smiling.

"You don't have to do this! You know I'll give you anything you want, Charlotte!"

"I know, but this is way, way more fun, Daddy."

"What else are you demanding?"

"In time, I want you to sign the company over to me."

His jaw dropped. "But…"

"There's going to be no debate. You're in my pocket now. And, whilst I'm at the office with you on Saturday and Sunday, I'll be running the show. You'll be letting me give you a good talking to in front of the staff, too."

He looked broken. His head dropped until his chin touched his chest.

"If I agree to these demands, will you promise to keep quiet? I'll never do anything like this again. We can start fresh…"

"Yes, I promise to keep quiet. But there will be more demands as I think stuff up. Humiliating such a powerful man will be so much fun, Daddy. I know how you feel now, when you push your staff around. Boy, do I!"

"You evil child," he muttered, unable to look at her.

"Come on, Daddy, I'm not the one who likes to play naughty games with little boys. Aren't I lucky you don't like little girls in the same way?!" she said, beaming.

"Get out," he whispered.

"Okay, but I'll be back with my birthday list later."

Just then, the front door banged shut.

"Charlotte?!" her mother called, "Come and help me with the shopping."

Their eyes fused.

A smile curled her lips.

****

Chaos lay on her bed and played with her pussy at the thought of her dad's face. It had been a long time since she'd thought of that moment in her life.

Oh, how he crumbled to my demands and wishes over the following days, weeks and months. He bowed down to me right up to the moment he died. God, how fun it had been to play him like a puppet on a string.

A powerful orgasm racked her body, causing her to scream as her fingers kept flicking her swollen G-spot.

He lavished me – showered me in gifts: clothes, money, jewellery…Anything I wanted, Daddy provided!

Another orgasm passed through her – her legs started to tremble once again. She could hear Simone moaning from inside his cage.

"This is the closest you will get to my pussy, slave-bitch!" she said through gritted teeth.

Daddy even bought me a pony.

Now she was screaming. Screaming and panting. She bit her lower lip so hard, she drew blood. Chaos tried to get her fingers to stop, but she couldn't override the extreme pleasure she felt, even if it was starting to hurt.

A life-sized doll house, too.

"Yes!" she bellowed, sucking in a deep breath. Sweat broke across her brow and ran down her face, into her eyes and mouth.

Satisfaction had her pinned to the mattress.

Her digits worked so fast, they seemed motorised.

Oh, how his dick had hardened at the thought of being pushed around by his little girl. His princess! Fucking pervert…

Chaos' mouth sagged as an almighty orgasm washed over her. Her fingers were soaked. Her juices poured from her.

She gasped, rolled onto her side, closed her eyes and tried to breathe steadily. Her entire body shook uncontrollably. Puckering her lips, she violently sucked air into her lungs and blew it back out just as viciously.

"*Fuck*!" she puffed.

I must remember to think about Daddy more often! How long did my games with him go on for? Must have been close to two years – yes, something like that. He died shortly after my thirteenth birthday.

A giggle escaped her.

"I loved my parents, or so I thought. When it came down to it, I didn't really give a shit about them. I don't give a shit about anyone."

I truly did love Dad, but something changed in me the day I caught him with that boy. I lost all my respect for him. He showed a weakness. And when the respect went, so did the love… she thought.

Chaos sighed, and rolled onto her side.

The pleasure and shakes had subsided.

A single tear slid down her cheek.

Crushing him had been satisfying…

****

For several weeks after she had caught her father up to his naughtiness, nothing had happened, even though she kept a close eye on him. He was totally unaware of her movements – she lived in his shadows.

"I'll be watching you!" had been her parting words that day in the office – the colour had drained from his face.

Then, one Wednesday after school, whilst she'd been watching his cabin in the woods, Charlotte had seen him greet a man at the door – the same thug-like man she had seen in the house. He was depositing a young boy to her father's cabin, to her disgust and joy.

She carried recording equipment – she had even been crafty in rigging audio and sound gear in his home office, work office and cabin. There was no escaping her watchful eye, no matter how hard he tried.

When she was in school, her monitors kept their silent eyes on him. Watching, recording, listening…

After her father took receipt of the lad, he scurried into the cabin. The thug left.

She crept through the woods from her hiding spot and inched her way up a tree. When she was high enough, she could see through some of the cabin's higher windows, which looked into the main bedroom, kitchen and lounge.

"It would seem I got here late," she whispered, removing a camcorder from her coat. Upon looking through the lens, Charlotte spotted not just one, but three boys with her father – they appeared much younger than the one she had caught him with in his office.

"What a weak, disgusting man," she uttered, catching the whole sordid act on tape.

All the sucking.

Buggery.

Kissing.

Exposing.

Undressing.

Fumbling.

Photo-taking…

She felt sick. Dirty.

Her father had even supplied hard drugs and spirits.

For the final act, he had the boys tie him up and beat him senseless.

When the show came to an end and the boys left via pick-up from their thug boss, who she also filmed, Charlotte approached the cabin.

Her father was crawling around on the floor, trying to stop his arse from bleeding – the boys had taken turns in ramming various objects into his anus, such as dildos and anal beads.

It was sickening.

Since all this had started, Charlotte had taken a keen interest in internet porn, and had done a lot of research into such things.

It was surprising what one could find…

"Well, well, Daddy…I see you've been up to your old tricks again!" she said, smiling. The camera was still rolling.

He collapsed onto the floor and looked up at her – his eyes were like pinheads.

"Princess…"

"Don't you princess me, you vile beast! You said this would never, ever happen again. What will Mummy think?!"

She spat on him before giving him a swift kick in his ribs.

Charlotte was starting to enjoy herself.

"Please…" he begged, grovelling at his twelve-year-old's feet.

She kneed him in the face with all the might she could muster, which hurt and sent him sprawling backwards.

His dick stood to attention – his old balls swinging.

She wrinkled her nose, then spotted a lit candle close by. The wick was melted down to a nub. On picking it up, Charlotte noticed the wax had pooled in the candle's centre.

She giggled before pouring it onto her father's crotch.

His screams were so loud she thought they would perforate her eardrums.

All the while, she kept the camera going.

"This is punishment for being such a dirty, naughty man!"

"I…I…"

"No! I'll never listen to you again."

"Don't…"

"Shut up! You were my everything, Daddy – you were my role model. 'Never show a weakness', that's what you told me. Well, I see yours, and, just like you taught me – I'll expose yours so bad, you'll wish you were dead!"

"…Tell…" he gasped.

"Oh, I wouldn't do that, Daddy. Where would the fun be in that?!" she asked, laughing.

"But…you said…"

"I know what I said!" She let another giggle slip on seeing his singed pubic hairs – his cock had started to blister.

"Mum…"

"No, I won't tell her. I just want to have all this hanging over you."

"Why…" he coughed and then gasped.

"Because it's fun. Just like you think it's fun to humiliate your staff, Daddy."

"*Ugh*!" he cried, grabbing his bollocks. "What have you done…?"

She covered her mouth and chuckled. "Well, I best get going – Mum will be wondering where I've got to!" she said, turning and then skipping out the door.

Behind her, she heard her father sobbing and wailing – he shouted something, but his words were unintelligible.

For the next eight months, things carried on this way. Sometimes she would catch her father up to his old tricks at the cabin, which seemed to be his favourite place to do his nasty deeds: It was discreet. Hidden. Also, it didn't seem to bother him about what she had done to him there. His blasé, somewhat smug attitude thrilled her – it was the stubborn man she had once respected. Nobody was going to tell him what to do.

Then, on other days she would have him cornered in the office at work or at home.

However, she didn't confront him on every occasion.

No.

She would let him think he was safe – she toyed with him.

Once, she let him have a dozen meetings with boys of various ages before ambushing him the very next time, informing him that she had all his delightful footage on tape.

Sometimes he would cry.

Other times he would piss himself.

But he would always beg, plead and explain how he couldn't help it.

He would ply her with more money.

More gifts.

Her tooth was kept sweet, and so he was allowed to continue with his depravity. What shocked Charlotte the most was how he never even tried to curb his ways or silence her. Silence her for good. He certainly had the power to do it.

But she knew how much he cherished her. How he would bend over backwards for her.

It truly was pitiful.

Not just pitiful, but sickening.

She was happy to keep milking him like a cash cow – that was, until he went too far; too far for even her to stomach.

After catching him with a bunch of lads no older than six or seven, she decided to finally blow the whistle on him and the sex gang who supplied him.

First, Charlotte went to her mother with the tapes she had accumulated while she had been watching her father. However, she only showed her the recordings of where she was watching from afar, not the ones where she had confronted her dad and mentally and physically abused him.

"Mum," she said, walking through the door to her house.

"I'm in the kitchen, sweetie. What is it?"

"Can you come into the living room, please? I have something I need to tell you."

"Okay, let me just dry my hands. I'm doing the dishes."

As she waited for her mother, Charlotte hooked the camera up to the TV and loaded the first tape, but didn't hit play.

"What is it, dear?"

Charlotte turned to face her mother, who was smiling, big and beautifully.

Then her face changed to confusion. "What's all this in aid of?" she asked.

"I'll show you now," Charlotte said, feeling a wave of excitement shoot up into her guts. *This is going to be pretty amusing!* she thought, looking at her mother's pretty face.

"Right, okay…" She sounded worried.

"You might want to sit down – what I have to tell and show you is going to shock you! Is Dad here yet? I was hoping to beat him home…"

"He's in his office. Charlotte, you're starting to scare me!"

Before she played the first tape for her mother, she told her everything she had witnessed her father do. And, before her mother could start yelling and screaming at her for saying such awful things about her own father, she got the tape rolling.

"Where…where did you get this, young lady?" her mother screamed.

"I told you, I kept tabs on him, Mum…I had to make sure I was right."

Her mother's mouth sagged. Tears started streaming down her face. Then she started to wail, which brought her father running.

"What's going on?!" he yelled.

His eyes were immediately drawn to the TV.

"You…told!" he whispered. In his hand, he held a letter-opening knife. "You little bitch!"

Charlotte shrank back, and grabbed the camera, violently. All the wires connecting it to the TV were yanked out. She hit record.

"Stop!" she said, pointing the camcorder at him.

"You fucking monster!" her mother bellowed, then attacked him – she beat her fists against his arms, body and face. As he tried to control her, she pulled the knife out of his hand and started swinging it wildly at his face. "I'll kill you! The shame this will bring!"

"No!" he yelped, jumping out of her path.

Breathlessly, she lunged at him again, only for him to punch her on the chin. Charlotte's mother collapsed onto the sofa – her nose was bleeding.

"What did you do?" he screamed at Charlotte. "You've destroyed everything!"

"No, you did!" Charlotte bit back. "You couldn't fight your weakness." She smiled. Then her eyes flicked to her mother, who held the letter-opening knife to her throat.

"Mum!" Charlotte had time to say before she witnessed her mother slice through her own neck.

Blood spurted out of her ruptured flesh, spraying the curtains, sofa and carpet.

"Jesus, no!" he screamed.

Charlotte watched and recorded the whole episode.

"No, no, no!" her father said, cradling his dying wife in his arms.

"I'll be sending all the tapes to the police, Father," she said just as her mother snatched at her last breath.

"You fucking little cunt!" he yelled, jumping to his feet and rushing her.

Charlotte ran screaming out of the door and down the hallway – her destination was his office. She knew he kept a gun in his desk drawer.

"I'll kill you!" he wailed.

She could feel his heated breath on her neck.

She crashed through his office door, ran around his desk, grabbed the gun and cocked it, but couldn't aim it in time. He crashed into her, sending the weapon flying into the air.

He put both of his big hands around her throat, strangling all the air from her.

"I loved you so much, even with all this shit you had over me!"

"*Ugh…*" she gasped.

Her eyes began to bulge. Turning her head as much as she could, she saw something lying on his desk. It sat next to a bowl of monkey nuts he always kept close by.

She fumbled for the object.

"I would have given you the world and everything in it. You would have wanted for nothing…" His words trailed off. He then started screaming a high-pitched wail as Charlotte wrapped the nutcracker around his privates and clamped them together as hard as she could.

His hold on her relaxed.

Tears poured down his cheeks.

The more pressure she applied, the more she could feel his balls yield.

"I'll pop 'em!" she said, forcing him backwards. He tripped over his own feet and sat down in his chair, hard – the nutcracker ripped free and he squealed.

"Bitch!" he said, grabbing his hurt.

She fell backwards, and crashed to the floor. Before she could scramble towards the gun, he picked it up off the floor and pointed it at her.

"You've made me do this!" he said, gritting his teeth.

He then opened his mouth, buried the muzzle and pulled the trigger – blood, brain and bone matter splashed up the wall behind him, leaving her to watch in shock, delight and absolute pleasure.

She had broken him beyond belief, causing a wetness between her legs like nothing she had ever felt before.

Once Charlotte had regained control over herself, she'd called the police. In her statement, she'd explained what her father had been up to – how she and her mother had found tapes he had made of his sick goings-on.

She'd also told them that her father had turned on her mother, killing her and intending to do the same to her.

"But I fought him off, and he took his own life," she had said, with crocodile tears streaming down her face.

A few weeks after the inquest, Gregory Ros' will and testament was read – he'd bequeathed all his money and assets to his daughter, who had been sent to live with her aunt, Sue Pass, in Porthcawl.

Charlotte also requested that the stories about her father be kept out of the media, which was met.

****

After thoughts of her aunt Sue had crossed her mind, Chaos decided to get up early the following morning – dawn had barely broken. Her Slave was still sleeping; she could hear his light snores.

Oh, you're in for a rude awakening, dog! she thought, tip-toeing by his kennel.

When she was out the bedroom door, Chaos made her way down to the kitchen and opened the chest freezer. Removing eight large bags of ice, she returned upstairs to the bathroom. Once there, she opened all the bags and dumped their contents into the empty bath.

She then filled it with cold water.

Nothing like a little water torture in the morning! This will sort his aches and pains right out.

Chaos felt a heat build between her legs at the thought of the punishment she had in store for him today.

That was one good thing about being left a ton of money – she didn't have to work, and so she could spend her time pleasing herself and doing whatever the hell she wanted. She also stopped Simone from working, too.

His sole job was to please her.

Well, it had been.

Now he was just a punching bag.

A broken plaything that she loved to abuse.

One day, he will just snap like Daddy! And when he does, oh, it'll be glorious! she thought, feeling her juices trickle down her inner thighs. She could barely concentrate on what she was doing.

Once the bath was filled to just under the runoff, she switched the cold tap off. She dipped her fingers in, trying her best to avoid the lumps of ice – a shiver tore down her spine.

Fuck! That's absolutely freezing. Time to wake the dog!

Chaos smiled as she walked back into the bedroom and heard Simone continue to snore. Grabbing her crop, she hit the bars to his cage as hard as she could.

"Wake up!" she screamed.

Chaos took the key from around her neck and opened the padlock.

Simone groaned.

"Get out, dog!"

"Water..." he gasped.

"You'll be getting all the water you can drink, sailor. Now, move!"

Slowly, on all fours, Simone came out of the cage like a dog. As he did, Chaos inspected his battered body.

He doesn't look as badly beaten as I'd first thought.

"Does anything feel broken, dog?" she asked, not that she gave a fuck.

"No...No, Mistress. Just a little sore..."

"I didn't ask for your fucking life story, I just asked if anything was broken!" She grabbed him by his hair, and pulled him along to the bathroom.

He didn't protest, just groaned.

This fucking cunt is starting to get me down with his stiff upper lip.

"Get in there!" she told him, pointing at the bath.

"No, not an ice bath!" he said.

"Oh, yes!" She gave him a kick in the arse for encouragement. "And when you're done sitting in there, I'll have anal hooks and wet ropes awaiting!"

"*Shibari*!" he said, looking at her.

She smiled, and then nodded, remembering her aunt Sue once again...

****

Aunt Sue had been a formidable woman. She was Charlotte's dad's sister, which had made her sceptical at first, when she'd learned of who she would be staying with.

"Can't I just go into care?" Charlotte had asked the authorities.

"No honey, it'll be better for you to stay with a relative. Besides, your aunt is looking forward to having you with her," had been the reply from a dumpy, red-headed woman with glasses and freckles. Her clothes had looked as cheap as the pen she wielded to write her notes on the paper she had fastened to a clipboard.

Charlotte had eyed her with contempt, not that the woman had realised.

When Charlotte had first clapped eyes on her aunt, who she had not seen in years, the word 'regal' came to mind. She wore a blue dress, high-heels, nude-coloured tights and a hat.

"Are you going to a wedding?!" had been Charlotte's childish words.

"Why, no, dear!" had been Sue's first words to her niece. Her smile had been kind. Welcoming, even.

She may have been regal to Charlotte at the time, but, over the course of the years she spent with Sue, Charlotte came to realise that her aunt was far from imperial.

Sure, she wore nice furs and pearls, but no knickers.

"I like my lettuce to be free, dear – it needs air, just like you and I!" she would tell Charlotte, who would blush. But, over time, she came to know and understand her aunt's ways.

"I'll mould you into a strong, take-no-shit woman, Charlotte. That father of yours had always been a pervert, you know! He'd been fiddling with little boys, hadn't he?"

It wasn't a question, but a statement.

"How did you know…There was nothing in the papers?"

"People talk, dear. I had to put up with his wicked ways when we were younger. Our parents never knew. He liked to spy on me whilst I showered."

"Oh…" had been Charlotte's blushed reply.

"I told your mother to keep a good eye on him; to keep him in his place with a firm hand. That's what men need, dear. They crave it – they secretly like to be controlled and chastised like the little boys they are!"

That was one of the first proper conversations they had about her father. It had taken place a few months after her fourteenth birthday. They never spoke of him again, or what he had done, until her sixteenth birthday had come and gone.

"I have tapes, Auntie Sue," Charlotte had blurted one evening whilst they had been drinking tea. She had no idea why she had said it, she just did.

"Please, dear – call me Sue! Tapes of what?!"

"Daddy, Aunt…I mean, Sue."

"Really?! And where has this come from all of a sudden? We haven't spoken about that monster in some time…" she said, smiling.

"I'm really not sure. I just felt like…sharing."

"I see. And where have you been keeping them, Charlotte?"

"I buried them in the garden of my house. My old house, that is."

"Interesting."

"You see, I was worried the police would get a hold of them. I didn't want Dad's shame dragged through the papers, even though he deserved it."

"Full of surprises, aren't you!"

"What did you mean when you said men need keeping in their place – that they crave it?" Charlotte asked, almost too scared and ashamed to look her aunt in the eye now, but she did, and saw that Sue was smiling.

"Oh, I have many things to teach you, Charlotte. Many."

"Such as…?"

"Remember I told you that I would turn you into a tough-as-nails woman?" Charlotte nodded. "Well, I plan to do just that. Now you're of age, I can show you and tell you all my dirty, naughty little secrets!"

The worry coursing through Charlotte must have shown on her face.

"Oh, there's no need to worry, dear – I'm certainly not like that father of yours, but I am naughty. Naughty in a good way, I promise. And I know you're going to love it!"

"When do we start?" Charlotte wanted to know. She had a tremor of excitement pass through her, and again she felt that heat between her legs.

"Have you started masturbating, dear?"

A heat like no other washed over Charlotte's face. "I…I…"

"Come, there's no need to act coy around me, flower. I know you're not. Have you been getting urges?"

"Urges…?"

"Yes, down below."

Can she read my mind…?

"There's no need to look so shocked – you're of age."

"I…I…"

"Come on, spit it out."

"I get an excited…*heat* almost. Between…my legs, Sue."

"Very good. Have you explored your body?"

Charlotte looked away. "No…"

"There's nothing to be embarrassed about. How long have you been getting these urges?"

"I started feeling them around the time I was…"

"Yes?" Sue pressed.

Charlotte thought she was going to pass out from the heat that was burning her neck and cheeks. "…When I was filming Dad…"

Sue gasped. "You enjoyed it?!"

Tears slid down Charlotte's face, and she thought they would evaporate once they rolled over her scorching cheeks. "I'm so ashamed, Sue," she said, "now that I think about it." She starting to bawl. "What's wrong with me? Am I like him? Am I broken too…?"

"Shh-shh-shh!" Sue said, getting up from her seat and making her way over to her niece. "There's certainly nothing wrong with you, dear. Did he ever…you know, try and touch you when you were filming him?"

"Ew! Gross! No, he didn't. He loved me. He was only ever interested in boys."

Sue let a giggle escape her. "You sound a lot like me, Charlotte. Did it excite you to see him caught? To see him flustered and embarrassed? Is that why you didn't blow the whistle on him immediately?"

Charlotte lowered her head again. "Yes…I know that was wrong of me – I let those poor boys suffer. If they weren't suffering with my dad, then they would have been suffering with some other pervert."

"Well, you did the right thing in the end, and a lot of bad people went to prison. I'm not going to hold it against you. A girl has to have a bit of fun!"

"Like I said, I still have the tapes. I also made him pay me for his silence…"

"You wicked thing. That's the trouble with men. They allow their dicks to think for them! Didn't he leave you everything in his will?"

Charlotte nodded.

"Huh, good girl. So, you started getting the urge to touch yourself in a sexual way when you were filming him. Why? I know, because he was humiliated."

"I think it was the begging. The pleading. It did something to me…I used to get a heat between my legs and in my belly, Sue. It would be all wet down there when I checked."

"Of course. There's nothing more satisfying than seeing a man squirm, Charlotte. Did you never think to explore your pussy?"

"My, *what*?!"

"Your pussy, dear. Your vagina, hatchet wound, lettuce…*cunt*."

Charlotte gasped. "No, never."

"When you go to bed tonight, I want you to explore your pussy, Charlotte. Learn. Tomorrow night, I will indulge that soft spot you have for seeing men writhe."

"But, why…?"

"You shouldn't be denied, dear. I'll help you explore it, as I too enjoy such a thing. I'll teach you how to handle – no, how to *control* a man like a dog!"

Charlotte felt the heat rise again. "I think…I would like that, Sue!" A smile crept across her face.

"Good. And, as I said, discover your body tonight. Tomorrow, we shall talk about things before I indulge you. I am going to make a strict, lean woman out of you, dear."

"But…but…I wouldn't know where to begin!"

"Oh, dear, you are silly! I tell you what, start thinking about how much you like men to suffer, and when that heat fills you, put your hand downstairs. The rest will come naturally," Sue said, winking.

After spending a further few hours with her aunt, watching TV and chatting. Charlotte made her way up to bed at eleven o'clock. As it was a Friday, Sue allowed her to stay up that little bit longer.

As she'd bid Sue a goodnight, her aunt had replied, "Have fun", which was followed by a wink and a smile.

Red-faced and turning her back on Sue, who was pouring herself a large glass of wine, Charlotte sloped off to bed.

And now, as she lay there, she felt her heart race in her chest. *What am I supposed to do?! Dad, she told me to think about catching him in the act. To think about his suffering…*

Closing her eyes, she tried to let her mind wander, but the sound from the TV downstairs was distracting.

*Block it out and think, damn it! Dad…Dad…Dad…*she repeated, and then her mind suddenly transported her back to a time she had almost forgotten. A time when she had caught her father unaware, but not when he was with boys. This was something completely different.

"Come on, Tracey – let's go inside and play for a while!" Charlotte said to her school friend, who had come to stay for the weekend.

"Why, what do you fancy doing?"

"I thought maybe we could go inside and watch some TV for a change."

"Yeah, okay – sounds like it could be fun. What about playing a board game?"

"With the TV on in the background?"

Tracey nodded eagerly, causing her pigtails to flap wildly.

"Sounds good. I have Monopoly?"

"Anything else?!" Tracey asked, wrinkling her nose.

"The Game of Life?"

"Buckaroo? I'm sure I saw that in your room!"

Ugh, she's positively a child! Charlotte thought, looking at her friend. Usually on weekends, Charlotte helped her father in his office where she learned money, business and politics. She thought better of herself, and didn't have time for silly games.

But, two days ago, her mother had insisted that she have a 'fun' weekend – that she should invite a friend over.

"You should keep your own kind of company now and then, Charlotte. It's all very well learning business, but you must learn how to be a child, too!"

Reluctantly, Charlotte had given in to her mother's demands and had asked Tracey over. Not that she was that keen on the girl. However, Tracey was the one she was the closest to at school, and she had jumped at the opportunity to spend the weekend at Charlotte's.

"If you want to play that silly game, then we shall, Tracey."

"Oh cool. Thanks, Char."

"Lotte!"

"Huh?!"

"Charlotte. That's my name, not 'Char'. Ew, that's just ghastly."

"Oh, sorry!"

"It's okay. Just remember to never call me that again!"

Both girls got off the two-seater swing set and headed towards the house.

"Are you sure your mother won't mind us going inside? She did tell us to stay outside and enjoy the sunshine, Char…lotte."

"Oh, she'll be fine!" she said, opening the door. At first, she thought there was nobody home, as the place sounded graveyard silent. But then she heard muffled voices, which were raised in frustration. Anger, almost.

"Are your parents arguing?!" Tracey asked.

"I don't know," she said, scrunching her face up in confusion.

"He-he, how embarrassing!"

"Shh! Follow me…This could be fun," Charlotte said, smiling.

As both girls edged closer to the kitchen, the voices of her parents became clearer.

"For God's sake, Gregory!"

"Look, I'm bloody trying. Are you sure the girls are outside?!"

"Yes, yes, they are playing on the swings. Are you ready?"

"No. Stop pressuring me!"

"I'm sure you don't have this problem with your slutty secretaries!"

"If that's how you're going to be!"

Silence. Then Charlotte heard the *clip-clack* of heels on the kitchen tiles.

"Shall I help?"

"You've already tried."

"Well, I can't just stand here with my knickers…"

Her mother stopped talking as Charlotte opened the door and saw her with her summer dress rucked up above her waist. Her virginal white knickers were around her ankles – her face went instantly scarlet.

"Oh…" her mother uttered.

Her father, who was naked, had his back to her.

"Look, I can't help it if I can't get it hard!" he said.

"Gregory!"

"What?!" he asked, turning around – he had his semi-hard prick in his hand. It looked like a mole's nose. His mouth sagged.

When Tracey tittered and pointed at him, his knob shrivelled even more. He blushed and covered it as quickly as he could.

"Get out!" her mother yelled. "Now!"

Giggling, both girls turned and left the kitchen. In the background, Charlotte heard her father say, "Do you think they saw it?!"

"Well of course they did! You were standing there stretching it in the hopes it would go hard and big. Well, as big as it can get!" her mother said, causing the girls to erupt into hysterics as they rushed from the kitchen.

As Charlotte lay and thought about that moment, a heat washed over her – moistness grew between her legs.

How could I have possibly forgotten about that?! It was during his tyranny over little boys! He probably couldn't get it hard with a woman…

The thought caused her to flush as her hand inched down her body. Before she knew it, the tips of her fingers were brushing against the top of her panties – her nipples stiffened.

A harsh breath escaped her as her fingers slid beneath the fabric of her underwear. The fine hair that covered her twat curled around her digits. She felt slightly ashamed, but couldn't stop.

"It'll come naturally," echoed Sue's words in her mind.

And it did.

Charlotte guided her fingers blindly towards the soft, wet folds of her pussy and worked one deep inside her.

She gasped.

As her finger slowly slid in and out of her, her thumb discovered the hard nub hidden in the hood of her twat. On rubbing it, she thought she was going to pass out in ecstasy.

"Oh!" she gasped, covering her mouth with her free hand, but she didn't stop pleasuring herself. It encouraged her to speed up. Taking her hand away from her mouth, she pressed it against her right breast.

She'd noticed they'd grown over the last twelve months, but had had no desire to touch them until tonight. Lifting her top up, she exposed her rock-hard nipples – she took the right one between her forefinger and thumb, then gently squeezed it.

Her eyes rolled in her head.

Her moans and groans became louder, but she didn't care.

Charlotte kicked her bedding off as her temperature soared. Sweat broke across her brow and her upper lip beaded with perspiration.

"*Oh-huh…*" she moaned, speeding her thumb and finger up.

It feels so good. I can't… "Ugh…ugh…" she panted as an orgasm started to engulf her.

She tried clamping her mouth shut, but she couldn't stop herself from groaning louder and louder until she broke into a scream.

So caught up in her experiment, Charlotte hadn't noticed the sound of the TV being lowered. Nor did she notice Sue standing in her bedroom doorway – she had a cigarette in one hand, with a half-empty glass of wine in the other.

"Oh, God!" Charlotte screamed, then finally managed to clamp her mouth shut. Her whole body shook as shockwaves of electricity shot through her.

Withdrawing her fingers, she huffed and wiped the sweat from her brow using her forearm. She looked down at the nipple she had been squeezing, and noticed light bruising around the areola.

"Shit!" she uttered, looking at her tit in sheer panic. "What have I done?!"

"My, you are a little screamer, aren't you?!" Sue said, blowing smoke free of her mouth.

Charlotte looked at her aunt in total shook – her jaw hung loose.

"Sue!" she blurted, pulling her top down as quickly as she could and covering her lower half with her duvet. "I'm naked!"

"Oh, please – you don't have anything I haven't seen, dear. Don't forget, I was a nurse for many years. I've seen it all."

"What do you want?!"

"Just seeing how you were getting on. Now that you've had your first orgasm, you'll be hungry for more. But you're not going to let any dirty boys and their unclean dicks near you. Do you hear?"

"Yes!" she gasped, still mortified at her aunt's presence.

"Get some sleep, dear – it's going to be a long day…and night tomorrow! I have a lot to show you."

"Sue…?"

"Yes, dear?"

"Do I have anything to fear with you? I know you said no, but still…"

"No. Of course not. I have only your best interests at heart. Now, off to sleep. Goodnight."

"Night, Sue."

It took Charlotte a good hour to drift off to sleep. Her mind kept spinning, throwing questions at her – questions she could not possibly answer.

What does she have to show me?

What does she want to teach me?

What does she have planned?

What, what, what…?

But then, just like that, when she thought her mind wouldn't shut off, it did. Charlotte fell into a deep sleep involving shrunken cocks, red faces, cries of pain and humiliation, her father and her aunt Sue.

The next morning around nine o'clock, Sue knocked on her door and entered. "Are you decent?"

Charlotte rolled over and pulled her top down, which had ridden up in the night.

"Yes," she squeaked and coughed.

"Hurry downstairs, Charlotte. I have breakfast ready. I'm dying to show you my Fun Room."

"Okay, I'll be down soon."

"Later today, I may have to take you to get a pretty dress."

"Why?" Charlotte asked.

"*Tut*, don't be dense, dear. We have male company this evening. I've invited a friend – he's bringing his son with him."

"*What*?!" Charlotte blurted. "But…but…You said no boys! You…you…"

"Stop repeating your words, dear. It's ugly – your mouth keeps flapping! I know what I said, but this is training, nothing else."

Charlotte had no words. She was terrified, yet a little excited at the same time.

I wonder if I have time to put my fingers between my legs before rushing down for breakfast…

Sue snapped her fingers. "Are you with me?" she asked, then laughed.

"Oh, uh…Yes, of course. Could you give me a few, before I come down – I'd like to use the bathroom and whatnot."

"Of course, dear. Try not to be too long, though. I wouldn't want breakfast to spoil."

"No, just five minutes."

When Sue closed the door, Charlotte slipped her hand inside her knickers and lay back. This time, she didn't need mental images to help her. Nor did she make as much noise as last night.

Within ten minutes, she was downstairs and eating breakfast at the kitchen table. Sue had put together a superb English breakfast.

"Hungry?" Sue asked, watching her niece wolf her food down.

"Mm, yes. This is good!"

"Yes, well, the horn will do that to you, dear. It gives you the munchies, as the children would say," she said, then smiled her regal smile.

"What's your 'Fun Room'?"

"I'll show you. Are you ready?"

"Yep!" Charlotte said, pushing her plate aside.

"Follow me." Sue led Charlotte out the kitchen and down the hallway. When she got to a padlocked door Charlotte had noticed on many occasions but had never questioned, Sue removed a key, which hung around her neck on a chain, from between her tits and used it to unlock the door.

She opened the door after placing the padlock in a safe place. With one hand, Sue reached out and flipped the light switch down. When light flooded the staircase, she continued down the steps.

"Mind your head, dear – the ceiling is a bit low here," she warned Charlotte. "This will be where we will be bringing our company tonight after dinner."

"But what's down here in a dusty old cellar?!"

"Oh, you'll see…"

When they reached the bottom, Charlotte couldn't believe her eyes. The walls were completely padded. Sound proofed. The lower room was also much bigger than she thought it would have been.

Adorning the back wall was an arsenal of lashing weapons – whips, chains, crops, paddles, bamboo shoots, sticks, canes, rulers...You name it, it was hanging there. There were also big rubber cocks, strap-ons, collars, leads, cuffs, ropes and masks. Charlotte had never seen anything like it.

"What is this place?!"

"It's a torture chamber, dear."

As Charlotte moved deeper into the room, she saw weird furniture, such as swings and chairs. "Is that a wine butt?!" she asked, pointing at the huge wooden barrel in the corner of the room.

"Why yes, dear," Sue said, all blasé.

"What on earth for?!"

Sue giggled. "It's one of my favourite torture devices."

"Oh…?"

"It's designed for water torture. Freezing water!"

The cellar even had a chest freezer situated in another corner.

"I don't think I like this, Sue. It's freaky!" she said, hearing the eerie rattle of chains as they lazily collided with each other on the wall.

"Don't be soft, girl! Once the party gets going later today, you'll be in your kinky element. Trust me."

"And you're definitely not going to hurt me?!"

Sue scoffed. "No! For the umpteenth time. I'm going to mould you. Teach you."

"Fine, okay. Are we going shopping?"

Sue smiled. "But of course. Go and get dressed – we shall go straightaway. Whilst you're getting ready, I'll text our guests!" she said, winking.

Thirty minutes later, as promised, Sue had Charlotte bundled in the car and they were heading to town for a shopping spree.

"This is my treat, dear. I know you have plenty of money now that your father has gone, but I'm paying this time," Sue stated as she powered her mighty Mercedes along the road.

Just like her brother, Charlotte's father, Sue had an ample amount of cash and wasn't afraid to splash it. But this was something else Charlotte didn't understand about her aunt, because she didn't work – she was a retired nurse, even though she wasn't old enough.

"Where did you get all your money, Sue?" Charlotte blurted, knowing how rude she must have sounded.

"My, you're not *that* shy, are you?! No wonder you had your father fooled. I'm sure he thought he was raising some kind of wallflower, until you taught him a thing or two, am I right?!"

"You could say that, yes. Well?" she pushed. *Just how fucked up is my family? I want to know.*

"It's a long story, Charlotte. But, in a nutshell, I was married once. A long time ago. He was a fool – a weak, pathetic fool, who loved whiskey, horses and pole dancers a bit too much. Just like your father, my Jim was a corporate man – did everything by the book, too. When I found out about his dirty pole dancers secret, I began to get even with him. I would play dirty sex games with him. I'd beat him and leave him tied up for days on end. Once, when I had him locked up, I got him to agree to give me a pile of his cash on the promise of the blowjob of his life."

Charlotte said nothing, just sat and listened.

"Of course, he agreed. When a man's dick is stiff and throbbing, he will agree to just about anything. So, as he lay there, dick swinging, I made him sign a cheque with a fuck load of zeros. You should have seen his face when I turned around, stuffed the check between my tits, and walked out the room, leaving him yelling and swearing."

"Ha-ha-ha!" Charlotte burst out laughing. "I bet that was a great sight, Sue!"

"Oh, very much so. He was so hot and bothered, until his heart gave out from all the shouting!"

"He *died*?!"

Now it was Sue's turn to laugh. "Oh, yes! It was hilarious. I rushed back into the room when I heard something wasn't quite right. He was thrashing about on the bed with foam coming out of his mouth – when I caught sight of his cock bouncing around, I burst into a fit of laughter. I have no idea why. It was just funny, seeing it bob around the place as though it was struggling, too. I tell you, I've never seen such a stiff dick go so soft, so fast!"

Charlotte erupted into laughter. "I saw it happen to my father a few times."

"When you caught him by surprise?"

"Uh-huh. I really am going to have to show you the tapes, Sue – you'll get a good rise out of them, I'm sure."

"Maybe after our shopping trip we can go and get them. Do you remember where you buried them?"

"Yes, I do. But it might be tricky. There may be people at the house?"

"Oh, you let your aunt Sue worry about things like that, dear!"

"I'll never forget this one time I caught him, Sue – he was with a couple of teenage lads, and he was flogging their naked arses. He was fully clothed, red-faced, and dripping sweat. When he saw I was standing there, filming him, he became a quivering wreck, and once again resorted to begging. 'You know I'll give you anything you want, Charlotte', he would always say. 'Money won't cut it this time,' I told him, looking at how badly the boys' skin had been shredded. There was blood everywhere."

"Gosh, what did you do?!"

"I made him strip, then I told him to give the whipping stick to the boys."

"Oh, you naughty thing! What did he say?"

"He started crying! It was hysterical. Myself and the boys just stood there and laughed at him. As he slowly undressed, the boys took his clothes away and threw them out of the door. Once he was down to his birthday suit, that's when the fun really began. I ridiculed his little dick, and compared it to the teens', who had impressive ones for their age. We then took turns in beating his arse until it was red raw. It was that red, planes could have used it as a landing beacon!"

"He-he! Oh, dear! How amusing."

As Sue continued to drive them to their destination, they went on swapping war stories. Sue concluded her story about her husband. About how she had masturbated at the sight of him struggling to draw breath right up to the moment he kicked the bucket. Once he was dead, she rang the authorities and said that he'd had a heart attack during sex.

"I didn't realise he had a problem with his heart!" she'd told one of the medics. "He always liked me to tie him up," she'd continued, letting the crocodile tears flood out of her. All the while, she'd smiled on the inside, her knickers damp.

Once they'd got to town, done their shopping and had a spot of lunch, Sue had driven Charlotte to her old home. When they got there, they had been in luck – the house and driveway were deserted, allowing Charlotte the chance to go around to the back of the home and dig up the tapes she had buried there with a garden spade that had been handily propped against the wall for her convenience.

They then made a quick escape back to Sue's, where they spent the rest of the afternoon trying on different dresses, drinking wine and telling more stories.

Sue took Charlotte back down to her cellar and demonstrated the use of a few different whipping implements, such as the bamboo shoots and crops.

"I had no idea you could use them in so many different ways."

"Oh yes, dear. And, if he's very unruly, never be scared to give him a few swift strikes to the balls – that normally puts them back in line."

After that, and with a few hours still left to kill before their company arrived, Sue and Charlotte took to watching a couple of the tapes.

"My, my, you do have a lot of me in you, Char... Hmmm…" Sue let her words trail off.

"What's the matter?"

"Your name, dear."

"Huh? What about it?"

"If you're going to be a ball-busting bitch from hell, you're going to need something more fitting."

"Oh…" Charlotte said.

"I'll need to think about that," Sue said. "For now, let's start getting ready. Our guests will be here in a short while."

"Are you going to let me…play with them?!"

"In what way, dear?"

"I want to make them suffer, Sue. I want to get back to how I was with my father."

"Ha-ha, you're such a sweet little thing, aren't you? Why yes, of course. I want you to get a full-on experience. This will be your first lesson in handling a man, dear."

Charlotte felt butterflies in her stomach.

The heat was back between her thighs.

"I'm very much looking forward to it, Sue!"

"Come on, come with me, and bring your wine. Do you like it, by the way?"

Charlotte looked down at the red liquid, shrugged, and said, "Yes, it's getting better by the mouthful!"

Sue laughed. "Come on, silly. I have a few surprises for you." She led her niece to her bedroom, where she had put all her shopping bags. "I picked up a few things for you in town."

"Oh, I didn't notice!"

"No, you were busy looking at the dresses in another shop." Sue upended a bag close to her, and a pile of cosmetics poured out of it. "Blusher, lippy, eyeshadow...Everything a lady needs to look a million, dear."

"Oh, wow! Mum never allowed me to wear make-up..."

"Well, you would have been young, dear."

"No, she put a ban on it – she told me that she never wanted to see me in make-up. She said that it would make me look like a cheap whore. I didn't know what a whore was, so she told me. 'It's a woman who goes with every man she can get her hands on. A whore sleeps with many men a day and does it for money. If you wear make-up, a man will think you're a cheap whore. A whore he can get into bed on a whim.' I'll never forget her words."

"Don't take this the wrong way, but your mother didn't have a fucking clue! Now, drink your wine, dear. I have more gifts!"

"More?!" she squealed.

"Oh, yes!" Sue said, spilling the contents of more bags onto her bed. "Try this one, dear." She handed Charlotte a black leather corset. "I hope it fits. I've done your washing, so I know your size."

"It's so pretty!"

"Come on, let's see it on you."

"Okay, I'll just go and change..."

"*Tut*, silly thing. You can change here. Like I told you, you haven't got anything I haven't seen before."

"Yes, true." With the wine swishing around inside her, Charlotte felt confident. As she started to slip her top off, Sue rifled through more bags.

"I bought you some nice lace knickers and matching bras," she said, passing everything over. "Oh, and just look at these stockings! They have pretty little pink bows on them."

Charlotte felt overwhelmed, and slightly tipsy, but she was happy to expose her body in front of her aunt, who was also undressing.

"I picked up a few new things for myself, too – a madam can never have enough nice things. You'll come to learn this, dear."

When she was down to her bra and panties, Sue advised her niece to remove her bra before trying the corset on. "You don't want your boobs to be constricted."

So she did. Charlotte took it off and threw it down on the bed. It was the first time she'd had her tits out in front of another person.

Picking up the corset, she slipped into it. "Do you mind fastening it at the back, Sue?"

"Of course not." Charlotte sucked in a breath as the laces were tugged and tied. She felt her waist being compressed. "Right, turn around. Let's have a look at you."

Facing Sue, Charlotte saw her aunt put her hands to her mouth – a tear had formed at the corner of her eye.

"You look breathtaking!" She moved in closer and adjusted the corset here and there. "You haven't got the biggest set of boobies, but they are divine. They will drive the men wild," she said, smiling.

Even though Charlotte blushed, she smiled. She knew women worried about their bust size, but it wasn't something that she herself had ever thought or worried about.

They're just tits!

"Thanks."

"Come on, get your knickers off! I want you to try these ones on first – I want to see if they match your corset."

Shrugging off the embarrassment, Charlotte took the black, lacy thong from Sue and whipped them up her legs. She'd never tried such underwear before.

"The bit at the back feels slightly uncomfortable, Sue."

"Ha! You'll get used to that – they look fabulous on you! But, we're going to have to give you a slight shave, young lady!"

Charlotte instantly put her hand to her face.

"No, down there!" Sue continued, smiling.

"Oh!" Charlotte said, feeling her face burn.

"Come here. Come and look at yourself in the mirror." Sue pulled Charlotte's hair back. "We'll put it in a tight ponytail later."

"Why?"

"Because men like to see a woman's neckline exposed, especially if you're wearing clothes that tease their pricks!"

"I look so…*sexy*!" Charlotte looked at her small yet full bust. Then she eyed her tight waist and sexy new thong. "I need a pair of heels…"

"Way ahead of you. I have a pair on the bed. Size four, right?"

"Sue, you're the best!" She turned and hugged her aunt.

"They fit perfectly, and make me so much taller!"

"I should think so – there's a six-inch heel on them. Just be careful – heels can be a dangerous!"

Once Sue had allowed Charlotte to strut around the bedroom a few times, and to then walk up and down the landing, she told her to get undressed and take a shower.

"Come on, on the double – I'm going to need one too!"

After showering and shaving her pussy bald, Charlotte had barely finished slipping back into her new corset, thong, stockings and heels before Sue was emerging from the shower – she had a towel wrapped around her.

"Want a hand with your make-up?" she asked Charlotte.

"Please!"

"Okay, finish getting dressed first. By then, I should be ready to help you."

Charlotte did as she was instructed. When she was done, she sat on the bed and awaited Sue. She couldn't help but eye her aunt after she discarded her towel – she had a lovely lean figure, with a tattoo of a mini devil on her bald pussy.

She's rather tall, too – much taller than me, that's for sure. Her tits are much bigger, too. Must be at least a C-cup, she thought, drinking her aunt in.

Sue put on a black thong with matching bra, followed by a pair of tights, tight leather skirt and blouse.

"How do I look?" she asked, slipping into a pair of heels, which added at least four or five inches to her height.

"Formidable!" Charlotte said.

"Aw, thanks. You look good yourself! Now, we don't want to be too heavy on your make-up."

"Agreed, Sue."

"Okay, let's see what we have."

Ten minutes later, Sue had finished dolling herself and her niece up, and had applied perfume to them both.

"Let's knock 'em dead," she said, just as the doorbell rang. "That's them. Let's give them a night to remember!" Going downstairs with Charlotte in tow, she answered the front door. A skinny, balding man of about fifty stood in the doorway. He looked as though a stiff breeze could carry him off into the ether.

"Hello, Sue!" he said, offering the half-alive bunch of flowers he was holding in his hands.

"Thank you, Paul," Sue said, having to bend over to kiss the short man on his cheek. "Is your son with you?"

"Yes," Paul said, stepping aside.

When Charlotte clapped eyes on the weedy, gangly thing behind Paul, she almost burst out laughing. He had his eyes down and his body appeared to be trembling.

"Shy, is he?" Sue asked.

"Very, but once you get Paul Junior going, there's no stopping the lad!"

"Well, you better both come in. This is my niece, Charlotte – she will be helping me satisfy you boys tonight."

"Oh, how lovely," Paul Sr. said.

When Sue closed and locked the front door, the fun began.

As the men, if you could call them that, walked down the hallway and into the living room, Sue sidled up to Charlotte. "That fine specimen is yours!" she said, pointing to Paul Jr. and sniggering.

"Gee, thanks!" Charlotte said, rolling her eyes and stifling a giggle.

Sue instructed both men to sit, while they fixed refreshments.

"You know this pair?!" Charlotte asked.

"I know Paul Senior, yes. He's been coming to me on and off for the last few years."

"Never brought his son along before?"

"Nope, I asked him to bring him along for you," Sue said, winking at her. "He's a real catch, isn't he?!"

Both woman laughed as they mixed cocktails and poured large glasses of wine for each other – they then took them into the living room.

Over the course of the next hour, they had dinner, drank, smoked and had a laugh, which helped bring Paul Jr. out of his shyness.

Once the drinks had been consumed and a large chunk of money had been exchanged between Paul Sr. and Sue, the mood in the room completely changed, as Sue became this completely different woman.

She had pre-warned Charlotte, but it still rattled her slightly.

"Up and on your fucking feet, you maggot cunts!" she raged, and then continued to rip and tear into them. "Strip, you fucking dogs. Now!"

Charlotte felt excitement flood through her as both men did as they were told and ripped their clothes off. When they were down to their birthday suits, with their stiff dicks swinging, Sue ordered them downstairs, where the butt was brimming with ice-cold water.

Before Sue could speak again, Charlotte found her voice.

"In the barrel, you cunting dog!" she told Paul Jr., yanking a crop off the wall as she went.

"But I…"

"I…I…I," Charlotte mocked. "I said in, you miserable piece of shit!" she barked, whipping the boy as hard as she could across the backs of his knees. He buckled and cried out as he crashed to the floor.

"Paul, it's…" his father was about to say, but he was cut off by Sue, who grabbed him by the balls and forced him to sit in a chair that had leather straps for the occupant's wrists and ankles.

Once he was in place, Sue put clamps on his nipples, causing him to yelp – a spring-loaded mouse trap with a safety catch on it was placed by his balls.

"One false move and you'll never fire another amount of love muck out of your grapes again!" Sue said, knowing the thing couldn't activate with the catch in place.

"*Ugh*!" Paul said, looking up at Sue. "Please, Mistress…"

She slapped him around the face once, twice, three times – a tooth was hit free. It pinged off a wall. Blood dribbled out of his mouth.

"This is going to be an experience you'll never forget. I'm feeling real bitchy tonight, Paul. You're not going to like me tonight, baby," she said, looking down at his rock-hard dick – pre-come had oozed out of its tip and was running down the exterior of the shaft. "My, my, you are a big boy! It would be a shame if your cannon's balls got squished!"

"But…But…"

"Shut the fuck up!" Sue said, putting a ball gag in his mouth and fastening it at the back of his head. She gave him a few more cracks around his face.

Sue looked up, and saw Charlotte was looking at her.

"Mm..." Charlotte moaned. "I love watching you in action, Sue!" she said, digging Paul Jr. in the small of his back with the haft of the crop. "Fucking move it!"

The boy cringed as he stepped into the barrel of cold, nut-shrivelling water. He yelped, then started pleading as Charlotte put the lid on, which had a hole big enough for his head to fit through. His chin rested on the wood and stopped him from drowning.

"Comfy?!" Charlotte asked, laughing.

"P-p-p-please..." he chattered. "L-l-l-let me out..."

"Not going to happen, you fucking pathetic excuse for a man!"

"Th-th-this was my dad's i-i-i-idea, I didn't want to c-c-c-come!" His teeth clashed together so fast and furiously that it reminded Charlotte of the wind-up toy teeth you could buy for children.

"No, and you won't be *coming*, either!" She laughed some more.

"B-b-b-bitch!"

"Oo, you are a feisty one! Keep that nasty talk up, and I may just have to let you drown..."

She could see his lips starting to lose their colour, along with his cheeks. Charlotte turned her back on him and strutted over to Sue, who was twisting the clamps on Paul's nipples.

"Do you like that, baby? Do you still love me?!" She sneered.

Paul's eyes flicked around frantically until they found Charlotte, who stared at him.

"What do you want me to do? Help you?!" She sniggered.

"I think he wants you to stroke his cock, dear!"

Charlotte lurched. *I don't think I could...*

"It's only a hard dick, dear. It won't bite your hand off. Give it a few gentle strokes. He might like it."

Charlotte nodded, and took Paul's erection in her small, delicate hand.

He groaned.

"I think you're doing it right!" Sue said, going over to her wall of toys and selecting a whip. She then began whipping him everywhere she could whilst Charlotte's hand movement became more rapid.

"This is fun!" Charlotte said, watching Paul's eyes roll.

"Charlotte, you can stop now – we can't let him have too much pleasure! Come here."

She did as instructed. "What is it, Sue."

"Him," she said, pointing at Paul Jr. "Remove your thong, step up on top of the barrel, crouch, and let him put his tongue inside you!"

The shock must have been evident on her face.

"It's okay – I'm here. It's just like what we spoke about!"

Sue had taught Charlotte many things about pleasure, self-pleasure, torture devices and how to get the most out of a good submissive male, so she wasn't that worried.

Charlotte nodded, steeled herself, then removed her underwear and heels before proceeding to climb above Paul Jr.'s face.

"Lick it!" she demanded.

"N-n-n-no!" he managed to say.

"If you don't, then you're never getting out of that barrel. Now, lick!"

Silence.

As the seconds ticked away, she thought he wasn't going to do it, which would make her look silly and weak.

"Sue, where's the hammer and nails – this fucker is going to spend the night—"

Before she could finish her sentence, she felt his warm, wet tongue push against her pussy's wet folds. She let out a loud gasp, which scared her. As she rocked on the balls of her feet, she kept in sync with his rapid tongue movements.

"Good boy!" she said, from behind gritted teeth. An orgasm was quick to wash over her, but she didn't allow him to stop until she had a fourth.

After a few more hours, the night was starting to come to an end. Paul Sr. had paid for four hours of brutal domination, and the seconds were running out.

This has been an unforgettable experience! Charlotte thought as she wrapped a warm towel around Paul Jr. – he snuggled into it like he'd never felt warmth before.

"Should we untie this maggot now?!" Charlotte asked, referring to Paul Sr. – he was slumped in his chair. Blood pissed from various wounds all over his face and body.

His cock remained hard.

"I think he's just about had enough!" Sue said, removing his gag and tossing it to one side.

"I can take anything you've got, you worthless whore!" Paul said. He spat blood at Sue's feet.

In that moment, everything changed.

"Oh, you think so, do you?!" Sue said, turning around sharply and cracking Paul Sr. across his face with a paddle she was holding. The smack was so hard, it rattled his teeth. His whole body quivered and his knees jerked violently, causing the trap between his legs to snap viciously closed on his scrotum, catching Sue completely off-guard.

His scream was ear-piercing, causing Charlotte and Paul Jr. to shrink away.

"Untie me!" he yelled, but Sue just stood there and watched.

"Well, that was unexpected. The safety catch was definitely engaged!" Sue said, tittering. "Charlotte, come and see this. Now!" she instructed. "Look!"

Gingerly, she walked over to her aunt and saw the blood pouring out from between Paul Sr.'s legs.

"*Ugh*…!" he gasped, the colour drained from his face.

"Have they…severed?!" Charlotte asked.

"Not quite," Sue said, putting her hand to the devastated nut sack. "One of his bollocks has been crushed to nothing!"

Charlotte giggled. "Rip it all free!" she said, beaming.

"No!" Paul gasped, but it didn't stop Sue, who ripped the hanging, flapping scrotum off – his one good testicle hit the floor, causing Paul Jr. to retch.

"*Ew*!" Charlotte said, wrinkling her nose. However, she didn't take her eyes off the ruptured area. "Look, his cock has all but shrivelled up and gone inside him!"

Both women laughed as Paul flopped, bucked and gasped.

"*Urgh*!" they heard Paul Jr. call from behind them. "You fucking killed him!" he yelled, then threw his towel aside. He went for the closest thing at hand, which was a whip. He ran at Sue and wrapped it around her throat. He pulled her tight to his body. "I'll fucking murder you, you fucking bitch!"

Paul Jr. was much stronger than his scrawny body suggested.

"*Argh*!" Sue squealed.

Charlotte backed off and tripped over something at her heel – she landed on her arse with a hard thump. "*Ow*!" she called out, but nobody paid her any attention. "Fuck!"

Paul Sr. had stopped thrashing at this point – below his seat, a neat puddle of blood had gathered. Some of it had splashed up his legs, with a small spattering on his left kneecap.

Forcing a look, she could see loose bits of flesh and veins drooping from where his nuts used to be – blood still trickled out of the wound. His face was ashen.

Charlotte then looked at Sue. Paul Jr. had her down on her knees and was screaming and swearing in her face.

"H-h-hel…elp!" Sue gasped.

Charlotte got to her hands and knees, then heard a crash.

Sue had managed to drag Paul across the room, where they had crashed into a table holding a small tray of items. Among those items lay a syringe.

"Die!" Paul yelled, still holding her. In the tussle that followed, Sue managed to plunge the needle into her attacker's left eyeball. He jumped off her, enabling Sue to roll onto her hands and knees.

Paul Jr. staggered around the room, crashing into furniture and walls before his hands found something.

"Sue! Watch out!" was all Charlotte had chance to say as she watched the lad crash down on top of her aunt for the second time. He plunged a pair of scissors into her throat.

Before she died, she managed to palm the syringe deeper into Paul's eye, killing him instantly. He collapsed onto her.

"*Ooph*!" Sue coughed and bloodied spittle flew from her mouth. "Call…"

"What?!" Charlotte said, crying uncontrollably.

"Nine…nine…"

"Sue!"

She gargled once more, and then died. Charlotte fell backwards and curled into a ball. She lay there crying for a long time before realising she had to call the police.

All she could remember thinking was, *What are they going to think? That's another family member who's died around me!*

When she finally managed to calm her hysteria, she did what needed doing.

She called the authorities.

****

"Poor dear Sue," Chaos said. "I'd swap a hundred of you for just one of her, you useless sack of shit!"

Simone's entire body shook. She heard his teeth chatter.

"You're lucky I don't have a wine barrel like my Sue, worm! I'd put the lid on and seal it for eternity."

"P-p-p-please…"

"Shut up, and get your head under the water!" she bellowed, giving the side of the bath a hard wallop with the crop she held. "Under. Now!"

Simone didn't need telling a third time.

She watched as he slipped beneath the surface, his form covered by the ice cubes that bobbed this way and that.

Not taking any chances, Chaos put her hand in the freezing water, found his head, and kept him under that little bit longer. When he started to thrash, she laughed. "Drown, piggy!"

After a few more seconds, she let him up. He smashed through the cubes and gulped air into his lungs. "Wh…why?!"

"Why not?!" she asked, slapping at his fingers that clung to the side of the bath. "Back under. Now!" she ordered, attacking his blue balls with the crop.

He submerged, and then broke the surface once again.

"Again!" she demanded.

"N-n-n-no more!" he pleaded.

"I'll decide when you've had enough, boy. Do you hear me?!"

He nodded. Water streaked paths down his face, and dripped from his chin."Hee…heee…heat…"

"Heat?! No, I'm afraid not. You're going to sit there for a few more minutes, dickhead. And once you get out, you'll be subject to more torture. I'm sure you're looking forward to that!"

"Yea…yeah, Mistress!" he said with chattering teeth.

"Now, you wait there like a good little doggy, and Mistress will be back to get you when she's good and ready. Understand?"

Simone nodded.

"I can't hear you, dog!"

"Yea…yea…yeah!"

"I beg your pardon?!"

"Y-y-yeah, Mistress!"

"That's better. Now, stay!" she said, turning to leave the bathroom. She walked back into her bedroom. *That motherfucker best stay put, or he'll be in for the leathering of his life!* she thought.

Putting her crop down, Chaos walked over to her wall of deadly dominatrix weapons and spied the ropes and anal hooks. "Oh, how he loves being suspended from the ceiling by his arse!" she uttered.

As she was about to take the hooks and rope down, her mobile started ringing. She picked it up and looked at the number.

Who the…

"Hello!" she snapped, annoyed by the sudden disruption.

"Chaos?" came the female voice. "Is that *you*?!"

That voice rings a bell… "Who is this?!" Chaos said, raising her voice.

"Don't you know?!"

"If I knew, stupid, I wouldn't be asking!"

"Ha-ha, same old Chaos," the person said.

"Look, if you don't start giving information, I'm hanging—"

"Wow, wait! It's me…"

"Me who, dipshit?!"

"Your little Texan Taco!"

"Dawn? Dawn Cano?! No!"

"*Yes*!"

The first thing to come to Chaos' mind was Dawn's young, tight body and thirty-six-D tits, along with her shaved pussy and small tattoo of a lizard on the left side of her neck.

I used to like to trace its lines with my fingers…

Even though she was five-nine in height, she was pretty petite, with light brown eyes and dark brown hair.

"Oh, my God! How long has it been?!" Chaos asked.

"Too long, darlin'!"

So many thoughts and memories came flooding back at that moment, causing Chaos to blurt questions.

"Are you still with Lisa?"

"Swearengin?!"

"Yeah, and Tallulah?!"

Chaos' mind drifted back to Lisa – she was as equally sexy, at five-six. Her tits were a shade smaller than Dawn's at thirty-six-C, but that didn't make her any less hot. She was a temptress who loved nothing more than teasing men's dicks with her very pink, stiff, and mighty nipples.

Like Dawn, she too had a tattoo, only hers was of Pegasus flying across her right shoulder blade.

That one I used to trace with my tongue! she thought, smiling.

"Sadly, Lisa has moved on and Tallulah has died…" Dawn said.

"That's a shame, I liked that snake…"

"Same."

Chaos was almost too excited to ask her next question, but she did. "Are you back in town?!" Before Dawn could answer, Chaos heard the smile in her friend's voice.

"You know it! That's why I'm calling. Are you able to meet up?"

"Our old stomping ground?!"

"The Fantasy Ranch in Cardiff?" Dawn asked.

"Damn right, sister!"

"You're on. Give me an hour or so, and I'll meet you there."

"Okay," Chaos said. "I have a few things to take care of, but I'll be there. I can't believe it!"

"He-he, soon!" Dawn said, and the line went dead.

Putting her mobile back down on the dresser, Chaos turned and looked at herself in the mirror. "I'm going to need to do something with my hair!"

God, I can't believe Dawn's back in town. How long has it been?

****

After Sue's funeral, Charlotte was presented with the opportunity to stay with another family member, but had declined.

"I'm over sixteen, plus I have money – I'll be buying my own place!" she'd told a concerned uncle, who liked to lick his lips far too often as he spied her young, bare legs.

And so she did – she took a large chunk of her inheritance and bought her own place in Porthcawl. The time she had spent with Sue had helped shape her into a strong-minded and challenging young lady.

When she had her own slice of property, Charlotte thought she was made. Also, when she finished school for the summer, she never went back. She had decided she was going to be a stay-at-home woman, and men would look after her.

"Just like Sue, I'll dominate them. I'll bend them this way and that until they give me everything. Once they're dry, I'll break them and throw them away, just like the filthy rubbish they are!"

But things didn't pan out the way she wanted them to at first. For one, Charlotte had no way to meet men, because she never went anywhere. Secondly, she didn't know *how* to find such men – men who wanted to be pushed around. Men who wanted to be tortured and humiliated.

So, she re-thought things.

"I think I need a bit of life experience before I try and settle into the same role as aunt Sue," she'd uttered. One day, whilst trawling the internet, she found the answer to her musing.

An advert popped up on the screen:

Like dancing? Entertaining? Men? Then why not try out to be a pole deviant at the Fantasy Ranch?

On closer inspection of the ad, Charlotte could see that they were looking for strippers. She read at the bottom:

Must be over 18 to apply – please call in for an audition/interview

Hmm, I'm sure I could pass for eighteen! I'm a pretty good dancer, too. It's pretty easy teaching yourself to move all slow and sexy. Sue would be so proud of me, she thought, looking down at her tits. *A splash of make-up, a short skirt…*

After writing the address down, Charlotte went to her wardrobe, which was filled with revealing, provocative clothing, and picked out the sluttiest items she could find.

After taking a quick shower, she dressed and marched down to the Fantasy Ranch at seven o'clock that evening. The bouncer didn't even question her age, just escorted her to the manager's office.

When she walked in, she noticed there were women on stage performing – men were stuffing money down their knickers. A variety of coloured laser lights helped to illuminate the dark room, reminding Charlotte of a fireworks display on a dark night. A normal sixteen-year-old would have been scared, surrounded by drunk, leery men, but not Charlotte. She loved how the sexy girls were stripping the stupid fucks for all the money they had just by shoving their tits into their faces.

It was a joke.

This will be easy money, and I'm sure the men will love my young, tight body…

"Here we are, miss," the ape of a doorman told her when they were stood outside a door marked 'Manager'.

"You don't say?!" she said with a look of mock astonishment.

"*Ugh*!" he grunted, and then walked off, leaving Charlotte to rap on the door.

"Come!" a voice boomed from beyond.

Charlotte gave herself the once-over, unbuttoned another button on her shirt, shoved her tits out, and walked in, all leg and attitude.

"Well, well, what do we have here!" the fat guy behind his desk said. "Take a seat, pretty thing."

Charlotte did as she was told, knowing immediately that this guy would be easy to wrap around her fingers if she played her cards right. On sitting, she pulled her skirt up that little bit higher, giving him a flash of her naked pussy.

His mouth sagged.

Got ya!

She smiled.

"Hi, my name's Charlotte," she said, extending her hand across the desk. "You are…?"

"Ugh…Oh, er…em… Herbert. Jim Herbert. But you can call me Herb. All the gals do!" he said, smiling and taking her hand into his huge, fat paw.

"Thanks, Herb!" she said, confidently. She returned his smile, and smiled wider when he dabbed his brow. "Hot?!" she asked.

"Yes, you are!" he blurted. "Oh…I…"

Charlotte giggled a school girl giggle. "Thanks," she winked. "Have you still got a job going?! I'm in desperate need of one. I can start tonight," she shot at him whilst he was still in a state of shock.

"Ha! You don't mess around, do you?!"

"Time is money, Herb, or so my dad used to say."

"A wise man, your father…"

"Not that wise – he's dead. So, job-wise?!"

He just looked at her. "You're a real piece of work, do you know that?!" he said, smiling.

"I like to think so."

"How old are you?"

"Eighteen."

"And you have the proof to back that up?!" he asked, letting his eyes wander down to her legs, which she had parted for him once again.

"If I don't?"

"Oh, well…" he said, his eyes glued to her crotch. "I'm sure we can work something out. Can you come down tomorrow? Do a few dance routines. I'd like to see how you move!"

I'm sure you would, you dirty old cunt.

"Sure! Shall we say five?"

"Make it four – we like to run a few hours before we get going."

"I'll be here," she said.

"Hey, and change that name of yours! We can't have a gorgeous thing like you up on that stage with such a name. Bring your tight arse and new name around tomorrow at four. I'll be waiting to greet you by the door."

"You got it." She winked, and then headed out the door.

That night, after a long, hot soak in the tub, a delicious pasta meal and a few large glasses of wine, Charlotte sat down and run through a load of names.

"It has to be something catchy!" she uttered, turning her music down low and taking a glug of wine. She had a pen and pad by her side.

"Raven!" she said, writing it down. "After all, I do have thick, black hair. I could wear my leather suits on stage...No, wait – I'll be a stripper. Less is best."

Putting a scratch through Raven, she wrote a few more down:

~~Raven~~
~~Amber~~
Destruction
~~Destroyer~~
Deviant
~~Foxy~~
~~Amber~~
~~Cherry~~

Hmm, I do kind of like Destruction and Deviant...They kind of sum me up, she thought, tapping her pen against her pad. *Think, damn it, think!*

"What about my own name?!"

She scribbled her name down on the pad and picked letters out to try and form a name.

~~Char~~
~~Lotte~~
~~Ros~~

"Damn it, I've never been any good with words!" she said, slamming her pen down, and that's when she saw it.

That's it!

Chaos.

"Chaos," she said, letting it roll off her tongue. "It's perfect. From this day forward, that's what I will be known as!"

Once she had her chosen name, Chaos decided to turn the music up high and get blind drunk.

"Not like I have anywhere to be early in the morning!"

The next day, Chaos awoke with a stinging headache.

Ugh…It feels as though there's a brass band going for it inside my head!

Undeterred, she got up and prepped herself for the day ahead. She started proceedings by going for a long jog, followed by a boiling hot shower, a full English breakfast and two mugs of strong coffee.

"Don't think I'll wait until four to make my way down there," she spoke aloud. "I'll get there for three-thirty. I want to make a good impression!" she decided, clearing her breakfast things away and pouring herself a third coffee.

With her hot drink in hand, she sat in front of the TV and listened to the news as she drained the last of her coffee. Once done, she put the mug in the kitchen and went upstairs to get dressed. She also packed a sports bag full of other clothes, including clean underwear, make-up and energy drinks.

"You never know!"

Once ready, she picked her bag up off her bed and checked herself in the mirror. She'd chosen her old school uniform, which consisted of a tight, white shirt, a short, pleated skirt, knee-high socks, sensible shoes and tie. Chaos had also put her luscious black hair into pigtails.

She was braless, and her nipples poked at the thin fabric of her shirt.

"And, to complete the look!" she said. Popping chewing gum into her mouth, she snapped a few bubbles. "Perfect."

With a nod, she turned around and left the house.

Within twenty minutes, she was standing outside the locked doors of the Fantasy Ranch.

"Damn, maybe this wasn't such a grand fucking idea!" she said, giving the door a few hard thumps. "Come on, open up."

At her back, a car full of men drove by and started shouting, heckling and whistling at her.

She turned around and yelled, "Fuck off!" whilst giving them the middle finger. "Arseholes!" she uttered. When she turned back to the door, she heard the locks disengage.

"Who the fuck is it?!" Chaos heard Herb say before the door flew open. "Oh, Charlotte! You're way too early," he said, looking at his watch.

"I know," she said, turning her torso this way and that, causing her skirt to flap.

She had his attention.

"I thought I'd come down early, you know – show how keen I am!" She snapped her gum and gave him a wink. "Also, I thought I could give you a private show, if you know what I mean!"

"Oh, well…"

"But, if it's a problem, I can always come back later," she said, pouting and lowering her head.

"No, no, no!" he protested. "Come in, please."

"Are you sure?!"

"Of course."

"Thanks," she said, walking through the door. The club smelt of stale booze and cigarettes, but everything was clean – the bar, stage and tables. "The cleaners have already been and gone?"

"Yep. Now, how about that private dance?!" he asked, pawing at her shoulder.

Fighting the vomit back, she nodded. "Of course. You sit yourself down there, and I'll get started!"

On turning, she saw him grin. "Sure!" he said, taking up a chair close to the stage. "If you can impress me, I'll give you the job here and now."

"Excellent."

"What are you doing?" he asked, watching Chaos set up a camcorder.

"I want to record my performance for my portfolio," she lied. *Oh, you'll be giving me a job, ya fat piece of shit.*

"Okay."

When she was ready, Chaos started writhing and shaking her small arse. Her petite tits bobbed and almost popped free of her loosely buttoned shirt as she strutted across the stage. As her routine progressed, off came her clothes, until she was naked, apart from a thong.

"So, what do you think? Do I have the moves?"

"Well, why don't you show me that pretty twat of yours and I'll consider it!"

"Hey! You just wanted a dance."

"Come on now, show me," he said, getting out of his chair. "You do want a job, don't you?" he said, smiling.

"Yes, and you're going to give me one."

"I don't have to give you shit, bitch! You came flouncing in here…"

Before he could drive his point home, Chaos got off the stage and grabbed her stuff, along with the camera.

"Fine," she said. "Ill be off, and I'll be taking this tape to the police – I'll tell them how you tried to rape and seduce a minor," she said, smiling.

His face reddened. She saw his jaw muscles flex.

"Bye, then!" she said, walking towards the door.

"*Wait*!"

"Yes?" she said, turning to face him.

"You can start tonight! How the fuck did you know?!"

"Know what, Herb?"

"That I wasn't going to hire you – that I was hoping…"

"Hoping for a cheap screw? That you would get me down here just to fuck me and then tell me to piss off?!"

"Yes!" he said from behind gritted teeth.

"Huh," she huffed. "You're a man – I can see right fucking through you! I'll be back in a few hours. Don't worry, I'll be here for my first show." Winking at him, Chaos strutted towards the door. "Oh, and Herb?"

"Yeah?!"

"My new name is Chaos, chick. You better make sure I do have a job when I return, or I am going to the police."

"Don't worry, you got my attention!" he said, smiling and shaking his head. "You truly are some piece of work. When you get here later, report to Dawn Cano – she goes by The Dark Delight. She's the head dancer, and looks after you girls."

"Thanks, I will!"

That night, on returning to the Fantasy Ranch, Chaos caught up with Dawn "The Dark Delight" Cano after she was told by the barman that her dance instructor was up on stage, doing her thing.

On approaching the stage, Chaos could see two women dancing closely. Their naked bodies touched – their stiffened nipples collided. Wrapped around the body of the shorter of the two, who Chaos came to know as Lisa "Ice Killer" Swearengin, was a fat-bodied Boa constrictor.

As their faces got closer to one another, their tongues emerged and tangled in a lovers' knot, which Chaos found extremely hot.

When the music finally came to an end, Dawn left the stage and addressed her.

"So, you're the newbie, huh? You look like a kid! But hey, you've got great tits. Herb has an eye for talent. Why don't you get your scrawny arse up here, and show me what you can do!"

Chaos found her bluntness irresistible, and soon a long and lasting friendship started, until Chaos left the company a few years later, after she met Simone in a dominatrix club in Cardiff.

****

When Chaos was dressed and ready for her rendezvous with her old friend, she ordered her Slave out of the bath and made him dress.

"Looks like you've been saved by the bell, maggot!"

"H-h-h-how so, M-M-Mistress?!"

"I have to go out, and I'm going to be gone for a few hours, but I'll be sure to continue the torture once I'm home!" she said, smiling.

"P-p-p-permission to have some time out of the house, Mistress? I n-n-need some fresh air!"

She thought about this for a moment. "Where will you go?!"

"I w-w-was going to go down to the fair…"

"If I allow this, I want you back by ten. Do you hear me?!"

He nodded. "Yea…yes, Mistress. I only want an hour or so, just to stretch…"

"Shut up, maggot!" she said, slapping him across the face. "You may have your time out," she said, looking down at his caged cock. "You stay out of trouble. And, if I have to come looking for you, there will be hell to pay!"

Again, he nodded. "Yes, Mistress."

"Good, now go and do what you have to. I'm off now, so behave!" she said, leaving the bedroom. As she got to the door, she thought she heard him giggle. She turned on her heel. "Something funny, Slave?"

"No, Mistress. I didn't say or do anything…" he said, laughing hard on the inside as he watched her leave him all alone.

****

Simone smiled at her back, and thought, *This is my chance to escape*… "I'll show you, bitch!" he whispered, then prepared to leave the house for the evening…

BROKEN PLAYTHING

"Forgive me, Father, for I have sinned…" Simone said, bowing his head.

"How long since your last confession, my child?"

"More years than I care to remember, Father."

"And what have you to confess, my son…?"

****

By the time Simone got to his front door, he'd managed to stop giggling like a little school girl, but the lopsided grin still remained – it was cartoonish in size, which, in turn, displayed his well-polished teeth and healthy gums.

"That's a real shit-eating grin you have there, love…" he could hear his mother say. She had one of the most radiant smiles he'd ever seen, and he couldn't wait to tell her what the women down at Bunnies had given him today for his twentieth birthday, which had been yesterday.

A belated gift, but still – it had been amazing.

The lovelies at his mother's workplace had lined up and given him a lap dance followed by a striptease. The manager, a close friend of his mother's, had even closed the place for a few hours so Simone could enjoy his birthday treat.

At the back of his mind, he knew she had probably sucked his dick to get it to happen, but he was cool with it. She loved him, as he did her, and so he let things like that slide. His mother was an adult. A beautiful woman who knew what she was doing.

Oh, if only Mr. Tickles had been there! he thought.

Crystal, his favourite, had lingered, and taken her time rubbing her arse against his dick, which had been a solid pillar beneath his trousers. When she was finished teasing, her striptease had been equally slow.

Simone, who had already blown his load twice, came a third time to Crystal and her performance.

What a woman, he thought, pushing his front door wide open. As he entered the hallway, a blast of music hit him. His smile grew wider. It was coming from his mother's dance room…*A final belated show for my birthday? She's such a wonderful mother. Maybe after her performance, she will want to take a shower with me! A bath is nice, but a shower is even better – her rubdowns are heavenly.*

When he got to the foot of the stairs, he looked up and called to his mother, but she didn't hear. Either that, or she did hear and wasn't answering. That was her way of telling him she wanted to be spied on, wanted his eyes on her.

He wasn't one for refusing either. Since he'd come of age, she'd relaxed about him watching her. He didn't have to peep any longer, but, like him, she knew half the thrill was in peeping from a hidden place.

*Oh, Mam…*he thought, excitement building in him.

After removing his shoes and coat and placing his keys on the hook close to the front door, Simone sauntered into the living room. All the lights were off, but he could still see. The afternoon sun may have been dying, but it was enough to light his path as he looked for Mr. Tickles.

I'm sure I left…

"Here, sir!" the clown called out.

"There you are!" Simone said, picking up his toy clown from the sofa. "You missed a treat at Bunnies, Mr. Tickles. Mam arranged a special show for me down there."

"Those dirty fuckers get their titties out for you, sir?!"

"Oh, yes! You should have seen the show Crystal gave me, man…Rubbed her arse, tits and *bush* in my face and crotch. It was amazing. She didn't hold back. None of them did, to be fair."

"Mother's in her dance room! Shall we…?"

Simone's smile grew wide once more as he clutched his clown close to his chest and marched upstairs.

"The new peephole, sir?"

"Hmm, why not!" Simone said. When he reached the second floor, he took a right and headed into the room directly in front of him. Opening the door, he looked inside before entering. Over the years, this space had become a dumping ground. It housed his old toys, clothes and some of his mother's costumes.

Before it had become like this, it had acted as Sian's room. Oh, how he'd had fun playing in this bedroom with her. But that was a long time ago now, and all he had left were memories of his sister.

Last month, when snooping around in here, Simone had stumbled into her walk-in wardrobe and discovered some plaster missing off the back wall. On further inspection, with prodding and picking, he'd opened up a hole. On looking through it, he pleasantly noticed he could see directly into his mother's dance room.

Having thought all the walls in his mother's room were sound proofed, he'd checked one night when she was out and discovered that the section supporting the hole was in fact missing some padding.

He used this to his advantage. The ceiling hole had become boring since his mother knew that's where he always spied from. Even though she knew he was doing it, something was removed from the peeping. The game. The façade that he and her played.

With a new hole in place, he could get excited about watching her again – she may have known his eyes were on her, but she didn't know from where they watched. It was hot. Erotic, even. It made his dick twice as solid, which impressed her.

"You don't think it's a small one?" he'd asked her last year, after a girl had laughed at him.

"No, honey, not at all. It's a very nice penis," she'd assured him.

Of course, some of the girls down at Bunnies had also assured Simone about his size. Not that women laughing at it bothered him. He found the experience rather kinky.

Once, one summer ago, a girl had laughed at his semi-hard cock under the pier down on the beach. At the time, he couldn't understand why he hadn't slugged her in the face, then kicked her ribs to dust when she was down, but the moment had thrilled him – his cock had grown in his hand, much to her fright.

"You're fucking weird!" she declared before storming off.

He'd pleaded with her to stay, to tough it out, but she'd thrown sand in his face and run away. "I'm going to tell my dad on you!" had been her parting words.

"Fucking tell, you whore!" had been his to her as he'd spat crunchy, golden particles from his mouth.

Stepping into the room, he drew in a deep breath. Even though it had been years since Sian had occupied the room, he could still smell her. He found that extraordinary, really. How could it be possible? It didn't matter, because he could.

Her womanly scent and perfume clung to the air like a ghost.

"I miss you so much…" he whispered.

"Chin up, sir. Mam is waiting!"

"You always know how to cheer me up, don't you?"

"Affirmative, sir –it's how you brought me and the other guys up. Krull Army would be nothing without you and your discipline, sir."

"Well, you're a good number two, Mr. Tickles," he told the stuffed toy as he held it from his body.

The clown nodded.

To Simone's surprise, the music in the opposite room came to a long silence.

The CD has probably finished, he thought. *Any minute now, I'll hear her change the disc…*

But it never came.

Intrigued, Simone quickened his pace and moved to the wardrobe. Upon opening the doors, the hole winked at him as light from behind it shone through. He moved forward and placed his eye against it.

She was nowhere to be seen.

Odd…

His heart started to race. Was she playing tricks on him? Was she hiding, about to jump out and scare him? She was prone to do such things. His smile returned. His hard-on faltered.

"Come on, you prick tease…"

"Anything, sir?"

Simone shook his head, about to speak, then the music kicked back in – Nazareth were singing about love hurting.

Getting onto tiptoes, Simone cast his eyeball downward. Nothing. Then he looked as far left as he could. Nothing. Before totally giving in, he shot his eye right, and that's when he saw her.

She was lying on the floor, her stiff nipples pointing at Simone's peephole in the ceiling directly above her.

A laugh escaped him. "What silly game is she up to now?!" he said, sniggering all the while. His shoulders skipped with his hearty chuckles.

"What is it, sir?"

"It's Mam, she's…" Then, something odd about her positioning struck him. Her left leg was bent at an awkward angle beneath her, as though she had collapsed onto it. Her arms were stretched out at her sides, with one slightly bent at the elbow.

He didn't know if it was his imagination or not, but he couldn't see the rise and fall of her stomach.

"Mam..." he said, sounding warbly. Tears were threatening. "Mammy?!" Simone's voice cracked. Mucus clogged his throat, stopping him from saying another word.

"Sir?" Mr. Tickles said.

Simone didn't answer. He exited the wardrobe as fast as he could, almost tripping over some of the junk which lay scattered about his feet.

"No..." he finally managed, wiping some of the tears off his cheeks, which were spilling from his eyes in abundance. "Please, no...Not her!"

Leaving the spare room, he went to her door and hammered his fist against it. When she didn't answer or open up for him, his fears were as good as confirmed – she was dead.

Trying the door handle, he found it locked.

"Mam!" he screamed. The tears leaking from him blurred his vision. "*Mammy*!"

Stepping back, he raised his leg and smashed his foot against the lock. Wood splintered with a sickening snap, but the door stood firm. Retracting his leg, he kicked out again. This time, the handle fell off the door and it opened a crack.

Pushing it fully open, a breath hitched in his throat – he was too terrified to look inside, but he knew he had to. After all, she could just be sleeping.

Maybe she's fainted?

Walking into the room, Simone went to the CD player and turned it off.

"Mam?" he called. He sniffled and wiped the tears from his cheeks. "*Mam*?!" His bottom lip trembled.

"Sir, maybe we should call for help?"

Ignoring Mr. Tickles, Simone edged closer and closer to his mother. He could feel his heart crumble beneath his ribcage. His skin turned cold. The hairs at his nape and on his arms stood on end.

He gulped. Hard.

When he got to her side, he put his fingers to the side of her neck – there was no pulse. To double check, he put his ear to her nostrils. She wasn't breathing.

"*Mammy*!" he screeched, scooping her body up in his arms and pressing her tightly to his chest. That was when he saw the multiple bottles of pills sprinkled across the floor like tossed confetti.

Mixed among the tablet containers were stray pills and a smashed glass.

His vision glazed over as he continued to scream and cry hysterically – his whole body shook.

"Wake up, Mammy! *Please*, wake up!"

"Sir, try and calm yourself!"

Putting her back down, he stood up and started lashing out – he put his fists and feet through her mirrors. He swept all her items off a dressing table she kept in the room. Make-up containers, brushes, wigs, fake eyelashes and nails, lipsticks and a mirror were thrown across the room.

The sound of smashing glass was deafening.

He roared like a jungle warrior and beat his chest like a gorilla. With all his might, he ripped his T-shirt to ribbons.

Finally, out of breath, he collapsed at her side.

"Why?!" he blubbered.

Her once pretty face had turned an ugly chalk-white and her previously rich red kissable lips had been replaced by a sickly blue-purple hue.

Looking down at her, he couldn't believe she was gone. Simone refused to let the information sink in, and, in his stubbornness, he leaned in and kissed her on the mouth.

The iciness he found there stirred something within him.

His loss and heartache was suddenly replaced by anger. Pulling back, he looked into her unblinking eyes.

"You were my world. How could you have done this?!" Rage coursed through him again. "You've betrayed me. Left me alone in this hateful world. Why?!"

He sucked up his tears and refused to spill any more over a woman he had given himself to.

"I loved you so dearly…"

He could feel spite working its way into his brain as his fingers fumbled at the button of her hot pants. Managing to unclasp it, he pulled the denims down her tight-covered thighs and tossed them to one side.

He ran both his hands over her legs and found the fabric to be most pleasing to his touch. His dick stiffened.

"Must I show you how much you mean to me?!" He slapped his dead mother across her cool cheek. "Fucking answer me!"

"Do it, sir – drill her fucking arse to the floorboards! We've waited to feel the inside of that pussy for a long time!"

"Her legs feel so good!" he said, then savagely tore the tights asunder. The horrific sound pleased him, and he smiled harder when he realised she wasn't wearing panties.

Before mounting her tiny frame, he ripped her flimsy bra apart, which exposed her small tits. Her nipples still stood erect.

He licked his lips and then turned her head so he could look into her eyes as he fucked her.

Once he was on her, he pushed his hardness into her, and thrust back and forth gently.

"I love you!" he said, feeling his orgasm quickly building…

"You *screwed* your mother?! Sorry, let me rephrase that – you screwed your *dead* mother?!" she said, bringing him out of the memory.

Turning to face her on the bed, he couldn't help but drink the woman in before answering her. *What's her name?* he thought. *Mary? No. Maggie? Mandy! Mandy Tyra. She's five-foot four-inches of pure heaven and legs. And those red fishnets…Damn!*

Her stockings were supported by matching red suspenders and she wore a garter around her left thigh. Beneath the material on the right thigh, Simone could see a tattoo of a large yellow rose. A fat-bodied snake was entwined around the flower of love, and its thorns were ripping into the cobra's scaly flesh, causing its blood to flow freely.

Moving his eyes to her crotch, he noticed how well-groomed it was, as there was only a thin strip of hair to be found. Earlier in the night, when he'd asked her how clean she was 'down there', she had joked with him about how she didn't cut shapes into her bush.

Just above her pubic bone, she sported more ink. This one, however, was not an image, but words. It read, in stunningly crafted calligraphy: *Tunnel of Love.*

Raising his eyes to her navel, he sought out the piercing she had there – a small hoop with a tiny pendant in the shape of a dream catcher.

"Did you hear me?!" she snapped.

But he wasn't paying any attention – her body had him hypnotized, much like it had put him in a trance earlier in the night. *She is beautiful,* he thought. *Such a flat stomach with well-rounded tits* (which were currently hidden beneath a bra that matched the suspenders). *Hang on, no panties? No, of course not – she explained that to me…*

"I never wear them, sailor – they get in the way of fun!" she'd said, winking at him.

Splendid.

"Hey, Simone!" she said, snapping her fingers.

His head shot up, and he found he was looking into her smouldering green eyes. Her medium brown-coloured hair flanked her pretty face, which was scant of make-up. *I hate it when they have so much make-up on, they look like a fucking clown!*

"Yes?" he said.

"I said, you screwed your dead mother?!"

He nodded. "Yeah, that's right," he said, adding, "multiple times."

"*What*?! Are you fucking crazy? Do you have wires touching?"

"Hey, you said you understood me. That you felt my pain!"

"Yeah, that's before I knew you screwed a dead body. And not just any dead body, but your mother's!"

"You said you'd listen to my problems. That you would help make all my pain go away – that you would love me, and never hurt me…" He started to raise his voice – he could feel his control slipping away.

"Love you?! Are you fucking nuts? I've only just met you…I thought you wanted to come back to this shitty hotel to fuck?! Isn't that why you picked me up at the strip club tonight?"

"No! I was hoping you would sit and listen to me. I wanted to talk. I wanted to—"

"Wow, hey, back up. I did sit and listen to you. We had a few slammers at the bar whilst we shot the shit, remember, stud?" she said.

"Yeah, and I thought you were lovely. That's why I brought you back – I wanted to keep talking. In private!"

"We have – you've been telling me how much you liked screwing your dead mother!"

A laugh escaped her, causing him to lash out. He backhanded her off the bed – her small frame crashed down on top of the nightstand. The phone was thrown to the floor, the cord ripped from the jack. Glass exploded under her, which he guessed was the lamp breaking.

He didn't care that she'd laughed. Humiliation had become his friend – it thrilled him when a woman belittled him. But he drew the line at a bitch being nasty about his relationship with his mother.

A bitch who worked a bar at Pole Puss.

Someone who liked nothing more than having strange men shove notes down her flimsy knickers. *I bet she loves the feel of tenners rubbing against her twat.*

"*Ugh*!" Mandy cried, rolling off the wreckage.

He'd been right about the lamp – it lay in hundreds of pieces at her side. Some shards had stabbed into her stomach.

It isn't so perfect now! he thought, ripping the length of wire out of the back of the phone. He wrapped it around his fists, making a garrotte out of it.

"No!" she whimpered. "Don't, please…I've done nothing to you! I have kids!"

"I thought you may have been the *one*, Mandy. I thought I had finally found my new Toni. But no. You bitches are all the same. You fuck us over. None of you are to be trusted."

"Toni?" she gasped.

"Yeah, long story…I haven't really got the time to go into it with you now," he said, wrapping the wire around her throat. He pulled her off the ground and applied as much pressure to the cord as he could.

"Fu…ck….f-fuc….k…" she gasped, spat and wheezed.

"Yeah, fuck. You're right. I fucked my mother until there was nothing left of her to fuck. I fucked her until parts of her started dropping off; until the body was so badly decomposed, I was forced to bury her in the sand at Porthcawl beach…You're the only person I've told. I never even told…*her* that!"

When Mandy stopped fighting, he threw her body to one side and collapsed onto the bed. He curled up and wept himself to sleep as he gently rocked back and forth.

"Mammy," he blubbered.

****

The priest muttered something before he spoke directly to Simone. "And when was this, my child?"

"Last night, Father…"

"I see. And what did you do next, my son? Did you call the police?"

"No, you fucking retard! We cut that cunt up with a hacksaw, starting with her head, then buried her under the floorboards of the—"

"*Shh*, Mr. Tickles!" Simone said as quiet as he possibly could, covering the clown's mouth with a hand. In the dimly lit confessional box, Simone could just about make out the form of his number two, who sat on his lap facing him. "I don't want to tell him stuff like that!"

"Are you okay, my son?"

"Yes, Father – I'm just…I'm feeling slightly overcome by it all," he lied. He fake sobbed.

"Take your time, my boy. There's no rush."

"No, I never alerted the authorities, Father…I was too scared," he lied, again. "After I killed her, I fell asleep. When I woke up today, I left the hotel and wandered the streets in the rain for hours before I decided to come here…I didn't know what else to do. I've been so, so bad, Father. I'm scared for my soul. Am I damned?!"

"No, child. Our Lord and saviour loves all his children, even the fallen ones. But you must do the right thing, my son. You must be able to see that?"

The priest's words struck a chord with Simone, causing genuine tears to roll down his face. *What have I done?* he thought.

"Yes, Father – I know what must be done, but first, I would like to talk to you more. Get things off my chest. Is that okay?"

"Of course, my boy. Here, in the house of our Lord and Father, we have plenty of time for a lost lamb such as yourself."

The Father's warm, tender words helped him to relax.

"Thanks. I need a friendly ear at the moment…"

"Of course. So, child, tell me – who is Toni? You mentioned her when you were telling me about Mandy and your mother."

"Oh, *her*...She's someone I knew. Sadly, she let me down and she's no longer with us. Just like my mother. Betrayed me. I found her in the arms of another. The *bitch* hurt me badly, Father!"

"Please, my boy, if you could refrain from foul language under the Lord's roof…"

"Yes, of course. I'm sorry. I just don't think I'm ready to talk about her just yet, Father."

"That's fine. Tell me what you want, when you want."

"It's their fault I've become this monster, this unholy thing that can't stop hurting people and lusting!"

"Who, child?"

"Women, Father."

"You blame your mother for the bad things you have done?"

"She's one of many, yes."

"Because she failed you as a parent?"

"No, she was a good mother. I blame her for leaving me all alone in this world. She abandoned me – left me to the wolves."

"Why did she do it, son?"

"Take her own life?"

"Yes."

"Because of how I turned out, Father – she blamed my wicked, perverse ways on herself."

"How do you know this?"

"She left a note. It was brief, but to the point."

"I see. That must have been hard on you."

"To this day, I still carry the note, Father. May I read it to you?"

"Of course, my son. But first, tell me: Didn't people wonder where your mother had gone to? You never alerted the police of her suicide."

"I told people she had abandoned me, Father. That she had fled back to Italy so she could be with my estranged father."

"I see. Please, read me the letter, son."

"Okay, let me see if I can get to it…" Simone said, standing up and removing his wallet from his back pocket. Before he could sit back down, his mobile started vibrating in his pocket. Digging that out too, he sat back down and opened his phone.

There was a new message awaiting his response.

Hmm, that's odd. I've not had a text or phone call in months. She *was probably one of the last people to text or ring me…*he thought, letting his mind drift as he opened his messages.

When he saw the name, a smile spread across his face. He'd very nearly forgotten about this person, and her friends.

"My God, *Chrissy…*" he whispered.

"Sandoval?" Mr. Tickles piped in. *'Fuck me, that name takes me back, sir."*

"Yeah, you're not the only one!" Simone said, looking at her message.

'Hey Simone, I hope you still have the same number, and that you receive this message. If you do, long time! I just wanted to let you know that I'm back in Wales with the girls, and I wondered if you'd like to catch up sometime soon?'

"What will you do, sir?"

"I…I'm not sure…"

"Are you okay, my boy?" the priest asked.

"Yes, Father. Could you give me two minutes, please? I'm gathering the strength to read this to you," he lied. Again.

"Of course, my child."

"Chrissy Sandoval," he whispered. He had not uttered her name in at least six years. *She'd always promised to get in touch if she was ever in the area. And by the sounds of things, she's back with her act,* he thought.

****

He couldn't stay inside forever. He knew that, but he couldn't face the world. Now, standing at his front window, Simone peeled the curtains back and looked outside. Summer had finally rolled around, which should have made him feel better.

How he loved seeing the lovelies out in their flimsy strappy tops, shorts/skirts and flip-flops.

It had been thirteen months since his mother had committed suicide – eight since he'd finally buried her remains on Porthcawl beach.

The sea has her now...

Huffing, he let his shoulders drop. "I need to get my life back on track," he said aloud. He looked around – the house, and everything in it, looked alien to him. "Maybe I should burn the place to the ground?"

"You can't spend any more of your time moping, sir!" Mr. Tickles said from somewhere behind him.

"I know…" he said, letting his words trail off. A large van stopped in his street due to traffic build-up. It was brightly coloured by the Stars and Stripes – a huge bald eagle with curled talons could be seen on the door. Simone couldn't see the passenger or driver of the vehicle, as the windows were blacked out.

Written over the red, white and blue on the side of the van were the words *'Flesh Flaying Fiends: the world's most deranged dominatrix act'*. The sound of it made his balls ache. There was a mobile number listed below the words. Quickly, he grabbed his own phone and took the number down.

As the van pulled off, Simone rang the number. A woman with a thick, south American accent answered. "Hello, Flesh Flaying Fiends, Chrissy speaking – how can I help you?"

His breath hitched in his throat.

"Hello?!" she repeated with a sharper edge to her tone.

"Who the fuck is it?" he heard another woman ask in the background.

"I don't know, Coops – some douchebag heavy breather! *Hello*?!"

Simone ended the call by snapping his phone closed. The American lady went away. "Dom…i…na…trix…" By breaking the word up, it helped him to digest it. "Can't say I've ever heard it before. What does it mean, Mr. Tickles? Have you heard that word before?"

"It probably means that they're a bunch of dirty whores that need a good whipping and fucking!"

He didn't have the internet in his house or on his phone, as he wasn't interested in it, so he couldn't check the meaning. Nervously, he opened his phone and redialled the number.

"Hello?!" the same woman said, clearly pissed.

"Oh, uh, h-hey…" he stuttered.

"Yeah?"

"I…"

"Are you the same person that called about five minutes ago?!"

"Oh…Er…Yeah, it was me…"

"Why you wasting peoples' time, bro?!"

"I'm sorry…I didn't know what to say," he confessed.

"Look, what can—"

"What does dom…i…na..trix mean?" he blurted. This provoked a shriek-like laugh from the other end of the phone. He smiled. *I like her…*A giggle escaped him.

"Dominatrix? Well, that would be telling, big boy. What do you think it means?!"

He looked at Mr. Tickles, licked his lips, and took a deep breath before answering. "That you're a bunch of dirty whores that need a good whipping and fucking!"

"*Atta-boy, sir! Tell the little strumpets how it is*!"

More shrieks of laughter, followed by her covering the phone and talking to the other person in the van. He couldn't quite work out what they were saying, but he guessed that they were making fun of him. He liked it.

"Ha-ha, is that so?!" she asked.

*Oh, boy, do I like her…*After so many months of living in the shadows, staying on the cusp of society, it was nice to finally have some interaction. He was starting to remember what it was like to talk to people. To talk to nice women, especially pretty ones.

"Are you pretty, Chrissy?!" He couldn't believe he had asked her that. *Fuck it.* "Bet you have nice legs, too!"

"Oh, you're a cheeky one! Mama's going to have to put a collar and lead on you, *dog*!"

He had no idea what she meant, but he liked it. His cock pulsed and pushed against the front of his trousers. Grabbing his zip with his free hand, he lowered it and reached inside for his dick.

As she spoke, he rubbed it to the sound of her voice.

"I bet you like the sounds of that, don't you, beast?"

All he could do was groan.

"Are you fucking playing with yourself, you dirty fuck?!"

Her giggling pushed him over the edge – he couldn't hold his orgasm back. His hot load erupted out the end of his cock and shot up the curtains and splashed the drapes.

"*Ugh*!" he gasped to the sound of her giggles.

"My, you're an interesting one, cowboy. Why don't you come on down to the Klitty Kingdom tonight?"

"On the front?" His breathing came in ragged tears.

"Yeah. I'll *show* you what a dominatrix is."

"Okay…"

"The show starts at nine sharp. Make sure you're there. And when you've seen the show, make sure you come over and say hi!"

The line went dead, which was followed by a dreadful buzzing sound. He pulled his mobile from his ear and hung up.

"Nine, she said. Should I, Mr. Tickles?"

"*Affirmative, sir – you need to get back in the saddle, as they say. Besides, it would be nice to have some clunge around here! It's been far, far too long.*"

A broad smile appeared on Simone's face. The call had been the thing he'd needed to help get him out of the doldrums.

Simone could feel the clouds of misery finally starting to lift.

Attention – that's the thing he craved most.

At precisely eight fifteen, Simone was standing outside the shithole named the Klitty Kingdom – a flea-bitten, ramshackle dump known locally as the Fuck Pit. The structure looked as though it was being held together by bubblegum and jism; most of the paint and plaster had come away from the exterior walls. It was the type of place where you wiped your feet on the way out.

As he was about to put his hand on the door handle to open it, he noticed the lacklustre brass was coated in dried blood and snot. His stomach back flipped and his eyes rolled like marbles.

"Dirty cunts." Carefully, he covered his hand with the cuff of his jacket and pulled the door outward – he was immediately hit by the smell of stale twat, cigarette smoke and suspect ale.

Releasing a held breath, Simone stepped inside and almost instantly regretted it – the place was rammed so full that he couldn't see the bar, let alone the stage. He'd never been very good at handling large crowds, but he was determined not to let that spoil his evening. *As if she's going to remember me after a brief conversation over the phone…I'm sure she's spoken to loads of guys today.* "Chrissy…" he said, letting the name roll off his tongue.

Lightly pushing past people to get to the bar, he excused himself as he went. When he finally got there, he realised he was standing next to a guy on a stool – he was slumped over the bar. A rank stench of shit and piss waved off him, bringing Simone to the conclusion that the guy had soiled himself in his intoxicated state.

"Devine," he muttered.

"Help you?!" asked the barman, who reminded Simone of a boxer, what with his flat nose, ravaged looks and missing teeth.

"Coke, please."

A few sniggers erupted from behind him, followed by "sissy", "faggot" and "fairy". He didn't care what the fuck others thought of him – he wasn't an ale, cider or lager drinker. He preferred wine, and he certainly wasn't ordering something like that in a bar full of brawler types.

When the barman returned, he slammed a can of Coke down on the bar. "That'll be three quid, pal," he barked.

"Next time, wear a mask, Turpin!" Simone uttered.

"Excuse me?!" the barman spat.

"I said, lovely." He handed the man his money and turned to leave. As he did, he looked down and noticed he'd been standing in a puddle of piss. "Delicious."

Moving on, Simone weaved, ducked and bobbed his way through the crowd until he was close to the stage. It wasn't as classy or clean as Bunnies, and lacked personality. The poles that the women used looked grubby.

Looking at his watch, he noticed it was almost five past nine.

Any minute now, surely…

As if the compere had heard him, he stepped from behind a pair of gaudy curtains at the back of the stage and addressed the crowd via the microphone he held in his fat hand. He seemed like just the kind of guy who would own/work a place such as the Klitty Kingdom – fat, sweaty, greasy-looking, and balding. No, not completely bald: He had a few strands of hair that acted as a combover. His jacket, much like the shades he wore, looked as though it had stepped out of the seventies.

Do the curtains act as a Tardis? he mused.

"Ladies and gentlemen, boys and girls of all ages…Welcome to the Klitty Kingdom!"

People all around him started to whistle, howl, applaud and cheer. "Bring out the Yankee fanny!" someone yelled as the raucous died down.

"Be patient, you little cunt!" the compere joked. "Tonight, and every night for the next fortnight, we are proud to present to you the lovely ladies from across the Atlantic Ocean, the Flesh Flaying Fiends!" he growled down the microphone. "The usual ladies will be around to strip, dance and tease you into comas as usual…But first, the wild, wet and devious threesome that's guaranteed to put a stiffness in your drawers…"

The loudmouth stepped aside and put his arm out in a sweeping motion. The lights dimmed and out from behind the curtain stepped three of the most glamorous girls Simone had ever seen.

"Making up the Flesh Flaying Fiends are Chrissy Sandoval, Marianne Elsie and Christina Cooper!" the compere bellowed from the shadows.

Simone's thoughts were drowned out by wolf whistles – not that he could think of much. Before him, the women came out in a line, led by whom he took to be Chrissy, considering the order the announcer had reeled off.

She was rather tall for a woman, five seven or eight, with good legs and prominent hips and a striking waistline. *Her tits are small, but perky and juicy,* he thought as he watched her naked form sashay across the stage. *The voice definitely matches the body!*

Her skin wasn't blemished by tattoos or piercings. He anticipated her turning around so he could see her arse, which he knew would be a perfect peach. But before he managed to glimpse it, he caught sight of her hairless twat.

*Ohh…*He groaned and fought the urge to touch his cock, even though he knew some of the other guys around him were doing it.

He didn't have time to keep looking at Chrissy, as his eyes were then drawn to the woman behind her. Marianne wore nothing but a bandanna. In her left hand, she held an impressive bullwhip; in her right, she twirled a nightstick coiled in barbed wire.

"Fuck! That thing looks painful," he said, smiling.

Marianne appeared to be slightly taller, fuller bodied and bigger breasted than Chrissy. Unlike her Flesh Flaying sister, she had tattoos. One visible above her left breast was in the design of Medusa's head. Her snake hair stretched out far on both sides, with all the heads spitting venom. Their beady eyes glowed yellow, and stood out in the garish lighting inside the Kingdom.

As Marianne strutted her stuff, she cracked her whip with a fierce flick of her wrist, which made Simone's hard-on waver but remain. She looked like hell on legs, which made him ache with pure lust and pleasure.

Pre-jism leaked out of his cock and glued his pants to his bits.

Behind Marianne was Christina, or "Coops" as Simone had heard her being referred to earlier in the day by Chrissy. Unlike her sordid sisters, she wore one article of clothing – a pair of hot pants with a huge strap-on cock, which was black in colour and glistened under the light. On her head, she had a leather punk cap, which was trimmed with spiked studs and small chains. She had her pierced tongue poking out.

Coops was the smallest of the three by far, breast and stature-wise, but Simone found her spattering of freckles a real turn-on, and he was eager to see what she had planned with her strap-on.

Pyros kicked to life and heavy metal music erupted through the speakers dotted around the room – a band was singing about how the torture never stops. Then, the lights were killed and coloured spotlights burst into action, flooding the bar area, stage and girls in a psychedelic glow, giving them the appearance of something psychotic lurking in the shadows.

Sparks flashed.

Bangs and puffs of smoke startled the punters as they watched on in complete bemusement and excited curiosity.

Who are these amazing women? Simone thought, barely able to hear the voice inside his own head as the crazy train before him chuffed on. *Amazing. I've never heard, let alone seen, anything like this before.*

"Dom…i…na…trix…" he mouthed. "Is this it?!"

Over the course of the next fifteen minutes, Simone watched on in wide-eyed wonderment as the ladies did their thing on stage.

Finally, the music was cut and Marianne stepped out of the pyro fog and slanted coloured beams, all tit and attitude. She addressed all the 'maggots' before her. "Who out there's man enough to take the kind of punishment me and my Flesh Flaying sisters are able to dish out?"

Simone's jaw slackened – they were looking for volunteers to disgrace and humiliate.

Behind Marianne, he saw Coops thrust her massive strap-on as she dangled a small, steel contraption before her. It looked like some form of cage and appeared homemade…

Simone gulped, but shook with the horn. Before he could shoot his arm skyward in a shrinking crowd, another beat him to it.

"Pick me!" the eager man bellowed. Looking over the audience, which seemed to breathe with relief, Simone saw a skinny arm sticking up – it looked as though someone's head had grown a limb. "Me, please!" the person continued, shoving his way to the front.

The tallish man with a shaved head rushed up the stage steps. He wore black leather trousers and a T-shirt that bore the words 'I love it in every hole' on its back. "Looks like we have a brave dog, girls!" Marianne said into the microphone. Behind her, Simone could see Coops and Chrissy laughing. "What's your name, beast?!" she asked him, then thrust the microphone in his face.

"Chris," he said. His voice sounded shaky.

Marianne, who was roughly the same height as her participant, turned the man around to face the crowd, who cheered.

On the front of his T-shirt, he had a huge, circumcised cock – the bell-end was pierced.

"Chris Hall!" Simone blurted. "Shit, I was in school with that fucker," he said to himself. "Give it to the bastard!"

"Strip, worm!" Marianne ordered him.

"Hey?! I thought I was going to get a lap—"

"Strip!" Marianne yelled, then struck her prey across the face with her barbed nightstick.

Chris went to ground and clutched his torn cheek. He cried in agony, but then gasped in shock as Coops and Chrissy ripped at his clothes. Within seconds, he was naked. Stocks were then rolled onto stage, and he was locked into them.

When Simone didn't think things could get any stranger, or exciting, Chris was tortured, beaten, fucked and humiliated to within an inch of his life – they pulverized his cock and balls before locking his bits into the homemade cage. As Marianne whipped him with her bullwhip, which took more than a pound of skin, Coops raped him with her strap-on.

Before he could start screaming, a ball with a couple of straps attached to it was rammed into his open gob – the belts fastened behind his head.

Some of the onlookers had walked out at this point. Others had thrown their guts up.

But not Simone – he was enthralled. It fed his devious side.

He wanted to know and experience more.

By the time Coops was finished pounding Chris' arse, the anus-busting wang was covered in shit and blood, and a pool of piss had spread out around the stocks that homed the humiliated man.

After an hour of punishment at the hands of the Flesh Flaying Fiends, Chris' eyes were rolling around inside his head and his knees were knocking. When they finally released him, he collapsed to the floor and rolled into his own urine. His body was spent, ruined and weeping red from multiple wounds.

His loose anus, which must have felt like he'd shit a rocket, emitted one fart after the other – it sounded like staggered machine-gun fire to Simone.

They totally dominated him! Then it finally clicked – "Dom…i…na…trix!"

"Any other brave—"

Before Marianne could finish her sentence, Simone put his hand high – his balls were that tight with excitement, he feared they would rupture in his pants.

"Get up here, *maggot*!" her voice boomed. "What's your name, you pathetic piece of shit?!"

"Simone," he said, his voice but a whisper.

"He has a girl's name!" Coops said.

"That's the fucker who kept ringing earlier!" Chrissy pointed out.

"Oh, so you're our heavy breather!" Marianne said. "Ladies, help him with his clothes."

As Simone was stripped, stagehands rolled Chris to the end of the stage and pushed him off. His body hit the floor with a dull thud. His clothes were thrown after him.

"What a little cock!" Coops said, pulling a crop from behind her back. She lashed his hardness repeatedly before ordering him into the stocks.

Her whipping had hurt at first – so too had the butt fucking – but he'd thoroughly enjoyed it, and he found he was able to take everything they gave him, much to Chrissy's obvious joy, as she'd masturbated in front of him.

After they finally broke him, he too was thrown off stage, just like Chris. He found he couldn't move – his legs didn't work and his body felt like jelly. Pain exuberated through him, which he welcomed. At some point, he slipped into unconsciousness and woke to find most people had left the club.

Rolling onto his side, he managed to get to all fours and crawled to a nearby chair with his clothes in tow.

"Hi," he heard someone say.

When he got to the chair, he found it hard in pulling himself up and sitting on it – he winced when he planted himself down.

"You okay there, cowboy?"

He knew the voice. Through squinted, tear-filled eyes, he looked about him and saw Chrissy sitting on a chair close by. She was fully clothed, much to his disappointment.

"You must have blacked out. The club's been closed for almost an hour," she said, smiling.

"Wha…wha…" he tried, but the words wouldn't come.

"You're quite the punch bag, sugar – you have a dom at home?"

"Water…" he gasped.

"Can we get a water over here, please?"

"Sure!" someone called back at Chrissy.

"Another beer, too," she asked.

"Coming up."

Simone snuck another glance at her – her legs looked very long, and shiny.

"You like my yams, sailor?"

"I don't have a…dom," he confessed. "This was my first time."

"You play the game like an expert, Simone. That is your name, right?"

He nodded. "Yeah. I think one of my ribs might be broken…"

"Nah, you're just bruised." Her beer was plonked in front of her. "Thanks."

"Here," the barman said, slamming his water down on the table.

Simone looked at the discoloured h20, which had bits floating around in it, and thanked the man. He took a hearty swallow before replacing the glass on the table. "That's fucking disgusting!" he said.

She giggled. "I like you!"

"Why are you still here? More to the point, why am I?!"

"I told them to leave you here."

"Why?"

"Because I wanted to take you back to my hotel room, sweetie," she said.

****

"Son, are you okay?!" the priest asked.

"Huh?!" Simone said, coming out of his thoughts.

"Are you okay?!"

"Oh, er…Yes. Sorry. I…"

"I thought something was wrong…"

"No, Father. Sorry," he said, giving the note he held in his hand a shake. "I was just about to start reading." But before he did, he replied to Chrissy's message.

"Okay."

"*Dear Simone, by the time you read this, I'll be gone. I'm sorry, baby boy, I just couldn't keep going the way we were – I've ruined the special bond between a mother and son, and I blame myself for the man you have become. One day, I hope you can find it in your heart to forgive me for everything I have put you through. I cling to the hope that we will meet again, in a place where we can be together forever. All my love, Mam. XXXX,*" Simone said, wiping a tear from his eye. He managed to keep himself together as he held Mr. Tickles close to his chest – he hugged his toy clown as fiercely as he could.

"I'm sorry to hear that, my child. What did she mean by ruining the special bond between mother and child?"

He didn't really want to answer the priest's question. After all, he hadn't told anyone what really went on between him and his mother. Not even *her. But isn't that why I came here? To finally get* everything *off my chest before I…*

"We were intimate, Father."

"You and *your* mother?!"

"Yes."

"Oh…" he gasped.

"I don't know why the fuck he's sounding so fucking appalled by your actions, sir – he probably touches the choir boys on the quiet!" Mr. Tickles said, smiling.

"I know how it must sound, Father…"

"My poor child."

"I can't say anything. After all, I did enjoy it – maybe I encouraged it more than I should have…"

"You can't blame yourself – she was the adult and should have known better. You poor lamb."

"She never allowed me to enter her body – we only played and bathed together, Father. I think she took her life before it got to that stage."

"What stage?"

"Sex. I think she may have been worried that's where the relationship was heading. I hate her for taking that from me, too. I loved her, Father. I loved her more than a son should love his mother, but I couldn't help it."

"Oh, my…"

"Will there be forgiveness for me, Father? Will I be allowed to enter into the Kingdom of Heaven – to walk through the pearly-white gates? Will I indeed meet my mother along with my maker? Please tell me! I need to know."

"Yes, my boy. As I told you earlier, our Lord is most forgiving of the sins his lambs commit. He died for them, after all."

"And my mother—will she be waiting for me?"

"Yes. Even your mother's sins will be forgiven. Her soul cleansed."

"It wasn't just my mother's fault, Father. Other women have helped push me down the wrong path."

"I see. Go on."

As if on cue, his mobile rumbled. Opening it, he saw it was Chrissy – she'd responded to his reply.

"There was once this American woman…"

****

After she finished her beer and he drained the last of his dirty water, she led him out of the Klitty Kingdom and to the streets beyond, which were dead quiet – not even a car drove by as they walked and talked. The only sound came from the crashing waves as they smashed against the rocks.

"What time is it?" he asked. "My watch was broken earlier…"

"Just past one A.M.," she said.

"Where are you taking me?"

"I told you, back to my hotel room."

"Where are you staying? Is it the Seabank Hotel?"

"Yes, how did you know that?!"

"It's the most popular…Are your friends staying there, too?"

"Look, let's cut the small talk – are you telling me you've never been whipped and beaten by a woman before? That was your first time?"

He nodded coyly. "Is it shameful that I enjoyed it?"

She smiled at him. "Come on!" she said, then led him down to the sands.

"Hey, where—"

"Come on!" she said, pulling him by his hand.

When she got him on the beach, she found them a secluded spot and started to strip.

"Leave your tights on…" he said nervously.

"Oo, does daddy like them?" she asked, strutting around in her panties, bra and tights – the rest of her clothes had been discarded. Thrown to the sands with gay abandon. As she did a little dance for him, she rubbed her thighs and blew him kisses.

All he could do was stand there and watch her. *I must look like a cardboard cut-out! Do something. Touch her,* his mind screamed. *She clearly wants you to.*

"You can't be shy, not after what you endured tonight – all the girls laughing at you! The crowd, too."

He shook his head. Slowly, he put one foot in front of the other, as though he was learning to walk for the first time – his legs were stiff. Simone felt like a reanimated corpse.

"Come on, baby!" she purred.

He halted and looked at her. He couldn't stop the words from tumbling out of his mouth – "I've never been with a woman!"

Sure, Sian and he had done things together, but that was a long time ago – he'd forgotten most of it. Besides, a fully grown, developed woman had never fucked him.

Chrissy stopped dancing and looked at him. Her smile faded.

"A woman has never touched me," he said. The thought that he was lying made him feel as though he was betraying his mother's memory. *Fuck her, she left me.* "I've been lonely…I have no one!"

Then, unexpectedly, tears raced down his cheeks.

"Hey, come on, it's okay!" she said, stepping closer to him and taking him by the hand. "You want to tell Chrissy what's wrong?"

No, I can't tell anyone what's wrong, especially a woman I've only known for five minutes, he thought.

"I'm twenty-one years old, and I've never been with a lady!"

"Sh!" she said, putting her arms around him.

He collapsed against her body and placed his head against her chest.

She smells like Mam…

The feel of her legs against his instantly turned him on – his hardness pushed against her thigh.

"Touch me!" she whispered down his ear.

"I…"

She took his hands in hers, and put them on her arse. "Go on, feel it…"

As she nibbled his neck, he caressed her arse and kissed her – it wasn't long before they were both naked and rolling around in the sand. When she had him underneath her, she rode his cock to the tune of multiple orgasms as he fumbled with her petite tits and teased her nipples.

When they were both spent, Chrissy collapsed onto his chest. It didn't take her long to drift off to sleep, leaving him to drink in what had happened. It was the first time he had been happy in over a year.

He may have still been broken at that point, but she had certainly helped in putting him back together.

Maybe I do have a chance at living a normal life now? he thought, looking up at the dark sky, which was starless and moonless. Looking down at Chrissy, who snored lightly, he wondered how different things could be if he found himself a nice girl like her. *Maybe she'll be my girl? I'm sure Mr. Tickles and the gang will love her.*

With that happy thought in mind, Simone closed his eyes and tried to drift off to sleep by listening to the waves roll and then collide against the rocks.

He awoke to the sound of gulls screaming. After clearing the sand of sleep from the corners of his eyes, Simone noticed Chrissy was nowhere to be seen.

Did I dream it?! No, that's impossible.

Slowly, he sat up and looked all around him – the only thing he could see were seagulls fighting over food and early morning fishermen casting lines. The sun was barely up.

"Chrissy?" he called, his throat bone dry. *I knew it was too good to be true.*

As his head dropped, he noticed something odd about the sand in front of him. Getting up, he took a closer look. Someone had scrawled something in it.

"Come to the Klitty Kingdom tonight! I'll be waiting for you… Chrissy. Kisses," he read aloud. A smile spread across his face. "So, she does like me!"

After kicking the sand message away, he ran up the beach and didn't stop until he got home.

By the time eight o'clock rolled around, Simone was about ready to climb the walls in frustration. The day had been spent pacing the floorboards of his house, looking out the upper and lower windows of the house, cleaning and doing anything else he could think of to waste time.

"I can't wait to see her again, Mr. Tickles. I think she could be the one, you know."

"Sir, just be careful. I don't want to see you hurt again. Not after mother…"

"No, I'll be fine. It's not like she's going to walk out on me. She wants me!"

"I'm sure you know what you're doing, sir. Do you plan to bring her back here tonight?"

"Yes, if she'll come. We might end up spending the night on the beach again!"

"Okay, sir. Just in case, I'll make sure myself and the rest of the Krulls are out of the way."

"Very good, Mr. Tickles. I'm going to head off soon, so if you can keep an eye on things around here, I'll be most grateful."

"Affirmative, sir – you have nothing to worry about with me at the helm."

"I know the place is in good hands. I'll hopefully see you later – I would like to bring her back here."

"Sir?"

"Yes?"

"I take it you know what dominatrix means now?" Mr. Tickles asked, smiling.

Simone smiled back, remembering the lashings Marianne had given him with her whip, along with the clamps Coops had used to crush his nuts – the thought of it got him turned on.

"Oh, yes! You could say I do, Mr. Tickles. They had this little cage with them – Chrissy called it a male chastity device – and they locked my cock up in it and I couldn't get it fully stiff. The bars restricted it. It was amazing."

"It sounds it. Maybe she'll do some kinky shit to you here tonight, sir. It sure would give me and the boys a few needed thrills."

"I'll see what I can do! Do you want me to put the TV on for you?"

"Please, sir."

"Okay. I need to get the hell out of here – time is moving on!" Once he'd switched the TV on, Simone left Mr. Tickles to it. "See you later!" he called, closing the front door behind him.

By the time he got to the Klitty Kingdom, the show had already started. He cursed himself for having left the house so late, but his bad mood soon turned to happiness when he saw the Flesh Flaying Fiends working their magic up on stage.

As Marianne, who was dressed in all leather, ordered a male member of the audience to strip, her girls worked the poles behind her.

Both Chrissy and Coops were dressed as schoolgirls – they wore pigtails, pleated skirts, knee-high socks and flimsy white shirts with loosened ties.

It was a marvel to watch.

When Chrissy spotted Simone in the crowd, she was upside-down on her pole with her skirt pulled back, revealing her pussy. She gave him a smile and a wave, which coaxed him to do the same. Some of the men in the audience turned to look at him with distaste.

He couldn't take his eyes off her. She was amazing, just like her smile.

When Marianne screamed at the 'maggot' at her feet, Simone looked at her – the poor bastard she had up on stage was now fitted with a collar and lead. She led him around like a dog before forcing him to take a shit and piss in front of everyone. When he whimpered he couldn't go, she kicked him in the nuts. Marianne continued to do this until the man finally pushed his waste out.

His humiliation seemed to go on and on, from having his nose rubbed in his own filth by Coops to licking the soles of Chrissy's high-heels.

Simone had never felt so turned on.

He knew he got off on shame at the hands of a woman, but he never thought he would have been turned on by being pushed around by one. To be beaten. This show had opened his mind – had broadened his horizon.

After the Flesh Flaying Fiends had finished with their latest victim, they wanted another. Immediately Simone put his hand in the air, but he was refused. He felt cheated as another male was picked from the crowd.

Turning his back on the show, Simone pushed his way to the bar, not watching where he was going.

"Hey, you fucking retard!" someone yelled at him. A rough hand grabbed his shoulder, and Simone was turned around to face a man roughly the same size as himself. "You made me spill my fucking drink!" he spat in Simone's face. His breath reeked of rum.

"Sorry, I'll buy you another…" Simone said, not looking for trouble. It had been a long time since he'd raised his hands in anger with another man.

Cartwright had been the last…

"Oh, is that so!" the man said, giving Simone a push. "How about a fucking sorry first, you little cunt!"

"I did apologise," Simone bit back. "Are you fucking deaf?" he continued, feeling his patience wane.

"You wha'?!" the man said, screwing his face up as though he couldn't understand what had been said to him. "Are you taking the piss out of me?!" He gave Simone another push.

He fell against a table, causing all the bottles and glasses that stood on it to rattle – contents were spilled.

"Hey, fucking watch it!" someone bellowed.

All the while, Simone could hear the Fiends doing their thing on stage, whilst he had some dickhead threatening him over something meaningless.

Before he knew it, his hand had wrapped around the neck of a beer bottle.

"Well?!" the man barked at Simone.

Without a second's hesitation, Simone brought the bottle up and cracked it across his attacker's face.

"*Argh*! My fucking eyes!" he said, clutching his face.

He wanted to plunge the ruined bottle into the guy's neck, but he managed to get a leash on his rage. *No, that would be stupid. Too many eyes.* He dropped his weapon and instead grabbed the man by his ears and pulled his head down swiftly. Simone brought his knee up to meet the guy's nose, which flattened like a ripe tomato.

The sound of bone crunching against his joint was beyond satisfying – within that moment, Simone could see why the girls on stage got a kick out of hurting people. It was exhilarating.

As his prey hit the deck, Simone dove on him and delivered lefts and rights to his wrecked face.

"I said I was fucking sorry!" he yelled as he punched and punched the man. "Maybe you'll fucking listen…"

Suddenly, Simone felt two sets of large hands on his arms.

"That's enough, sunshine!" someone said.

"He's had enough, and you're out of here!" said a second person.

"Wait, no! Chrissy!" Simone yelled.

"We don't want any more trouble!" the second voice said.

Someone punched Simone hard in his kidney, causing his breath to catch in his throat. He was led out the back of the club, where a pair of double doors were opened.

"One…Two…Three!" his escorts said as they threw him out into the alley.

His body crashed against a dozen bins. A cat pounced onto his stomach before scampering off into the night.

"Ugh!" Simone said, rolling onto his side.

"And fucking stay out!" one of them said to him.

"Yeah, we catch you back here again, we'll kick your arse, pal!" the other said.

Opening his eyes, Simone saw the two for the first time – they were huge. It was as if someone had stuffed a pair of gorillas into ill-fitting dinner suits.

He said nothing, just lay there and accepted his fate. "Chrissy…" he mouthed, holding his ribs.

Groaning, he got to his feet and dusted himself down – a banana skin and other bits of rubbish had clung to his shirt and jeans. "Ugh, fucking disgusting."

Undeterred by the thug-like bouncers, Simone stayed in the lane and waited for the girls to finish their show in the hope that Chrissy would come outside and look for him.

After a few hours passed, however, he was on the verge of surrender.

"She ain't coming!" he said to himself, sitting among the scattered bins. Rats scurried about him, but he didn't care.

Getting up to leave, he was stopped by the same doors he'd been thrown through opening at his back.

"Simone?" he heard a female voice whisper.

"Chrissy?!" he said into the gloom.

The next thing he heard was her high-heels clacking along the stone floor.

"Aw, I'm sorry," she said, throwing her arms around him. "Are you okay? They didn't hurt you, did they?"

"No," he said. The pain in his side had long since subsided. "Why didn't you allow me up on stage? Had you, I probably wouldn't have got attacked by that fucking bozo!"

She lowered her head to look at her feet – she still wore her schoolgirl outfit. "Sorry about that, too. It was my fault Marianne didn't pick you…"

"Why?!" he said, stepping out of the shadows to loom over her.

"Is that fucking shitbag bothering you, love?!" one of the gorillas asked from the doorway.

"Piss off!" Simone yelled back.

"You little fucking—"

"No, stop. It's okay. He's my friend," Chrissy told the bouncer.

"Are you sure about that?" Simone asked her.

"Yes, silly!" she said, smiling. "Want to take me home?!"

He saw that sparkle in her eye again – the same one he had seen last night. Her smile was beyond sexy. It was cheeky.

That night, they made love until the early hours. In the morning, before he had awoken, she had gone, just like she had done on the beach. A note had been left in his kitchen.

"Pick me up from the Klitty Kingdom tonight – I'll come back to yours…" he read.

For the following fortnight, that's pretty much how it went down between Simone and Chrissy: He would pick her up from work, take her home to fuck, and she would be gone by the next day.

Some nights, on his request, she would dominate him – spank him, tease him, dress him like a girl. Anything he wanted, she was only too glad to participate. She confessed to really liking him and wanting him to go back to the States with her.

"I can't, Chrissy. As much as I would love to," he'd told her.

"Why not? You could sell this house…Come with me! We could build a life together in America. You have nothing keeping you here."

"I'll think about it," had been his answer to the opportunity of a lifetime. To a woman he could see himself being truly happy with. Deep down, he had hoped she would stay to be with him…

And, on her last night in Wales, he thought she was going to tell him just that – that she was going nowhere. That the act would have to find a replacement. But no. Just like that, she had walked out of his life. Before going, she had taken his number and had promised to get in touch if she was in his neck of the woods ever again.

"You have my contact information: e-mail and both telephone numbers – home and mobile. If you change your mind about coming to the States, contact me. I'd love to have you over."

When she'd kissed him goodbye, he'd made a promise to himself – *I'll never wash my lips again.*

The night she left, Simone dwindled back into his black hole of depression. Thoughts of his mother returned to haunt him, making him think he was destined to be miserable for the rest of his life.

"You were right, Mr. Tickles – I should have watched myself. I've been let down by another woman. First my mother, and now Chrissy…"

****

"Do you also blame this woman you speak of for your ways, child?!"

"Until we started talking, Father, no, I didn't. But now, the more I think about it, yes, I do."

"Why, my son? She presented you with an opportunity – you could have taken it. You could have avoided the sins you were to commit, had you left with her."

"You're right, but I couldn't. I just could not leave here, Father. Porthcawl is my home. It's where my mother brought me up. And, as much as I hated my mother for leaving me, I just wasn't ready to move on."

"Yet you expected her to drop everything and stay with you?"

"I thought you weren't supposed to judge, Father?!" Simone said with a harshness to his tone.

"Sorry if it sounded unsympathetic, my boy, but you have to see it from her side too."

Simone sighed. "I don't just blame her for leaving me, Father."

"Oh?"

"If it weren't for meeting her, then I would never have met Chaos. The woman who finally tipped me over the edge."

"Chaos?!"

"Yes, it was her dominatrix name."

"Oh, yes. I see. And how was Chrissy to blame for you meeting this, this Chaos person?"

"She'd given me a taste of the dominatrix ways. I wanted it. And as I sat at home, crippled by depression once more, it started to dwell on my mind. Not just the sex, but the punishment she had given me. I started to crave it, and so I went looking for it."

"I see. Go on."

"At first, I took it as a good sign. I mean, it got me out of the house – something which I hadn't done since Chrissy had left a couple of months prior. I was meeting people, going to clubs…I felt great. I felt alive once more, Father."

"Hmm, I see. And was it in one of these clubs that you met Chaos?"

"Yes. It was in a club in Cardiff. You see, these types of places can only be found in the city; here in Porthcawl, a place like that could never thrive. Bunnies, the place where my mother used to work, closed down due to lack of interest, which was a shame. It was a safe haven of mine."

"Did you immediately find this Chaos character, my child?!"

"Oh no, Father…It took a lot of searching, and a lot of acceptable mistakes, until I found her…"

****

When you're into the depraved, it's hard to find a place to play. A clean, healthy and decent place. A place where you feel safe. Simone hadn't been outside of Porthcawl much, and so city life, fun and games were new to him.

But that's where he needed to be if he was ever going to get his new kind of jollies.

He would never have thought of going to Cardiff had he not heard the whispers on the streets of Porthcawl; during off-season, a seaside town can be one of the murkiest places on the planet. One Saturday night, whilst trying to score a bit of debauched kink, Simone had overheard a couple of fairground hands talking about the seedier side of Cardiff city. About how a bloke can get "any kind of fuck" he wanted. About how the "boys like to dress as women" and how the "men like to get whipped and have big black dicks stuffed up their arses." About how you can "pay to sniff cocaine out of the arse-crack of a stripper." And about how a few dodgy alleys in the middle of the city were home to such places for perverts, freaks and weirdos.

The city was the place to play.

The rich kids knew it.

The businessmen knew it.

And, after eavesdropping, Simone knew it…

At the time, he had wondered if he would find dominatrix fun in the city, on top of everything else he had heard.

He'd planned to find out, and so, that very next weekend, he'd hit the streets of Cardiff.

Getting off the train at ten P.M. in the city felt strange. As he stood among a scant amount of people on the platform, he couldn't help but feel like a rabbit caught in headlights.

Simone had to admit, he was scared.

He'd heard lots of horror stories about the city – the crime, the violence.

I wish Mr. Tickles was with me, he thought. *Come on, I'll be fine. It's not like I can't take care of myself.*

Before he exited the train station, Simone removed his wallet from his back pocket and stored it in the breast pocket of his jacket, along with his train ticket.

Even though the night had settled in, the city was bustling as though it was the middle of the day. The neon lights lit his way as he went in search for something beyond explicit.

Would he find it?

He didn't know, but he was sure as hell going to try.

Firstly, he decided to hit a few pubs to help loosen himself up. Not only that, he thought he may catch people talking about 'parties' going on at certain clubs around the city.

When that failed, Simone decided to keep moving. To keep searching and checking out all the different pubs and clubs he came across.

After an hour or so of being on the street, he finally found a place he thought he might be in luck with.

The name of the joint, which was lit up in pink, gaudy lettering, told him all he thought he would need to know: *Leather and Ice.*

"Sounds just like what I'm looking for!" he said aloud. As he was about to enter, someone from behind called him a "shit-shoveller". Simone thought nothing of it and continued to make his entrance.

Once through one set of double saloon doors, he found another set – beyond the frosted glass, he could see coloured disco lights flashing. They kept in sync with the heavy thud of cheesy nightclub music.

Ugh! Not my type of music by a far cry! he thought. *Still, I might find the exact kind of person I'm looking for.* Taking a quick look down at himself, Simone smoothed his shirt, ran a hand through his thick black hair, and walked through the next set of doors with bated breath.

"Here goes nothing!" he said, exhaling.

As he walked through the doors, the disco music cut, and on came "Legs" by ZZ Top, which Simone found to be pretty apt – the sight before him was breathtaking. The dance and bar area crawled with women. Not a man, other than himself, was in sight.

There were legs on display everywhere.

Most of the women wore tiny, ridiculously short skirts with either heels or boots. Some wore corsets; others wore just bras or flimsy see-through tops. Erect nipples were illuminated by the flashy-flicky-coloured lights that were both headache inducing and luring to the spectacle before him.

Above, women danced in steel cages suspended from the ceiling.

Waiters, who appeared to be the only men in sight, worked in nothing but black trousers, shoes and dickie bows – they wore cuffs, but no shirts. Their bodies rippled with muscle and shone with sleek sheens.

Even though there were multiple barmen, they all appeared to be the same, as though there was a conveyor belt somewhere spitting them out of a backroom acting as a warehouse. With their matching attire and stature, they all had luscious black hair, blue eyes which screamed "*take me to bed*", and smiles that could melt the hardest of hearts.

But it wasn't the boys he was interested in, even though he found their role fascinating, and was certainly a job vacancy he could fill – it was the women and their legs he wanted.

He'd always been a leg man. Tits and arse were nice, but not as good as a cracking set of pins. Of course, the thigh had to be just right. In his mind, the perfect thighs were ones that were slightly thicker.

Oh, how they look good in tights.

And, as he roamed among the cougars, tarts and teens, Simone sought out his thick-thighed lady – maybe he would find one with a panache for whipping and beating men with a bamboo shoot, whip, crop or anything else that came to hand.

Cheekily, he whipped a large glass of wine off a tray a waiter was carrying and kept walking, much to the squeaky protest at his back.

Sue me, dickhead! he thought, taking a large gulp of red and smiling.

As a scantily clad female passed him, he grabbed a handful of her arse cheek and kept moving.

Her little yelp of shock, possibly pleasure, caused a current of excitement to jolt his cock awake – not that it was in that much of a slumber. Not with the amount of pins on display.

Hot pants, stockings, tights, short-shorts, French knickers, g-strings…It was endless.

And the boots they are wearing!

Simone had seen a lot of different attire for women, having grown up around strippers, but some of the things on display here were new to him.

Some of the lovelies wore boots that went right up their thighs.

Breathtaking!

When "Legs" came to an end, a song Simone didn't know came over the speakers, but it had a hard edge to it.

I hope they keep these kinds of song choices up! he thought, moving through the crowd and allowing his hand to grab and caress buttock and thigh alike.

A few of the women gave him black looks; others squealed in delight. The odd one or two spat something at him, but he didn't care – he felt like a lion parading through his jungle. They were his playthings, whether they liked it or not.

Fucking whores.

Smiling, he took another sip of wine.

Then, he stepped into a clearing – at the back of the club was a seating area. It was cordoned off by velvet cords and signs that read "VIP Lounge." As he was about to turn to walk back the way he had come, a voice chirped, "A *man*!"

"Huh?!" Simone said, turning back.

"*Oo*! An outsider. Love it. How dangerous of you, babe!" the cougar said. At a guess, he would have pegged her to be in her fifties, but she had the prettiest face he had ever seen. Her accent wasn't local, either.

"Dangerous?!" Simone said. He wondered if he looked as stupid as he sounded.

"And such attire! Oh, you're just divine. A damp patch waiting to happen!" she said.

"Are you talking to me?!" Simone asked, pointing a finger at his chest.

"Why, yes, you silly thing. Come, take a seat next to Francesca."

"It says it's a VIP area, er…Fran…"

"Cesca, my dear. And do ignore that – I'm a regular. I do as I please. Come!" she said, patting the spare sofa cushion at her side. "I won't bite!"

Yeah? You may get somewhere with me if you do, you fucking stinker!

He felt a smile crease his face as he watched her pull her very short skirt up that little bit further. *Any more, and I'll be able to see your furry cup!*

Stepping across the room, he loomed over her – her legs looked amazing beneath the black stockings she wore. As she crossed her leg over the other, he noticed she was wearing suspenders, heels and a garter.

At her side, he spotted a crop and leather mask with a zipper for a mouth.

On seeing the crop, he couldn't believe his luck.

She wore very little make-up, which caused her beautiful brown eyes to stand out, along with her high cheekbones. Her hands were gloved in lace and her torso was tied into a corset, which enhanced her very small tits.

He could tell she was excited, as her nipples were poking through the fabric that encased them.

"Rather delicious, aren't you!" Simone confessed.

"My, what a big handsome charmer you are!" She giggled. "Please, sit."

"Thank you," Simone said, saddling up next to her. She was much smaller than he'd first thought, now he was sat at her side.

"Would you like another wine?" she asked, spying his near-empty glass.

"Please." Swallowing the dregs, he put the glass on a table in front of him.

"Excuse me!" Francesca called one of the Adonis-like waiters.

"Yes, ma'am?" he said, giving Simone a funny look.

What's his fucking problem? he thought.

"Another G&T for me and a large glass of the house's finest red, please," she said. Her tone was smooth. Silk-like.

Her exposed thighs kept catching Simone's eyes – he couldn't help but snatch looks here and there.

"Are you drawn to them, dear?" she asked him, rucking her skirt up that little bit more.

"Oh, I'm sorry…I didn't mean to stare…"

"No, that's quite all right. Would you like to touch?"

He nodded, but not in an eager way.

She smiled. "What's your name?"

"Simone."

"Oo, how exotic. Isn't that Italian for Simon?"

"Yes," he said, nodding and smiling.

"What's so funny?" she asked, a smile spreading across her face.

"Nothing. Well, not really."

"Go on, don't be coy."

Before Simone could answer, the waiter butted in with their drinks.

"Leave them on the table," she said, not taking her eyes off Simone. "Start me a tab."

"Sure," the waiter said, turning to leave.

Simone gave him a quick look. *There's that fucking look again – what is his problem?* Simone saw a smirk develop on the waiter's cocky-looking mug.

"Why does he keep looking at me as though I'm an alien?!"

Now it was Francesca's turn to giggle. "They don't tend to like out-of-towners in here, sweetie. Don't sweat it."

Then he put his hand on her thigh. "Better?" he asked.

"Mm, much."

"What's the mask for?"

"My gimp," she said.

"What's a gimp?"

She smiled. "Let's just say it's a man that I keep under control…"

"Where is he?!"

"I haven't found him. Yet!" she said, looking at Simone. She looked hungry, but not for food.

"Will you whip me? Make me parade around like a girl? Put a collar and lead on me?"

"Wow! Steady on! You're making me hot!" she admitted. His hand crept up her thigh. "You have the Midas touch!"

He watched in wide-eye wonder as her bottom lip trembled. Her teeth could be heard chattering.

These fucking legs! he thought. *Amazing.* They were the right side of chunky – not too fat and not too skinny.

"How would you like to worship them?"

His hand retracted as he looked at her. "What do you mean?"

"Well, my little deviant Simone, how would you like to play with them until your heart was content, but only if you were good to your mistress?"

"A mistress as in a dominatrix?"

She giggled, then smiled. "Yes."

"Please!" he said, which almost sounded like a beg.

She had him hooked, causing him to keep moving his hand closer to her crotch. By the time he discovered she had a cock and was indeed a man dressed as a woman with tits, he didn't care.

His dick was leaking come into his pants – he was practically panting. His ache was great. His hand curled around her fat, stubby hardness, and slid up and down her shaft…

Before leaving the sofa and club, they both came. Twice.

That night, Simone left Leather and Ice with Francesca, and a new friendship blossomed.

Over the course of the three months they were 'friends', Francesca taught Simone many things about the underground sex scene he so craved to be a part of. After he told her about the Flesh Flaying Fiends and his relationship with Chrissy, and how he longed for a dominatrix in his life, she told him it wasn't as "simple as that."

That you didn't just *get* a dominatrix.

That you had to get to know the person.

That trust needed to be built up between the dom and sub.

As she taught him the ways, how and what clubs to visit and not, Francesca allowed him to worship her legs for the three months they stayed in each other's company.

It was during this relationship that Simone learned more about the usage of a cock cage, and the relationship between the wearer of the chastity device and the 'key holder', which was very straightforward, really.

When the man/slave agreed to surrender himself to his mistress/dom, his cock and balls were then locked away so he couldn't fuck or touch it – unless his key keeper allowed it, of course.

Francesca was a good mistress, but that was only because Simone was such a good slave – he looked after her legs as though they were his own. He'd wash them, shave them, cream them, dress them...

The best part for Francesca? She didn't need to satisfy him. He was happy to have his cock locked away as long as he got to play with her legs.

However, after three months, she got bored.

She was bored by the fact that Simone never wanted to fuck, suck or pleasure her arsehole in some way.

And so she called it off, leaving Simone heartbroken once again.

Although he'd had his heart and head fucked with once more, Simone refused to go back to the person he had been: the recluse.

This time, Simone pushed on with his life.

Did it matter women kept letting him down?

There was a whole world of them out there – he just had to find the right one.

Not long after his relationship with Francesca ended, Simone struck up a new friendship with another she-male named Porsche.

Like Simone, she too was new to the underground sex scene, and was very much an interesting character.

After meeting in a club by the name of Whips and Chains, which was buried down a side street out of harm's way, Simone came to learn very quickly what Porsche was all about.

Unlike Francesca, Porsche liked to be kept as a sissy slave – to be dressed up all pretty in stockings and ribbons. She existed for one reason and one reason only: to suck dick and please her master in any way he wanted.

She wasn't interested in being pleasured, and so kept her cock and balls in a cage – the padlock had been glued in place, so it was never coming off. Porsche had once been married, but her wife had left when he'd decided to go full transsexual.

"She couldn't put up with me taking boys back to the house, Simone. She hated what I was. What I couldn't control," Porsche had confided in him one evening whilst she was drinking.

Porsche had also told Simone that she had killed his wife and buried her in their garden, but Simone had discarded that, taking it as being the ravings of a bitter drunk.

He'd allowed her to pleasure him, just like he'd had fun and games with Francesca – Simone always took himself as a red-blooded male that loved nothing more than pussy, tits and arse, but since entering into the depraved, he found he was liking all sorts of fun and games.

Besides, he'd argued with himself, *they are womanly. They have breasts, slinky bodies, and pretty faces. And, I never let Francesca fuck me. I'll never allow Porsche too, either. That's never going to happen. I'm not a complete fucking poof.*

Truth be told, Simone was in his element.

At this point, he wasn't sure what he was looking for.

And then it happened.

After a few months of good times with Porsche, Simone moved on after meeting and falling in love with a woman by the name of Chaos, or Charlotte Ros, as he later found out.

****

"You see, Father, when Chaos came along, I thought all my worries were finally over. I thought I'd found my perfect dream woman. Even though I was having fun at this point, and Porsche and Francesca had pulled me out of my despondency, I still felt as though I was missing something. That a part of my jigsaw was amiss."

"Yes, my son. And was Chaos not what you were hoping her to be? Did she too let you down?"

Before he could answer, his phone bleeped. He removed it from his pocket – it was Chrissy. *'Are you kidding? Yes! I'd love to hook up. Where and when?'*

After replying, he put his phone away. A smile spread across his face.

"*That bitch is going to get hers, right?*" Mr Tickles asked.

Simone nodded and whispered, "You can count on it!"

"*I can't wait to see her naked, bleeding and screaming!*"

"Yes, Father. She let me down, too – in fact, she was the one that drove me to hurting people. She broke me. Caused me to snap."

"Dear, dear. It sounds as though you have had bad experiences with women, my child. Can that justify your actions? I'm not so sure. But I say unto you, that ye resist not evil; but whosoever shall smite thee on thy right cheek, turn to him the other also. And if any man will sue thee at the law, and take away thy coat, let him have thy cloak also!"

"I'm weak, Father."

"Yes, my child. A lot of His lambs are. And when they are lost and scared, he welcomes them into his house. He will forgive you for your sins, child, but you *must* do the right thing to warrant his forgiveness. Confessing all your sins to me alone will not save your soul from total damnation."

"Yes, Father. I know I must tell the police of my crimes."

His phone bleeped again. He opened his messages. '*I have something totally awesome to tell you*!'

Intrigued, he responded immediately, leaving the Father to waffle.

'*Sounds exciting!*' he replied.

Instantly, a response: '*It's a surprise, so I'm not telling you until I see you!*'

"*What the fuck is that cunt up to, sir*?!" Mr. Tickles blurted.

"I have no idea, but she's not going to live to tell me – not once I get her back to ours!"

"*Excellent, sir. Let it be known, you don't fuck with us*!"

"…so you see, my child, by confessing all your sins, your soul will be cleansed by our Lord and master. Our saviour."

"But I've killed a lot of people, Father, and not just the girl from last night."

"Oh, child. Will you tell me about them? Will you confess it all to me, then go tell the police the same thing? Will you seek total redemption?"

"It all started when Chaos came along, Father. Like I said, I thought I'd found what I was looking for, but I was wrong. So very wrong…"

****

Whips and Chains – it was a club Francesca had told him about. At the time, it was one of the hottest new clubs in the city. It wasn't the sort of place Francesca was interested in, because it was too full-on for her liking.

She had liked the tamer side of dom and sub.

What you got with Whips and Chains was something a whole lot heavier, much to Simone's excitement. And now he wasn't with Francesca, or Porsche, he was free to do as he pleased.

And so he did.

The first opportunity he got, he went to Whips and Chains, but was not expecting to meet and fall in love with a woman he met on his first visit.

As soon as he laid his eyes on her, he knew she was the one – she came out of the pyro gloom inside the club like a wave of destruction. Her leather cat suit could be heard creaking over the loud music, along with the clicking of her heeled boots, which rode her thighs. Her long black-as-night hair flanked her pretty face, causing her ice-blue-coloured eyes to stand out. She had a bullwhip hanging from her left hip, with a crop holstered at her right. She didn't so much walk, but saunter. Stride, even.

All eyes were on her, and by fuck, she knew it.

She lapped it up.

Her body seemed to absorb the attention, which helped it move in that prick-teasing manner. All her curves danced and played to the awareness of the hundreds of stiff dicks that surrounded her.

Jaws sagged.

Offers of drinks, pleasure and being used as a whipping boy were given, but she ignored them all – her steely gaze had found him, and she knew what she wanted. She *always* knew what she wanted, and what she wanted, she got. *Nothing* got in her way.

If it did, she crushed it beneath her boot heels.

She was a ball-busting temptress that rode the high, searing waters of hell; she was as hot as the lava that carried her forth.

She was Chaos, and everybody knew that, bar him. But that didn't matter – he was about to find out everything there was to know about her as she got closer to him.

As she strutted her stuff, a smile spread across her face. He couldn't move. His breath had jammed in his throat, and his legs had turned to pillars of jelly. No woman bar his mother had ever had such an effect on him.

His face flushed. His cheeks felt as though bacon could easily sizzle on them.

Simone's cock grew so stiff, he thought he was going to faint.

When she stood directly in front of him, all five-foot-nothing of her, and said "Hi!" his dick exploded in his trousers – his hot spunk drizzled out of his pants and ran down his thighs.

He buckled and quivered.

She giggled, which caused his cock to keep on pulsating and shooting.

Simone reached a hand out and slammed it down on a table in front of him. His body felt flimsy; his knees knocked. Shocks of pleasure skipped through him, causing a trembling sensation only a raging sexual urge could provoke.

Her hand reached up and grabbed his bollocks. She lightly squeezed his package as she whispered into his ear, "If it's any consolation, you've made my knickers damp!"

"*Ugh*!" he groaned, enjoying the tightness of her hand around his bits, which did nothing to stop his ejaculate. It was starting to seep through the front of his trousers, much to his discomfort.

"Jesus, you come like a fucking racehorse!" she said. "I can still feel it pulsating out the tip of your dick." Her grip tightened.

"*Ahh*!" he groaned, getting onto tiptoes.

"You like that, don't you! Naughty beast," she said, giving his nuts a twist in her small, not-so-delicate hand. "Maybe I should rip 'em off? Make a eunuch out of you…How would you like to be my sissy eunuch? My ball-less little bitch?! By the feel of your package, you ain't packing much – not much of a real man, are you?!" she continued, her grip getting fiercer.

"No!" he gasped.

"No, *Mistress*!" she said, twisting his balls that extra bit harder, which took him to his knees. She followed, her grip not loosening.

"No…M-m-m…Mis…tress…" he managed with a warbled tone. He could feel tears beginning to form. Bile gathered in his throat, burning.

"That's a good Slave! Would you like Mistress to take you home with her?"

He nodded. "Yes."

"Yes what?!" she said, giving his privates a savage squeeze and twist.

Tears streamed down his cheeks, his voice but a squeak. "Please, Mistress!"

"Good Slave dog," she said, finally releasing her vice-like grip. "I'm glad you finally got the message," she whispered in his ear. "I exercise my grip daily, which I've been doing for many years now, and could easily pop your grapes. After all, I can crush apples! Be advised, do not cross me, sissy, for I will squash them to pulp if need be."

"Yes," he said, adding "Mistress!" as quick as he could.

"Good," she said. "Now, get me a drink, Slave, then come and join me."

"Of course, Mistress."

For fear of losing his sperm factory, Simone got her a drink. It wasn't just fright, it was lust – he really liked her, even though her greeting was a little unorthodox. As he continued towards the bar, he was able to straighten up.

Small sparks of a smile crossed his face.

He was going to enjoy the night, thanks to his new friend.

His new madam had been true to her word. After several drinks and being used as her personal footstool, Simone had been taken to her home for a good cropping and whipping – she had beaten him until he had fainted.

As she unleashed on him, she had told him this was her way of breaking in her new plaything, her toy, which she liked to tease and wind-up at first – she liked to know if the nut could be easily cracked. And, if so, she would discard it without a second thought.

When he'd awoken from his unconscious state, he'd found that he was still chained in a starfish position inside her torture chamber, which was her converted cellar. Her "*Pussy Pleasing Palace*", as she liked to call it.

As he hung there, which felt like weeks on end due to all the windows being blacked out, he started to think she'd forgotten about him, but he knew it was another test.

A test he was not going to fail.

As minutes turned to hours and hours into days, Simone's stomach tightened with hunger. His lips began to crack. He soiled the floor below him multiple times.

When delirium started to kick in, she appeared like an angel of mercy.

"Many would have been crying and begging by now, Slave!"

"How…how…long…" he panted.

"Long enough, Slave," she said, undoing the cuffs at his ankles and then his wrists. "There's food and water over there for you." She pointed to a table close by. "When you've regained control over yourself, clean your mess up, Slave, then join me upstairs like a good dog."

From her tone, he couldn't tell whether she was pleased or displeased at his stamina and being able to put up with her hard tasks.

But he soon found out how pleased she was with him when she allowed him to eat her cunt, which was something she never authorized a brand new Slave to do. They had to earn it, but most never got that far due to her brutal initiation.

Had things continued in the same vein, Simone had thought he too would have succumbed to her viciousness, but, thankfully, he'd earned his keep. His place, even. Rather easily, too, he'd thought.

After finishing his meal, Simone cleared the floor of his shit and piss, took his empty dishes up to the kitchen, and then joined his Mistress, who was waiting for him spread-eagle on her bed.

"Well, don't just fucking look at it. Eat it!" she'd barked. Never had he been kept on his knees for so long – he remembered thinking how numb her clit must have been by the time he'd finished. "You're a very good Slave. Mistress likes you. You're not one for breaking, are you?"

"No, Mistress. I will serve you for as long as you want me to." And he wasn't lying, either. In that short time, he'd fallen in love with her. He didn't know or care if the feelings were reciprocated, he just knew that she was his madam.

"What a lovely thing to say, my little wind-up toy."

"Thank you, Mistress. I hope I'm not bold in saying this, but you have lovely legs, Mistress. I hope you will allow me to worship them one day."

"Oh, is that what my little Slave likes?!"

"Yes, Mistress."

"Well, we shall see. First thing tomorrow, I am having your cock and balls locked away, Slave. Don't think you will be touching me with that thing of yours. All I'm interested in is your tongue and what you can do for me. Is that clear, Slave?"

"Crystal, Mistress. I would not expect it of you – I only want to please you."

"That's good to hear. If you're a good boy, which you're fast proving to be, then I shall from time-to-time take you out of your cage and give you a release. I may even parade around in tights and stockings for you. And, if you're really lucky, I will allow you to worship my legs."

"Oh, thank you, Mistress!" he said, truly happy and eager.

She allowed a smile to appear on her face in front of him.

"Well, this is promising, Slave. From now on, you will live with me – anything you need from your own home, do so tomorrow. After that, this will be your new place, Slave. You will be given the spare room, which is kitted out with a single bed. I also have a cage big enough to house you should you be naughty."

The next day, as told, he was allowed to return home to pack a few things, arrange his bills and was then outfitted with his very own cock cage – she'd been slightly taken aback by his knowing of such a device, but at the same time, it pleased her.

"Don't forget, you will only have this removed when I see fit to do so. Any begging, crying or otherwise will earn you a harsh punishment, along with having the cage kept in place for *much* longer," she told him.

The key to the device was then placed on a rope necklace, which she wore at all times. It dangled between her tits, which he constantly thought about.

As days turned into weeks, Simone found he was in bliss. He behaved, obeyed and found himself to be the most obedient sub servant he ever thought he could be. *Then again*, he thought to himself, *it's easy because I have the best Mistress.*

His loyalty and dedication to pleasing and pleasuring her were not unrewarded. She constantly reminded him how *excellent* he was at his 'job' and how *contented* she was with how selfless and caring he was.

Simone never craved, whined or drew attention to his needs. No matter how hard his cock swelled within the confines of his cage, or how much his body sometimes shook with extreme horn, he focused on her.

Mistress Chaos was the light of his life.

He not only worshipped the ground she walked on, but licked it clean before approving her to step foot on it.

In his eyes, she could do no wrong. He didn't care if she did, or ever could, love him.

All he cared about was her keeping him around.

She was unlike anything he had ever encountered in his life, and maintaining her contentment meant everything to him. Her delight ensured he was staying put.

As the weeks turned into months, it looked as though they were going to be happily engaged in this relationship of dom and sub for a long time to come.

With the passing of time, he got better and better at pleasing her – he sought out all her pleasure zones and could take her to a place beyond paradise. With this, she freed his cock from its cell more frequently and gave it the release it deserved.

Not only did she do this for him, but she also paraded around in skirts, stockings, tights, French knickers, hot pants, thigh-high boots and anything else he asked for.

Simone especially liked being told how much she "loved" her Slave. That she was "blissfully happy to have such a delicious pet around."

He could do no wrong.

She never punished, screamed, or lashed out at him and always allowed him to pleasure her pussy and legs and make her feel comfortable.

After the first three of four years of their relationship, he had even earned himself a place to sleep at the bottom of her bed like a good dog.

But things soon after started to change.

By the time they'd been together five years, things had got sour. Little matters began changing, such as being told he was no longer allowed to sleep on her bed, which were telltale signs of things not being as rosy as they once were.

His leg privileges and releases became less recurrent, until the former was non-existent; the latter became borderline extinct, too.

He couldn't work out what was causing these changes, but it upset him. He didn't care about the loss of bed and leg rights, nor did it bother him that he wasn't getting his orgasms. Well, not to begin, at least.

Simone still loved her.

Then the beatings started.

She would take her frustration out on him by locking him up in her *Pussy Pleasuring Palace* and beating him within an inch of his life. Mistress Chaos wouldn't just use a whip or crop, but chains, sticks and bamboo shoots – skin would be torn from his body.

Because there hadn't been any beatings until now, the pain had been unbearable to begin with, but his body soon toughed to it, so frequent the thrashings became.

He didn't know what he had done to deserve such treatment, and he was never told. Simone continued to go along with it all in the hope he would get his old Mistress back, but if anything it worsened, along with her moods.

She would also go out every weekend and not return. He would be left locked up or lashed to his bed.

It pushed him over the edge. It broke him.

She not only broke his body, but his heart, too.

His Mistress had let him down, and now he needed out.

Chaos would allow him to go so long without a release that Simone would feel delirious every time he was aroused.

When she realised he was not going to give her the satisfaction of breaking, Mistress started using other tactics to smash his spirit: ice baths, stringing him upside-down, lack of nutrition, making him stand outside in the nude from dusk until dawn, telling him to clean the floors with a toothbrush, parading him around on a collar and lead, along with many other things.

It never worked. All it did was make him hate. To resent her.

Simone started becoming insubordinate on purpose – he found pleasure in pissing her off to the point where she would scream, yell, curse and lash out at him in sheer anger and frustration.

Then she began bringing different men home.

Mistress Chaos was now visiting Whips and Chains throughout the week, not just on the weekend. Whenever she brought a new Slave home, Simone would be forced to watch as the Slave got to fuck her – something he had never been allowed to do. Something she had told him no Slave had ever been granted the right to do.

She'd become so low that she was willing to sacrifice her own rule to make him suffer.

Mistress had also told him that she would never, ever allow him to leave her care until he was a broken, stuttering and crying wreck of a man.

When she occasionally let him out of the house, he thought about running away, but he never could. And, much to his annoyance, he knew she knew that. Mistress had him under her spell, and not just her lock and key.

But he knew something had to be done, and so, on a rare night out, Simone decided he'd had enough. He could no longer go on living like this. His sanity, what was left of it, was on the cusp of dropping into a black hole. He knew he wasn't that stable of mind, and now that he had lost another love of his life, Simone was uncertain he could stop his understanding from tipping over the edge. If that happened, he knew he would be put on a path of total destruction.

And so, whilst out one evening, he'd come to the rational choice of reaching out for help. At first, he hadn't known whom to turn to, but it soon became clear.

After seeing a flier advertising a Samaritans hotline, Simone knew it was his only chance at getting out from under the black cloud above him.

"There's always help at the end of a line, right?" he said, snatching the mini poster from off the lamppost it had been glued to.

As he entered the numbers into a payphone on the outskirts of the town's fair, Simone's heart raced. His mind ran amok.

What if a bloke answers? I'm not telling no guy about all this!

What if the person is old?

What if I say too much and the person goes blabbing to someone else, such as the police?

After hanging up on a few operators, Simone was about to give up, then *she* answered. She with the soft voice of an angel…

****

"Who is this *she*?!" the priest asked

"*She is the cat's mother, you boy-touching faggot. There are just too many up-hill miners in the church nowadays!*" Mr. Tickles said.

Simone sniggered.

"Are you all right, my child?!"

"Yes, Father. Just a sneeze."

"But I thought…"

"She is—*was*—Toni. The voice at the other end of the phone – the one I thought would save me."

"Ah, I see."

"Just like the rest, she let me down. She was beyond the final nail in the coffin, but she helped seal my fate."

"What did she do, my child?"

"I told you, I caught her in the arms of another man, after she swore her feelings for me, Father. She not only crushed my heart, but tore it from my chest. She flaunted her affections for this other in my face. Mocked me. Then, when I confronted her, she lied. Lied like the dirty, filthy whore she was!"

"You keep saying *was*, child…"

"That's right, Father. I do." *You want to know why; you fuck…?!*

"Why…" The priest's tone wasn't as strong – as fire and brimstone – as it had been.

"I killed her, Father. Slowly. It took nine months until she drew her final breath."

"Dear God!" Simone heard the priest say, which was followed by a series of whispers. "What did you do, my child?!"

"I cut her, Father. Firstly, I started with her feet, and then I gradually stripped each of her legs to the bone over a period of time and feasted on her flesh. She tasted good."

"*Ohh…*"

"After hearing about a cannibalistic kink, I just had to give it a go. After nine months, I'd practically picked her clean. I then cut her into sections, harvested the organs, and buried the remains on the beach."

"Sweet Jesus!"

"Something like that, yes. She tasted pure – I would have thought a liar would have had a rotten tang, but no. She was as sweet as she used to look."

"How long ago was this, child?"

Simone thought the priest sounded as though he was going to throw his lunch up.

"I buried her scraps a few weeks ago, Father. Since her, I've killed six young girls, two women and a fella. The man was an accident – he caught me killing one of the women. I've come under suspicion from the police, but they are yet to press charges."

"Now you've told me, you must go further to cleanse your soul and to seek total absolution, son!"

"Yes, I plan to, Father. I see no other way out of the situation I am in. I've been very bad, I know. But it wasn't all my fault. My biggest mistake, and regret, was allowing that bitch Chaos to break me. Once broken, I should have left, but I stood defiant to her abuse – I didn't want her to think she had won. That she had crushed my resilience."

"My poor child."

"It's my own doing, Father."

"Who else have you killed?"

"I don't know if I want to go into it."

"Please, my child – if you seek amnesty, then you must get everything off your chest. Do you remember the names of your latest victims?"

"No, Father. I don't remember any of the ones from my past, either. All I remember is, I killed two young teenage girls, a man walking his dog, four university students, Chaos, a Jehovah witness, and Toni…If there's more, I can't remember. My mind is a cesspit, Father. I didn't want this life of debauch. It was thrust upon me from a young age."

"Yes, my child. I see that. But now you are doing the right thing. Please, don't stop here. Go forth and unburden yourself, I beg of you!"

"I intend to, Father. If I don't, and nobody catches me, then I will keep on killing. I know I'll never be able to stop."

His phone bleeped. It was Chrissy – '*I just wanted to let you know that I'm at the Klitty. Can't wait to see you later. X*'

"*That bitch has to have hers!*" Mr. Tickles said.

"Go now, my child. Strike whilst the iron is at its hottest!"

"Thanks for listening, padre," Simone said, exiting his booth with Mr. Tickles held close to him.

When he got back to his house, it was gone six, and so he knew he had a good few hours to kill before he had to leave to pick Chrissy up from work.

"What could be so important that she couldn't just text me about it, Mr. Tickles?!"

"*I have no idea, sir. But don't let her fuck with your mind!*"

"No, I don't intend to let her!" Although, deep down and tucked just underneath the need to kill her, Simone was actually looking forward to seeing her once again. It had been too long.

"*Maybe fuck her guts out first. You know, one for the road!*"

"That's what I was just thinking!"

"*Great minds, sir…*"

"Mm, yes."

"*Are you thinking of hearing her out first, sir?*"

"Not really, no. I want to hurt her as much as she hurt me! I'll firstly fuck her, and then fuck her over!"

"*Eat the bitch!*"

"Oh, I'll do more than that!"

"*The fucking cunt should have stayed away, boss. Or, if she was going to come back, why not stay silent – why did she have to go and drag up the past? She must want a short existence.*"

"Ha! Maybe. Perhaps she owes some nasty people a lot of money, and is hoping I'll do her the fuck in?!"

Simone and Mr. Tickles both laughed.

When midnight came, Simone left his house for the Klitty Kingdom. He arrived there and was waiting outside the back entrance for Chrissy at exactly ten past the hour.

Drunks and rabble-rousers passed the entrance to the alley in which Simone stood – they were cheering, shouting and spilling their chips all over the pavement as they zigzagged their way home.

"Fucking pissheads!" Simone said, smiling as he watched the crowds of men and women stagger by. "Chucking out time is certainly something to see around here," he uttered.

He placed his hands inside his pocket and lightly stamped his feet to try and keep warm. "Come on, where the hell are you?!"

Then his fingers brushed against the large blade he had inside his left jacket pocket. It was his butcher knife that he usually kept in a wooden block by his microwave.

The inches of steel had gleamed when he'd removed it from its home.

"I'll cut her open like a warm loaf of bread. Maybe I'll do it here, or maybe I'll do it back at mine. Let's wait and see…" he told himself.

As a smile crept across his face, the stage door flew open – Chrissy burst out and screeched his name.

"Simone! Oh, my God!" She ran down the steel steps and threw her arms around him.

She smelt good. Her warmth radiated through his clothes and seemed to melt his rage.

Passion aroused within him.

He wanted her.

Needed her.

Before he could attempt to remove the knife, she planted kiss after kiss on his lips. "I never thought I would get to see you again. Why did you stop sending me e-mails? I was scared you hated me. When I sent you that text this morning, I wasn't sure you were going to respond. I also thought that maybe you had changed your number."

"What if I had?" he said, pushing her lightly away from him.

"I would have come looking for you. I still remember where you live, Simone."

"You're kissing me and hugging me like you're my woman. I may already have a woman!"

"If you do, then what are you doing here?!" she asked, smiling. "Come on, don't be mean. I've been dying to see you. I've not been with another since you, Simone. I knew I would be back this way soon, so I was keeping myself. Plus, I have a surprise for you!" she said, barely able to contain her excitement.

"What is it?" he asked her coolly. At the back of his mind, all he could think about was what he was going to tell the police in the morning, once he'd dumped this bitch down at the beach.

I lied. It was *me, not the one-armed man!* he thought, smiling.

"I'm not telling you here, Simone! I thought maybe you would like to get some takeout and a few bottles of wine? What do you say?"

"I…I'm not sure, Chrissy. I mean…It's been a long time. I've changed. Moved on…" He knew he'd hurt her – the look in her eye told him everything.

"Oh, I see..."

Looking at her, Simone saw himself. *Is that how I appeared when I was crushed, time and again?*

"Look, maybe that was a bit harsh." His grip loosened on his knife. "Come back to mine. We can talk."

Her face regained its happy glow.

When they got back to Simone's house, he poured them both a glass of wine – he'd had reservations of spiking her drink, but he didn't want her numb to the pain he planned to dish out later in the evening.

"I was hoping you'd have been extremely happy to see me, Simone. Before I left here the last time, you were all over me. You were begging me to stay..."

"Yes, but you left, Chrissy. You left and you broke my heart. You let me down, much like every other woman in my life has at one point or another."

"If you felt like that, why did you bother keeping in touch for so long?!"

"I guess I was hoping..."

"Look, I'm here now. Why don't we try and get back to where we were?"

Oh, I'm sure you'd fucking love that, wouldn't you, bitch? Build me up, just to fucking smash me down again? he thought. His grip on the wine glass intensified, which put the stem under threat of snapping.

"Why don't you stop beating around the bush and tell me what this whole surprise is?"

"I'm not sure there's much point in me saying, now..."

He felt like throwing his glass to one side, removing his knife, and scalping her. Simone was about to do so – she must have seen the rage cloud over his pupils.

Putting her glass down, she picked up her bag.

She's thinking of leaving. Stop her! his mind yelled.

She removed an envelope from inside, which stopped him from attacking. "Here, for you," she said, handing it to him. "I'll completely understand, of course..."

Setting his own glass aside, Simone looked at what he'd been given.

"Go on," she urged.

Ripping the envelope open, he removed what was inside. "What's this?" he asked.

"It's a one-way ticket to the States, Simone. I was hoping you'd come home with me at the end of my stay. I'll be leaving here in two weeks."

"But—"

"Before you say anything, I just want to say that you'll be fine living with me, and you won't have to worry about a job, as I've cleared it with the girls."

"Cleared what?!" He felt numb. Staggered. He didn't know what to say. She'd dropped a bombshell.

"To work the show with us – we'll figure out a role for you. You could put this place up for rent, right? Come on, what do you say? Throw caution to the wind!"

He hesitated. He'd sought absolution and spoken about his sins. Had his prayers been answered? Was this a sign from God? A message? *Go forth, child*, he heard his judicious Lord say. *Maybe I should*, he thought. He'd be in a new place, with Chrissy and her friends, doing a new line of work.

New thrills.

New kills.

And Chrissy wouldn't be the wiser…or safe from him.

A smile spread across his face. *I guess miracles can happen!* Simone thought, looking at Chrissy. "Yes, I'll come with you," he said. "You've made me the happiest man alive."

"Oh, marvellous!" she shrieked, throwing her arms around him.

"Before we go…" he told her.

"Yes?"

"I have to *kill* some time with an old priest," he told her, touching the blade in his pocket.

INTO THE PLAYPEN

Bosco Brown was your typical schoolyard bully – big, stupid and lumbering. *You couldn't really call him an ape.* Simone thought, watching Bosco saunter across the cafeteria floor to a bench where he sat down to eat his food. *Why? Because it would be insulting to the mammal in question, that's why.*

But they weren't in school. Oh, no. They were in Cardiff prison. Their schooldays long behind them. Nevertheless, you didn't have to be in school to encounter a bully. *They never grow up. Never leave the schoolyard, and there's only one way to deal with them,* he thought, watching Bosco intently.

Simone'd had contact with such people before. Namely Cartwright and his goons.

Cartwright. What a cunt. Well, I sorted that fuck!

"Give me your fucking bread!" Simone heard Bosco say to one of the weaker inmates he sat by. "Or I'll put my fucking fist through your face!"

"*Huh*!" Simone grunted. *Pricks like him think fear tactics work on everyone. Well, every dog has its day…*

When Simone had been placed here three weeks ago, Bosco had been the name constantly mentioned. He'd heard things like "Bosco owns these walls", or "Bosco is the Top Dog", or "This is *his* house".

His house? What the fuck does that even mean? Simone pondered, watching the big man thieve the food from off the other inmates around him. *What an utter fuckbag.*

This was Simone's first real look at the man nicknamed "Bos-Berserk'o", or "Berserk'o" for short.

"He's a fucking lunatic, man!" Simone's cellmate had warned. "Stay out of his way. At all costs!"

As he spooned soup into his mouth, Simone wondered about the life the man had led outside the walls he now found himself behind. By all accounts, Bosco had been a fella living a life of brutality. He'd worked as a security and bodyguard after coming out of the Royal Air Force, before finding himself shovelling shit for a living.

Luckily for Bosco, he was at the right end of a shitty spade after 'accidentally' killing a man he was supposed to be protecting. Subsequent to the court hearing, which was a not guilty verdict, Bosco could only find menial work.

However, in a twist of fate in a place where double-jeopardy no longer lived, new, condemning evidence came to light, sealing Bosco's fate to two life sentences.

Word was, Bosco didn't take the guilty verdict too well. He'd flattened his defence attorney with a brutal left and right before head-butting the man into oblivion. The lawyer's nose had broken, the bone splinters stabbing into his brain. He'd died on the courtroom floor in a violent fit of spasms, or Simone had heard.

It had taken ten coppers to restrain Bosco, get the cuffs on him, and then escort him down to the holding cells below the courtroom.

The lunatic had currently served twelve years, and would be looking at dying behind these walls.

Couldn't have happened to a nicer fella! Simone thought, smiling. As he got to the bottom of his soup, he tilted the bowl and scraped up the last of the shit-coloured liquid. Once finished, he used his bread to mop his bowl clean.

"Hey! That's mine!" Simone heard someone shriek, causing him to look up from his dish – he saw Bosco robbing an inmate of his soup. The other man tried to grapple his meal back from off the bully, but Bosco viciously rammed his fork into the other guy's eyeball.

"*Argh*! My fucking eye!" he screamed, getting up from his seat and stumbling to the floor. Pus-like liquid and blood jettisoned from the burst orb. The cafeteria erupted into whoops, cheers, laughter and applause. The rest of the jailbirds liked to appear to be on Bosco's side for fear they would get a midnight call from the man and get shivved or sugared.

Simone looked over both shoulders and all around him. The guards were slow to react. They didn't much care. The way they saw it, every last one of the pricks inside H.M. Cardiff Prison deserved everything they got, guilty or not.

"Fuck the scum!" Simone had heard one guard say to another one night as they patrolled past his cell.

As the prison officers approached the man sprawled on the floor, with blood pouring from his eye, they laughed.

"This your doing, Bosco?!" the one guard asked.

"He cut himself shaving!" Bosco said, shoving a mouthful of bread into his mouth.

"Very funny!" the second guard said, before addressing his colleague. "Come on, we best get this bag of shit down to the infirmary, Davis."

As they were about to drag the injured man off, Bosco halted them.

"Wait! That motherfucker has my fork," he said, standing up and ripping the eating implement from the eyeball, which made a wet, sucking sound as it popped free.

Bosco licked it clean. "Delicious, boys!" he said, laughing and baring his blood-stained teeth. He then sat back down and watched as the wardens dragged the man off to the prison's hospital. All the while, Bosco belly-laughed and pointed as he continued to stuff his face – the happy-clapping fucks around him began to quieten.

"*Psycho*!" Simone could hear the walls whisper.

Simone neither cheered nor smiled at Bosco's antics. He just stared at the bully, who always seemed to get his own way. Even the guards turned their cheeks. He had them all in his pocket.

"Be on your toes, new boy – he'll come for you soon!" Simone's roommate had also warned. When Simone had asked him why, the answer had not shocked him. "Because he likes to assert his authority rapidly. He likes the new boys to know what's what, especially when the new boy fancies himself as an ice-cold killer."

Simone hadn't bothered trying to explain to his newfound friend that he was not an ice-cold killer. That life had dealt him a clichéd shitty hand. That his mother had been a no-good come-dumpster and that his sister fucked him, then fucked off. That everyone he had come in contact with had shit on him.

There's so much shit on me, he thought, *that I look like a victim of a squabble of nervous seagulls!*

Besides, letting them all think he was a 'cold fish' was probably for the best, Simone had thought at the time. *That way, people will stay out of my way. And that's best for everyone.*

Although he could control his temper, it didn't take much to spark it, and he wasn't prone to keeping it in check when pushed too hard by someone.

Keep your eyes off him, Simone, he thought, trying to tear his gaze off Bosco. *What would Mr. Tickles advise if he was here? I know exactly what he would say. "Take the big cunt down, before he takes us out, sir."* This thought made him smile at an inappropriate moment, as Bosco turned to look at him. Their eyes fused and Bosco saw Simone's shit-eating grin.

"What the *fuck* are you looking at, newbie?" Bosco yelled across the cafeteria floor – remnants of chewed food blasted from the gorilla's mouth. When he stood, Simone hadn't recalled the man being so tall. And now, as he drank Bosco in, he saw the man's neck tattoos, which included the words 'New-Aged Skinhead' and designs of swastikas, knives dripping blood and the heart-wrenching 'I Love Mum', which had been crafted in a delightful calligraphy.

His shoulders were as wide as a door – his head was devoid of hair. He cracked his knuckles as he kicked his chair to one side.

A hush fell over the canteen.

"I said, what the fuck you looking at, pencil dick?!"

An '*Oo*' rippled through the spectators.

Simone looked around – the guards just stood and watched as the events unfolded.

Fucking bastards. There's no way I'm begging…

"I wasn't looking at you, Bosco…"

"You were grinning like a fucking arsehole, fuckstick!"

As Bosco got closer, Simone could see the man bore the mark of The Boas down his left arm, which was an outlaw biker gang operating in and around Cardiff.

"I promise you, I was not!" Simone said, slowly removing his bowl off his metal tray.

"Then why the Cheshire cat routine, pin-dick?!"

"I was thinking of something personal!"

"About how you fucked your mammy?!" Bosco bellowed, erupting into a fit of laughter. This set off most of the other inmates. "Yeah, we all know the rumours, ya fucking faggot."

Simone's grip tightened around his tray.

"Oo, are you going to cry, baby girl?!" he continued to needle. "We have a princess on our hands, boys!"

The whole room seemed to close in on Simone – his vision became tunnel-like, and the sound around him muffled. He thought he was going to blackout. His whole body trembled.

Then he felt a hand on his arm. "Don't think about fighting back, newbie – he'll eat you for breakfast!" the burly inmate at his side said.

Simone pulled his arm free. "Fuck off!" he said to the man, who had a Hispanic look about him.

"Your funeral, amigo!"

Turning back to face Bosco, Simone noticed the man was now towering over him. The smell from his unwashed pits and vile breath pounded against his nostrils.

"Is it true about all 'em women you killed?!" he asked. Simone nodded. "Think you're real cold, don't ya!"

"Not at all…"

Bosco unexpectedly grabbed Simone by his prison fatigues and hurled him across the floor before he could react. His tray, which he'd had a firm grip on, went sailing through the air and crash-landed on a table in the near distance.

"Yo! What the fuck, brother!" Simone heard someone call as plates, bowls and cutlery crashed to the floor around him.

Simone rolled onto his back. His blurred vision cleared, and he saw Bosco standing over him – he stamped one of his massive feet on Simone's chest, causing him to cough and wheeze. He thought his torso was going to cave in on itself.

Then he was off the floor and floating through the air again. He smashed down on top of another table, much to the protests of the men around him.

"You're bleeding all over my dripping, man!"

Simone garbled something in his semi-conscious state, but he didn't know what.

"Kick his arse!" someone yelled.

"Go on Bos, we love ya!" another screamed.

Simone felt a harsh tug at his legs, and then his body smashed against the hard canteen floor once again. A rib popped.

"*Argh*!" he cried. "*Fuck*!"

He was then rolled onto his back to see a huge furious fist fly towards him. His nose exploded across his face. Fireworks went off behind his eyes – blood and spittle marred his vision.

Another punch.

Followed by a third, fourth, fifth…

He felt his jaw slacken.

A tooth rattled across the floor.

I need to get to my…

His thoughts were head-butted from his mind. A cheek collapsed. His mouth filled with blood and then dribbled down his chin.

More punches – one, two, four, six…More teeth rattled free.

"He's killing him!" someone from close by yelled.

Simone felt Bosco's weight being dragged off him, allowing him to crawl to the closest bench.

"Get the fuck off me!" he heard Bosco shout.

The guards, they must have stepped in…

When he got to his shaking legs, Simone spotted his tray on a table in front of him – his one eye was completely closed, but the other was half open. Grabbing the tray, he turned around and saw Bosco being held by two guards – they had an arm each.

As fast as he could, Simone stepped forward, swung the tray over his shoulder like a golf club, and then swiped at Bosco with all his might. The edge of the steel tray smashed into the huge man's throat – a burst of blood popped from his mouth. At that moment, the guards let him go, and so Bosco was free to grab his injury.

Simone didn't stop there. He hit the man across the face, sending him to the floor. When he was down and on his back, Simone attacked the man's throat again and again – blood spurted from Bosco's mouth. When he heard the bully's windpipe crush and his neck snap, he threw the buckled tray to one side.

The cafeteria erupted into applause.

Before Simone knew what was happening, he felt taser barbs puncture the skin at the side of his neck. A body-numbing burst of electricity shot through him, sending him to ground.

Then he blacked out.

****

"Father, where am I?" Simone asked the priest, who was standing half-in, half-out of the shadows surrounding them.

"Safe, my son."

"My face… It hurts."

"Those wounds will heal, my child. You should be more concerned about the injuries to your damned soul! They will not mend. Not now, not ever. I tried my best. Did I not warn you of the wrath of God?!"

"You did, Father!" Simone said. His salty tears slid down his cheeks and found their way into the splits and cracks – the pain made him wince. "Why am I not at the infirmary?!" he whined like a child. "I want my mother…" he pouted.

"I'm afraid it's too late for that, boy!" the priest said, his tone taking on a harder edge as he stepped out of the shadows. The light, which was coming from underneath the door, illuminated the old man and his blood-spattered clerical collar and black gown. "Look what you did to me!" he preached with fire and brimstone. "You will burn in hell for killing one of God's servants!"

Simone couldn't look. Instead, he bowed his head and stared into the darkness. He tried to make out his feet, but couldn't. "Am I in hell?!"

"I said *look* at me!" the priest all but screeched, his voice cracking. Simone thought the old codger had ruptured his voice box, but he dared not to look up.

He couldn't.

Simone remembered the large shard of stained glass he had used on the priest. It had been taken from one of the old boy's church windows. Simone had caved one in by using a chair. Once he'd cornered the priest, he'd pinned him down and carved chunks of meat out of his face, before cutting his lips off and digging his eyeballs out.

He'd also taken the man's saintly tongue.

A trophy.

"You carved me up like a fucking Christmas turkey, Simone. You and that fucking clown doll of yours!"

"Stop it!" Simone screamed, covering his ears. "You're not real! You're not here – you're dead!" And then he did look up. The eyeless priest stood a few feet from him. His empty eye sockets wept fresh blood onto his torn cheeks and nose, which made Simone think of a haphazard roadmap. The father's teeth were perfectly visible and clenched shut – they glistened red. Saliva coated his chin and lipless mouth. "What are you?!" Simone blubbered. "A visage of hell?!"

"There's much worse awaiting you on the other side, *boy*! If you think this is scary, just wait until you meet your hoofed, horned master. He'll devour your soul, slowly. But not before making you bleed leisurely, like a stuck pig!" The priest's laugh was harsh, witch-like, which tore through Simone's eardrums; it pierced his brain, driving more hot tears down his cheeks and into his cuts.

"I want to go home…"

"Hell is home!" the priest continued to torment. "The noose is waiting, boy!"

"There is no capital punishment!" Simone screamed, and then his breath hitched in his throat as a hangman's noose was thrown over his head and tightened around his neck. "*Ugh!*" he gasped.

He watched, bug-eyed, as the priest pulled on the rope – the noose constricted his throat that little bit extra. His tongue protruded and flopped. "Let…me…" he gasped. "Go…"

"You'll swing by the neck until dead, dead, dead!" the priest said, and then laughed a crazed, psycho ward laugh. "*Die!*" he screamed.

Simone kicked his legs and thrashed like a fish out of water. His fingertips tried desperately to pull the rope from his neck, but it was all in vain. Black spots appeared in his vision – he could feel himself slipping into unconsciousness.

A bright light appeared before him.

The image of his mother stepped forward.

"Mum…" he gargled, putting his hand out in front of him. Her sight was heavenly.

"Come," she said, holding her hand out.

Then he pulled his hand back, remembering her treachery. "You left me!" he yelled the best he could, allowing the rope to keep strangling him.

The light, along with his mother, disappeared.

"She can't save you!" the priest screamed, pulling the rope harder.

As Simone let himself slip away, he heard a thumping sound in the distance, which grew louder and louder, until it was pounding in his ears.

Looking up one last time, Simone saw Mr. Tickles behind the priest – he wasn't a small, twenty-four-inch doll as he remembered him. No, he was a seven-foot monster of a man.

When Simone's right-hand man grabbed the father by his scruff, the rope at Simone's neck loosened. He hit the deck hard and started a coughing fit.

"Mr. Tickles…" Simone wheezed, but could hardly hear the sound of his own voice over the awful banging noise that assaulted his ears.

A shocking coldness washed over his face, and then he was awake – two guards stood over him.

"Wake the fuck up! You've been screaming like a little bitch in here!" one of the officers said.

"Wh…wha…what the fuck!" Simone blurted. Speaking caused his mouth and face intense pain. He huddled back into a ball and covered his eyes – even the outside brightness caused him hurt. "Turn the light off!"

"Get the fuck up, cunt!" the second officer said. "We have orders to take you down to the infirmary, now you've had the chance to cool off. You know killing Bosco is going to earn you another life sentence, right?"

"He's dead?!"

"That's right, killer!" the first guard said. "Looks like you're the new Top Dog." Both guards laughed.

"Now, get on your feet!"

"How long have I been in here…I need water…?"

"Long enough. Now, up!"

"I can't move my right leg…Where am I?"

"Solitary confinement, killer. Jenkins, grab his left arm," one of the guards said to the other.

"Right'o."

"I'll get his other."

Before Simone knew what was what, he was being dragged out into the brightly lit corridor. The strobe-lighting molested his one, partly opened eye, which wept when he strained it against the light.

His shoes came off as his heels dragged along the ground. With his feet bare, his skin started to burn as he was quickly pulled down the long hallway. His arms and shoulders felt ablaze.

"Please, slow down!" Simone rasped.

"Oh, so you want some mercy?!" one of the guards said, causing the other to chirp in.

"Did you show any of your victims mercy, you piece of shit?!"

The haft of a baton was pounded into his guts, causing him to double. "Fuckers…" he wheezed.

"You've got that right, pal!"

Simone didn't say anything else, just allowed himself to be dragged as he tried to shake the last of the priestly nightmare from his mind.

It's guilt, that's all… No, it's not guilt. It was brought on by that massive beating I took. That combined with the lack of food and water is playing tricks on my mind. I'm suffering mild delirium! he argued with himself.

"This fucker is heavier than he looks!" one of the guards said.

That's it, pricks – work, work, work… He smiled. *Once I'm in the sick bay, at least I'll be left alone. I'll be able to recover in peace. And now that I've taken out the biggest wolf in here, I'll be set for life.*

"Here's another one for you, doc!"

Simone was dropped to the floor. His back connected with it first.

"Jesus!" he said, curling into a ball.

"Do you mind throwing him onto one of the beds over there?"

Simone didn't know the voice, but guessed that it belonged to the doctor.

"Sure," one of the guards said.

Simone was picked up again, dragged across the floor, and then lugged up and onto one of the beds.

"Get well soon, princess!"

As the guards left, Simone heard them talk about him as they walked back down the corridor – their laughter reverberated off the walls.

"Fuckers!" he spluttered, then huddled into a ball. "Shit! My ribs." When he coughed, blood spattered the bed sheet. "Doc!" he called, his voice hoarse. "*Help*...Please."

Then a coughing fit racked his body – more blood splashed against his sheets and pillows. Some found its way onto his prison jumpsuit. Trying to roll onto his back, Simone fell off the bed and cracked his head against the floor.

"*Ugh*!" Getting slowly to his knees, he grabbed the bed sheets and tried to haul himself back up.

"Oh, God!" he heard a voice say from behind. "Doctor, this man needs serious attention!"

Then there were hands on him. Soft, warm hands; they were not the sort of hands associated with a man.

"Here, let me help you," she said, putting his arm over her shoulder to steady him. After regaining his balance, he was able to ease himself back onto the bed with her help. "Lie down. I've got your legs."

"*Water*!"

"Yes, of course. *Doctor*!" she called, and then readdressed Simone. "I'll be right with you."

He couldn't make out her image due to his swollen eyes, but her scent filled his nostrils and made him feel slightly light-headed.

"Who are you?" he asked nobody. "*Hello*?!" Then the coughing started again. The pain in his chest and sides was beyond anything like he'd ever felt before. Chaos had given him brutal beatings, but this was something else. He hurt everywhere.

And that dream...Why the priest? Why now? It's been years...

"I'm here," she said. "Take a few small sips."

A straw was inserted into his mouth and he drank greedily.

"Easy, easy!" she said, pulling the straw from him. "The doctor will be with you shortly."

"Thanks!" he panted. Simone tried his best to open his one eye to its fullest, but failed miserably. "Who are you?!"

"I'm a nurse here at the prison's medical unit."

"Do you have a name?"

"Yes, Nurse Sinnamond." He could hear her smile in her tone.

"Sin…" he said, which was barely audible. "Do you have a first name, Miss Sin?!" He felt himself smile. It hurt, but he didn't care.

"Jessica."

"That's a pretty name…"

"Thanks, I—"

"Nurse, why isn't this man restrained?!"

"Hey, Doc. How nice of you to show up!" Simone sneered, but the doctor didn't respond to him.

"I didn't think there was a need. He's in a bad way, Doctor."

"Nurse Sinnamond, how long have you been here? You, above anyone, should know the rules and procedures regarding an inmate."

"But—"

"Not another word or I'll see to it that you are reprimanded!"

"But this man was held in solitary confinement in his condition. He could have died. How many times are we going to sit back and allow this to happen?!"

"Nurse, I'm warning you! Back. *Off*."

"Doctor…"

"Sinnamond, I won't tell you again! You know very well how dangerous these inmates are – most of them are killers and rapists. They won't think anything of hurting you where you stand should the opportunity arise."

"No…" Simone said, weakly.

"Now, restrain this man. Until that happens, I'm not treating him."

"*Huh*," Jessica huffed. Simone then felt the restraints being put in place around his ankles and wrists. "I'm sorry!" she whispered in his ear.

"Your trust and sympathy for *these* individuals is rather disturbing, Nurse."

"They're human, just like us."

"No, they are monsters. The system put them here for a purpose. Now, see to it that I don't catch you neglecting your duties again, Jessica. Consider this your *final* warning."

"Yes, Doctor."

"Fine, right. Now, help him out of his fatigues and into a fresh pair of hospital pyjamas. See to it that you dress the wounds that you are able to. I'll be back shortly to sort that rib and eye socket of his."

"Yes, Doctor."

Simone heard the doctor's footfalls as he walked from him and Jessica. She was saying something in his ear, but he couldn't make it out – he felt himself slip into darkness. The nightmares came back for him, as a face from the past appeared before him.

Chrissy…

****

That night, four years ago, when she'd walked back into his life and offered him a second chance at going to the States, he'd taken it. Of course, the priest had tried to convince him to put things right.

With the police closing in, he'd seriously considered it. Wholeheartedly. What was left to live for? Prison seemed like the best option. But then he'd come to his senses. First and foremost, he wanted Chrissy to pay for breaking his heart. That could not go unpunished. Secondly, he wanted to kill her friends – the Flesh Flaying Fiends. Why? Simple: because they'd been the whores who helped steer him into a world of filth he found himself in at the time.

Dom…i…nat…rix… I'd never heard of the word before them…

Had they not walked into his life, then he could have carried on living an existence of misery. Also, had he not met them then Chaos would never have come onto the scene and totally ruined his life.

Thirdly, he knew the priest had to die if he was going to go to America with Chrissy – he couldn't leave any loose ends.

If Chrissy had come back sooner, then I wouldn't have confessed all to the father. It's her fault he died.

After agreeing to go to the States with Chrissy that night, they'd then toasted their new life to come in America. Once Chrissy had passed out drunk on the sofa, he'd carried her to bed and tucked her in. With the level of alcohol he'd helped pour down her throat, he'd left the house with confidence – there was no way she would wake and find him gone.

When he'd arrived at the church, Simone had snuck around the back of the building and found a lower window open. He'd then tip-toed upstairs to where he found the old priest on his knees at the foot of his pulpit.

"I've been expecting you," he'd said to Simone, not turning to look at him. "I purposely left the window open for you, son."

"But…how?!"

"There's no curing you. Just before you left, I saw the devil in your eye. I knew then, in that moment, that you would be back to kill me at some point."

"If you were so sure," Simone said, stepping forward, "why didn't you call the police? You could have turned me in!"

"I guess, deep down, I was hoping I'd be wrong."

"Well, that was just plain fucking silly, Father!"

"Let's get this over with."

"I wouldn't be too keen on getting to your demise, old man. It's going to be painful, not to mention messy."

"God will protect me, son. Where…"

"Get off your knees and walk us to your presbytery, oh man of God!" Simone said, smiling.

The priest didn't protest; instead he did what was asked of him.

"There's still a chance…"

"Get the fuck in there!" Simone had then shoved the old man in his back, sending him sprawling through the open door to the presbytery. He'd then broken one of the windows inside the room, taken a large shard of glass, and cut the priest to ribbons.

For a man who had a god protecting him, he didn't half scream and cry.

Simone had then disposed of the body by hiding it in the rat-infested cellar. Before leaving the room, he'd watched with morbid fascination as the rats tore, nibbled and ate the old man.

With a smile on his face, he'd then closed the door and made his way back to Chrissy, who was still in bed, snoring.

Two weeks after killing the priest, the Flesh Flaying Fiends' stay in the U.K. was over. It was time for them to return to the States, Simone included. In the build-up to them leaving, Simone had become very anxious, making him wish he hadn't killed the priest as soon as he had.

But there was nothing he could do about it. It was done, and had he not finished the father off when he had, then he may have gone to the police and sold Simone down the river.

To try and starve off his anxiousness, Simone had repeatedly visited the church at the dead of night, just to check on the rats' progress. After a week of being munched on, most of the holy man remained – the rodents had only managed to eat away the face and parts of the neck.

By this time, the priest had been reported missing, presumed dead. Another person gone astray from the small seaside town.

It was heat Simone could do without, considering he'd already been pulled in for questioning once before.

The second week couldn't have dragged any slower, as police trolls scoured the town and neighbouring villages, hamlets and cities. Now that a man of the cloth had been taken, the police were ever more determined to find the person or persons responsible for the killings.

They went house to house, turned over every doghouse, shed and outhouse in search of their man. Question after question was asked of people. Nobody knew a thing.

By the time they'd finally managed to get around to Simone's house, he'd fled the country with the Fiends. When they finally got to Baltimore, Maryland, he felt safe. Free and safe. It was the first time in a long time he'd felt that way. But he wondered for how long…

He knew he couldn't run forever, and that he wouldn't be able to stay in the States after killing Chrissy and her friends.

He knew he was on course for a life on the run. But how? He had no assets. No money. The only worthy possession he had was his house back home, which was currently on the housing market. The only disposable money he had was what he had on him right then and there. He would now have to wait for his home to sell, which could take weeks, months even.

Chrissy had promised him work on stage with the Fiends, so he wasn't that destitute. She would also be giving him a roof over his head and a bed to sleep in, which was all hers.

"If we're going to be husband and wife in time to come, you may as well start living with me!" had been her words back in the U.K.

And so they did. She took him back to her house and showed him off to her neighbours and around her small town. The locals found his accent hypnotic, soothing. They fell in love with him, just like she had.

As promised, Chrissy had found him a job within the Flesh Flaying Fiends as their on-stage assistant. Much to his surprise, he'd enjoyed it, making him slightly reconsider his original plan.

He still wanted them all to die, especially Chrissy, but he'd decided to take things a lot slower. To plan what he was going to do and how to make his escape. Simone figured that if he let them live long enough for him to be able to bankroll enough cash then he could easily disappear into the wide blue yonder.

Simone allowed his plan three years, and in that three years leading up to his killing spree, he accomplished many things: He married Chrissy and successfully worked with the Fiends. He also managed to bankroll a stack of cash and fuck as much American fanny behind her back as he could.

As for killing? No, not a single person whilst he was State-side, apart from the Flesh Flaying Fiends – he stayed off the radar, managing to keep his blood-lust on ice; as much as he wanted to murder some women he came into contact with, he didn't.

He found the States to be big, bright and full of potential victims as he and the Fiends travelled the vast land of the good ol' US of A. And that was another reason he was able to keep his killing in check. He was around Chrissy most of his time, not to mention Marianne and Coops. If he wasn't working, then he was spending his time with Chrissy, as much as he loathed her.

He managed to lull the women into a false sense of security. They loved him, thinking the sun shone out of his well-formed Welsh arse.

When his third year came to an end, it was time to ditch the girls and America, as planned, and so Simone thought of starting with Marianne before moving on to Coops – he wanted to keep Chrissy until last. He wanted to make sure she suffered the most.

After keeping his rage at bay for so long, it would be a good thing to start with someone other than his wife of two years. Why? *Because it's like having a wank or sex after being locked in a cage for far too long – you go off like a fucking hair-trigger…* he'd thought at the time.

Even though Marianne never saw it coming, which reminded Simone of a cow being led to the slaughter – one moment they're chewing their cud, the next, they have a steel bolt slammed between their eyes. Lights out. Goodnight. Auf Wiedersehen, pet – his plan didn't work out the way he'd hoped…

"I'll be glad to get to my nest!" Marianne said as she drove them all home from their final gig for the summer.

"Fuck yeah!" Coops said. "Not sure about you gals, but that felt like one long-ass tour."

"It felt very fucking long!" Chrissy agreed. "We've never done eight states before, man. *Fuck*. How many towns and cities do you think we covered?!"

"A fuck ton!" Marianne said, not taking her eyes off the road.

As the girls spoke among themselves, Simone lay at the back of the van, all the while plotting the moves he would be playing over the next few days. He knew he had to kill these three as soon as possible before skipping the country, because he'd already bought a ticket to Argentina – his flight left in four days' time.

Chrissy nor the other two knew, of course.

They were completely in the dark.

He even had Chrissy thinking he was taking her away for a second honeymoon whilst they were off the road. All the while he was having fantasies about skinning her and eating her flesh.

I'm surrounded by dead women! he thought, sniggering.

"Now we have fall to look forward to!" Coops said. "*Whoop!* I'm going to get wasted tonight, then probably sleep the rest of the week. What about you and Si, Chris?"

"My baby and me are going away. Isn't that right, Simone?"

"Hm? Oh, yeah… Second honeymoon, Coops," he said. "I've got to treat my hardworking lady every now and then."

"Nice, guys – where are you heading?" she asked.

"He won't tell me!"

"That's right, I won't. You know it's a surprise, Chrissy," he said. *It's a one-way ticket to the afterlife, bitch!* he thought, smiling at them like a Cheshire cat.

"I'm sure it'll be somewhere exotic, knowing our boy Simone!" Marianne said.

"Yeah, hot and spicy!" Coops chirped in.

"*Ugh*, I don't think I could put up with any more seediness!" Chrissy said. "Please don't tell me you're taking us to Thailand or somewhere like that?!"

"Oo, like the lady boys, Si?!" Coops giggled.

That's right, laugh it up, motherfuckers. "I can't go giving all my secrets away," he said.

"What about you, Marianne?"

"What about me, Coops?"

"What's your plan, now that we're off?"

"Well, tonight I plan to kick it up in the hot tub with a few beers and a couple of fat ones!"

The girls laughed. Simone just lay there, staring at the van's roof. *Tonight would be the perfect time to take her, and then Coops tomorrow night. That would give me two days with Chrissy before I have to go.*

"Coops, we're coming up on your house, baby girl," Marianne said.

"Thank fook! Nothing against you girls or anything, but this year has really taken it out of me."

"They call that getting *old*!" Chrissy ribbed.

"Hey, fuck you, bitch!" Coops said, putting Chrissy in a headlock. Both women screeched with laughter.

"Pack it in!" Marianne said. She applied the brakes sharply, which in turn, caused Simone to slide along the floor and the two women to shoot forward in their seat.

"Hey!" he yelled. "What's the big idea?!"

"Chill, Si – I was only messing with y'all!"

"Can't say I like being skidded across a fucking floor, Marianne."

"What's eating your man, Chris?" Coops asked.

"You okay, babe?"

"Yeah, fine."

"No, you might not be," Marianne said, "but you *luurve* having your bits butchered on stage!"

Simone felt the rage build inside him. He wanted nothing more than to get up, go over to her, and smash her face in against the van's steering wheel. But he didn't. He choked the anger down.

I can't let three years of hard work go down the pan… Soon, it will all be over. Soon. Tonight!

He smiled up at Marianne, who was eyeing him in the rear-view. They were all looking at him as though he had just magically appeared from another planet. "Ha! I'm only twisting your tits," Simone said. "God! Lighten up, ladies."

Marianne laughed, sparking Chrissy and Coops off.

"Fuck, you had me going!" Coops said.

"Me, too!" Chrissy confessed.

I've had you all going for the past three years. Welcome to my parlour, said the spider to the fly…

"Coops, we're at yours. Want us to stick around, make sure you get in safe?"

"Hell, no! I'm ten paces from my home. And the last time I checked, us badasses can take care of ourselves!"

"True, dat!" Chrissy said.

Once they'd dropped Coops off, Marianne proceeded towards Chrissy and Simone's place, which took less than thirty minutes. When they arrived, Simone and Chrissy got out of the van and headed towards their home.

"Check you guys in a few days!" Marianne called from her driver's side window. "Once my booze and weed haze has worn off." Before pulling away, she howled and thumped the roof above her head.

Chrissy laughed.

Simone watched Marianne with squinted eyes. *I'll be seeing you much sooner, bitch.*

"Come on, babe – let's get some beers inside us!" Chrissy said.

"Sounds like a good idea. That was one long fucking trip!"

"Agreed, my Flesh Flaying friend!"

She smiled.

He didn't. When her back was turned, he scowled at her. *I could kill this cunt first. Take the next few days and really strip her to the bone! No, the others must come first.*

"Want to get freaky in the bedroom?" he asked. Since stepping foot on American soil, a lot of Simone's perverse side had deserted him. His bitterness towards Chrissy and the others had taken over. Set root in him. Over the three years that followed, his character had changed slightly.

His sexual behaviour had slowed down.

He didn't need releases as much, not now.

Simone guessed age was starting to play a part in it, too.

Not like I'm getting any younger.

But, deep down, he knew it was his rage that was blinding him. It was keeping all aspects of his brain quiet. When he fucked pussy behind Chrissy's back, it was out of spite. Nothing else, which tasted sweet.

Also, work with the Fiends had kept him very busy and tired. After all the years of not working, just being a plaything for Chaos, it had taken its toll. He wasn't used to life in the rat race.

That was another thing he intended to break free of. A worker's life was not for him.

When I get to my next destination, I plan to settle down with a woman who will take care of me, just like Chaos but without the whole brutal domination. I want to be truly loved by a woman… Will it ever happen? He thought this as he walked up the path behind Chrissy to their house. *There's enough time to worry about love. Firstly, I need to think about wrapping* this *life up.*

"Oo, is my bad boy up for a bit of naughty, spanky fun?!" she asked, turning to put her arms around him. He had to stop himself from jumping out of her hold in repulsion, especially when she grabbed his hand and placed it on her arse. "Go on," she rasped, "smack and squeeze it. You know how it drives me wild."

Lightly, he pushed her away. "Let's wait until we get inside, yeah?"

"*Wow*, when did you become such a prude?" she asked, sniggering.

It was fun to fuck you at the start out of malice, but that wore off a long time ago, whore, he thought.

"I'm not, I just feel a bit tired, that's all."

"Okay, baby. Come on, I'll fix us a couple of drinks and then you can tie me up with my stockings!" She giggled and bit her lip.

I wonder if she can see the disgust on my face? "Sounds good to me!" he said, and that's when the final pieces of his plan clicked into place. *Tie her up?* A smile pulled across his face.

"You like the sounds of that, baby?" she asked.

"Yeah, damn right!" *I'll make sure she's well fastened to the bed before leaving her there to kill the other pair. It'll be perfect. When I return, I'll be able to have all the fun in the world with Chrissy,* he thought, feeling his smile pull tighter.

When they got inside, Simone hit the lights and Chrissy slipped on over to the bar they had in their living room.

"Beer or something stronger?"

"Er, no, I'll stick with a cold beer."

"Coming up!" she said. "Do you want to put some music on?"

"No!" he snapped, not really wanting the drink. He just wanted to get the bitch trussed up like a turkey as soon as possible.

"*Wow*! What's up with you? You're not still pissed about Marianne, are you?!"

"I told you, I was joking." He snatched the beer out of Chrissy's hand. "Besides, I don't want to fuck around down here, I want to fuck around up there!" he said, flicking his eyes towards the ceiling.

"Well, all right. You got it, sailor."

She forgot about the drinks and took his hand in hers. She led him upstairs to the bedroom, where she bent over the bed and stuck her arse in the air. "Want to see what's under my skirt?"

A smile briefly played across his face.

He walked up behind her and smacked her arse as hard as he could, causing her to groan. "*Fuck*, do it again!" she urged. "That ripple you just caused in my arse cheek tickled my pussy."

Simone walloped her again and again, until she climaxed hard. He noticed her juices flowing down her legs.

"What a dirty, naughty girl!" he said, shoving her onto the bed. She grunted.

"And what happens to dirty, naughty girls?!" she asked, giggling.

Opening the bedside drawer, he spied two sets of handcuffs, stockings, a whip and blindfold.

"Perfect!" he said, removing the cuffs and stockings. "I'll show you what happens to them." He proceeded to cuff her hands to the bed's posts before bounding her legs with the use of her stockings.

"Rip my skirt…"

She didn't have chance to finish her sentence, as Simone smashed his fist into her mouth. Teeth flew. A splash of blood found its way up the wall behind the bed.

When he retracted his fist to hit her again, Chrissy became hysterical. At first he hadn't noticed that she'd bitten her tongue in half, which lay on her chest.

Simone became frenzied with laughter. Getting off her, he watched her with morbid curiosity. He liked how the stump of tongue inside her mouth flapped as she screamed and balled.

"Can I touch it?" he asked.

Tears flooded down her cheeks. Blood spilled out of her mouth.

"Well, I didn't actually plan on this playing out like it has," he confessed. "Marianne was first on my list. I was going to draw your death out."

As her screaming continued, his patience became thin.

"Shut up with that wretched noise, woman!" he yelled, slamming his fist against a wall. When she didn't, he grabbed a pair of her knickers that lay by the side of the bed and rammed them down her throat. "Fucking *shush*!" he demanded, shoving at the silk garment until she made gagging sounds.

"You know that kind of sound is only appealing if you're choking on my cock!" He watched as her mouth opened and closed, but no words came. "You can't talk, you've only got half a tongue and your panties are rammed down your gullet!" He laughed.

Simone then tore the clothes from her body. He'd always admired her shape, especially her legs. "You know, it's going to be a real shame, me having to cut you up into tiny pieces."

Her sobbing became violent. She grunted and screamed, which came out as nothing more than muffles.

"Now, what do we have around here that I could use…" He let his words trail off when he saw what was leaning against the wall. "Shall we do a Richard Ramirez?" he asked, grabbing the brush. "It was reported that he stuck broom handles up some of his female victims, but I'm sure others did it too!" His smile broadened. "I guess I'm going to give you the fuck of your life, whore!"

Chrissy furiously shook her head.

"You're probably wondering what the fuck you've done to deserve this? Well, in a nutshell, I'm just one fucked-up bastard," he said, stepping closer to her. "Come on – open up 'em pretty piss flaps for daddy!"

Then she was screaming as he violently shoved the brush's three-foot wooden shaft deep inside her. He proceeded to pump it in and out of her like a huge, rampant dildo. Blood slicked its rough surface and poured out onto the bedspread.

When it looked as though she was going to pass out, he ripped the brush free of her and started hitting her as hard as he could with it.

Her jaw cracked.

An arm snapped.

When he'd had enough with the brush, he flung it to one side and clamped his teeth down hard on one of her nipples. He ripped the appendage away with such malice that one of his teeth chipped.

Her whole body started to spasm as it closed down and went into shock.

"Night-night, bitch!" he said, spitting her nipple out of his mouth.

****

The memory of Chrissy disappeared as Simone was violently shaken out of his nightmares.

"Wake up!"

"Who…what?!" His face still hurt. "I'm having nightmares," he blurted.

"It's me, Nurse Sinnamond, Simone."

"How long have I been out?"

"Two or three days. You've been running a very high fever – I've been trying to knock it out of you."

"Terrible nightmares," he muttered.

"That will be the fever – it can cause hallucinations."

"Huh?"

"Mind phantoms. Delirium, you know? They're not real. Don't worry about them, they will pass," she said, putting the back of her hand to his forehead. "You're cooling down, but they may persist for the next twenty-four hours. Try not to move too much, as you're hooked up to drips for nutrition."

"Okay, but I need water." When he gulped, it felt as though he was trying to swallow a plot of cacti.

"Here," she said, putting a freshly poured glass of water in his hand. "I need you to listen to me, Simone. I have some very important information from a mutual friend."

His mind raced: *A friend? I don't have a friend. Certainly not on the outside, and most definitely not in a place like this!*

"Who?!" he snapped. His spittle coated his chin. "I don't have such people…"

"Shut up and listen. I can't tell you too much at the moment, because if others find out, heads will roll. I've been put in place to protect you – to make sure you get out of this sick bay unharmed. Tonight, at around midnight, two of Bosco's men are going to come in here and attempt to kill you whilst you sleep. I'm not going to be able to protect you, but I can give you this," she said, placing a cool, metallic object in his hand.

"A scalpel…?"

"Yes. I'm also going to loosen your wrist and ankle straps, so you can get out of bed and surprise them," she said, unfastening his restraints.

"Why are you doing this?!"

"I told you, we have a mutual friend who very much wants to see you live. They're working on trying to get you out of here."

"The hospital?"

"No, the prison."

"An escape?!"

"Yes. Look, I don't have much time. If the doctor catches me here, we'll all be fucked. Take this, also," she said, slipping something inside his blanket.

"What is that?"

"It's a sports watch – I've set the alarm for eleven o'clock. That will give you plenty of time to make your move. I'll come back to see you again tomorrow."

"How can they just come in here and kill me? They'll be locked up, won't they?"

"They've bought the guards and the doctor, Simone. This will be one of many attacks. Don't worry, though. Myself and our friend will keep you safe. Also, because of your critical condition, the doctor had you moved to a side room. You're in here alone."

"Shit, okay. But who's this mutual friend?!"

"I can't say. They won't allow me to."

"They?!" Simone said.

"Look, I'll try and tell you more tomorrow – I'll ask for permission. For now, get some rest and deal with the oncoming threat." She bent over and kissed him on the forehead, which was totally unexpected. His nostrils filled with her exotic perfume. As she was so close, he could just about make her out through his partly open eye.

Jessica was very pleasing to look at – her hair smelled of coconuts and her breath of ice-cool spearmint. Her dark shoulder-length hair flanked her pretty face.

"You smell wonderful," he said, inhaling her deeply.

"Thank you. Take care of yourself, Simone. Bye." Before he could answer, Simone heard her high-heels click-clack as she walked away.

"*Jessica…*" he whispered, and then remembered the scalpel in his hand. He clutched it tightly. "So, they think they can take *me*? Simone? Not a fucking chance. What gutless fuckbag attacks a sleeping man? Well, let them come. I'll be waiting!"

Putting the scalpel down by his side, he searched for the watch and brought it close to his eye. Simone made out that it was almost nine-thirty, which didn't give him much time.

Thanks for cutting it so fine, Jess! he thought, looking down at his feet. His ankle straps were completely undone, allowing him to throw his legs off the bed. Both hands were also free so Simone lowered himself to the floor as gently as possible. The tile flooring was cool against his face as he slid under his bed with the scalpel and watch in his hands. *Surprise, motherfuckers.*

Once he was settled, Simone put the watch and medical tool by his side. When he squinted his good eye, he could just about see beyond the end of his bed, so spotting his attackers coming was going to be a trial.

"I'll just wait until they're on top of me," he said, smiling.

Doesn't look like any of the guards are going to come around and do their checks tonight. Bastards. They're leaving the door wide open for Bosco's boys. Well, fuck 'em – I'll make sure nobody wants to fuck with me ever again after tonight, he thought. *I'll be sending a message of my own.*

Lighting the watch's face, he looked at the time and saw it was approaching ten o'clock. Simone closed his eyes and rested his head against his arm – a headache had kicked in from the exertion of moving down to the floor.

Two chopped up douchebags coming right up!

Before he could stop himself, Simone slipped into another troubled sleep as the headache pressed itself upon him – a cold chill ran down his back, followed by beads of perspiration.

****

He cut her into the smallest pieces possible.

Simone didn't have to, because he'd already done an adequate job by chopping her arms and legs off to fit her into a few black bags.

But it wasn't enough for him.

His bloodlust hadn't been slaked in a few years.

He needed it.

Had been craving it.

Simone didn't just dice her up, but fucked her, pissed on her and popped his seed all over the legs that he had loved so much.

He'd even pulled her guts out and rolled around in them. Whilst her blood had been hot and spurting, he'd lapped at it; tasted her salty, metallic life source.

When he finally come to chopping her up, he realised he'd spent the best part of seven hours playing with her carcass.

After finding a hacksaw in her garage, he'd started with her legs, then arms, before removing her head and ripping the tongue out. He'd even smashed her teeth out for the fuck of it.

Once Simone had sectioned her into tiny pieces and bagged her, he'd buried Chrissy in her back garden. He'd then showered, changed his clothes and made his way over to Marianne's house, even though it was well past midnight.

Simone pulled up at Marianne's at exactly one A.M. At first, he'd considered turning back. Going home.

It's too late to be creeping around – anyone could spot me! No, it has to end tonight, he'd argued with himself.

He took a deep breath, put his hand to the door handle, and pulled. *No turning back now.*

The thrill of chopping Chrissy up was still pumping through him. He could feel his blood whiz around his veins. His heart rate galloped. He felt alive, which he hadn't in a long time.

Fucking women. If they're not breaking your heart, they're holding you back! Maybe I will go solo from here on in? Who needs a woman – think of the fun I could have! Fuck love.

As he walked across the street to Marianne's house, Simone let the hacksaw dangle at his side. When he got to her door, he tried the doorknob. Locked. He moved to the window and noticed there was a slight parting in the curtains. Putting his face to the glass, he could just about see into the room beyond. It was dark, but there was a light shining towards the rear of the house.

Hmm… How best to handle this?

Simone moved towards the back garden. All the while, he checked over his shoulder to make sure there was nobody watching.

When he got to the flimsy back door, he took a chance in kicking it open. The lock at the back flew off, causing the door to spring backwards and slam against the wall. Before moving through the entrance, he pricked his ears.

Nobody was coming.

Nobody had heard his destructiveness.

As he walked into the garden, he heard soft music.

Water was rippling. Splashing.

Simone then listened with intensity – someone was singing.

"*Marianne*!" he blurted, gripping the hacksaw that little bit tighter.

He made sure to close the wooden gate, even though he couldn't lock it.

After walking that little bit further, Simone came to a corner of the house. He put his back flat against the wall and peeped around it. Sure enough, Marianne was in her hot tub as promised.

How fucking long as she been in that thing?!

There were a couple of empty champagne bottles on the side of the tub, along with a couple of fat ones. She had headphones on and didn't alert to his approach. He put the hacksaw down and picked up one of the empty bottles.

As he drew it back, ready to strike, he noticed she was naked. A breath hitched in his throat. Why this sudden interest bothered him he didn't know – he'd seen Marianne, much like the other Fiends, naked many times on stage.

The water... The bubbles… It's making her skin glisten.

Then he saw her tits, her big pink nipples.

His cock grew hard.

He shook his head and brought the bottle crashing down on her head – the glass exploded in his hand. The bubbling, broiling water turned red. She didn't even have time to yelp.

Simone watched her body float on top of the crimson water. She didn't appear to be alive, but he couldn't take any chances. He picked up another empty bottle and waded into the water.

"Come here, you fucking bitch!" he yelled. The crimson tides crashed around his thighs, sticking his jeans to his legs. Water even cascaded up his torso, plastering his T-shirt to his trunk.

When he got to Marianne, he grabbed her by the hair, lifted her head out of the water, and began slamming the bottle against her skull time and again. He heard something crack.

More blood helped colour the already dense water.

After his arm went weak and he became breathless, Simone stopped hitting her. Her cranium was pulverised, her hair thick with blood.

He made his way back to the hot tub's edge and got out on shaking legs. Tripping, Simone sprawled along the floor and lay there, panting.

"Jesus…fucking…hell…!" he gasped between ragged breaths.

A light came on in a neighbouring house.

"Marianne?!" a voice called. "Are you okay?! Marianne!"

Simone clutched his breath and listened.

"Jim, call the police – I think something has happened to Marianne."

Fuck! Simone's mind screamed. He then heard a muffled voice in the background and decided it was Jim's.

"I'm sure I saw someone creeping around outside. Marianne! Go on, Jim – get them on the phone. Now, man!"

Shit, shit, shit! I need to get the fuck out of here. Now!

He rolled onto his stomach, got to his knees and then listened some more.

"Jesus, Jim! She's been killed!" Looking up, Simone saw the old woman from next door – she had her head over the fence. "He's still in the yard, Jim!"

Simone hopped to his feet and ran for the back gate. When he made it out onto the street, he heard the bolts on the neighbour's front door disengage.

"*Fuck*!" Simone bellowed, making it to the car and slamming his body against it. He fumbled for his key. When he looked over his shoulder, he saw Jim standing on his porch with his twelve-gage in his hands.

"*Stop*!" he yelled, but Simone jumped in his car and slotted the key into the ignition. He fired the car up just as Jim took a shot at him. The back window blew out.

"Fucking hell!" he screamed, feeling glass wash over him. Just then, his car kicked to life. He stamped down on the accelerator and brought his foot up off the clutch as quickly as possible; being in the States, he'd learned to drive a shift, but favoured a car with a gear stick.

The tyres screeched as he pulled away from the curb, kicking up black smoke and loose stones.

He thought about aborting and heading to the airport – to get as far away as possible – but decided against it. *There's no point in hitting the panic button. Stick with the plan.* And so he did.

Simone headed towards Coops' house.

I need to see this through. Once I'm done, I'll grab my shit and head to the airport. I don't care if I have to wait a day or two for my flight. Once I'm there, I'll be safe.

The roads were deserted as he drove to his next destination.

****

The pithy alarm on the sports watch woke him from his unsettled, fever-laden sleep, which was filled with blood and murder. When Simone pulled his head up off his arm, he left behind a wet, sticky patch of saliva. Strings of drool hung from his bottom lip and chin.

"*Ugh*!" he said, putting a hand to his face to wipe the fluid off him. "Fucking disgusting!"

He shook his head to try and clear the sleepy fog that clouded his brain and then grabbed the watch – it was just past the eleven o'clock mark.

Plenty of time yet, he thought, moving the scalpel close.

After a few stretches and rubs of his eyes, Simone felt alert and ready. Then he noticed the light in the hallway was off, which he found odd. *Wasn't it on earlier?* Crushing darkness surrounded him, not that it bothered him.

The darkness is going to affect my visibility – I may not even be able to see my attackers standing by the bed. It was fine when the hallway light was on, but not now. Shit. No, surely they'll turn the light on…? Fuck, if they do, then they'll see that my bed is empty.

He crawled from under his bed and got to his feet as fast as possible – it took him more than ten minutes to slide from under the bed, and then a further ten to get to his shaking legs.

Simone threw the sheets back and placed his pillows in a straight line down the centre of the bed. Happy, he covered them and got to his knees again. Once he was back under the bed, sweating profusely, he checked the time.

Eleven forty-five.

Fucking hell – that took some effort. Not to mention time! Shit, my body is completely fucked. That big bastard give me a worse battering than I had first thought. I mean, I've taken a lot of punishment in the past, but that was intense.

After lying there resting for twenty minutes, Simone felt fit again – well, as fit as he could possibly get with regards to the state he was in.

At ten-past midnight, Simone was starting to give up.

Nobody was coming.

Then, in the distance, he saw a light wink on and then off quickly.

Whispered voices drew closer.

His heart rate started to pick up beyond its normal pace.

Simone made sure he had the scalpel tight in his palm, which was starting to feel icy and tacky from his sweat.

His door lightly squeaked, which had been part-open.

Soft footfalls could be heard approaching.

More whispers.

Not the quietest cats on the block, are they? Then again, if I hadn't been warned, I would have been out of it. I would never have known what was coming.

Then the door to his room creaked some more.

A breath hitched in his throat.

The sound of shuffling feet felt closer to his ear, but he couldn't see anything. Not even a faint shape.

Come on, show your-fucking-selves! Then he heard footsteps to his other side. *They're flanking the bed.*

As if his hopes and prayers had been answered, a blinding light filled the room, causing Simone to shield his eyes.

"This is for Bosco, yo!" someone yelled.

Then Simone heard the awful sound of two men pummelling the bed sheets and pillows with shivs. Feathers fluttered down to the ground. The attack was as frenzied as it was brutal.

Both assailants screamed as they ripped into the empty bed.

When Simone's vision adjusted to the sudden brightness, he could see a blurred set of feet to his right. He lashed out with the medical instrument, making sure his aim was deadly. The sharp blade cut through the man's Achilles tendon with ferocity.

"*Argh*!" he screamed, hopping. Blood gushed across the floor. Simone didn't stop there and took no time in slashing through the man's other Achilles, causing him to drop to the floor, hard. This brought him eye-level with Simone.

"*Surprise*!" Simone said, ramming the blade into the man's eye. He twisted the scalpel before retracting it. When he did, it dripped blood and popped eye gloop. As the man did the jig of death, Simone rolled quickly onto his other side and slashed the second attacker's Achilles tendons.

When he was down, screaming and begging, Simone slipped from under the bed. Both men had an Italian/Spanish look about them. They also had the mark of the Boas stamped all over their necks.

"Fucks like you never learn, do you?!" Simone said, standing. He had to hold on to the bed due to his legs trembling and his feet slipping in the copious amounts of blood. "It looks like a fucking slaughterhouse in here!" he said, smiling.

"Please, don't kill me, man. I was only following orders…"

"What's your name, wop?!"

"André," the man said – his face was scrunched. "Can you get me the doctor? I'm bleeding badly."

"Now why would I want to do that?!" Simone said, bending over the man. He placed the tip of the scalpel to the man's throat.

"Please. I beg you. I'll give you any information you want."

"Don't you pricks have a code?" he asked, slashing at one of the man's Boas tattoos.

"Yes, but I like you."

Simone scoffed and then laughed. "You lying piece of shit! Tell me who ordered this hit?"

André gulped, but said nothing.

"Just as I thought – you won't surrender any information. Maybe I should cut your balls off?!"

"No! It was Maddie!"

"*Who*?!"

"Maddie. After Bosco, Maddie's next in chain of command behind these walls."

"So, if I was to take that cunt down, would the rest of you pricks leave me alone?!"

"Only…"

"*Yes*?!" Simone pushed, pressing the point of the blade harder against André's neck. A trickle of blood escaped a vein.

"Only if you can make an example of Maddie, I suppose. We were impressed that you managed to kill Bosco, but you had to be dealt with. If Maddie should die, that would be all our high-ranking officers dead. There would only be us foot soldiers left!"

"Thanks," Simone said, smiling. He then slashed André's throat. "Tell Satan hi from me!"

After André stopped bucking and thrashing his arms and legs, Simone got back into bed. It didn't take him long to fall into a deep, dream-filled sleep once again, as he thought about Marianne and Coops.

****

With Marianne's house behind him, Simone took his foot off the accelerator. A few cop cars flew past him, their blues and twos screaming out in the dead of night.

"Got to keep my speed under control – I don't want them to stop me for something silly or they will see all this blood," he uttered, looking down at himself. His top was covered in thick red and pink-ish stains. His jeans were completely saturated and stuck to his legs. Even with the car's heater on full blast, it did little to air them out.

His teeth chattered.

"Once Coops is dead, I can get back to mine and shower. After that, I'll grab a bite to eat, pack and then hit the road. In the morning, I'll drain my bank account on the way to the airport."

Simone looked in the rear-view mirror – he wasn't being followed.

"With any luck, the old fucker didn't get my licence plate number," he said, hitting the steering wheel with his hand. "That was so fucking careless of me. Shit!"

His eyes flicked to the rear-view once more.

Nothing.

Stay calm! I need to keep my shit together… The radio!

Simone clicked it on and tuned it to the local station – there were already reports going out about the murder of Marianne. They were also broadcasting descriptions of Simone and his car; they even had a part of his licence plate.

"Holy fuck, this is bad!"

More police cars whizzed past him.

Maybe I should leave Coops after all – just get the fuck out of here. Now! I can't. If she lives, then she will be able to give them the full rundown on me. She must die!

With that in mind, he put his foot down on the accelerator and cut his car through the cool, night air.

After driving another twenty minutes, Simone finally pulled up outside Coops' home. The radio was still going crazy with reports of what had happened, putting Simone in a state of unease.

The sooner I get this over and done with, the sooner I can disappear.

He got out of his car and closed his door as quietly as possible before running across the street to the house he needed.

There were lights on inside – upstairs and down.

"Mmm…She's still awake. This could be fun!"

When he checked the front door, he found it to be unlocked. Pushing it open, Simone casually walked into the passageway. The hacksaw was in his hand once again.

A TV was playing in the distance.

Simone could hear the police reports.

I need to take her down before she realises it's me they are talking about, he thought as he crept down the hallway to the open door at his right.

He kept his back flat to the wall, just like he had done at Marianne's place. When he got to the entrance, he quickly poked his head around the doorjamb and that's when he saw Coops. She was passed out on her sofa – there was a scattering of empty beer cans on the floor.

She was lightly snoring.

Simone walked into the room and switched the TV off.

Coops didn't stir.

A smile pulled across his face.

"Sweet." Like Marianne, she too was naked, right down to her juicy pink twat. "Ain't you delicious, Coops? It's such a shame I have to put you to sleep for good!"

He didn't bother waking her – he needed to make this kill quick. Had the walls not been closing in around him, then Simone would have taken his time.

There will be plenty of women to kill on the road! he thought, and then viciously shoved his hand into Coops' face. He pushed her head back, exposing her neck.

She awoke, screaming and clawing at his hand and face but it was futile.

He placed the saw to her throat and ripped it across to the right, then fluently swept it to the left – the blade bit through her flesh with ease. Blood splashed up Simone's face.

The noise the saw made was much like that of leather being torn, giving him an instant erection. He was in fear of coming in his pants, much like he had done when he'd killed Marianne, but he didn't care.

Simone didn't stop sawing until he was cutting into the sofa cushions under her.

After the first couple of swipes with the hacksaw, she had succumbed.

When he held her severed head up to his face, he noticed her mouth was open – fixed in a silent scream.

Spitefully, he got his hard dick out, which hadn't fired off a milky round, and shoved it down her throat. He feverishly moved her head back and forth whilst fingering her stump as he did so – it felt warm and wet, which eventually caused him to climax.

With his dick spent, Simone removed it from her in a hurry, suddenly fearing Coops would clamp down on it.

Don't be silly, it's not fucking attached to her body!

He threw the head to one side and rushed out of the house.

Before he could reach his car, squad cars came screeching onto the road from every direction, hemming him in.

"Get on the fucking ground, now!" someone yelled from beyond a stream of blinking red and blue lights.

Guns could be heard cocking.

Red beads scattered across his chest.

He dropped his car keys. He knew he was done for.

Rough hands grabbed his arms and placed them behind his back. Simone was thrown against his vehicle and placed under arrest. Cool cuffs were snapped into place.

Within minutes, he was in the back of a police car and being hauled off to the nearest station.

What will become of me…? he thought, looking at Coops' house as the cop car he was in pulled away from the curb.

****

He wasn't scared. In fact, he was relieved. Relieved that he'd been caught and that the killings would finally come to an end – the women in the world would sleep and rest easy, for Simone was off the streets. For good.

"Thank you," he told the arresting officer as he was led into a small room with no air conditioning. "I can see why people call these interrogations rooms 'sweat boxes'. There's no worries about me not talking – I'll tell you everything you want to know."

"It won't be me, son – my superior officers will be along shortly to talk to you." Simone was then placed in a chair and cuffed to the bars that were set into the middle of the table in front of him. "Shouldn't be long now," the copper said, leaving the room.

Alone, Simone looked at the opposite wall – there was a large two-way mirror set in its centre.

"I know you're watching me. There's no need. As I told your man, I'm happy to answer all your questions. I just want this over with." He smiled and hoped that the show of emotion would illustrate his sincerity.

Within minutes, the door to the room he was being detained in opened. Three men in low-class suits walked in. The one in the lead, a big, burly son-of-a-bitch, extended his hand. His round face was flanked by mutton chops – a slug-like moustache covered his upper lip, with a bushy goatee gracing his chin. His gut hung over his gun belt.

"Simone, I'm Detective Inspector Grater – this is Sergeant Smithers," he said, pointing at the skinny man directly behind him and then at the balding, bespectacled fella who now stood alone. "That's Dr. Stevens – he wanted to sit in on this chat."

"Why, so you can determine whether or not I'm nuts?!"

"No, no…" the doctor started, but was cut short by Simone.

"Chat? Don't you mean interrogation!" He smiled and then winked at Smithers. "I'm more than willing to open up to my crimes. But, if I do so, I want to be sent home. I don't want to do my time here in the States. Can you arrange that, Detective?"

"I'll see what I can…"

"I want your word. No, scrap that. I want it in *writing*. I want to go home and serve my time. Until you can guarantee that, I'm not saying diddly shit!"

"Okay, Simone. Have it your way," the detective said. "Smithers, come here," he said, beckoning with his fingers. He then whispered into his officer's ear, and the sergeant then sloped out of the room.

"Where's he going? What did you say to him?" Simone asked.

"Now, now – cool your engines, Mary-Jane. He's just going to make a few phone calls. See if we can't work things out for you," said the detective.

"Who's nutsack does a guy have to drain around here to get a cup of tea?!" Simone gave the detective a smug look.

"Doc, would you mind popping down the hall and getting us some refreshments." It wasn't a question.

"Of course," the doctor said, and then left.

"Now, Simone, you seem like a real smart kind of guy, so why don't you just tell me everything you have to, there's a good lad."

"I told you, I ain't saying fuck-all until you can say for definite you will be sending me home."

"Fine, son. But I want that confession. I want to know what else you've been up to."

Simone smiled at the big cop. He liked him. "I'll be more than happy to cooperate, Detective."

At that moment, the doctor came in with three mugs of tea.

Two hours after that, Smithers returned and whispered in the detective's ear.

"Well, Simone it would seem you're very much in luck," Grater said, beaming. "The British police *want* you back – it would seem you've been a naughty boy there, too. They said as soon as we have what we want, we can deport you. Of course, we'll have to wait for the paperwork, but that shouldn't take too long. Besides, it's cost effective and it seems you don't have an American citizenship? No work visa, either! Naughty. But I guess it helped us bag your sorry arse nice and quick – it all led back to Chrissy's home."

Chrissy had begged him to get a citizenship, but he'd managed to fend her off every time she brought the subject up because he'd never intended on staying. She was easily distracted, especially when he got fruity with her.

"Sounds pretty good to me. Where will I be held until then?"

"We have holding cells here – shouldn't take more than a few days to sort you out and have you on a plane back home. I hear the prisons are much tougher, too – especially for people like you, friend. It will save us a hell of a lot of paperwork, that's for damn sure! Let the Brits have you, I say."

"I want this in writing. I'm still not cooperating until I know for definite!"

"That's fine, son. I'll get that sorted now. Whilst I'm at it, I'll get the ball rolling on those deportation forms. Give me a couple of hours."

"Fine," Simone said. "It's not like I'm going anywhere!" He winked, and then blew a kiss at the doctor. "Do you like having your balls beaten by a hot dominatrix, Doc? Please, tell me."

The coppers laughed but the doctor blushed. "Oh, my!" he said, taking his glasses off to clean them.

Within seventy-two hours, Simone's business with the American officials was complete: He'd had his guarantee in writing, confessed everything to the detective and had his deportation papers drawn up and signed.

He'd then been placed on a plane home the next morning, with four FBI agents escorting him.

Fourteen hours after boarding the jumbo jet, Simone found himself back on British soil, with a police convoy awaiting his arrival.

After he'd been placed in their care and the papers were handed over and signed, Simone was taken in to custody in Cardiff. Once there, Simone didn't hold back. He spilled his guts about everything, even his mother and sister.

He'd felt like a great weight had been lifted from off him.

It wasn't long then until he was caged with the rest of the animals where he would stay until his dying days.

****

He felt himself lift out of the deep sleep he was in. A hand roughly shook his shoulder.

"Simone, are you awake?!"

It was her. Jessica. He wanted to respond but he was sleepy – his mouth felt slack. *Are there more people coming to kill me?* he thought.

Cold water hit his face, shocking him fully awake.

"Wha…what?!" he blurted, wiping the liquid from his eyes. When he could finally focus, he saw Jessica – his vision had slightly improved. "You're beautiful!"

She blushed.

He eyed her up and down – she didn't look like your typical nurse. She looked more like a counsellor with her pinstriped skirt and jacket, which was open and revealing a black, silky blouse. She wore chic glasses with her black hair tied up into a ponytail. Her legs were long – Route 66 long – and were covered in black tights. Her skirt didn't quite reach her knees, which was very pleasing to his eye. She wore heels and cradled a clipboard in her arm.

"Why, thanks."

"I've been having awful dreams again," he said, sitting up and looking down at the floor, which was spotless. No bodies. No blood. "But…but…" he stammered, not able to form the words and sentences he wanted to. He felt his whole body start to shake. "I don't know what's real anymore…"

"Simone, take it easy!" Jessica said, pushing him lightly backwards by his shoulders. "I took care of them."

"They were right *there.* I killed them! I did, I swear it. I could smell…"

She struck him across the face. "Stop it!" He looked at her, and at that precise moment, he felt like he was back with Chaos. That he was instantly under the thumb of a new mistress. A new woman. "Sorry, but I had to stop you. You were becoming hysterical."

He went to lift his hand to his face to soothe the sting that was developing there, but couldn't. The straps were back in place. On his ankles, too.

"What happened?" he whispered. For the first time in many years, Simone was scared. He felt like a little boy.

She intensified her grip on his shoulders and looked him square in the eye. "I took care of the bodies, Simone. Nobody knows you killed your attackers apart from Maddie. He runs…"

"I know, he's taken over from Bosco."

"How…"

"One of those shitbags told me. I need to take Maddie down."

"Not yet, you don't. You're not fit enough. Besides, by this time next week, our mutual friend should have you out of here. There's an escape plan in motion."

"But…"

"No buts, Simone. Before you're fully recovered, you'll be out of here. Things are being prepared as we speak."

"How long since they attacked me?"

"The pair that came in here?" she asked. He nodded. "Three nights ago – I've had you on strong pain killers. Some of your injuries were not as bad as first suspected. Your broken rib was the worst of it. Your cheek and eye socket were pretty much fine."

"All those years of not being beaten by Chaos has turned me soft," he muttered.

"Excuse me?"

"Huh? Oh, nothing. Just thinking. When I do get out, where do I go?"

"That will be revealed to you by our friend. Just get plenty of rest."

"Can I take a shower?" he asked.

"Supervised, yes. I'll arrange it."

"Thank you, Jessica. I don't mean to be bad. I…"

She held her hand up. "I don't need you to tell me. I know everything there is to know about you, Simone. I know about your upbringing, everything."

"Who told you?"

"Your files, Simone," she said, giving him a quick examination. "Everything seems to be coming along just fine. Now, get some rest – you're going to need it." She turned from him and started to walk away.

"The shower?"

"Yes, I'll try and organise one for this evening. You must be rather…ripe – you've been in that bed awhile."

"No bed bath?" he asked, smiling.

"Not here, no, but I'll get your need sorted, don't worry."

"Thanks."

She smiled. He winked.

What I wouldn't give to see her whispering eye! he thought, lowering his gaze to her crotch.

She didn't seem to notice as she turned and continued to walk away. "Don't forget, get plenty of rest!" she said over her shoulder.

"I will," he uttered.

Who the fuck is *this mutual friend, and what do they want with me?* His mind raced, making him drowsy. Simone relaxed and let himself slip into a deep sleep once again.

****

"Get up, woman!" someone yelled in Simone's face. He felt their hot breath against his cheek – it stank of onion.

Close by, something was being run back and forth across the bars to his bed, irritating him. "Stop it!" he yelled. This earned him a powerful punch to the guts. "*Oof!*" he coughed.

"I said up! Now, sister!"

"Huh, if he was your sister, you'd still be bathing her, amigo," a new voice said.

"Hey, shut up!"

Simone opened his eyes. Two prison guards hovered over him.

"What do you want?" he coughed.

"I want you to get up!" the first voice raged again. Simone felt hands at his wrists and ankles. "You ordered a shower, didn't you? *Mary!*"

"I've got to tell you, I don't much like the room service you guys are providing in this place!" Simone said, earning himself another punch to the guts. "And those toilets…*Phew*!" he continued, showing as much defiance as he could. "I want to speak to your manager," he said, laughing. "You'll have to excuse me – the drugs are making me loopy."

"He's fucking crazy!" the other man said.

"Grab his arm. We'll drag this motherfucker over to the showers."

"What about his clothes?"

"Fuck his clothes – this cunt seems tough enough."

"Are you strapping lads going to help me scrub my bollock bag?" Simone asked. "It could do with a strong hand…" A robust punch to the jaw threw his head to one side. He spat blood free. "A no would have been…" Another punch to the face. "You fucks are making my flaccid love stick thick and ready."

"This bastard's going to get it!" the second man said.

"Not much further. We're almost there."

"Maybe you fairies can help me…" Simone started, but when he picked his head up and saw what was waiting for him in the shower area, he let his words trail off.

"Throw that piece of fucking shit in here!" the man in the shower room ordered. He was large, but not Bosco large. He was flanked by two other men – they all had the Boas mark on their necks and hands.

Simone gulped.

The two guards holding him dropped him to the floor.

"We softened him up a little for ya, Maddie!" one of the guards said. "He's one stubborn son-of-a-bitch!"

"We'll see just how fucking stubborn he is!" Maddie said, cracking his knuckles. He then removed his prison shirt to reveal a bare, tattooed chest – he had the Welsh dragon ripped into his flesh, along with an impressive swastika on his right pectoral. His hair was a long, greasy mess. When he smiled, Simone could see the inside of the man's mouth was made up of mostly gold.

Simone got to his knees and scrabbled backwards.

The guards backed away, but Simone managed to relieve them of their batons, much to their protests.

Before they could catch him, he rushed into the opposite corner of the shower room.

"I can see you like it rough! Dogs, get that mother-fucking piece of shit!" Maddie said, signalling his troops to move in. "Get those batons off him."

"Right'o, boss!" the one goon said, closing in on Simone. His pal backed him up. "Give 'em up, fuck…"

Simone allowed the first punk within arm's reach before lashing out with the baton in his left hand – teeth could be heard pinging off the shower heads, pipes and tile-flooring.

"*Argh*!" the man screamed, putting his hands to his smashed mouth – his jaw hung off its hinges. Blood pooled into his cupped palms. As he crumpled to his knees, his mate moved in fast, but not fast enough – Simone managed to club his fresh attacker across the back of his head with both sticks, killing him outright. His body slid across the slick floor, coming to a halt at Maddie's feet.

"*Fuck*!" the biker boss bellowed. "Get him, you fucking pig bastards!"

Simone looked at the guards.

"Not a fucking chance – we don't want no part in this, Maddie!" the one said.

"I pay you fucks to do as I say!"

"Touch me and I'll make sure you cock-suckers die in this prison," Simone warned the guards. "I have pull, too!"

"Okay, okay…If you're going to kill Maddie, get it over with!" the second guard said.

"You fucking double-crossing pig scum!" the biker yelled.

Simone smiled. "Oh, you're so dead, Maddie!" Moving closer to the man, he held the bloody batons over his head.

"Come get some, punk bitch!" Maddie spat on his knuckles and moved to meet Simone in the centre of the shower room.

Simone took a swipe with the right baton but it was blocked by his opponent, who ploughed his head into Simone's nose, which hadn't recovered from the first breakage. Tears and blood stung his eyes, causing him to swing the batons blindly.

One was knocked out of his hand by Maddie, who savagely flung himself at Simone and clamped his teeth down on his neck.

"*Argh*!" Simone cried, feeling his veins pop and squirt. He tried to dislodge Maddie by turning in circles. When that didn't work, Simone managed to get a finger to the man's eye, which he gouged.

"*Ugh*, you bastard!"

As Maddie clutched his weeping eye, Simone let rip with the baton. He struck the guy in the back of his knees, which took him down, but he was far from defeated. He gripped Simone's balls and squeezed them. At first, Simone could take the pain, but Maddie's grip became intense. Fast.

In a blind panic, he started clubbing the man around the base of his skull until he heard something crack.

Blood spurted.

Bone burst through the side of Maddie's left eye socket as he was sent flying across the floor.

Simone doubled over and held his nuts – pain shot through his guts and into his head. Brain freeze took him to his knees.

"Shit!" he gasped. Looking up, he could see Maddie getting to his feet. "Does this faggot ever give up?!"

"You're going to fucking die!"

Simone twirled the baton in his hand. "I don't think so, big boy!"

Maddie bull charged. Simone sidestepped and clubbed his attacker around the back of his head, sending him skidding across the floor once again.

"Stay down if you want to live!"

"*Aargh*! You fucking cunt." Maddie got to his feet once again and charged. This time, Simone wasn't fast enough to get out of the raging bull's path, and was caught up in a bear hug to end all bear hugs – his back clicked. Due to the severe pain, Simone dropped the baton and tried to get a finger to Maddie's eye once again, but the man buried his face in Simone's chest.

"*Help*…!" He felt his chest tighten. His air supply became thin. Simone started to feel a numbing sensation wash over him.

The guards watched on, exchanged money and laughed.

"Goodnight, fuck face!" Maddie screamed, applying as much pressure as he could.

More clicks and creaks of bones, which sounded like the groaning of an old ship's rigging.

Simone felt like a rag doll – his arms flopped at his sides. Black spots appeared in his vision as the walls closed in around him. In a desperate attempt, he brought his knee up. Fast. It connected with Maddie's bollocks.

To Simone's shock, the man took it with a gasp and a grunt. His lock didn't waver.

"What the bloody hell is the meaning of this!" someone yelled. "Are you men *betting*?!"

The pressure from Simone's back vanished. He could breathe. He gasped and spluttered as he tried to drag air into his lungs.

"Sir, we—" one of the guards tried to speak, but he was cut short by the suited fella standing behind him.

"Why are these prisoners here and why are they fighting? I'll have your bloody jobs for this!"

"I…ugh…er…" the second guard spluttered.

"Get these men back to their respective cells. *Immediately!* Then you come and see me in my office – I and the prison governor will be wanting words with you. I suggest you get moving."

"Yes, sir!" the guards spoke in unison. Without another word, they unclasped the Tasers they had and advanced on Simone and Maddie.

"*Hey*! There's no fucking need for—" Maddie started to protest, but one of the guards stuck his shocker into the biker's neck – a jolt of electricity passed through his body, taking him to ground.

Simone didn't fight it – it was coming, whether he liked it or not.

As soon as the electrodes hit him, he blacked out.

****

After being Tasered, Simone had been taken back to his room on the infirmary ward, where he had awoken a few hours later. He'd found the good doctor standing over him, who had told Simone that he had examined him and that he would soon be fit enough to return to his cell.

That bit of information had pleased Simone, because here in the hospital he was a sitting duck to Maddie and his goons.

After the doctor left, Simone decided to sit up in bed – he didn't feel like sleeping any longer. Also, he wanted to be alert in case someone should try to make another attempt on his life.

He examined his fresh wounds – they didn't seem to hurt him that much.

I have Chaos to thank for that; all those years of abuse... The pain barrier is kicking back in.

"Fucking hell, I need to get out of this shit hole. I know I thought it was good at first, being taken out of civilisation, but I can't live like this. I need out. I need to find peace," he uttered.

Simone looked up at the window which was set high in the wall. The sun was starting to go down – shadows cut across his bed sheets. Within them, he thought he could see the faces of his many victims.

"I'm sorry," he whispered, wiping a tear from his eye. "I deserve to be stuck in a hole like this, and more than deserve being kicked about by mean sons-of-bitches." More tears rolled down his cheeks. "Where the fuck did it all go wrong?! I should have let that big bastard kill me yesterday. Hell, I could have let Bosco do it. I don't deserve to live."

"You really shouldn't talk like that, you know." He looked up and saw Jessica standing by the door. "I just heard what happened with Maddie. I'm sorry, I didn't think…"

"Were you behind that attack?" he asked.

"*No*! I'm on your side, Simone. I've done nothing but try and protect you. Our mutual friend…"

"Yeah, yeah, our mutual friend wants me alive, or some shit. When is all this fucking crap going to end? I want to know what's going on, Jessica!" he yelled, trying to fling his arms in the air, but they were anchored to the bed. "Who is this man who claims to be my friend, and why does he want to help me?!"

She came closer and stroked his face.

He tried to snap at her fingers.

"Calm down! I'm only trying to help and our friend has been working hard to get you out of here, which will be happening tonight. In a few hours, I'm to lead you from here to the offices on the top floor of the prison. Once there, they will be waiting to escort you to freedom."

"What then?" he said with a sullen expression on his face. "I'll never change. I'll just go on killing until I'm dead. I'm not capable of altering."

"Deep down, I think there's a good person inside you, Simone." Jessica continued to stroke his face. "Like I said, I know all about you – the struggles and pains you've been through. I could love you," she admitted.

He looked at her, shocked. "You don't even know me!"

"I know enough. You need someone in your life that you can fully trust. People keep letting you down…"

Simone looked into her eyes. "Are you saying you want to be that person?"

"I can't be, no. But the person getting you..." She stopped herself from saying too much, not that he seemed to notice.

"Who is it?!"

"I can't tell you, but all will be revealed tonight." She continued to stroke his face – her long nails gently scratched his skin. She slipped a finger into his mouth which he started to suck.

Her skin tasted of strawberries.

"*Wait*!" she said, going to the door. After locking it, she returned to him and took her white medical coat off. Underneath, she wore the same pinstripe skirt she had on the other day, but the jacket was different.

She hitched her tight skirt up to reveal her stockings.

"I'm not wearing any knickers!" she whispered in his ear, but he didn't need to be told that.

His eyes were working perfectly.

"Loosen my..."

"Not a chance!" Jessica threw his bed sheets back – his cock was making a tent out of his pyjama bottoms. He watched as she slipped his trousers down his legs to free his pulsating dick. Pre-come had gathered in its head – she licked it clean. "You taste nice."

She removed her hair tie and let her locks flank her face. Jessica then climbed onto the bed and straddled him. She bit her bottom lip and grunted as she rocked gently back and forth.

"I want to see your tits!" he said. "Please." Jessica smiled down at him and undid her jacket and shirt, but didn't remove them. "Come a little closer," he said, and so she did. He took her left nipple in his mouth and teased it with his tongue and lightly nuzzled it with his teeth.

He felt her pussy muscles spasm and then tighten around him.

"*Ugh...*" he grunted, closing his eyes and forcing his head back into his pillow. He could feel his orgasm building.

Jessica quickened her movement, causing her hair to fling about her. She made very little noise, but the small gasps she did make told him everything he needed to know.

Then she flung herself backwards, arching her back as much as possible – her tits were thrust skyward and her hands clamped his ankles. She made circular movements with her hips, which ground her pussy against his cock.

Fuck, she's coming! The thought rushed through his mind, causing him to push his hips up and grind against her – the feeling was beyond immense.

When she sat upright, Jessica started bouncing wildly. Her mouth was closed but her lips were drawn back, revealing her gritted teeth.

She then buried her head in his chest and let out louder sounds of pleasure.

It was too much for him. Simone lost control and all concentration as his own orgasm racked his body, causing him to shout out.

She put a hand over his mouth.

After a few minutes of lying on his chest, Jessica got up and straightened herself.

"*Fuck*!" Simone gasped – his breathing was still uncontrolled. It came in ragged rips. "I needed that."

"You can't tell *anyone* about this!" she demanded.

He shook his head. "Who the fuck am I going to tell?!"

"Nobody, that's who! I wouldn't want our friend knowing."

"Our secret is safe, don't worry."

"Good. Right, I'll be back to collect you later this evening – the rendezvous has been set for midnight, just as the guards change over."

"I need to do one thing before you take me out of here, Jessica."

"What?"

"Maddie. I need to end it with him – I can't leave that stone unturned."

"I know. I'll find out where he is and get you access to him. I'll see you in a short while. In the meantime, rest."

He nodded.

After fixing her hair, Jessica turned to leave. "I've acquired the key to your room. On my way out, I'll be locking you in, just in case of another surprise attack."

She then left without another word, leaving him with his mind once again, which swirled with thoughts of who he would be meeting, and whether or not it was a trap.

I'll need to be on guard, he thought. *I'm not going to let some jailbird scum take me down. No way. I could be walking into anything this evening. Anything. With the amount of people I've pissed off in here, and on the outside, I have enough enemies who want to harm me.*

He tried to relax, seeing no point in getting himself worked up into knots.

Whatever happens, fucking happens. I'm not scared, he continued to muse, looking up at the ceiling. *Let's just get this fucking shit over with.*

When the locks to his bedroom door clacked, a breath hitched in his throat. He wanted to call out, but he didn't dare.

Do I get back under the bed? I don't have a weapon! Plus, I'm tied down!

The door was pushed inwards, causing light from the hallway to spill through and cast Jessica's form into a silhouette. Her face was dark, so he couldn't see what type of expression she wore. However, knowing it was indeed her, and just her, allowed Simone to breathe with ease.

"What time is it?" he asked, looking up at the window. The sky outside had turned dark.

"A few minutes after eleven. I need to get you out of here now, if you're to strike Maddie – we only have a small window of opportunity."

"Well, untie me!" he said, rattling his restraints.

She went to him and undid them. "Come on, quick. If we get there in time, you'll be able to get two for the price of one!"

"What do you mean?" He threw his legs off the bed, stood and then stretched. His body was starting to feel like his own again.

"The guard that set you up for Maddie in the showers should be with him. They usually have a meeting around eleven, eleven thirty," she said.

He nodded. "Do you have anything for me?"

"Here!" She pressed a bottle in his one hand and a carving knife in the other.

"What the...?" he said, holding the Molotov cocktail up to her face.

"I'll light it for you once we get to where Maddie is being kept."

"He's not in a cell?"

"No, he's in confinement. Now, no more questions!" She took him by the arm and led him down a series of dark, dank corridors.

"Are we heading downwards?!"

"Yes."

Is this bitch setting me up for a fall? he thought, gripping the knife tight in his hand. *Well, if she is, I'll make sure I take the cunt with me!*

When they approached another corner, Jessica indicated for him to put his back to the wall, just like her.

"Don't say a word."

In the distance, they could hear voices.

He watched as Jessica poked her head around the corner. "Perfect!" she said.

"What is it?!" he whispered.

"The guard is currently standing outside Maddie's cell," she said, turning to face him. "I'll go down and distract him and you sneak up on him. Use the knife."

"Won't that alert Maddie?"

"Doesn't matter – he's tied to the bed," she said. Simone smiled. All of a sudden, the Molotov felt good in his hand. "Once you've killed Maddie, it should cause a massive distraction, which is what we want."

He nodded. "Okay, let's get the show on the road."

"Wait here. Once I'm down there talking to him, make your move." Then she was gone.

He listened to her heels as they clacked along the floor until they stopped. Then he heard her voice. He took his chance and peeped around the corner. The guard had his back to Simone.

"You crafty bitch!" he uttered. As silent as he could, Simone slipped down the hall and jammed the knife into the guard's neck. He retracted it and stabbed again and again – blood cascaded up Simone's face and the wall.

"What the fuck?" Maddie called from inside his cell. "Help! Help!"

When the guard hit the deck, Jessica handed Simone the lighter and he lit the rag that was stuck down the bottle's neck. Before tossing it in, he let the fuse burn.

"Goodbye, Maddie!" Stepping close to the cell's bars, he threw the bottle against the wall beside the biker's bed. The mattress caught immediately and Maddie screamed like a girl as the fire started to consume him.

"Come on! We have to go!" Jessica said, pulling on Simone's shirt.

As he was led away, Simone watched the big man thrash on his bed as his lava-like blood pooled on the floor along with his skin. Black, cloying smoke started to fill the hallway – an alarm was triggered, which, in turn, activated the sprinkler system.

Simone moved a few cells along and was distracted by the noise coming from within one to his left. He glanced in, seeing a familiar face: Chris Hall, the guy he'd known in school and who had had his arse pulverized at the Klitty Kingdom, was being fucked doggy-style by a chick with a dick. In the corner of the room, a prison officer was masturbating whilst getting it on film.

"Harder, Skiddy! Harder!" Chris cried. The he-she had an extremely pretty face, with long blonde curly hair – her face was heavily made-up, taking nothing away from her beauty. Her tits were massive, matching her cock.

Blood could be seen trickling out of Chris' anus, but he didn't seem to care.

"You like that, baby?" Skiddy said. "You want it harder?!"

Chris cried and begged for more. "Uh-huh!" he gasped. "More, Skiddy Banger, more, more, more!"

Then, what the he-she did next almost sickened Simone – she stuck her fingers up her arse and smeared her shit in Chris' face. He licked at her digits and smacked his chops.

"Ugh, fuck!" Simone belched, quickly moving on.

He tried to stay as close to Jessica as possible, but she was moving too fast as she led him down more corridors, through doors and up flights of stairs.

"Where the hell are you taking me?!" he demanded. "This better not be a fucking trap, bitch!"

"Shut up!" she called back, taking him up a third flight of steps. They appeared to be out of the main prison area and looked to be in a more administrative part of the rabbit-warren-like building. "We're almost there."

"Where the hell are all the guards?!"

"Most of them have been paid off," she admitted. "The ones that couldn't be bought have been sent to different parts of the prison."

"Fucking hell, this person you're taking me to must have some great pull…" He let his words trail off when he noticed they were now standing in front of the governor's room. "*Ha*!" he couldn't help but laugh. "You're trying to tell me that the main man is the one helping me escape?"

"Yes. I couldn't tell you before, just in case…"

"What type of idiot do you take me for?!" he screamed, rushing her. He held the knife to her throat. She gasped. "You better start talking!"

"Please…you don't understand. If you walk through that door, you'll…"

"Ladies first!" he said, knotting her hair around his fist. He pulled her head back, leaving her throat at his mercy. "*In*!"

Slowly, Jessica put her hand to the doorknob and turned it. "There really isn't any need for this. Do you honestly think I would have fucked you if I planned to kill you? I could have done you as you slept."

"Shut up!" Simone shoved her through the opening door.

"*Ugh*!" she grunted, falling headlong. She hit the carpet and slid towards the huge desk in the centre of the room. If there was a person sat in the chair behind the desk, then they didn't acknowledge their presence.

"What the fuck is going on here!"

"Distrusting as ever, I see!" a voice from within the room said.

"Who are you, and what do you want with me?!" he demanded. "Answer me, or I'll fucking gut her!" Simone moved to Jessica and put the knife to her throat once again. A trickle of blood leaked from her.

"You're hurting me!"

"I'm surprised you don't recognise my voice, Simone."

"Who are you? Where are you?! I'll stab her in the fucking face, I'm not messing about!"

"Leave her alone. She's done nothing to you! Oh, how I have longed for this moment. I never thought it would come," the person said. Simone looked up and at the chair, figuring that's where they were. "I've missed you, brother."

It's a woman, not a man!

Simone's mouth opened. His jaw swung loose.

The woman in the desk chair swivelled around to face him.

"*Sian*?!" he screeched.

"Yes, Simone. I see you've been busy!" she said, smiling.

He ran to his sister and threw his arms around her. "*Jesus*! How...What..." He couldn't form the words. Tears rolled down his cheeks. "I thought I'd lost you forever. I tried to find you, but couldn't..." Hard sobs racked his body.

"*Shh*!" she said, holding him close to her body. "You wouldn't have found me because I changed my name. However, I've been keeping track of you, Simone."

"Fucking hell!" he cried.

She pulled his head close and whispered down his ear.

He felt an excitement grow in his guts. And in his pants.

"Can I be excused now?" Jessica asked.

Simone looked over his shoulder and smiled.

Jessica shuffled her feet.

"Not just yet, Jessica," Sian said, letting go of Simone.

"She's a most loyal, delicious pet..." Simone said, standing to face Jessica.

"Yes, very."

"I think we should take her with us... A ménage à trois of fucking and killing," he said, feeling Sian push something into his hand, which was behind his back in readiness.

"Agreed," she said, getting up to stand by his side. "What do you think, Jessica?"

"I think it sounds like a cracking idea," she admitted, smiling.

Simone watched as Sian walked over to Jessica and put her arm around her. "How about a fuck before we leave for the plane?!"

He licked his lips. His dick pushed against his zip.

"We really should get going..." Jessica said.

Simone could tell she was getting nervous. Sweat broke across her brow – her eyes made frantic movements as they flicked between Sian and him.

"No, there's plenty of time. After all, you made time to fuck my brother. Didn't you?!"

"How—" Jessica started to speak, but was cut dead by her superior.

"Spies, my dear. Spies. My walls have ears and eyes. Eyes and ears everywhere. The whole place is my playpen, Jessica. And everyone within it is my plaything." In one swift, sudden movement, Sian grabbed Jessica by her long hair and yanked her head back, exposing her throat.

"Please..." she begged.

Simone could only watch on in excited pleasure as the front of Jessica's trousers darkened with piss. He wanted nothing more than to free his stiff cock and wank it to climax.

"Hu...mil...i...ation," he uttered, fondling his dick through his prison jumpsuit.

Sian brought a police baton from behind her back in a stealth movement and chopped it across Jessica's throat.

"Ugh-uch..." Jessica gargled, grabbing her injury and then hitting the deck.

"Let's fuck this cunt up!" Sian looked over at her brother.

He liked the sadistic glint she had in her eye. Come drizzled out the end of his cock as he stepped forward and produced the shiv from behind his back. "Sticking her like a pig would be too easy."

"What do you suggest?"

"That we take our time..."

They both smiled.

"Let's strip her!" Sian said.

"I like the new Sian – when did you become such an evil fucking cunt?"

"I've always been bad. You just didn't get to see it in its entirety. The motherfuckers took me away, remember?" She stepped close to him and slid his zip down, freeing his dick, which sprang into her hand. "What the hell have you been feeding this fat fucking monster?!"

"Dirty bitches... Most of whom are buried under the sand at Porthcawl beach." He groaned, feeling his love muck race up his fuck stick.

She worked her hand faster as Jessica rolled about the floor, gasping and crying.

When he came, his hot sauce launched out of him and into Jessica's hair, which Sian took great delight in smearing.

"Make her lick your fingers clean!" he gasped, still reeling from his orgasm.

Sian obliged by ramming her digits into Jessica's mouth. All the while, she screamed, gargled and begged not to be hurt further.

Recovered, Simone walked over to Jessica and kneeled by her side. He took no time in ripping her trousers off and tearing her blouse and bra from her body.

"Open wide!" he screamed, and then shoved the shiv deep into her anus – a gush of blood drenched the carpet, soaked Simone's hand, and raced up his forearms. "Stop the bitch from screaming."

Sian rushed to her table, grabbed the ashtray that sat there, and smashed Jessica across the face with it – some of her teeth danced across the floor and rattled off the skirting board; half of her tongue surfed out on the blood that pumped from her flapping mouth as Simone shiv-raped her.

Excrement mixed with blood and piss.

"Rip her fucking guts out!" Simone screamed, continuing to drill the girl's arse – the shiv was at this point almost completely buried in Jessica's arsehole. "Come on, Sian."

He watched as his sister threw the ashtray to one side and picked up the letter-opening knife that rested on her desk.

"*Aaargh*!" Jessica screamed over and over again, until Sian rolled her over and stabbed the knife into her guts and ripped it upward to her throat.

"How's that taste, bitch?!" She pulled the blade free and put it by her side. Sian then ploughed her fists into the opening and ripped Jessica's intestines out.

Her guts hit the carpet like a dropped lasagne.

Simone had been forced to stop 'fucking' her and stood up. He watched Jessica's body twitch, buck and then finally shut down.

"Fuck me!" Sian bellowed, ripping her jacket and shirt open and smearing her exposed flesh with the gore that covered her hands.

Simone lay her down next to Jessica, and proceeded to fuck his sister among the blood and guts, which squished and popped with every hard thrust he delivered to Sian's overly wet cunt.

But she didn't allow him to jizz. Instead, she took control by rolling him off and getting on top. She rode him. Cowgirl style.

"Oh, fuck!" she gasped. "Fuck, fuck, fuck…" As she orgasamed, Simone rubbed more of Jessica's still relatively warm blood into her tits, face and hair.

He tasted it – licked his fingers cleaned.

"Harder! Pound me fucking harder, just like when we were younger… Oh, that's it!" she squealed, feeling him pump faster until both of them exploded into orgasmic screams of pleasure.

She collapsed onto his chest, and then rolled off onto her back – her juices ran down her thighs and mixed with the chunks of guts that lay beneath her, which she scooped up and rubbed against her bald twat.

"I needed that…" she panted.

Simone got to his feet and looked down at his half-naked sister – her skirt was up around her waist. "Are we going to Cardiff airport? Is that where your plane is?"

"Yes, Simone. It's taking us to a little island just off Hawaii."

He smiled. "How do you plan on getting me out of here?"

"The doors have all been left unlocked. The cameras switched off," she said, smiling. "And, of course, all the guards have been paid off."

"Excellent!" he said, pulling the shiv out of Jessica's arse – it made a slurping, sucky sound as it came free, much like a penis does after energetic sex. "Why didn't you find me sooner?" he asked.

"Huh?" she said, not looking at him. "What are you talking about?"

"You really are no better than the rest, are you? First, you fuck me up, then you fuck me over. You're the catalyst, Sian. Don't you see?"

"Sim, what are you talking about?" she said, lifting her head up to look at him.

"With you dead, I'll be free…"

"Hey, come on. I tried to find you sooner – do you know how hard it is…" Her words turned into a howl of agony as Simone stabbed the shiv through her eye and dug it out of her skull. "*Urrrgh-argh*! My eye!" she shrieked. "My fucking eye! Simone…*Ugh*…" Her good eye rolled around in her head as dizziness kicked in.

Simone ripped the orb off its cord and shoved it into his mouth. He bit down on it, hard. Juice exploded onto his tongue, cheeks and palate. "Mm, damn! Tasty."

His dick started to stiffen once again.

"You know, I once fucked a woman's empty eye-socket. I would do it to you, but I don't like being repetitive. I'm more creative than that, sister!" he said, and then laughed.

Kneeling by her side, he rolled her onto her back and shoved his hand into her mouth. "I've been told the tongue of a liar is delicious."

"*Arrrrgh*!" she wailed as he grabbed a hold of it and proceeded to pull on it.

Muscle tore.

Blood squirted.

As the organ detached, Simone wiggled it in front of his sister's face. "I guess it's bon appetite, Simone!" he said, shoving it into his mouth and licking his fingers clean.

Once he was finished munching on it, he decided to free her other eyeball and devoured that one too.

"I guess you're going to be a part of me forever!"

Simone spotted the letter-opening knife entangled in Jessica's intestines and picked it up. He then proceeded in sawing through Sian's nipples, before taking to her teeth with the ashtray. After the fiftieth smack around her mouth, he was happy to see her toothless. Her jaw hung on its hinges.

"Oh, she's passed out on me!" he said. "Never mind, this should wake the fucking bitch up." He firstly rolled her onto her stomach and then stuck his hard cock into her anus for one last orgasm.

Sian didn't come around screaming as he'd hoped. Instead, she awoke whimpering and crying, causing his dick to explode a third and final time as he grabbed her by the hair and yanked her head back.

"I think I'll wear the top of your head as a hat! I'm going to need something pretty for my trip to Hawaii…"

"*No-uch…argh…!*" she garbled as Simone took the letter opener to her scalp and started to saw through it.

Once he'd scalped her, Simone rolled her onto her back and got to his feet. "Before you die, I want you to see how pretty I am… Oh, I forgot. I ate your eyes. Silly me!" He laughed, and then put her hair on his head – blood trails ran down his face and into his mouth. "Ta-da!" he screamed. "I guess you'll have to take my word for how gorgeous I look…"

She coughed and spluttered, causing blood to fountain out of her mouth. "I loved…" Sian managed, before gasping and dying.

"Loved? You didn't know what the fuck the word meant!" he screamed, and then lay into her corpse with fists and kicks, before picking up the knife and shiv and stabbing her all over until he was breathless.

Forty-five minutes later, Simone walked out of Cardiff prison as his sister. He'd straightened her hair on his head and cleaned the blood off his arms and face the best he could with bottles of water he'd found in her office; he'd also stripped her of her skirt and wore it along with the shirt and jacket she'd been wearing, even though the clothes were a tight fit.

"Good thing I'm a slim fuck!" he'd uttered.

But there had been no need for the disguise, because nobody had stopped him – Simone had been free to walk out the door and up to her car, which had taken him a further ten minutes to find.

Once at the airport, he'd boarded the small private jet and taken the pilot by knife point. He'd promised to let him live if he should take Simone to the intended destination.

Of course, the pilot had agreed.

Unfortunately, Simone had not kept up his end of the bargain. As soon as the plane had landed on the remote airstrip in the middle of nowhere, he'd killed him and fled the makeshift airport.

Simone walked off into the sunset, not looking back – with his sister dead, he felt as though a great weight had finally been lifted from off his shoulders.

I'm now free to start a new life in a place where nobody knows me... he thought. *Let the screaming begin…*

HIS NAME WAS SIMONE

Halloween was James' favourite time of year. It had been ever since he'd been a little boy growing up with his parents at their home in the small seaside town of Porthcawl, south Wales. The spooky holiday eclipsed the likes of fireworks night and Christmas in his eyes, and he could still remember the first year he'd dressed up at the age of four and gone trick-or-treatin' with his older brother Luke. James had been Wolfman; Luke, Dracula.

But those days were long gone.

James didn't live with his family now, as he was attending university and lived close to campus with a bunch of friends in a student accommodation.

When Halloween rolled around, he would get nostalgic and think about past parties, costumes and the fun he and his brother used to get up to as they got older, such as pranking neighbours, scaring smaller children, telling ghost stories and playing ghoulish games like ducking and swinging apples.

James, whenever thinking about Halloween, could on occasion smell the toffee apples and cookies their mother used to make, along with the taste of the sweets they would gather from neighbours. James could even recall watching episodes of *The Simpson's Halloween Tree House of Terror* specials and classic films such as *The Thing* and *Halloween.*

As he aged into his teens, until he moved out, James continued to celebrate the holiday by dressing up and walking the streets – he had to. He loved it. Even though his brother had stopped, thinking it childish and stupid, it hadn't deterred James.

"You don't know what you're missing!" James would tell Luke, rattling his plastic Jack-o'-lantern he'd used for treats ever since he'd been a boy.

If his parents had found his behaviour around the holiday a little strange, they'd never voiced their concern or opinion. They'd just allowed him get on with it.

However, after starting his studious days at University, James soon found that he was around some like-minded people – people who liked to party, get drunk and have fun times. People who also liked to dress up on Halloween and go wild.

It was perfect.

Whilst in his first term, James had learned of a serial killer who had lived and operated locally.

"His name was Simone," a fellow student and friend had told him. "Thirty years ago, the small seaside town of Porthcawl had been thrown into a hellish nightmare as Simone had prowled the streets, beach and fairground at night. For people unfamiliar with the area, they wouldn't have heard about this vicious killer's heinous acts of deranged sex and violence."

"*Bullshit!*" James had said, laughing. "I've lived in Porthcawl my whole life and never once have I heard of such a person and his crimes!"

"That's probably because the police buried it, kept it a secret – they told the parents to never tell the future generations…"

"Then how the hell do you know?!" James had said.

"Information leaks… Besides, most people on campus know about it."

James had scoffed, shrugged the story off, but something had nagged away at him. Being the kind of person he is, stories about haunted places, ghosts and killers interested him. He'd researched Simone and found fictional books and newspaper clippings about the man and his murder spree. Worryingly, James became obsessed with the stories revolving around the charismatic serial murderer who had claimed multiple lives within the seaside town.

By the time James was in his second term of study, he was completely absorbed by the life and crimes of Simone. He made it his mission to know all there was to know about the killer, such as how Simone, as a child, had had a bunch of G.I. Joe action figures that were a part of his murderous 'Krull Army', along with a stuffed clown by the name of Mr. Tickles, his right-hand man. The Krull Army would help Simone butcher his other toys, along with his female victims he managed to lure into his home.

But of course, they were only toys, suggesting their voices and actions were in the killer's mind, but still. It fascinated James – thrilled him.

James also came to discover that Simone had been an extreme pervert who liked having his cock and balls locked away in a male chastity device. His girlfriend had been a dominatrix – one who took role-playing games a bit too far: She would regularly beat him into a state of oblivion by breaking bones and taking copious amounts of blood.

That is until Simone put a stop to her and cut her into tiny pieces, along with a whole mess of others.

Some said Simone still prowled the nights. That he was never caught. Others would say he was killed by a woman he failed to murder and that his ghost haunted the house he used to share with his dominatrix called Chaos. James had even heard rumours about Simone being apprehended and dying in jail. He'd also heard that Simone had fled the country many years ago.

Finding the correct version of the story had proved impossible, as anyone outside of the University didn't like to talk about it. People were still scared by the past events; even his own parents had refused to discuss it when he'd asked them about it.

"I have no idea what you're talking about, James!" his mother had said.

Towards the end of his second year, James had met and fallen in love with a Goth girl by the name of Neen Hunter – they, along with a couple of their other friends, quickly came to realise their shared intoxicating obsession with Simone.

Not just rumours, paper articles and works of fiction had been written about Simone and his sordid life, but also true crime books, bios and articles of interest. But since nobody had ever spoken in-depth with the murderer, no real hard evidence about him could be found.

The works of fiction presented James, Neen and their small circle of friends a lot of titillating information, even if most of it was made up. James, in particular, would read the novel *Wind-Up Toy* repeatedly, which detailed most of Simone's life, including those closest to him, such as Chaos and his toys.

"The author must have been a sick motherfucker!" Neen had said. "But you have to admire him for wanting to research something so fucked up and writing a book about it."

When Halloween drew close that year, James had suggested they dress up as Simone and his gang and visit the old home of the killer and his dom.

"Think of the fun we'd have! We could get wasted and do a bit of partying at the old killing house. I'll dress as the man himself and you could be my Chaos!" he'd told Neen at a private party they were having at the beach.

"Sounds like a ton of fucking fun!" John Ratcliff said. "I could dress as one of Simone's toys."

"Hell yeah! You can deal me in too," Darren Dilnott had butted in.

"Me, three!" Lyndon Johnson had confirmed, along with the rest of their friends.

Halloween rolled around a few weeks later, and they all planned to meet at James' student accommodation for pre-party drinks, music and some basic foolishness.

As James applied false blood to his slicked-back hair, face, exposed chest and shoulders, the door to his house opened. John entered, carrying a crate of beer. On his back, he had his rucksack.

"I thought you were dressing before coming over, man?" James said.

"Nah, I decided to grab some booze and snacks – I thought I'd change here, if that's okay?"

"Of course. Have you heard off the rest of the guys?"

"Darren told me he and the boys would be here around nine," John said, removing two cans of Carlsberg from its packaging. "Want one?"

"Please," he said, catching the can that was gently thrown to him. After popping the tab, James took a long drink. "Tastes damn fine! How do I look?"

"You're only half dressed! However, the blood looks good."

"Cheers. It's pretty hard to dress like Simone because I've only seen photos of him in a prison jumpsuit, which is what I'm going with."

"Sweet! Where's Neen?"

"She's in the shower, man. Wait until you see what she's fucking wearing! Or rather, *not* wearing," James said, smiling.

"Nice, dude – this is going to be a blast!"

"Agreed."

"Hey, do you really believe in half of the sick things Simone did?"

"Like keep his mother's dead body so he could fuck her?" James said.

"Yeah, like that!"

"Definitely."

"I'm glad you think so, because I do too. I'm pumped to be dressing up as one of his gang members, even if it is just a toy I'm representing."

"Yeah, but the names he gave his Krull Army members were cool as fuck. Who are you going as again?"

"Rape Charge!" John said.

James smiled. "Too awesome. I believe Darren is going as Mr. Tickles," he said, causing them to laugh.

"What were the names of the other toys?"

"Cumslot, Incest, Neck Snap and Spiked Mace – all G.I. Joes, just like you!"

Again, the boys laughed

Just then, a door opened and closed at their backs, causing them to look. Neen strutted out of the bathroom in nothing but her birthday suit, not caring if John or indeed the rest of the gang was there; she was a total exhibitionist, which James loved about her.

"When I graduate, I want to be a model," she often told James.

"You certainly have the arse for it!" would be his response.

Her body was a work of art, not just because of its slim tightness but in respect to the tattoos that covered it – she was a patchwork of beauty, a golden-haired bombshell. Her tits were small but perky, her hair long and luscious. James found her smile to be infectious, along with her laugh and silky-smooth tone.

John had known Neen for as long as James had been dating her – her blasé attitude towards being naked around him was no surprise. He was wise to her minx-like ways and brazen, wild attitude.

"Lager?" he asked her.

"Aye, wing us one," she said, snatching the cold tin out of the air as it sailed towards her. She then moved close to James and rubbed her bald snatch against his exposed forearm. "See anything you like, Simone?" she asked before licking his earlobe and stalking back towards the door she had appeared from. "I'm off to get changed, boys. See you in a while." She laughed and smacked her arse as she did so.

"Man, she's off-the-hook crazy!"

"I know, and I love her for it," James said, grabbing his prison jumpsuit and putting it on. Once it was in place, he applied more spatters of blood to his face before adding copious amounts to his costume. "Now how do I look?"

"Much better! Got a knife?"

"Here," James said, lifting the real butcher's blade off the table in front of him.

John smiled and nodded, and then turned his attention to his backpack. When he unzipped it, he removed his G.I. Joe outfit and started to dress.

Thirty minutes later, there was a knock at the front door. James answered and found himself face-to-face with Darren, who was already dressed as Mr. Tickles. The black, purple and chalk-white make-up he wore was enough to send a shiver down to James' bollock-bag, making his nuts and pecker shrink in a covert operation of hide-and-go-peep.

Darren wasn't wearing a normal clown wig – instead, he wore a green, Mohican-like hairpiece. He also carried a fake chainsaw that dripped blood.

"Boo!" he yelled, pushing his face close to James'.

James could see the rest of his friends at Darren's back, all dressed like G.I. Joe action figures. He backed away from the door and let them enter.

As John handed out cans, Neen reappeared to a chorus of wolf whistles. She wore stockings and suspenders, a leather thong with matching bra and thigh-high boots. Her blonde hair had been hidden beneath a hairpiece of black, which had been tied into pigtails.

"You look smokin', Neen!" Lyndon said. "When you stop fucking this loser, give me a call!"

"Ha! Fuck you, man!" James said. "Or shall I just refer to you as Neck Snap for the rest of the evening?"

"Just call me Snappy!"

"And me Rapey!" John said, winking.

"Rapey, break out some more beers," Neen said, cracking the whip she held in her hand. On her hip was a leather crop, which had been stuffed down her thong to keep it in place.

Over the course of the next hour they played music, drank, ate nibbles and got up to raucous fun, such as acting out sick scenes from the books and newspaper clippings they had read regarding Simone.

When they were finished having fun inside, they decided it was time for the main attraction and headed out onto the streets. As they made their way towards Simone's and Chaos' old home, the posse had fun along the way: They picked on small children trick-or-treating, egged cars, lit bags of dog shit and put them on doorsteps, pranked people and generally raised hell as they drank and sung their way along the partly lit streets.

They even managed to have some banter with a group of men who were out on a stag do, with Neen putting on a slap'n'tickle performance for the stag himself. This drove James wild with sexual excitement.

"I'm going to fuck your brains out in Simone's house!" he told her once they had continued walking.

After rounding the next corner, the group found themselves standing in front of the killer's old home.

"Shit, I forgot to bring my crowbar!" John said, looking up at the house. All of the windows were boarded over, with a piece of sheet metal covering the door. Most of the brickwork was decorated in colourful graffiti – words such as 'pervert' and 'killer' could be found among the many interesting and crude images.

"It's okay," James said. "I think there might be a way in around back."

"I fucking hope so!" Lyndon said. "I'm freezing my clams off out here."

"Settle down, cowboy," Neen told him. "We'll be in there having some fun before you know it."

"Follow me," James said. "And try to keep the noise down – people around here already hate this fucking building, without having a bunch of half-drunk students turning up for a shindig!"

"Half-drunk?" someone at the back said, burping and hiccupping. "More like pissed as a fart!"

They trooped down a nearby alley that led them to the rear of the house. Once there, James saw that one of the top windows was missing any kind of barring, and it was open. "Right, who volunteers to shimmy up the drainpipe? Once in, you'll be able to run downstairs and let the rest of us in."

The group fell silent.

"Fuck, I'll do it!" John said, stepping forward – the plastic grenades strapped to his chest rattled as he did so.

"Cool. Let's go, soldier."

James and the rest watched as John heaved, huffed and puffed his way up the pipe and then through the small window. When he was in, he poked his head out and gave them a thumbs-up.

"Right, we should be inside before we know it," James said.

As the minutes ticked by, James started to wonder where John may have got to, until he finally heard the rattle of chains and clacking of bolts.

When the back door opened, James jumped. "Jesus, man!"

"What?" John asked, a smile spreading across his face.

"What the hell took you so long?"

"Well, it's pretty damn dark inside – I had to take my time! I'm not falling and breaking bones for anyone. Come on," John said, flicking his head as an invitation to enter.

"You'd swear you owned the fucking place the way you're acting!" Darren said, laughing.

Once the group were inside, James closed the door behind them and guided them into the living room. When they got there, they started setting up the CD player and lighting candles. The booze was unloaded and someone passed a bag of weed around.

"Fuck yeah! Let's get totally wankered!" John said, dancing and drinking.

"Just try and keep the noise level down a bit, guys," James said.

"Fancy doing some exploring?!" Neen said, grabbing James' crotch and then a couple of flashlights from out of her bag. "I heard Simone did some pretty nasty things down in the cellar…"

"You kinky bitch!" he said. "I'd love to get you down there, but how about we explore the rest of the house first? We may find some interesting trophies."

"Yeah, sounds good to me, baby! After all, every serial killer needs a keepsake."

"Yes, they do! Go on, lead the way." As she turned and walked off, he reached his hand out and gave her arse a hard crack.

"Naughty, naughty!" she said, wiggling a finger at him. "That's going to cost you a good beating from off your mistress."

As Neen and James left the room, they saw John, Darren and Lyndon pass a fat one between them.

"Don't worry," Neen said, looking back at James. "They're not even going to notice we're gone."

"Very true," he said, following Neen into the kitchen. There, they took their time in exploring the room – it had been stripped of its white goods: freezer, toaster, kettle… Doors were missing from cupboards and the table was a shattered mess in the centre of the floor.

Spots of dried blood were found on the back wall and floor by the kitchen sink – an acrid stench of piss and shit mixed with vomit and stale booze clung to the air.

"I think people may have been using this place as a squatting zone!" he said.

"Yeah, agreed!"

"Doesn't look like we're going to find much in here."

"I don't think we'll find anything, James."

"Shall we try the bedrooms?"

"Yes!" she said, exiting the kitchen and entering the hallway.

He was about to follow when he heard strange whispers. "Do you hear that?" he asked Neen, but she was already climbing the stairs to the second floor. In the distance, and over the sound of the music coming from the other room, James was sure he heard the faint sound of a whip cracking.

"*Kill her!*" a whisper said.

"*Drain her blood all over the fucking floor,*" said another ghostly voice.

James felt something change within him – a gross need to hurt, maim and kill washed over him. He felt at home in the old house.

"Simone's back!" he whispered. When he heard footsteps above him, he went after Neen. The weight of the knife in his pocket felt good.

As he ascended the stairs, he heard her call him. "James, come quick! You'll never guess what I've found."

Over her excited pleas, he could hear the voices of the long-ago murdered inside the house – they were coming from behind the walls and under the floorboards. They echoed screams of death, pain and blood. So much blood.

"What is it, Neen?!" he said, his voice not sounding his own.

"His toys! I've found Simone's old gang!"

This snapped him out of his trance-like state. He rushed into the room and saw her holding Mr. Tickles and a couple of the action figures.

"Holy shit!" he blurted. "That's fucking amazing. Where did you find them?"

"They were under the floorboards by the door – when I stepped on them, I felt that they were loose and decided to investigate."

"Come on, we—" He stopped dead. The feeling of excitement and his old self were once again cast aside as the sound of a cracking whip could be heard somewhere from within the house. The voices were also back, egging him into butchering his beloved Neen.

"What the hell is wrong with you?" she asked. "Let's show these to the guys." As she made to push past him, he gripped her arm in a vice-like hold. "*Ow*! James, you're hurting me."

Without protest, he let her go and she rushed downstairs, all eager to share her find.

"*Bitch*!" he muttered, and headed after her. When he re-entered the living room, he instantly recognised the massive shift in his friends' moods. Nobody was singing. They were just staring at Neen.

"What the fuck is wrong with you all?!" she said, her voice rising.

James could hear the whispers. They were much stronger now. So too was the sound of the whip being cracked. "Jesus," he said, holding his head. "Make it stop!"

"Huh?!" Neen said, turning to face him.

"Nothing," he said, shaking his head.

He thought the place was having some kind effect on him, but he didn't want to say it in front of them – he didn't want to be ridiculed.

What the fuck is wrong with me?!

Before he knew what was happening, James was being led down to the lower floor by Neen and her torch. He sensed a slight change in her, too. The home was turning them into someone or something else.

We need to get the fuck out of here! he thought, but his mind fought back. *No! You need to kill this bitch and assemble your men to go out into the night.*

But why?

To kill. To spread fear.

Then all he could think about was ripping her clothes off and fucking her as hard as possible. Of course, he'd had these kinds of thoughts towards her before. However, this time they felt different. He didn't just want to fuck her, but also hurt her. Slap her and pull her hair.

When they got into the cellar, he noted there was a table of sorts in the centre of the room – it had ankle and wrist cuffs tied to it. Other articles lay strewn across the floor: latex and rubber clothing, masks, sex toys, whips and various bits of debris.

"I bet he killed Chaos on that!" Neen said, putting a hand down her knickers. "Will you fuck your mistress on there, Simone?!" she asked James.

He liked where she was going with this, which confirmed in him that she too was not quite herself.

James grabbed her bra and tore it from her body; he wanted her like he'd never wanted her before. The music from above thudded through the floorboards, keeping in sync with his throbbing dick.

After he ripped her panties down her legs, he tossed her onto the table and tied her wrists and ankles in the straps provided.

"I bet he cut that Samaritan up on here, too!"

"The girl he fell in love with?" James asked.

"Yes. I can smell her blood."

Had she said that to him on a different day, in a different situation, he would have laughed at her, as much as it thrilled him. But he too could smell and *see* the blood spatters about the room.

It can't be! It must be the way the torch is shining…

"Tongue me, Slave! Or I'll beat you hard," she said.

As he parted her legs, a strange sensation came over him, as though someone were standing over his shoulder.

"*Do her…*" a ghostly voice whispered in his ear.

He didn't feel scared. In fact, he felt exhilarated, and he knew Neen felt the same way. "Can you feel the presence of his victims?" he asked her.

"*Yes*!" she panted.

"Are you *coming*?!"

"Mmm!" she moaned. "Lick me faster. Harder!" Neen begged.

"I'm not touching you!" James admitted.

"It's them – the ghosts."

"Yes…" he said, letting his words trail off. He climbed on the table and straddled Neen – her body spasmed from orgasm after orgasm. James bent over and took her nipple in his mouth – he sucked, teased and bit it.

"*Kill her*!" a new voice uttered in his ear.

The thought excited him and brought his attention to the weight of the carving knife in his pocket.

No! I can't kill her… I love her. Or do I?!

James got off Neen, put his hand in his pocket and closed it around the haft of his knife.

"What are you waiting for?!" she panted. "Keep going."

"Oh, I have something better in mind!" With his free hand, he lowered his zip and pulled his hard cock out. Before she could speak, he eased it into her mouth, and she willingly took it.

"*Do it, now*!" the voice demanded.

James slammed his blade into Neen's stomach and pulled it back out just as fast – blood sprayed from her and hit the ceiling. In shock, she gasped, but didn't scream. When she tried to speak, blood dribbled out of her flapping mouth.

"Oh, I'm going to give it to you, all right!" he said, plunging the knife deep into her stomach again, and again, and again… He felt magnificent as he watched her thrash on the table, her blood leaking from several stab wounds and forming a neat puddle on the floor.

"*Assemble the others*," the voice continued.

Before leaving Neen, he put the knife to her throat and whispered in her ear, "You'll never tell me what to do again, Chaos!" After removing his cock from her mouth, he sliced the knife across her neck.

A loud thump and scream from above caused him to look up at the ceiling. His friends were shouting and whooping.

As he turned to leave, he took one last look at his dead, naked girlfriend.

"See you in hell, *bitch*!" James then proceeded up the cellar steps.

"What the fuck happened to you?!" Lyndon asked James, who entered the main room.

He had no fear of saying what he had done, because deep down, he knew his friends had come under the spell of the house. "I killed that fucking whore of a girlfriend of mine!" he said, smiling.

A laugh escaped Lyndon. "Well, I'm glad you got here in time! We were worried you were going to miss the show. Look," he said, pointing at John, who had a naked woman pinned to the floor – he was raping her in the most violent way James could ever imagine.

A pool of blood had gathered on the floor between her legs. She didn't scream, just whimpered.

"Have at her, Rape Charge!" James bellowed.

"I thought Rapey liked the cock?!" Darren said.

"Nah, one in the pink every so often is good by me! Hell, one in the pink and stink at the same time is even better," John said between gritted teeth as he kept fucking.

James then noticed a couple of terrified children and a man by the door leading to the kitchen – they were being guarded by Lyndon, Darren and the other action men.

"Where they fuck did this lot come from?" James asked.

"The stupid pricks came trick-or-treating here!" Darren said. He then put his clown face near the children. "I have a sharp knife in my tunic!" he told them. "I think I'll cut your toes and fingers off first – I like a digit sandwich!" he said, giggling.

The children cried for their mother, who was now being pulverized by John. He bucked as he spent his load inside her.

When she was half-dead, he got off her and dragged the man into the centre of the room. "Your turn, pal!"

The excitement bubbling within James was barely containable.

"Darren – I mean, Mr. Tickles, drag those children over here. Let's hack them into tiny bits and eat them," James said.

"*No*!" the little girl dressed as a bumblebee pleaded.

The boy who James guessed to be her brother, adorned in the uniform of a chimney sweeper complete with flat cap and brushes, stared blankly into space as the chaos ensued around him.

He didn't even flinch as James and Darren cut his sister's toes and fingers off, followed by her arms, legs and tongue.

Some of the gang snacked on the hacked off bits before joining John in buggering, torturing and beating the man to death.

After they were finished with their victims, the floor was awash with blood and guts – their bodies and costumes were slicked with the stuff, their hair gelled by it.

"The fun doesn't end here!" James said. "Mr. Tickles! Assemble the troops – we're taking this party to the streets!"

"Yes, sir!" the clown said. "Rape Charge, Incest, Cumslot, Spiked Mace and Neck Snap, fall in."

James watched as his – no, Simone's – troops gathered before him.

"We're taking our mission to the outdoors, men," Mr. Tickles continued. "Grab all your necessary shit – we're going to paint the town red!"

The men whooped and cheered before scattering to find all the weapons they could.

"Sir, the men have been briefed," Mr. Tickles told Simone.

"Good. Let's go!" Simone said. "On the double."

Lyndon threw open the back door, charged around the house and into the street and grabbed the first person he saw. Without hesitation, he broke the neck of the small female he held and proceeded to bite her nose off.

Darren was second outside, followed by John and the rest of them.

As James was about to close the door at his back and join them, he heard that faint sound of a cracking whip once again. Looking back, he saw his mistress. His Neen, standing by the bodies of the family.

When she stepped forward, he noticed it wasn't Neen, but the spirit of Chaos.

A smile played across his face as he shut the door and joined his gang.

The night came alive with the shouts and cries of pain as Simone and his boys took to every person they found with their knives and other weapons of slaughter.

This truly is the best Halloween ever! James thought, hacking and slashing at a small boy before moving on to his next victim…

Acknowledgements

No book can be published without acknowledging the wonderful people who helped to make it happen. Both David and Darkerwood Publishing would like to thank Nic and Jon for their hard work and multiple readings of the manuscript to catch errant commas and double words (among other things) that would have likely been missed. One of the banes of being a small publisher is that sometimes funding and staffing is limited. At the time Darkerwood Publishing Group accepted this manuscript we had two content editors and one line editor. By the time the manuscript went into editing and production, Darkerwood had zero line editors, except for the acquisitions editor who knowingly admits she may be a good content editor, but not always so good at catching line edits. So again, thank you Nic and Jon. David and Darkerwood Publishing are forever indebted to your keen eyes and patience.

About The Author

David Owain Hughes is a horror freak! He grew up on ninja, pirate and horror movies from the age of five, which helped rapidly install in him a vivid imagination. When he grows up, he wishes to be a serial killer with a part-time job in women's lingerie…He's had several short stories published in various online magazines and anthologies, along with articles, reviews and interviews. He's written for This Is Horror, Blood Magazine and Horror Geeks Magazine. He's the author of the popular novels "Walled In" (2014) and "Wind-Up Toy" (2016), along with his short story collections "White Walls and Straitjackets" (2015) and "Choice Cuts" (2015).

Links

Facebook: www.facebook.com/DOHughesAuthor/?ref=hl

Twitter: DOHUGHES32

Website: http://david-owain-hughes.wix.com/horrorwriter

www.ingramcontent.com/pod-product-compliance
Lightning Source LLC
Chambersburg PA
CBHW060543310726
48982CB00009B/1355/J

* 9 7 8 1 9 3 8 8 3 9 0 7 8 *